STORMING THE REICH

LEE JACKSON

SEVERN RIVER PUBLISHING

Severn River Publishing
www.SevernRiverPublishing.com

This is a work of fiction based on actual events. Names, characters, places, historical events, and incidents are the product of the author's imagination or have been used fictitiously. Although many locations such as cities, towns, villages, airports, restaurants, roads, islands, etc. used in this work actually exist, they are used fictitiously and might have been relocated, exaggerated, or otherwise modified by creative license for the purpose of this work. Although many characters are based on personalities, physical attributes, skills, or intellect of actual individuals, all of the characters in this work are products of the author's imagination.

ISBN: 978-1-64875-640-5 (Paperback)

ALSO BY LEE JACKSON

The After Dunkirk Series

After Dunkirk

Eagles Over Britain

Turning the Storm

The Giant Awakens

Riding the Tempest

Driving the Tide

Into the Cauldron

Storming the Reich

Crossing the Rhine

The Reluctant Assassin Series

The Reluctant Assassin

Rasputin's Legacy

Vortex: Berlin

Fahrenheit Kuwait

Target: New York

Never miss a new release! Sign up to receive exclusive updates from author Lee Jackson.

severnriverbooks.com

DEDICATED TO:

General Philippe Leclerc de Hauteclocque
Your unremitting dedication and courage were crucial to restoring your country.
You were and are an example to all people of principle

Jan Van Hoof, Agardus Leegsma, and Captain Arie "Harry" Bestebreurtje
Of the Dutch Resistance
You prevented a greater tragedy and helped save the Netherlands and Europe

Major Florence Conrad, Suzanne "Toto" Rosambert Torrès
And all the Women of the Rochambelles
No greater courage, dedication, or kindness was ever shown

Private George Sakato and the Men of the 442nd "Go For Broke" Regimental
Combat Team
Never has patriotism or love of country been more exemplary

US Marine Private First Class Guy Gabaldon
Your demonstrated toughness and compassion saved many of your Marine
brothers' lives

US Army Lieutenant Martin "Marty" Higgins and the Men of the 141st Infantry
Regiment
The Lost Battalion

You met overwhelming odds with tenacity

Commander Ernest "Big Chief" Evans and the Men of Taffy 3
But for your actions and sacrifice, the pacific war might have been lost

The numbers of Unsung Heroes and Heroines of WWII
Are Incalculable.
Without them, the world might have been enslaved.
Because of them, we live in freedom.

PROLOGUE

September 12, 1944
Sark, Guernsey Bailiwick, Channel Islands

A rapid knock against the panes on her back door in the hours past midnight brought the Dame of Sark, Marian Littlefield, scurrying through the halls of her medieval stone mansion. She hurried as fast as her skeletal frame could carry her across her kitchen amid the frantic barking of her equally starved white poodles. She feared no unwelcome intruders at this hour—Sark's Nazi occupiers had thus far treated her with measured respect.

Biting cold compelled her to pull a woolen shawl over her layered night clothes. As she turned the doorknob, an anxious voice called out just above a whisper in *Sercquiais*, the island's native dialect. "Madame, I must speak with you. I have terrible news." Marian recognized the voice of Otto, a farmer and butcher living farther down the same road from her home.

"What are you doing out at this hour?" she chided gently as she let him in and closed the door. "You've put us both at risk by coming here during curfew. Does your wife know you're out and about?"

Otto bobbed his head. His bald scalp with a band of hair around the back and sides glowed in the light of a waning moon streaming through the window. "The situation is serious. I came the back way through the brush. I'm sure I wasn't seen."

Having been rotund as the island's butcher before the German occupation had blighted the lives of Sark's islanders, he now appeared as a walking cadaver peering at Marian with worried eyes barely visible within their shadowed sockets. "You'll have to stay here until daylight," she replied brusquely. "We can't have you running through the night and tripping over a landmine or getting shot by an overzealous guard. Come into the drawing room. There's still some warmth from the fireplace." She chuckled with a trace of irony. "I must say, though, that I'm running out of furniture and doorframes to chop up for firewood."

"It's that way all over the island," Otto replied as they felt their way through the dark halls. "Do you think we'll be liberated soon? The Germans are losing. They must know that. They've been pushed off the beaches at Normandy. Sark is now behind their enemy lines. Why are they still here?"

Marian stopped in mid-stride and turned toward him. They were in total darkness now, neither seeing the other. "I don't know," she said. "I wish I had a better answer, but I can only guess that we'll be rescued after a major push to force the *Wehrmacht* back into Germany."

"Well the news just got worse. That's what I came to tell you. The Germans are preparing to commandeer all of our stored grain and ninety percent of our potatoes. I overheard two officers talking outside my shop today. Their troops are going hungry too. They'll confiscate the island's store of vegetables very soon."

"I'd heard that might happen on Guernsey," Marian replied. Her voice, already shrill from lack of nourishment, took on a hoarse quality. "The *Wehrmacht* doctor was kind enough to tip me off yesterday afternoon. I'd hoped *that* misfortune might pass us by. We're such a small population and have so little as it is." She sighed. "That action will starve us completely."

"Yes, mum. I'm sure."

"Oh, dear." Marian leaned against a wall and rubbed her hand across her face. Overwhelming guilt gripped her as she wrestled with the news, and her mind darted between alternative actions. A vision played before her eyes of the full population of Sark, more than four hundred people, gathered in the stone Chief Pleas Assembly building nearly four years earlier. Her husband, Stephen, had stood by her side within the ancient walls as she had implored her fellow citizens to stay rather than accept an offer from the British government to evacuate them ahead of imminent German occupation. She had told those dear friends that the preservation of their unique culture compelled them to remain on the island. To do otherwise would surely thrust Sark's way of life into forgotten history. Meanwhile, her own sons, Paul, Lance, and Jeremy, were scattered to places unknown to fight in the war, and her daughter Claire had moved to London two years earlier to play piano in the London Philharmonic Orchestra.

Everyone had stayed and endured the privations of the German presence. Some had since been deported to prison and work camps in France and Germany. Among them was her beloved Stephen, for being a Royal Air Force veteran of World War I. As the years ground on, minefields, barriers, and armed troops had shrunk the available farmland on which to grow food for themselves and their livestock, and much of their produce was requisitioned by the *kommandant* at a fixed rate of exchange that converted the transaction into virtual theft.

Babies went without milk. Children wore out their shoes. Men and women outfitted themselves in all sorts of mismatched clothing that served to provide inadequate warmth while meeting the expectations of a modest society.

"Our people will starve." Otto's voice caught. "The children..."

"We won't let that happen," Marian said resolutely. She straightened her spine and continued on her way through the dark hall to the drawing room. "Come. Tell me the details, and we'll plan what to do."

1

Five Days Earlier, September 7, 1944
London, England

On arriving at Special Operations Executive offices at 64 Baker Street while banishing nagging thoughts that he might never again see his fiancée, Amélie Boulier, and being too tired and annoyed to care that he was being borderline disrespectful to a superior officer, Major Jeremy Littlefield expressed his displeasure. "Why was I brought back from France?" he asked irritably. "There's plenty still to be done there."

"And plenty of capable SOE people to do it," the lieutenant colonel who greeted him snapped. His tone jarred Jeremy to normal respectfulness.

On his way from Paris, Jeremy had noticed that changes since the early days of the war had been monumental. On prior flights while being transported between France and England, he had scurried surreptitiously out to open fields on moonlit nights where Lysanders were guided to land by people with flashlights positioned to indicate wind direction and the length and width of the field. After such landings, the pilots immediately turned their planes into the wind, discharged passengers and cargo, took on whatever or whoever was to fly with them, and returned into the night skies, all within three minutes.

This time, on leaving Paris, Jeremy had been driven to the plane in broad daylight. The aircraft was waiting on an apron adjacent to a paved runway, and the pilot took his time to relax and refresh. Then, instead of landing under a cloak of secrecy at an airfield along Britain's southern coast, Jeremy had been flown straight into RAF Tempsford Airfield on London's edge. He was met by a driver, who whisked him by government automobile to SOE headquarters.

On traveling through the city, Jeremy took note of many scorched relics of bombed-out buildings still standing as somber reminders of the worst of the *blitz*, but gone were sandbags along the streets in front of shops and office buildings. People moved about their business with alacrity. Absent were fearful faces alert to any disturbance that might herald yet another attack from the sky.

As Jeremy passed near St. Paul's Cathedral, a sacred crucible of Anglican faith the world over, he relived the memory of the city in flames on a dark night while flying a Bristol Beaufighter in pursuit of a German Heinkel He III bomber that had targeted the revered church with incendiary bombs. He had shot down the intruder.

Did I really do that? The thought seemed too surreal to believe.

"Here's the thing," the lieutenant colonel said, pulling Jeremy back to the present. "The RAF needs pilots just now. Bomber pilots in particular."

"I was a fighter pilot. I've never flown bombers."

"Take that up with your commander at No. 9 Squadron. SOE loaned you to the RAF, and I'm told to advise you to make haste. Time is short. And one other thing." He furrowed his brow and leaned forward with a hush-hush expression. "You are not to let friends and family know you're back in England. In fact, you're to go straight over to RAF Woodhall Spa in Lincolnshire and meet with Wing Commander Tait of No. 617 Squadron. He's expecting you. A car will drive you. It's over a three-hour trip."

"I thought you said I was assigned to No. 9?"

"Yes, that's right."

Jeremy quelled rising irascibility. "Sir, can I get a proper briefing?"

"Wing Commander Tait will explain it all when you arrive there, *Major*," came the strident reply.

Irritated by the officer's patronizing tone and with memories floating through his mind of aerial dogfights in which he had engaged over Britain and the heated combat that had nearly brought his end so often in France, Jeremy cocked his head to one side. "Out of curiosity, sir," he said with labored civility, "where have *you* fought in the war?"

Realizing that he had just been borderline insubordinate by letting fatigue and irritation get the best of him, Jeremy snapped to attention. "Sorry, sir. I was out of line."

The lieutenant colonel stared and turned red. "I was here," he stammered with a cough, "doing my assigned job. Now, if you'll follow me, I'll turn you over to the clerk who'll provide all the documents and details to get you to the squadron. And remember, mum's the word."

"Of course."

While meeting Wing Commander James Brian "Willy" Tait later that evening, Jeremy regarded the officer in awe on learning that Tait had flown with the No. 617 Squadron in the famous "Dambusters Raid" in Germany's Ruhr Valley last year. Further, Tait had succeeded the legendary Guy Gibson, who had led the raid.

Tait was tall, dark-haired, lean, and clean-shaven, and his naturally serious countenance, resulting from his sharp features, was softened by an easy manner and a ready sense of humor. He smoked a pipe while they spoke.

"That jaunt was a bit of a nail-biter," he said, referring to the dam busting raid, "but it had to be done. Fortunately, it succeeded better than we had a right to expect. We have another one coming up that might challenge our wits to similar bounds."

Jeremy's concern mounted. "Sir, I've never flown bombers. I've always been a fighter pilot, and it's been over two years since I've flown anything."

Tait grinned. "We'll try to make the most from your poor life choices." Sensing Jeremy's genuine discomfiture, he said, "Look here, you're the last of the replacement pilots coming in and I've got time now, so I'll give you the full briefing. I've perused your file and know some of what you've done. *I'm* in awe of *you.*

"Frankly, I wouldn't have brought you on if I didn't think you could do the job. We're thin on pilots these days. A lot are being shipped off to the Pacific War." He took the pipe from his mouth and held it in his hand while he gathered his next thought. "You've heard of the *Tirpitz*?"

Jeremy sat up in surprise. "Of course, the sister ship to the German battleship *Bismarck,* which our navy sank in mid-'41. I was on a raid to muck up the only dry-dock on the French coast large enough to handle repairs for it. The idea was to deny it service facilities to keep it out of the Atlantic. Otherwise, ship convoys from the US to the UK would once again have been at the mercy of German U-boats. Britain would have starved."

Tait rose to his feet in astonishment. "You were in the raid at Saint-Nazaire?"

"Yes, sir. That's the one. I guess we caused a row."

Tait came around his desk and took the chair next to Jeremy's. "I must have scanned over your file too quickly. I missed that. You'll have to tell me about it sometime. You're a commando?"

Jeremy nodded. "I was at the time." To divert attention from himself, he said, "I recall the *Tirpitz* being in the news when it was launched, a year before the war. I was then posted to my first assignment as an army engineer in northern France to build roads and airfields. Isn't the *Tirpitz* the largest ship ever built?"

"It *was,*" Tait affirmed. "*Yamato*, the Japanese battleship, took over that honor, but the *Tirpitz* is big, and it's deadly. Winston Churchill calls it the 'Beast.' Fully loaded, it displaces over fifty-two thousand tons, and it carries that load at thirty-four knots. That's faster than any British battleship, and it does it with armor so thick that regular bombs bounce off of it. It's manned by a crew of twenty-eight hundred, and its eight big guns can be elevated to shoot down aircraft at high altitude."

He leaned toward Jeremy to emphasize a point. "It can hit another ship seventeen miles away, over the horizon, without ever seeing it." He arched his brows and added, "Keep in mind, that is precisely how the *Bismark* took out our HMS *Hood.*"

Jeremy raised his eyebrows in acknowledgment. "German U-boats ruled that ocean until the *Bismark* was taken out."

"Exactly, and the same thing is happening in the North Sea with the

Tirpitz. At the beginning of '42, the Admiralty learned that Hitler ordered it into that war zone below the Arctic Circle to threaten Allied shipping to the Soviet Union."

Tait drew on his pipe and mused, "I don't think the world knows the extent to which the war is being fought up there. It's quite extensive really." He grasped his pipe and waved it in a dismissive gesture. "In any event, on June 27 in '42, a convoy, PQ 17, sailed from Hvalfjörður in Iceland with thirty-seven ships on a supply run to Arkhangelsk on the Soviet northern coast. It was the largest supply convoy of the war to date."

Tait let out smoke from his pipe. The scent wafted. "The convoy had started out with a massive escort, but after it set sail, word of *Tirpitz's* presence in the area prompted the admiralty, on that news alone, to issue a 'scatter' order. That meant the entire escort fleet returned to home port, including the battleship *King George V*." He sighed. "Only eleven merchant ships of the convoy made it through to Arkhangelsk."

He scoffed while shaking his head. "The *Tirpitz* never fired a single shot, but its mere presence caused us to remove our own naval assets, which turned those supply ships into sitting ducks for German subs and other surface warships. That was the psychological effect of the Beast on shipping in the North Sea, the Norwegian Sea, the Barents Sea, and the Greenland Sea."

"That's one hell of an expanse of water," Jeremy interjected.

Tait drew on his pipe again while nodding. "The prime minister was furious at the losses. He had promised Soviet General Secretary Stalin that we'd keep that supply line open. He went so far as to issue a statement that, 'The destruction of this ship is the greatest event at sea at the present time. No other target is comparable to it.'"

The wing commander blew out smoke rings and watched them ascend and dissipate. "The thing is," he continued, "without that supply line, the Soviet war effort would collapse. The Allies would likely lose the war."

Given the gravity of his last statement, Tait remained silent a moment. Then he grunted. "To add another degree of difficulty, in two months, the arctic winter will set in. Our navy will then be inoperable in the area until the spring thaw."

Jeremy's mind had been working rapidly while he listened. Dread formed in the pit of his stomach. He broke in. "You're proposing to sink the *Tirpitz*."

Tait leaned back and laughed a full-belly laugh. "I'm proposing nothing, ol' boy. I've been ordered to do just that." He stood and paced. "It's a difficult mission, and we'd be stupid to think otherwise. Our navy's Fleet Air Arm tried thirty-one times to sink it, but their strike aircraft weren't designed for the task. The navy also sent a minisub attack against her last year that kept the ship out of commission for seven months. And last December, the Fleet Air Arm sank the *Scharnhorst*, another battleship in the North Sea that supported the *Tirpitz*, but it was nowhere near as formidable. So, the efforts have not been wasted, but they haven't delivered a knock-out blow. Repairs were made on the *Tirpitz*, and it threatens again."

He chuckled. "The Germans know the *Tirpitz* is an essential target for us. It's now anchored at Kåfjord in Norway's far north, well within its inlets."

"Why there?"

Tait grunted. "Several reasons. The location is deep and wide enough for the ship to maneuver. The mountains surrounding it are tall, steep, and protected by radar and anti-aircraft guns, so attacking it there is difficult. But it can move rapidly back out to sea and threaten shipping to and from Soviet northern ports. Attempts to destroy or keep it penned up tie down Allied naval assets, which means that our merchant shipping can't get through."

Jeremy took a deep breath and let it out. "What's the plan to get me up to speed on the Lancaster?"

"At first light tomorrow morning, you'll be at the controls on one, and you'll practice every day for the next three days until I get the green light from my adjutant. By the way, you're seeing me now because I like to get to know all pilots on a mission that I'm leading. You're actually billeted to No. 9 Squadron. You'll be in good company with that lot. It has a sterling reputation in its own right, having bombed enemy shipping in the early days of the war. It also supported our raids into Norway back in '40, and it participated in the strategic bombing the RAF did over Germany.

"So No. 9 has kindly loaned us six planes and crews for this mission. I've divided the total into Forces A and B, and I've assigned six of my own aircraft and crew into Force B." He chuckled. "Just keep Johnnie Walker in mind."

Puzzled, Jeremy asked, "The whisky, sir?"

"As I said, just keep it in mind. I should tell you that the crews are practicing a lot of dinghy drills."

"Sir?"

Tait nodded seriously and pursed his lips. "Dinghy drills, the process of escaping from the aircraft in a dinghy should you be forced down at sea. Unfortunately, you won't have time to practice it, but your crew's been rehearsing with other pilots. They'll be able to guide you should the occasion arise."

"Ahh, well, that's comforting."

Tait ignored Jeremy's barely concealed irony. "Do you have any other questions?"

Jeremy furrowed his brow. "I'm sure I'll have many more, but my head's spinning with what you've just told me. The main question that comes to mind now is, when do we do this thing?"

"Four days from now. On the 11th, we fly to Arkhangelsk. We'll prepare for and stage the attack from there on the 15th."

Seeing Jeremy's concerned reaction, Tait chuckled. "Don't worry, ol' chap, you'll have a crew of seven, including yourself, with a flight engineer, a navigator, and a bombardier. You fly the airplane. They'll do the rest. During the mission, follow along with the other aircraft and do as they do. I have faith in you." He beamed. "And why wouldn't I? You were a commando at Saint-Nazaire."

Jeremy shot him a doleful glance.

2

September 11, 1944
Over The North Sea

Jeremy fought off fatigue as the vibrations of four Rolls-Royce Merlin V-12 piston engines on the big Lancaster bomber pulsed through his arms and legs, numbing his mind. He scanned the dark clouds above and the choppy seas below. A strong wind blowing out of the north tossed his aircraft about. He had no fear of enemy aircraft attacks—the *Luftwaffe* had abandoned this part of the skies to the Allies. However, the weather could be just as deadly.

He had barely had time to acquaint with his crew, and even less time to get to know the leader of Force B. The past three days of becoming marginally flight certified on his Lancaster were grueling, leaving him exhausted at day's end. The crew performed well, providing him with rising confidence in its competence.

He could only hope he provided back the same sense. Each crewmember was a blooded veteran. They had lost their pilot on their most recent mission during which he had been mortally wounded from enemy gunfire, but he had landed the aircraft safely before dying.

For the last three evenings, Jeremy spent time with each crew member at a local pub and found all of them to be congenial, but their loss showed in their haunted eyes. They spoke nothing about their shared tragedy and little about themselves, instead concentrating on operational aspects of their specific systems and responsibilities.

The formation of thirty-nine Lancasters that comprised Forces A and B had flown out at dusk for a two-thousand-mile night flight to Yagodnik Airfield near Arkhangelsk. They flew high, at twelve thousand feet, because their intended route would take them over enemy territory in Norway and across neutral Sweden.

They also planned to fly over Finland, which Jeremy found interesting. What to expect there was anybody's guess. The country had been allied with Germany and fought fiercely against Russia for most of the war, but its president had signed a cease-fire with the Allies only eleven days ago, and was expected to enter a peace agreement in a few days. *With Soviet designs on Finland, that might not go well for them. But meanwhile, will they shoot at us?*

The rhythmic turbulence allowed Jeremy's mind to wander. As always in such moments, his thoughts turned to Amélie and their last moments together. She had just told him she had decided to join the Rochambelles.

Was that really only four days ago?

The Rochambelles, a unit of female ambulance drivers and nurses organic to French General Philippe Leclerc's 2nd Armored Division, had been part of his organization since Morocco. He was a major then, commanding a loose force of six thousand North Africans and over four hundred French soldiers. The Rochambelles had rescued wounded men, often under fire, from both sides of the front lines, including during Operation Fezzan II when Leclerc led thirty-five hundred soldiers up through Italy. And, they had landed with him at Normandy and crossed France with his newly constituted armored division.

Jeremy had vehemently protested Amélie's plan to join the Rochambelles. "You'll be killed," he gasped, embracing her tightly. "Don't go. Please —" Running through his mind were the long separations imposed by the war that they had endured and the close brushes with death each had experienced.

"Maybe not," Amélie replied while brushing loose hair from his forehead. "*Les boches* are retreating rapidly. The Soviets are closing in from the east. Some people think the war will be over by Christmas."

Jeremy shrugged. "I'd like to believe that, but I have my doubts. The Germans will be defending their homeland. The mountains between here and there are rugged, and we have the Maginot and the Siegfried lines to cross. That will be fierce fighting." He took a deep breath. "And you'll be in the middle of it."

That had been just before Jeremy flew to London. It seemed to him like decades had passed.

Dull explosions from anti-aircraft guns jarred him back to the present as the bombers crossed over Norway's coast. The barrage was ineffective at high altitude, but increasingly hostile weather continued to toss his Lancaster. Then he heard other pilots calling to Wing Commander Tait, one by one, informing him that they were breaking away to head back to home base.

A sudden downdraft battered Jeremy's Lancaster and drove it toward the ground. He pulled hard on his stick and worked it to the left and right in concert with his pedals as the plane twisted one way and then another. It continued to plunge, and visions of a fiery disaster on the side of a remote mountain loomed in his mind. Then gradually, the nose came up, the wings leveled out, and he regained control.

Breathing hard and sweating, he called over the intercom, "Time to go." Then he instructed his navigator, "Scout, set a course for home." He could almost hear the crew's collective sigh of relief.

He was about to key his mic to transmit his decision to Tait when the commander's voice sounded in his headphone. "This is Willie. Abort. Seek nearest shelter. Over."

Jeremy listened as other pilots acknowledged, and then called in. "This is Labrador. Roger. Out."

3

September 15, 1944
Yagodnik Airfield, Arkhangelsk, Soviet Union

The flight back from Norway four days ago had not gone well. The formation was scattered, and planes landed in Shetland, Scotland, northern England, and anywhere else their pilots thought they could get down safely. Some ditched in the North Sea.

Jeremy had managed to set down at RAF Sumburgh at the southern tip of Shetland, and there, over the course of two days while waiting out the gales, he had learned the fate of the special formation in general. In all, sixteen aircraft and crews had gone down. Force B had lost six bombers and crews, and Force A had lost ten.

Early yesterday morning, orders had come down to fly straight to Yagodnik, their original destination from which they would launch their attack on the *Tirpitz*. The weather was better, but still daunting, as thick clouds and snow flurries made finding the field difficult and landing there a precarious enterprise. Nevertheless, the remaining twenty-six of Wing Commander Tait's Lancaster bombers landed safely late that night.

The pilots assembled the next morning in a cold building offered by their Soviet hosts. No social exchanges had been scheduled due to the press of time to complete the mission. "If we don't get it done this time, we'll have to try again and again," Tait told the very tired and somber audience. "And we're down four more days before winter sets in. The good news is that weather over the target is reported to be clear."

He gazed over his audience, recognizing the crews' deep fatigue that he shared. No rousing speech would raise their spirits, nor was one needed. "You know the mission. We'll do a map rehearsal, make sure everyone knows the critical turning points, landmarks, plan of attack, and escape routes—" He straightened and took a deep breath. "We fly out in one hour."

Jeremy listened distantly, as he was sure his fellow pilots did. Aside from being on flight status for only eight days in an aircraft still new to him, the mission itself gave him pause. At the back of his mind was Tait's comment that thirty-one attempts to destroy the *Tirpitz* had failed.

This special formation of Nos. 9 and 617 Squadrons had not made a single bombing run for this mission, yet it had already lost sixteen aircraft and crews to bad weather. *We'll fly over seven hundred miles of mountains in similar conditions. If we have to bail on the way, dinghies won't help.* Jeremy wondered if any of those who had ditched in the North Sea four days ago had survived.

If the current formation endured the mountains, managed to stay on course, find the ship, and evade flak and anti-aircraft guns, they would drop their payloads and then fly eleven hundred miles over the North Sea back home to England. "If you see that you won't make it all the way to Lincolnshire," Tait advised during his final comments, "head for the airfields in Shetland." He ended on a jocular note. "The local residents love visitors—so long as they're from our side of the North Sea."

His attempt at humor fell flat. He looked into a sea of somber eyes.

"No fighter escort?" someone asked.

Tait shook his head grimly. "None. Our fighters don't have the range. But there are also no *Luftwaffe* bases in the area."

"That we know of."

"True." Tait straightened to full height. "I've kept nothing from you. We all know the stakes and the danger. It's my honor to serve with you." He paused, scanning the tired, serious faces. All eyes were locked on his, and the pilots grasped his unspoken message, a farewell wish for a peaceful rest for those who did not return. "Let's go."

As Jeremy filed out with the other pilots, he recalled the similar briefing just before the Saint-Nazaire raid had launched. He was struck by the circle of events that had brought him to address the *Tirpitz* once again, this time directly. In both cases, the participants knew that some or all of them might not live through their mission.

At the final briefing for the earlier raid at Saint-Nazaire, an air of bravado had permeated. It was absent from this mission. The group was smaller, one hundred and eighty-two pilots and crewmen as opposed to six hundred and eleven commandos at Saint-Nazaire—yet the stakes were every bit as high. The commandos had been training for months before the raid and were eager to get into action. This mission had been thrown together in a matter of days with crewmen who had been fighting the war for four years.

Thinking of the time that had passed since Saint-Nazaire, Jeremy was suddenly dumbfounded. The earlier raid had launched, nearly thirty months ago, in 1942. Put another way, it had occurred only two and a half years ago. So much had happened in the war since then. *So many people came into my life. I cared for them, and now where are they? Where is Amélie? She must be in the field by now.*

He forced the thoughts away and watched the air crews. They were tired to the bone. They had lost a full third of their number before heading in for the attack, and the nature of the mission assured that more of them, perhaps all of them, would not return home. Nevertheless, at the appointed time, they sauntered out to their aircraft to do their sworn duty, Jeremy and his crew among them.

With his engines fully primed, the checklist completed, and waiting his turn to taxi, Jeremy basked in the warm recollection of the last day that he had been with Amélie, his brother Paul, Chantal, and Madame Fourcade, all of them together. That had been the day that the US 28th Infantry marched in parade through Paris to show Allied support for General de Gaulle's fledgling provisional government, and it occurred three days after General Leclerc had liberated the city. The SOE had granted Jeremy seven days of leave, and he had spent every possible moment with Amélie. Unfortunately, that time had been cut short by his sudden recall to London.

He took a photograph of Amélie from his jacket pocket and gazed at it a moment. Then he touched it to his lips and placed it in plain sight on the Lancaster's instrument panel, wedged under the rim of the altimeter. He glanced at it again. *Wish me luck! Next stop, the* Tirpitz.

His deep weariness brought on by the swirl of events caused his mind to fixate, unbidden and inexplicably, on the strange tail of the bomber waiting in line ahead of his own. Like all Lancasters, it had no center vertical stabilizer. Instead, at the end of each horizontal stabilizer was a small vertical one.

Jeremy had inquired about the configuration and learned that the design provided several advantages, including a more spacious bay for larger bomb loads and enhanced aerodynamic efficiency, resulting in better maneuverability and control. It also allowed a space for a tail gunner that looked directly out the aircraft's rear. As Jeremy watched, the gunner in the aircraft ahead of him settled into position and checked the movement of his wicked-looking machine gun.

Jeremy approved of the unusual design. *The tradeoffs seem good.*

The aircraft ahead of him started its taxi. The tail bounced, and the gunner in his bubble waved. Startled to full awareness, Jeremy waved back.

In anticipation of a command to follow the departing Lancaster, he revved all four engines to taxi-power and pushed down hard on the brakes. Strong vibrations shook the aircraft, rattled every loose object, and jarred through the arms and legs of each of the seven-man crew.

Seconds later, through his headphones, Jeremy heard the controller's voice from the tower, reduced to a thin tone by electronics. "Your turn, Labrador. Begin your taxi."

Jeremy smiled while he let up on the brakes. When he had been asked what callsign he preferred, he gave the codename that he had used with the

French Resistance, Labrador. Hearing it on this mission provided a sense of continuity, however vague and distant, within the chaos ever present since the war's onset.

He taxied into position and watched the aircraft ahead speed down the runway and elevate into the sky. On receiving clearance from the tower, he began his own takeoff run. The bomber's tires rumbled over the tarmac, adding to the jumble of noises. Then Jeremy pulled back on the stick, and with a tremor, the Lancaster lifted into the air and the relative quiet, broken only by the droning engines.

As he flew out over the port of Arkhangelsk on the Northern Dvina River, inland from the Soviet Union's northern coast, Jeremy looked along the river's eastern bank for the golden domes and fine architecture of Saint Nicholas Cathedral. He had spotted them on approach last night by ambient light reflecting from its white walls and smooth domes, and he wished that he could spend time to satisfy his engineer's curiosity about the building and the town's surrounding topography. The area was character-ized by low hills created long ago by glaciers that had ground boulders into rocks, pebbles, and sand.

Force B led on a northwestern heading that would take them over Finland and neutral Sweden. They climbed to twelve thousand feet, high above the mountains, and hopefully, the weather.

As the Lancaster ascended, Jeremy glanced over his right shoulder at his engineer, Flight Sergeant Thomas Andrew. With hours ahead and nothing to do but keep the aircraft in trim and on course while monitoring its creaks and groans for anything amiss, the thought occurred that Jeremy had placed his life in the hands of people he barely knew, and they had placed their lives in his. *Will we live out the day together? I hardly know their names.*

Always before, he had taken time to get to know his mates, subordi-nates, and superiors. Andrew had taught Jeremy all he could about the Lancaster in a short time, but during off hours in a pub near RAF Bardney, and over the days of waiting out the weather, nearly all conversation had been about the aircraft and the mission.

Jeremy was glad to have Andrew as his flight engineer. The non-com knew every detail of every system on the plane, and he made sure that each of the other crew members knew their specific systems just as well. He was gruff, and the crew called him Flight Sergeant, but he gave each of them nicknames. The radio operator was "Sparks," and the navigator, "Scout." The bomb aimer, who lay flat in the nose of the aircraft, was "Mark," short for marksman. The mid-upper gunner, sitting in a bubble protruding through the top of the fuselage, was "Sky," and the tail gunner was "Stal," for "Stay Alert."

Jeremy knew their nicknames and their functions. He had quizzed them on the technical aspects of their jobs, but he suddenly realized that he could not be sure of their real names, where they were from, whether they had families, what they did before the war, or what their ambitions were for after the war.

His deficiency gnawed at him. *How sad to die among strangers.*

As the formation drew closer to Kåfjord, he directed his thoughts to the plan of attack and the payload his Lancaster carried. The entire Force B, pilots and crewmembers alike, were disgruntled about those munitions, so-called JW mines, and they had let their displeasure be known to their superiors.

"They're ugly," Andrew had said when he first showed one of the devices to Jeremy. "They're unproven, and they're dangerous."

After studying the one then before him, Jeremy shared the concerns. From an engineer's viewpoint, they were ungainly, appearing as two half-cylinders welded together around the middle, with pipes extending along its sides, and a propeller within a protective collar fixed on the bottom. Spikes protruded at the top.

"Tell me about this thing, Flight Sergeant," Jeremy said. "What is it?"

Andrew stared at it and scoffed. "That is a JW mine," he said, "and we're all fools many times over in Force B, because only fools would fly with those monstrosities, and each Lancaster carries twelve of them."

"How do they work?"

"The real question is, *do* they work?" came the derisive reply. "Theoretically they do, and I'm sure they've been tested, but they've never been used in combat." He blew out a breath in disgust. "What's supposed to happen is that after we drop them, they deploy parachutes to break their fall into the water. As they sink to the bottom, a buoyancy chamber activates, and they rise to the surface. As they do, a stream of propellant pushes them side-ways. Those spikes on the top act like the ones on any submersible mine—when they contact a hard surface, they set off explosives in the cylinder. If they haven't found a target, they sink again, rise to the surface, and repeat, and repeat, and repeat until they either come up under a vessel, or run out of energy.

"Essentially, they're mines wandering around to find a target. Force B will drop a total of seventy-two of them. The idea is that some of them will meander under the *Tirpitz*, explode against its thin underside, and sink it."

Jeremy had listened with his arms crossed while scrutinizing the mine. Now he rubbed his chin with an absorbed expression. "Well, they're certainly ugly, but the concept sounds brilliant. What's your issue with it? And what does JW stand for?"

Andrew smirked. "Johnnie Walker."

Bewildered, Jeremy replied, "Excuse me?"

Andrew laughed. "The rumor is that the concept was born in a pub where a group of designers had drunk too much—"

"Johnnie Walker," Jeremy breathed, and then chuckled as he recalled Tait's humorous admonition to remember the name. "That would explain a lot."

"Depending on whom you believe, they weigh about a thousand pounds each, and a third of the volume in those tubes is filled with hydrogen—highly flammable—with explosives below that. Our standing orders are that if we're fired upon, we ditch 'em. If we go off course and can't see the target, we ditch 'em. And under no circumstances are we to return home with them still in our bomb bay. That's why I say that we must be fools to fly with them."

Jeremy displayed a rare smirk. "Ours to do or die."

Andrew nodded. "Aye, sir." He gestured at the mine. "No one lays claim to this Frankenstein weapon," he growled. "Force A is carrying 'Tallboy' bombs, and we know exactly who designed them, Sir Barnes Wallis, and he's right proud of them."

"Explain."

"The Tallboys weigh in at over five tons. They're sleek, shaped like rockets with fins, and when they drop, the nose goes down, and it spins, which seems to keep it on course. It's called a 'precision bomb.' It hits where it's aimed, at least most of the time, and it penetrates a ship's steel deck before it explodes. If it hits on or near the ammo magazine— whoosh!" He raised his arms to simulate the effect.

Jeremy cut in. "So, the reason that Force B is leading the attack must be that Johnnie Walkers hit the water softly and submerge, while Group A's Tallboys explode after penetration."

Andrew shrugged. "Makes sense, but I don't know for sure."

Subsequent briefings confirmed Andrew's descriptions of the JWs and the Tallboys as well as Jeremy's conclusions about putting Force B out front. *Let's hope the flak doesn't reach us. But that would be the case irrespective of Johnnie Walker.*

The flight toward the Kåfjord area was uneventful. Maintaining an altitude between ten and twelve thousand feet along the way had kept them above the worst of the turbulence. Only intermittent clouds floated over the mountain peaks.

At roughly sixty miles from the target, Wing Commander Tait's voice sounded through the wireless. "Enemy radar imminent. Ascend to attack altitude."

Immediately, Major Evans, Force B's leader, relayed the order. Jeremy flexed his hands against immediate tension in his extremities and tightening in his stomach. "We're starting our run," he called over the intercom. "Mark?"

"Ready," the bombardier replied.

"Scout?"

"We'll be over the target in six minutes."

"Sky and Stal?"

They both confirmed their readiness by squawking the mics.

"When we get to home base," Jeremy called, "I want to get to know each of you better. I couldn't ask for a better team."

The crew members squawked back acknowledgment.

The target area crawled into view and was immediately recognizable by thick clouds of many hues of black, gray, brown, and white rising into the sky. Jeremy heard Evans radio to Tait, "Willie, they're saturating the target area with smoke."

"Roger. Do what you can, but don't leave without dropping your payload."

"Roger. Out," Evans replied. Then to Force B, he ordered, "Starting our run. Acknowledge."

Jeremy pressed his mic sharply and heard five other electronic signals. Seconds later, the six bombers ascended to sixteen thousand feet. They had flown northwest almost constantly since leaving Arkhangelsk. The fjord where the *Tirpitz* lay at anchor was oriented almost parallel to their direction of flight, but south of the formation. To get a clean bombing run required the Lancasters to fly north, turn southward, and attack to the southwest.

Jeremy banked his plane, keeping an eye on the spot below where dark smoke billowed into the air. He circled wide so that when he lined up on the fjord, he would be behind the group leader. The other bombers of Force B would form up similarly behind him. Force A would ascend to twenty thousand feet and execute a similar maneuver well behind Force B.

Surface gusts intermittently cleared the area sufficiently that, ahead of the lead plane, Jeremy saw the body of water and its shoreline. From this altitude, the fjord appeared as a wide horseshoe bay closed off at its southeast end, almost as if manmade. At the northwest end, also seen only in glimpses, the fjord merged into another larger one that led north to the open sea.

During a break in the smoke, Jeremy pointed the nose of his aircraft on a line that ran through the near and far end of the fjord. "Scout," he called to his navigator, "keep me on this course. Let me know if I veer off. Mark, did you get that view of the fjord?"

"Roger, and I saw the *Tirpitz*. It's a long speck near the south bank. We'll be lucky to see it again. The jerries are pouring out smoke from machines all along the shore."

Jeremy grimaced at the impossibility. "We're trying to hit a speck in a spot under thick, dark smoke," he muttered to himself. To the bombardier, he said, "Mark, listen carefully. In this soup, I'm losing sight of our group leader and the target area. I'll do my best to get you a clear shot, but if I can't, use your judgment to estimate time and distance, and drop at will."

"Roger."

"Scout," Jeremy called again, "as soon as Mark drops, give me a bearing to get out over the sea, and chart a course to the Shetlands. I'm not sure we've got enough fuel to get all the way to Bardney."

"We don't," Andrew broke in. "As soon as you can, start conserving."

Jeremy's Lancaster flew at or near top speed of two hundred and fifty knots. Ahead, Evans' Lancaster disappeared into the clouds.

"Bombs away," Mark called. "I saw the forward plane's drop too."

"Set course for two-sixty degrees," Scout chimed in. "We should be over safe waters in just under three hours."

Moments later, they heard massive explosions behind them. "That must be Force A's bombs," Andrew called out, his tone filled with sarcasm. "Our skinny little mines wouldn't make such noise. They're probably bobbing about, still looking for a target."

Despite the tension, Jeremy had to laugh. "Let's head for home."

Jeremy and his crew trudged into the flight hut at RAF Sumburgh. Evans was there with his bunch. His expression was dour. His eyes met Jeremy's and he shook his head. "No dice," he growled. "By the time Group A flew over, the target was completely obscured. They dropped blind. We don't know if there were any hits."

Jeremy scrutinized Evans' face. He liked the man but had not had an opportunity to know him well. Short and stubby with unruly brown hair and a brusque manner, he was a competent pilot and leader, but in the rush of preparing for the mission, he and Jeremy had concentrated on their crews and aircraft to the neglect of deepening their mutual acquaintance. As an officer of equal rank, Evans had accepted Jeremy as a peer, counting on Jeremy's professionalism to defer to his decisions, and both had relied on the various briefings to stay abreast of crucial mission details and changes.

Andrew and the rest of the crew grouped around the two pilots, listening to Evans' comments. Jeremy turned back to him. "Any losses?"

"Not from our group, at least none reported yet. One from Force A ditched near Shetland's coast. We don't know the status of the crew. A rescue plane is on its way."

Jeremy pursed his lips dolefully. *I hope they practiced their dinghy drill.* He caught Evans' eye again. "What's next?"

The group leader grunted sardonically. "We'll see what the after-action reports say. If we didn't sink the ship, we'll do this again. The *Tirpitz* must go down."

4

Three Days Earlier, September 12, 1944
Vittel, Lorraine, France

Lieutenant Colonel Paul Littlefield watched General Philippe Leclerc's expression harden into controlled fury as they walked together to a closed barbed-wire-reinforced chain-link gate barring entry into the town. Mid-morning sun glinted off the barrier as they approached. Within its confines, men and women peered at them through sunken eyes and gaunt faces. Their tattered clothes hung on thin frames. Behind them, the fine buildings of the erstwhile resort showed signs of recent combat and long neglect. Most disturbing was that, pressed against the fence while avoiding being torn by the barbs, rows of malnourished, awestruck children gazed at them.

At the flick of Leclerc's wrist, a sergeant hurried forward with bolt cutters and sliced through the thick chain and padlock holding the gates closed. Meanwhile, Paul observed what had been, until moments before, *Frontstalag* 121, a dismal German internment camp for political prisoners.

As the chain clinked to the ground, the officer stepped back. Leclerc strode forward, seized the right portal disgustedly, yanked hard, and threw it open. It swung its full arc to the right and bounced against the adjoining fence. The general then grabbed the other side and rammed it in the opposite direction. Then he stood at the entry onto the main street, scrutinizing his surroundings.

Jagged, twelve-foot-high horizontal barbed wire strands stretched from pole to pole, with the intervals between them reinforced with more barbed wire strung diagonally across the face of each section. The fence disappeared into the distance along its perimeter with more rolls of barbed wire affixed at its top. Intermittent guard towers and spotlight housings and a worn footpath along the outside periphery for armed patrols and guard dogs had completed conversion of the town into a prison.

Lieutenant Colonel Jacques Massu, a sub-group commander from one of Leclerc's combat groups, had encountered the gloomy spectacle only minutes earlier and immediately informed his higher headquarters by radio. "You might not want to come here, sir," he advised when he had been connected directly with Leclerc. "The conditions are deplorable." He provided details.

"I'm coming," the general had growled. "I'll open the gate personally."

Paul joined him in his scout car to drive the short distance to the barred entrance. Nestled in a shallow valley among wide fields and forested hillocks nearly two hundred miles east of Paris, Vittel should have been a place to enjoy nature, particularly on such a day as this, with blue skies, fair weather, magnificent landscapes, and the first chill of autumn in the air. Further, Leclerc and his troops were still flushed with the triumph of liberating their own capital, Paris, from German control less than three weeks earlier. Fresh in Paul's mind were visions of the Eiffel Tower, and atop it, France's tricolors flying proudly once more in the wind. That victory had culminated after Leclerc's 2nd Armored Division had fought across France from Normandy.

Paul, chosen for his fluency in French and German as well as his experience as an intelligence officer and combat infantry battalion commander, had joined Leclerc as a liaison officer as the unit had emerged from the beach at Normandy six weeks earlier. He had been at the general's shoulder for the demoralizing drive through the "capital of ruins," Saint-Lô, so called for being leveled to allow Allied forces to break out of *bocage* country that had kept them penned in Normandy for nine weeks after D-Day.

Together, Paul and Leclerc had toured the battlefield at the Falaise Gap, strewn with blood and bodies of dead soldiers, livestock, and wild animals as well as the hulks of myriad burned-out war machines. Paul saw then that the glint of determination never left the general's eyes, but fury, compassion, and dismay often attended as well.

Paul had been in awe of the young general who walked with a cane as a result of a wound received during the German *blitzkrieg* through the Netherlands, Belgium, and France at the beginning of the war. While fighting in Libya, Leclerc had entreated his command to swear "not to lay down arms until our colors, our beautiful colors, float again above the cathedral at Strasbourg." Known as the Oath of Kufra, the commitment had sustained the general and served as an ideal to rally his troops throughout their many battles and loss of comrades.

Now that he was within one hundred and thirty miles of fulfilling his vow and on the road to seize his current objective, a river crossing at Épinal along the Moselle, Leclerc's excitement had been subdued by the sight before him at Vittel.

After opening the gate, the three officers stood in momentary shock at the sight they beheld before walking through the gate at a measured pace, lean and weathered in their combat uniforms from many days in action. Paul and Leclerc were both of medium height, Massu a half-head taller. The two Frenchmen had dark hair cropped short and thin faces, and both men sported narrow, well-trimmed mustaches. Paul's face was wider, his hair sandy-colored, but his cheeks were also hollowed out from the campaign's physical demands.

Only the anger in Leclerc's eyes hinted at his revulsion for the sight before him.

Inside the gate, Vittel's detainee population drew back and parted as he started toward them. Sensing their fearful uncertainty, he forced a smile, lifted a hand, and waved. "My friends," he called out, "I am General Leclerc, commander of the French 2nd Armored Division. We are here to set you free."

Audible gasps rose from the crowd. Tears rolled down the cheeks of men and women, old and young. Then a cheer resounded and fists stabbed the air as people pressed around him. Seeing the celebration of their elders, children joined in, jumping up and down and scrambling between legs to get closer to this stern-looking man who had just opened the forbidden gate.

At the rear of the crowd, an elderly man in a British officer's uniform so ragged that his rank was indeterminate pushed his way through. As people realized his presence, they moved willingly out of the way to allow him passage.

He approached Leclerc and the two men exchanged salutes. "I am Captain Brown," he said, "senior person among the prisoners, and I'm British. I expect that you'll want to meet with the French among us."

Leclerc studied the old man solemnly. Then he shook his head as he laid a hand on Brown's shoulder. "No. I want to meet everyone." He smiled compassionately. "I was treated kindly when I escaped to England in 1940, and the British have supported us during the war with money, weapons, equipment, and supplies. Let me return the favor. Tell me who's here."

Brown took a deep breath. "This is a family camp that ranges between two and three thousand inmates. We have eighteen hundred of my countrymen here. Mostly we have political prisoners, French, British, and some Americans who were trapped here when the US entered the war. The Nazis thought these people could be used for bargaining chips."

He grinned, exposing yellowed teeth in need of dental care. "Obviously, our captors gave up on that idea." He sighed and looked around. "This town was a resort before the war. As prison camps go, it's not so bad. The hotels are in dire need of maintenance, but they were built for luxury." He chuckled. "I don't think anyone will want to pay to stay in them now, but we have running water, and we've mainly governed ourselves—" He paused and stared at the stark barbs on the fence. "Within limits."

His expression suddenly turned sad. "Our Jewish population was recently shrunk. Three hundred of them were just deported. We don't know where they were taken. Somewhere east, that's all we know."

Leclerc absorbed the information grimly, but before he could respond, Massu approached. "General, our right flank is completely exposed to the south and east, and the enemy is forming to defend Épinal and all along the Moselle River. We've also received intelligence that the 112th *Panzer* Brigade has been ordered to re-take Vittel. They appear to be forming to do just that, at Dompaire."

Leclerc nodded and turned to Paul. "Radio my deputy. Tell him to move food supplies and troop trucks forward and provide whatever these people need, including medical attention. Tell him to seek guidance from Corps headquarters on how to handle their release. We need to move the people out of here. Fast. Tell Operations to reposition at once and to relocate my headquarters east of Vittel. Stay here until all that's done and then join me. I'll head to my command post. We attack tonight."

Paul regarded him doubtfully. "Sir, I'm your liaison to the British. Your command might not—"

"My staff knows you," Leclerc snapped. "You speak for me. They'll do as you say."

Captain Brown interrupted. "Sir, I should tell you that former Prime Minister Reynaud's wife is here with us."

Leclerc swung around in astonishment. "Reynaud's wife? Madame Henri-Robert?"

Brown nodded. "And their daughter."

Paul moved closer to listen. Reynaud had been appointed as prime minister of France just weeks before the German invasion. In the interim, he had pushed for increased military preparedness and tried to rally France to meet an expected German threat. One of his actions was to appoint Charles de Gaulle as undersecretary of state for war. When Germany invaded, Reynaud found himself overridden by the influence of General Pétain, the World War I Hero of Verdun, who promptly pushed to negotiate an armistice with Germany. Unable to further influence events, Reynaud had resigned. Pétain succeeded him and arrested him, and subsequently turned him over to German authorities, where he still remained in prison.

Leclerc once again addressed Massu and gave further instruction. Then he told Brown, "Send a messenger to Madame Henri-Robert. Tell her to prepare to leave for Paris with her daughter at once. We'll have them safely home tonight."

Turning once again to Paul, he ordered, "See to it."

5

Same Day, September 12, 1944
West of Dompaire, Lorraine, France

"You can't think that way," Amélie Boulier chided Lieutenant Louis Gendron.

"Really, you mustn't," Danièle Heintz chimed in. Her concerned pallor diminished the effect of the freckles on her face and her red hair. "You know there is a God, and He's watched over you all this time."

The tall, slender officer smiled dispassionately. "To the exclusion of all my comrades who've died?" He grunted. "I grapple with that notion."

"I'll pray for you nevertheless," Danièle replied. Born into a religious family, she professed her faith without being overbearing, and she was known for her spunk. In mid-afternoon on D-Day, Allied bombs fell all around her home in Caen. She rushed with her brother to help out in the hospital where she was a nursing student.

When Allied bombers dropped ordnance on their building, she wiped blood with a white sheet from the floor of the treatment rooms and ran outside to fashion a red cross on the front lawn. Bombs ceased to be dropped on their facility.

She and Amélie conversed with Gendron in a muddy orchard behind a

Rochambelle ambulance, which gleamed wet from recent heavy rain. "We're outnumbered," he said matter-of-factly. "I'm confident that we'll win the battle, or General Leclerc would not commit us. But we'll take casualties and I've cheated death too many times. I don't expect to live through the day."

"But you fought all across Africa and Italy," Amélie protested. "You must have felt the same way at times, yet here you are. Look at the news today. Patton's 3rd Army just linked up with General Patch's 7th Army near Châtillon-sur-Seine. That's only sixty miles southwest of here. The *Wehrmacht* has fallen back all across their western front, from the Channel to the Mediterranean. What's left of their armies in southeastern France is trapped with General Patch's army closing in on them."

"But here in the northeast, we're approaching the Moselle River," Gendron said. "Just forty miles beyond is Germany and its Siegfried Line. *Les boches* pulled their troops back to reinforce it, and before we get there, we'll have to go through our own Maginot Line, which they occupy, and they'll defend it against our advance. Even before that, we'll have to cross the river, which is heavily defended, and then we'll be attacking into the Vosges Mountains." He glanced at dark clouds in the sky and noted water dripping from the leaves of the peach trees. "This incessant rain isn't helping either. The enemy has all the advantages of defending in the worst autumn weather in a century, which will probably lead to a horrendous winter. And before we do any of that, we'll have to get through tomorrow's battle at Dompaire."

Gendron sighed. "We'll have to do all of that before we can even think of crossing the Rhine, and every inch of the way will be heavily defended." He grunted. "Look, Épinal is our next major objective. The Germans don't want to give it up because it's an important transit point across the Moselle, so they've sent a force out to stop us.

"Intelligence says that we're facing the 112th *Panzer* Brigade. It was formed only last week with new recruits. That means they're poorly trained. But they're armed with Panthers and Mark IV *panzers*. Both of those outgun our Shermans, and they have so many of them, nearly a division's worth."

He paused and sighed. "I know we came across France rapidly, but the fight ahead will be much harder. I feel it in my bones."

He stood, stretched, and clasped his hands behind his head. Then, straightening, he let out an ironic laugh. "Don't pay attention to me. I'm being morose. We'll win. But I believe I've outlived my luck."

Amélie and Danièle regarded him somberly. "Thinking like that could cause a self-fulfilling prophecy," Amélie said. "Please don't do it."

"At least pray as you head into battle," Danièle added.

"I'll try on both counts," Gendron said, grinning without conviction. He waved slightly as he walked away. "May we see each other in better times."

Amélie's heart sank as she watched him go. Standing next to her, Danièle sighed. She had joined the Rochambelles shortly after her home was destroyed in Caen. "I hope he makes it."

Amélie had been in Paris during the capital's liberation. With her sister Chantal, she had attended General Charles de Gaulle's triumphal parade down the Champs-Élysées, secured by Leclerc's armored division. Included in the procession was a unit of ambulances driven by women. That was not unusual—in both the last world war and in the current one, women had volunteered as ambulance drivers, but they were not members of the units they served and did not travel with them.

The women in Leclerc's unit wore the French Army uniform and they moved and acted as a unit, and one that was accepted with pride by their comrades. Over the next few days, Amélie inquired about them at division headquarters, and what she learned was startling.

The unit was known as the Rochambeau Group, named for a French lieutenant general who had led his forces to Yorktown, Virginia, to help win the American Revolution. The Rochambelles, as its members came to be called by their 2nd Division compatriots, had decided to use a name that Americans would easily remember, but because "Lafayette" had already been taken by a World War I group of flying aces, they settled on "Rochambeau."

They were led by Major Florence Conrad, a wealthy American widow who had driven a battlefield ambulance during the First World War. She was legendary for her exploits in that earlier conflict. One episode that was particularly poignant for the current setting at Dompaire occurred when, during that war, she had found herself trapped in enemy territory on the east side of the Moselle River.

Because her job had been to pick up wounded soldiers, she was often under fire between combatants. On one occasion, as she retraced her route to a bridge, she discovered that it had been bombed and was impassable. Skirting along the river, she encountered a German roadblock and was taken into custody.

The United States had not yet entered that war, so she showed her American passport to the commanding officer. He ordered her to drive to his encampment at Dompaire and sent a soldier along to ensure she complied. There she found herself among twenty thousand French prisoners. She then presented her passport to the prison camp commandant and received a permit to transport wounded soldiers between Etain and Paris. In that capacity, she drove on empty streets through Paris on the night the opposing forces signed the armistice to end the Great War.

Twenty-five years later in New York City, Florence purchased nineteen new Dodge ambulances. She recruited twelve young women, ten being French, one Austrian, and one Romanian, three of them nurses. She arranged extensive training for her team and persuaded the military to ship them to Morocco. They arrived in October of that year.

There, she recruited twenty-two more women, most of them French expatriates, to join her group as drivers and nurses, and put them through additional training. When she was ready, she presented herself to General Leclerc via telephone and proposed that he accept her organization and the ambulances as a unit in his division.

Reluctant to introduce women into his ranks, he proposed to take the ambulances without the nurses and drivers. Florence was resolute. "The crews come with the ambulances," she told him. "You cannot have the ambulances without them."

Leclerc, ever a pragmatist and innovator, accepted.

Amélie was astounded to learn that the Rochambelles, even before the 2nd Armored Division had been formed, had served with the general through some of the worst fighting in North Africa, up through Italy, and across France from Normandy. Their diligence, bravery, and dedication in rescuing wounded soldiers under heavy fire had earned them respect and proud acceptance among the 2nd Division's troops. They arrived in Paris with Leclerc's liberating force and participated fully in celebrating the city's liberation. When Leclerc's troops deployed north and east to recapture other parts of France and storm into the Third *Reich*, the Rochambelles went with him.

After learning all she could about the Rochambelles, Amélie inquired about joining them and was gratified to learn that they needed to recruit ten more women. She promptly applied, certain that she would be accepted.

"You're a trained SOE operator in the French Resistance?" Florence pressed, startled when Amélie divulged her background.

Amélie nodded. "Please don't mention it to the others. I can put you in touch with people who can vouch for me. In fact, if you know Lieutenant Colonel Paul Littlefield, he can not only provide more information, but he can also put you in touch with the SOE if you need a more thorough check. He's a liaison with General Leclerc—"

"I know him," Florence interrupted. "I'll have a word with him." She was a tall woman with white, puffy hair cut short around her face, and a merry disposition revealed by a constant wide smile. "If things are as you say, we'll be glad to have you. You'll find our group to be a congenial bunch. We have to get along in good humor to maintain our own sanity. You'll have to practice first aid, and I'll warn you that what you'll see and handle is gruesome more often than not."

As Florence spoke, Amélie's mind flitted back over the past four years. She and Chantal were native to Dunkirk and had witnessed the furious German thrust that pushed the British and French armies off the northwest French coast in 1940, resulting in the massive boatlift to evacuate the stranded soldiers.

Shortly after the German occupation of Dunkirk, Amélie had beat a German soldier to death with a shovel while he tried to rape Chantal. German retaliation had driven the two girls and their widowed father to flee their home. Subsequently, a German major leading the search for them had murdered their father. Enraged, then fourteen-year-old Chantal had rushed the officer and pushed him over a cliff onto rocks far below. He did not survive.

The two sisters then joined the French Resistance. Flown back to England by surreptitious night flights, they had both been trained at Winston Churchill's Special Operations Executive spy school and returned to France where they had been active in missions with the French Resistance.

"I can handle anything that comes my way," Amélie told Florence flatly, "including use of weapons and communications equipment. I can meld into a crowd, get through German checkpoints, carry concealed documents —I've done it all before. I'm stronger than I look. I heard that your women must be able to maintain their vehicles, including repairs. I'm not a mechanic, but I learn quickly. Driving your ambulances and helping the wounded is an imperative that someone must do. I can, so I must."

Florence had contemplated the petite woman before her in silence for a few moments. Amélie's natural beauty had been worn by the war, manifested in lines at the corners of her eyes, and her auburn hair hung straight around her oval face. But the light of determination shone from her honey-colored eyes.

The major stood and extended her hand. "I'll speak with Colonel Littlefield, but I'm sure we'd love to have you. Let me be the first to welcome you."

Paul had tracked down Amélie that same evening. "Are you sure about this? Those ambulance drivers come under constant fire. They're in front of the front, picking up the wounded, including enemy soldiers, while battles rage all around them. I know Jeremy doesn't want you to do this."

Jeremy and Amélie had met at Dunkirk when he found himself abandoned by the evacuating British army. Amélie and her father had risked their lives to go out into a storm to rescue him from certain capture by the Germans. The same plight had befallen thousands of British and French soldiers. For most of the intervening four years, their romance had blossomed despite their constant separation, forced by war.

"I know," Amélie replied to Paul's comment. "I wish none of us were doing any of the things we do. But I must find and free Jeannie. I'll be guilt-ridden for years if I don't. Leclerc intends to go all the way to the German capital, and the Rochambelles will be with him every step."

Jeannie Rousseau was an elegant socialite whom Amélie had recruited to spy, first at Dinard in the German *Wehrmacht* headquarters charged with planning the invasion of the United Kingdom, and then in Paris inside the German high command. Amélie had served as her courier in both places, bearing secret documents to the Allies.

So successful were their efforts that Churchill himself requested that Jeannie be brought back to London so that his staff could explore her knowledge in person. She had agreed on condition that Amélie accompany her. However, as the two women were about to rendezvous with a Royal Navy boat along the coast, Jeannie was captured by the *Gestapo*, but not before giving warning. Amélie escaped.

"We know Jeannie was sent to Ravensbrück," she said, resuming her conversation with Paul. "That's where they send most female prisoners and it's not far from Berlin. With the Rochambelles, I can do some good along the way, and when we get to Berlin, I can look for her."

"If you're not killed first."

Amélie sighed. "I know," she said, "but those soldiers and those ambulance drivers put their lives at risk constantly. I can't stay in safe places while that goes on."

"And what of Jeremy?"

Now under the tree in the orchard near Dompaire and thinking of her conversation with Paul, Amélie's mind went to the last time she had seen Jeremy, just over a week ago, and she teared up. She could not rid her mind of the horror in his eyes when she told him that she had joined Florence's group.

Also not lost on her was that this town, Dompaire, was the very one where Florence had been captured while treating prisoners during World War I.

Amélie had left Jeremy that evening, five days ago. During those days before leaving Paris, Amélie had worked hard with her new compatriots. The bond between the veteran crews was deep and unmistakable, but they extended a warm welcome to the ten new members who brought the unit back to full strength. Together, they worked to change tires, check fluid levels, and change them out as needed. They helped with repairs under the hood and practiced administering first aid.

At each day's end, covered in dust and grease smudges, her body aching and her hands blistered and scraped raw from mechanical work, Amélie had only minimal facilities to clean herself. Nevertheless, when she finally lay down on the hard cot inside her assigned ambulance, she fell fast asleep.

On the last day in Paris, with Danièle, she watched as the French 2nd Armored Division's war machines formed up for departure. To the two women's surprise, some soldiers limped past the ambulances on canes or crutches. Others with bandaged arms, heads, or other body parts hurried to rejoin their units. Refusing to be left behind, they had discharged themselves from the hospitals. Having fought across continents, crossed seas, endured freezing mountain crests in the dead of winter, and liberated Paris, they were determined to be part of the final thrust to fulfill their Oath of Kufra to free Strasbourg, now only three hundred miles away.

Amélie, Danièle, and their fellow Rochambelles had departed Paris in convoy with the French 2nd Armored Division. The route to seize Leclerc's next objective, Épinal on the Moselle River, led through Vittel and Dompaire.

6

That Night, September 12, 1944
Valleroy-le-Sec, Lorraine, France

Paul Littlefield drove through heavy rain at dusk, arriving at Leclerc's command post as darkness settled on this ancient town four miles east of Vittel. The operations staff was briefing on the current situation as Paul made his way into the room inside a schoolhouse where the field headquarters had been established. He made eye contact with the general, but then stood back while the presentation continued.

A map on the wall delineated General Patton's 3rd Army area of operations. Blue arrows drawn on the map indicated Patton's thrust along a wide front toward Germany, with the leading element headed toward Saarbrücken, a city on the German side of the border. Red arrows depicted an anticipated armored German counterattack against the southern flank to halt Patton's advance. The tip of the enemy arrow was aimed at General Haislip's XV Corps, situated to block the *Wehrmacht* maneuver. Leclerc's division was currently attached to that corps, and stood right in the path of the expected German onslaught.

The briefing's presenter, a major, summarized that the day before, Leclerc had deployed one of his battle groups forward, commanded by

Colonel Paul de Langlade, to probe enemy forces. "Today, we captured hundreds of prisoners and extracted valuable information," the major said. "The combat unit that opposed us on the right flank centered its defenses in villages, and the men were mainly occupation troops, not combat-hardened veterans. On the left side, we met the 16th Infantry Division, which was composed of reserve members of the *Luftwaffe* field commands. As fighting forces, they're known to be as effective and equal in status to SS combat units. However, they were spread thin along nearly forty miles and were poorly equipped.

"The American 319th Infantry engaged them from the north. Group de Langlade penetrated easily at the seam between the two units and moved at will behind their lines. That was when Sub-Group Massu encountered *Frontstalag* 121 at Vittel."

At the mention of the former prison town, Leclerc turned sharply and called to Paul, "Colonel Littlefield, how are those matters I left in your hands?"

Paul stood. "Completed for the most part, sir. Most of the people at Vittel were transported away from the village and set free to make their own way home. The adjutant coordinated with logistics to get food and other necessities to them. A security detail met me halfway back to Paris and escorted Madame Henri-Robert and her daughter there." He looked at his watch. "By now, they should be home."

Leclerc nodded, apparently satisfied, and directed his attention to his intelligence officer, a full colonel. "So, the *Wehrmacht* deployed this 112th *Panzer* Brigade against us in reaction to de Langlade's actions today. What else do we know about them?"

The officer stood. "They appear to be well-equipped 'fair weather soldiers,'" he began. "As we've discussed before, we know they were formed only a week ago. We thought at first that they must be hardened combat veterans because they were issued ninety brand-new *panzers*. But they're acting as if they've had only the most fundamental training."

"That's curious," Leclerc broke in. "How so?"

The colonel arched his brows and chuckled. "They're organized with two *panzer* battalions, one grenadier battalion and one reconnaissance company. Their objective seems to have been to re-take Vittel, but they've taken shelter against the rain in the northern part of Dompaire despite that we hit them with field artillery this afternoon, killing their commander. Their soldiers were assigned to sleep in houses, shops, and barns. Those are easy targets, and the unit seems to have done no recon at all. Otherwise, they'd know that they're in a shallow valley surrounded by forested hills. They've given up the high ground and its cover and concealment without a fight, and we have yet to encounter a single security outpost. When the battle starts, they'll be fighting blind."

Leclerc absorbed the information with no expression. "We only have a third of our division to meet the threat," he mused out loud. "The rest is still screening the length of Patton's southern flank. But the Americans are engaging the German 16th Infantry's right flank, and we have close air support and four times the 112th *Panzer's* artillery. They have no air assets at all.

"This battle is critically important to them. If they lose, we'll take Épinal, which could collapse their entire defense along the Moselle south of Nancy." Leclerc turned to his operations officer. "We must win. Show me where de Langlade's forces are deployed now."

The officer stood and pointed out three other locations on the map. "De Langlade positioned his command post here in Ville-sur-Illon, four miles south of Dompaire. He's held one sub-group in reserve there under his personal command. He stationed Sub-Group Massu along high ground overlooking the town and centered here on Hill 380.

"Sub-Group Minjonnet conducted its planned reconnaissance-in-force to the east at Damas, a hamlet just outside of Dompaire. He encountered German *panzers*, and in the engagement, four of our tank destroyers knocked out two Panthers, forcing an enemy retreat."

Enthusiastic whoops accompanied by broad smiles and fist pumping circulated through the staff. Leclerc quickly silenced them. "Go on."

The operations officer continued. "Minjonnet pulled his troops back to Ville-sur-Illon to prepare for a full attack tomorrow morning.

"With the American's 319th Infantry blocking in the north and the Germans hunkered down in the town, Massu will launch his attack from the north and southwest. Meanwhile, Minjonnet will launch his attack to seize Damas and cut off Route Nacional 166. With the high ground, surprise, and enemy inexperience, we'll neutralize much of their numerical advantage and cut off their escape.

"The US 19th Tactical Air Command dedicated six P-47 Thunderbolts to us for close-air support by the 406th Fighter Group. Each one carries three bombs and they're equipped with eight .50 cal machine guns. They'll help even out our numerical disadvantage. And we've seen no sign of enemy anti-aircraft weapons."

Paul listened intently. He had noticed a rise of reserve in Leclerc's demeanor. In the romp across France from Normandy, Paul had enjoyed personal camaraderie with the general. The campaign resulting in Paris' liberation had incurred horrific moments. That was certainly the case at Falaise, but the difference between then and now seemed to be that then the Germans were retreating to their own borders. Having nearly reached them, they were prepared to stand and defend. That perception apparently bore down on the general with a sobering effect.

Leclerc now projected a sense of steely resolve beyond that which had carried him and his men all the way from Libya to this place. "Listen to me," he said, addressing the entire staff. "Inexperience is not the same as incompetence. No classroom can match combat for training. I like the plan and its progress, but in evaluating our foe, the worst thing we could do is underestimate him.

"Those German soldiers who live through tomorrow's battle and escape to fight again will not forget the lessons we are about to teach them. Therefore, our imperative is to execute rapidly, relentlessly, and allow no escape. That brigade has the weaponry and manpower of nearly a full division, and we have only a third of our assets to deploy against them. Nevertheless, what they lack most is initiative, and the net advantage is ours." He paused in reflection. "When we win this one, we'll take a major step closer to Strasbourg."

September 13, 1944

Amélie and Danièle maneuvered their ambulance with difficulty in the night, seeing their way through a mud-spattered windshield under torrential rain, the result of following immediately behind the lead tanks of Combat Sub-Group Minjonnet, a battalion-sized unit named for its commander. They skirted behind low ridges southeast of Dompaire.

Long before dawn, they positioned themselves within a security perimeter inside a tree line overlooking Damas. From that vantage, at daybreak, they could view much of the battlefield. Meanwhile, trying to sleep was useless, so they stayed in their seats, peering into the night and conversing while rain beat a steady drumbeat on the metal roof.

"Are you all right?" Danièle asked after a time. "You seemed nervous as we were leaving. I'd heard that you've been in combat before."

Amélie laughed lightly. "Am I that transparent?" Florence had not divulged Amélie's association with the SOE, but she had mentioned her involvement in blowing up a train inside a tunnel at Buttes-Chaumont park on the east side of Paris the day the city was liberated. Enemy casualties had been high, and the correct conclusion among the Rochambelles was that Amélie must have directly caused at least a few of them. She had—by lobbing hand grenades down on enemy soldiers as they inspected railroad tracks, and then she helped dynamite the locomotive. Amélie had never spoken of it, inferring that Paul must have informed Florence during the vetting process. Word had spread.

Just before leaving Paris, the Rochambelle group had been dismayed to learn that Florence would no longer lead them. "I'm afraid this fifty-eight-year-old body has run the limit of what it can take in this war," she had told her group, laughing at herself in her usual way as she bade them farewell and good fortune. "I've passed command to Toto. I'll remain here at headquarters and monitor your progress."

Florence's choice of her successor had been no surprise. When Florence had first introduced Toto to the Rochambelles, one of the women, Lulu Arpels, jumped to her feet in astonishment and called out, "Toto!"

The two had been childhood friends in Paris, and the nickname stuck.

Suzanne "Toto" Rosambert Torrès had been a prominent Parisian attorney in her mid-thirties when Germany invaded France. She immediately volunteered as an ambulance driver on the front. She also liaised between the volunteers and the French command.

After General Pétain surrendered the country, Toto heeded General Charles de Gaulle's radio call from London to his countrymen to resist and fight, and she fled to the south of France. Arriving there overland, she convinced a friend, famed aviator and author of a newly released sensation, *The Little Prince*, Antoine de Saint-Exupéry, to fly her to Oran and then Algiers.

There, she found French colonial authorities enforcing adherence to Pétain's Nazi-sympathetic dictates, thus putting her under constant threat of arrest. So, she moved on to Morocco, and then back to southern France, staying in Marseille.

Shortly after moving there, the *Wehrmacht* extended its control over the whole country, and she escaped to Spain. There she took a ship to Brazil, and eventually traveled to New York City where she mixed with communities of French expatriates who had escaped the Nazis. A friend introduced her to Florence Conrad at a dinner party.

Florence had been informed of Toto's background and immediately recognized her abilities. When the Rochambelles shipped out to Morocco, Toto was with them.

Resuming the conversation with Danièle in the dark ambulance, Amélie asked, "What do you think of our new leader? I haven't had time to know her."

"She's very good," Danièle replied. "I only came on board with the Rochambelles after Normandy, but I've seen Toto in action. She's very much like Florence in drive and determination, and she knows how to organize and get things done. Her demeanor is always serious, but she cares every bit as much about us as Florence did, and about what we do, and our soldiers. I have no reservations about her."

"That's good to hear." Amélie dropped her head in her hands and blew out a breath. "You were right when you thought I was nervous," she said. "I am. I haven't been on this side of a lethal battle where my job is to save soldiers, German ones too. I'm not sure I can do it."

"Do you mean all the blood? That can't be new—"

"No," Amélie said. "I know first aid very well. I've had to apply it a time or two. If one of our soldiers needs my care, I can do it—but the thought of saving a German..." Her voice trailed off. She remained quiet a few moments, and then stifled sobs as unhappy memories pervaded. "They drove us from our home," she said hoarsely. "They killed my father."

Danièle reached across in the dark and massaged her shoulder. "Did you get a chance to talk much with Arlette Hautefeuille?"

Amélie sniffed. "Are you joking?" Breaking out of stoicism, she laughed. "With that grand wedding and all."

Danièle chuckled softly. "We were thrilled for Arlette and shared her happiness. We'll miss her. Have you heard the story of how that wedding came off? It's incredible."

"No."

"I'll make it quick. Captain George Ratard, one of Leclerc's officers who is now Arlette's husband, knew her in Rabat where he rented a room from her family while French troops were training there. *He* suggested that she join the Rochambelles.

"On the day that we liberated Paris, crowds were all around celebrating. Arlette was in the streets, tired, confused, and not quite knowing what to do next. A woman saw her in her uniform, approached, and asked if she could do anything for Arlette.

"Arlette muttered that she could use a shower. She was kidding, of course, but the woman took her to a very elegant apartment and let her clean up. They hit it off and talked for hours. During that conversation, Arlette said that she and Georges wanted to get married in Paris, but didn't know how to get it done.

"Arlette didn't know that her new friend, Elina Labourdette, was a famous movie star. Both of them are in their early twenties, like us. Elina immediately took things in hand and coordinated with Florence.

"Florence still had her apartment in Paris from before the war. Her daughter's wedding gown was stored there. She loaned it to Arlette and had it altered to fit her. Meanwhile, she took Georges to ask General Koenig's permission to marry Arlette."

Danièle laughed out loud. "Can you imagine that? He had to go to the most senior officer in the whole French army after de Gaulle." She paused to enjoy the moment. "Elina wanted them to marry in Notre-Dame, but the bishop refused, saying that it was reserved for royalty. So, they married in Elina's parents' very posh apartment. It was beautiful, and so was the reception."

While Danièle continued the story, Amélie found herself thinking of Jeremy. An ache formed in her chest. She lapsed into inattention. *Will I ever see him again?*

Sensing her dejection, Danièle said, "I'm sorry. I'm prattling on about a wedding, and you just said farewell to your fiancé. How did the two of you meet?"

Amélie related some of what had taken place at Dunkirk and the various times she and Jeremy had seen each other since then. "We haven't had much time to spend together over the past four years."

"Ah, but yours is a wonderfully romantic story, and I'm sure you'll spend long lives together."

"Let's hope." Amélie grimaced in the dark. "What was the other story you were telling about Arlette?"

Danièle inhaled. "It's not as happy. Just one month ago, our division was fighting at the Falaise Gap. It was very intense. Dead bodies were everywhere, the sun was setting, and we were out tending to the wounded.

"I should tell you first that Arlette's father fought in the last big war, and he brought back with him hatred for anything German. He passed that along to Arlette, and when she joined the Rochambelles, she was steeped in it.

"On that field at Falaise, sometimes we couldn't tell right away whether the bodies or the badly wounded were friend or foe—they were so covered in blood and coated with dirt."

Danièle's tone changed as she spoke, losing the merriment of moments before and sounding hollow. "Arlette treated a soldier who was so badly wounded that he couldn't be moved. He turned out to be enemy. She stayed with him all night, speaking with him in her high-school German. He told of his wife and children and showed pictures of them."

Danièle's voice became taut as she continued. "He died that night. Arlette was not the same. His death broke her heart. She told us, 'So many are just boys out here. They love their families. They don't want to hate us. They're doing what they're trained to do.'

"She said that her hatred was gone. And then she said something I'll never forget." Danièle paused. "I want to get this right. Arlette said, 'Hate cannot stand in the face of suffering.'"

Amélie let out a deep breath. "That's a wonderful sentiment and a noble ideal," she said quietly. "But I've seen the cattle cars of Jews and political prisoners sent off to God-knows-where. I saw no compassion on the faces of those delivering pain. They had snarling dogs, they herded people at gunpoint, even children and the elderly, and they seemed to enjoy it."

"I see your point," Danièle said softly.

The two sat quietly in the dark for a time, then Danièle chuckled. "Have you seen those rules Toto's been putting out."

"I have," Amélie replied, laughing softly, involuntarily. "They're hilarious, like that one that says not to strike a match within a few feet of certain officers because their alcohol content might start a fire. I guess that's her way of being humorous."

"How about the one that outlaws the use of the words 'my' and 'mine.' She uses as an example that we should speak only of 'our' toothbrush."

They shared a few more, now bursting with laughter. "I've lost count of how many proclamations like that she's made, and she keeps adding to them."

With the previous somber mood broken for the moment, they guffawed over as many as they could remember. Struggling to catch her breath, Amélie said, "My favorite is the one where she says that a Rochambelle should not receive a male visitor wearing anything less than her long underwear, and army-issued at that." She let out a peal of laughter.

After a few more exchanges and having exhausted themselves with hilarity, the two settled into quiet. Danièle looked at her luminous watch. "We should try to grab some sleep," she said. "The sun will be up in an hour or so, and then..." She left the thought unstated.

At daybreak, the rain had stopped, and a mist rose from the valley. Almost precisely at 06:30 hours, Lieutenant Colonel Massu's field artillery unleashed blistering salvos onto Dompaire from Hill 380. Even at two miles' distance, the ground shook and clouds of smoke darkened the sky. The explosions continued with only intermittent breaks for a seeming eternity, but by Amélie's watch, they lasted only ninety minutes. Then, as one, the big guns ceased.

A new sound rode a stiff breeze, the roar of aircraft.

Viewing the western sky, Amélie spotted six dark specks that grew rapidly in size until wings and a tail were recognizable on each of them, and the sun glinted off the cockpits of six P-47 Thunderbolts. They banked to the north, circled, and screamed south over Lavieville, a town that abutted Dompaire to its immediate north. Then the fighters flew along the entire length of the battlefield. As they swept above the villages, flames spewed from the leading edges of their wings, and smoke trails angled to the ground followed by horrendous explosions as *panzers* and dug-in positions were hit, their ammunition ignited, and chunks of heavy debris flew into the air.

The aircraft skimmed above the ground past Dompaire heading toward Damas. Amélie's throat constricted as she watched their approach, gripped with fear of becoming a target herself even as she envisioned the human carnage that would soon be hers and the other Rochambelles' to contend with.

As soon as the six fighters had lifted their noses skyward at the end of their runs, Minjonnet set his combat sub-group in motion. Another hour and a half passed with unceasing fire and more sweeps by Thunderbolts across the battlefield. Then Sub-Group Minjonnet, while quickly quelling light resistance, descended into Damas against a foe still reeling from the aerial onslaught. The bulk of Minjonett's troops sped to Route Nacional

166, cutting off that means of German escape from Dompaire, and setting up blocking positions on two secondary roads. The German 112th *Panzer* Brigade, already much reduced, was completely surrounded.

With Danièle at the wheel, the two Rochambelles drove down into Damas. Exchanges of gunfire persisted as they entered the hamlet, trusting that, per the Geneva Convention, enemy fire would be directed away from the big red crosses on the sides of their vehicle.

German gunfire was light compared to that delivered by the French forces.

Danièle's face transformed into a stoic mask as she navigated the small roads, but Amélie's eyes widened in shock as the ambulance reached the hamlet's southern edge. Bodies lay in unthinkable positions among scorched *panzers* and along the streets, some with eyes staring in whatever direction they faced at time of death, others with their faces buried in the ground. Disconnected arms and limbs lay about, and blood had sprayed on vehicles' sides, and pools of it had gathered in low places.

Both women had seen the destruction that war machines had wrought on towns and villages, so neither was shocked at the sight of rubbled buildings with roofs and walls missing or flattened with only the floors marking where homes had been. Unbelievably, some of the stone structures still stood.

The sight of so much carnage was new to Amélie. The smell of spent ammunition invading her nostrils mixed with the stench of burning flesh. Nausea threatened to overwhelm.

French combat troops combed through the ruins, taking prisoners and searching for pockets of resistance. Amélie and Danièle dismounted inside the village and ran from body to body, checking for signs of life among the prone figures.

"Over here," Danièle called.

Amélie ran to her. On the ground next to a burned-out *panzer*, a German soldier writhed, gasping for air. His face was charred and almost unrecognizable as human, but his open eyes moved all about while blood streamed from open cuts.

"Morphine," Danièle yelled. "Give it to him now."

Amélie froze.

"I'll do the morphine," Danièle screamed. "Get the stretcher."

The ambulance suddenly seemed a far distance, and Amélie's muscles refused to respond. She stood staring at the badly burned German soldier.

"Go," Danièle screamed again. "He'll die."

Shocked into awareness, Amélie ran to the ambulance as if in a nightmare, her feet like dead weights on the end of unresponsive legs. In reality, she took only seconds, but as she returned, she saw Danièle stand and shake her head.

"He's gone," she said. "Let's get to the others." She glanced around. "Over there," she said, pointing. "I see another man moving."

By mid-afternoon, the battlefield had quieted to sporadic small-arms exchanges as mop-up operations began. Vehicles smoldered, and intermittently, others exploded from fire that had previously not reached them. German prisoners streamed to collection points under the watchful guard of French soldiers.

After hours of applying tourniquets on legs and arms, pressure bandages on open bullet holes, protecting sucking chest wounds and protruding entrails, struggling with stretchers, and driving many round trips with wounded men stuffed to capacity inside the ambulance and transporting them to an aid tent, the battle ended for the day. Rumor spread that a large German force had circumvented to the south and turned to attack from Minjonnet's rear, but that Leclerc had already sent a reserve unit to block it. Hence, some fighting might resume the next day, but essentially, the battle was won.

Casualty counts trickled in from French officers seeking medical attention, and to Amélie, the numbers would have been unbelievable but for having seen the destruction taking place and treating the wounded. The Germans had lost sixty Panther and Mark IV *panzers* and over three hundred men killed against French losses of eight tanks and forty-four soldiers killed.

Exhausted physically and spent emotionally after transporting the last of the wounded to the aid station, Amélie and Danièle joined the other

Rochambelles in their parking area to clean out their ambulances, scrub off blood that had splattered onto their walls and floors, and pull maintenance on their vehicles.

As the sun descended against the western sky, they attended to their personal care, shared experiences of the day with the other Rochambelles, and chatted with those men of the division who were not currently planning, guarding, patrolling, or doing other related functions.

Sitting cross-legged in her uniform outside her pup tent with her compatriots after a heated battle was another new experience for Amélie. Somberness pervaded with attempts at humor. The women brought their meals in their small mess kits from the field kitchen and ate while sitting on the ground.

At one point, Danièle left the group and wandered toward Group de Langlade's headquarters. After some time had passed and she had not returned, Amélie went to find her. As she approached the front of their ambulance stationed among the others in a line, she heard muffled sobs coming from the rear of the vehicle. Rounding the left side, she found Danièle.

The rear doors were opened wide, and Danièle sat on the edge of the floor, bent over, her feet on the ground, her face in her hands.

Amélie ran to her and wrapped an arm over her shoulder. "Danièle, what's wrong? Are you hurt?"

Danièle looked up momentarily. Tears streamed from bloodshot eyes. She shook her head and buried her face once again in her hands, weeping uncontrollably. "It's Lieutenant Gendron," she managed at last. "He led a platoon in Sub-Group Massu to the north of Dompaire. He was in the first infantry assault—" Her breath caught. She could not speak. Finally she gasped, "He was killed, and I could do nothing for him."

7

Same Day, September 13, 1944
Sark, Guernsey Bailiwick, Channel Islands

Dame Marian Littlefield scanned the fields and the road in front of the village hall. Successive German *kommandanten* had ordered for all of the island's wheat harvest to be stored in the building. Whether from oversight or reliance on the population's acquiescence to their living conditions under occupation, no guard had ever been posted at its entrance. However, a sentry was usually stationed at the top of the old mill where the road led to the hall, although incongruously, not during mealtimes. Fortunately, the entrance itself was screened by trees.

In consultation with Otto, the emaciated butcher; Mr. Baker, the new *seneschal* now responsible for the island's judicial and administrative matters; Mr. Bishop, Marian's farm manager; and Philip Le Feuvre, a carter, Marian had determined that the best time to raid the hall was at six o'clock. That would leave them roughly an hour of daylight and three hours before curfew to complete their mission to rescue as much of the island's stored grain and potatoes as possible.

Otto could not be present because his absence ahead of dinner would be noticed. Those who participated recognized that what they set out to do could result in their summary executions, probably by firing squad.

Although a cart traveling that road and disappearing behind the trees near the hall would not be unusual, if it did not reappear within a short time, an inquisitive sentry might investigate. Hence the emphasis on raiding at dinnertime, counting on fabled German punctuality to avert curiosity.

Philip drove his cart within a few hundred feet of the entrance and halted in deep shade behind the remaining wall of a ruined shed. Marian stood to one side of the hall's entrance where she could observe him as well as the sentry. Baker and Bishop waited behind the hall.

Precisely at six, the sonorous tones of the big bell in the square tower of the stone church resounded across Sark's plateau. The guard disappeared from his station on top of the old mill. Marian waved her scarf. Philip flipped his reins, and his horse plodded forward, pulling its cart with empty bags scattered across its bed.

When the cart arrived, Baker and Bishop were already inside with shovels, and while Marian stood watch, the three men worked as rapidly as they could, filling bags and depositing them in the wagon. A cool autumn breeze blowing from the English Channel made their work easier. Nevertheless, they broke into perspiration, and malnourished as they had been for years, they soon found themselves exhausted.

Seven o'clock approached too rapidly, and Marian did not care to have the cart reappear on the road from behind the trees after the guard had returned to duty. Ten minutes before the hour, she walked through the door into the hall.

"It's time," she said somberly. The men glanced around at the remaining wheat piled high around the storage room and gazed at her with expressions of resignation. "We got at least a ton," Marian said in an attempt at encouragement.

Seneschal Baker grunted. "To feed over four hundred people indefinitely?" He shook his head as he threw down his shovel and carried his last bag to the wagon. "At least we'll live to fight another day."

While he and Bishop disappeared into the gathering dusk, Philip prodded his horse and started toward Marian's *Seigneurie*. She took up the rear, watching to ensure that the cart was a sufficient distance away before the guard appeared.

Marian's status granted her perfunctory respect among the Germans, so she was unlikely to be stopped and questioned by any roving patrol she might encounter. She had noticed that the German troops themselves showed signs of war weariness. Although their conditions were not as stark as those of Sark's residents, their short rations resulted in visible effects of malnutrition.

Marian had heard rumors spread among them about the state of the war, and if behavior was a guide, resulting troop morale was abysmal. Buttressed by her observations and the news gained from the BBC over her hidden radio, she thrilled at the notion that the Huns' days were numbered.

She arrived at the *Seigneurie* and made her way straight to her barn. The cart and horse stood inside, and Philip, Baker, and Bishop were unloading the precious cargo into a small mill. "I'll go check on the potatoes," Marian told them.

She made her way to the back of her house where the garden she had tended for so many years lay desolate. That was heartbreaking to see, but the scene that met her reached into the depths of her soul. Men, women, and children waited for her in ragged clothing, with wide eyes sunk in lined, anxious faces. Each carried bags of potatoes.

Marian put her hand to her mouth to hold back a gasp, surprised at her own reaction. She had seen them individually and in couples or normal groups going about their business around the island, and they had even come together for celebrations and gatherings sanctioned by their German occupiers. She had never seen her friends and neighbors in such a pitiable state with fear written on their faces as they braved fatal retribution to entrust Marian with the safekeeping of perhaps their last scraps of food.

Swallowing hard against her devastation, Marian forced a smile. "Let's do this as orderly as possible," she called out. "Form a line, stay in the shadows, remain silent, leave the back way, and go straight home. We must hurry to store everyone's potatoes. Do not even attempt to break the curfew tonight."

The strange silence of a large group of people moving about carefully in the dark was one that Marian thought she would always remember. They quickly formed a queue, and she led the first ones through the same door where Otto had tapped on the window the night before to bring her news of German plans.

Was that only last night? Marian marveled that so much had taken place in so short a time.

She continued on through the kitchen, down the main hall, and into her drawing room. There, she moved a sofa aside and pulled back a rug, revealing a trap door. After releasing a latch and allowing the wooden cover to swing down, she turned to two young men near the front of the line.

"Take your bags down the stairs and place them at the back of this cellar. As the people come up, they'll drop their bags to you, and you can stack them."

While the work continued, Marian stationed her two poodles at the front door to perform their regular early-warning duty. Other men had taken positions around the mansion's exterior and down the road for the same purpose, and she moved between a front window and a position where she could monitor progress.

Strangely, as the process continued and people turned to leave, Marian saw that often they did so with smiles on their faces. The atmosphere seemed to have lifted.

The only single hour that Marian could recall that was more suspense-laden was the one immediately preceding with the wagon being loaded at the village hall. But the queue finally delivered its last participant, the last potatoes were stored, the trap door replaced and covered, and the wheat safely hidden away in the barn.

When only *Seneschal* Baker remained, he and Marian collapsed on the sofa in the sitting room. She looked at her watch. "You'd best be going," she told Baker tiredly. "Curfew starts in ten minutes."

He nodded and regained his feet. "Before I go, Madame," he said, "I want to say what a wonderful thing you pulled off."

"It was a rather small thing, and not nearly enough—"

"It was a magnificent thing. The Allies are winning. Everyone knows it, even the jerries. And here, on tiny Sark, we pulled off a flawless operation right under the noses of our Nazi occupiers, in broad daylight. It might be enough to let over four hundred people survive the rest of the war.

"You led us, and we won't forget. It was *our* victory, and best of all, everyone participated in his or her own rescue. You gave us hope."

Marian regarded Baker without expression. "You give me too much credit," she said at last, gruffly. "*Bon nuit, Monsieur Seneschal.*"

He reached for her hand and kissed it. "Good night, Dame Marian."

8

Three Days Earlier, September 10, 1944
An Allied Airfield Outside of Brussels, Belgium

"I get your concept," General Eisenhower, Supreme Commander of Allied Forces-Europe told Field Marshal Bernard Montgomery, Commander of the British 21st Army Group. "I like it, but I'm not sold. I'm anxious to hear the details."

The two officers sat next to each other at a map on a narrow table that ran the length of the passenger compartment of the North American B-25 Mitchell, serial number 43-4030, that Eisenhower used to move about the European Theater. The aircraft had been heavily insulated, fitted with five commercial-grade seats on each side of the table, and the walls had been trimmed with blue fabric over wood panels.

The meeting was held in the parked airplane because Eisenhower had injured his leg and moved about with great difficulty. Also present were the Deputy Supreme Commander, Air Chief Marshal Tedder; Eisenhower's chief administrative officer, Lieutenant General Gale; and Montgomery's chief administrative officer, Major General Miles Graham.

Two maps were open on the table. They were almost identical, showing France, Germany, and the "Low Countries" of Belgium, Holland, and

Luxembourg, so called because much of the land in the first two countries was below sea level, resulting in widespread marshes that inhibited military maneuvers. Luxembourg shared the characterization for being in the same region and sharing a common culture.

The two maps differed in the displays of military symbology drawn onto them. The first showed Eisenhower's plan for defeating Germany. The second illustrated Montgomery's alternative plan.

"My 'broad-front' strategy got us here, Monty. It's slowed because of logistics. We're outrunning them. When you've opened up Antwerp, and the other ports in Brittany are captured and functional, that bottleneck will be relieved."

Eisenhower was a fair-complected, average-sized man with light hair and blue eyes over an ever-present phantom smile. He had been selected for supreme command in Europe due to his dedication, even temperament, strategic thinking, and diplomatic skills. Those, among other traits, had served the Allies well in campaigns across North Africa and western France.

"After St. Lo, Brad's army group pushed westward faster than we expected," he said, continuing his discussion with Montgomery. "His armies under Hodges and Patton are nearing the German border from the west. General Patch's 7th Army cleared the Rhône Valley in the south. They're moving north of Lyon now and are linking up with Patton's 3rd Army. With your group expected to move through the Low Countries and across northern France, we'll be poised to—"

"Sir, your 'operational pause' due to 'offensive culmination' is costing us momentum."

Eisenhower chuckled. "So now you're questioning Clausewitz? I happen to think he was right. An army that pushes itself too far too fast will run out of steam and write its own defeat."

"Sir," Montgomery countered, "since the breakout at Normandy, we've crossed France at breakneck speed. In some places, we must be within a hundred miles of the German border."

Eisenhower glanced at the field marshal sharply. "Victims of our own success, I suppose," he muttered. "You don't think they'll fight like fiends to defend their homeland? We don't enjoy endless supply or manpower, and don't forget that the war extends to the other side of the planet. There's a major assault building at a place called Peleliu in the Pacific as we speak. Allied forces there require food, fuel, guns, and ammo the same as we do. And on this side of the world, our supply routes must open up, or all the materiel will be useless. You must have heard about the fate of the bombing mission to take out the *Tirpitz* in Norway?"

When Montgomery nodded reluctantly, Eisenhower continued, "If we don't take care of that situation soon, we're dead there. The Soviet effort would grind to a halt, and we need them to keep pushing the *Wehrmacht* from the east. Failure there could end the war." He added grimly, "Not happily for us, I'm afraid."

"I understand, sir." Montgomery said with an edgy tone, "Peleliu? I've never heard of it."

"Nor had I, and it's a strictly US operation," Eisenhower replied, meeting the field marshal's acerbic tenor, "but my point is that we can't open the spigot and let it run. We're six months ahead of our expected progress. Ultra-level intelligence reports indicate that German losses in their retreat from France are over a hundred thousand men. Over ten thousand officers. Some units report that they are completely out of fuel, and they have only one man to replace every fifteen lost. So, while we're bemoaning our own difficulties, they don't approach those of the Germans.

"We can fix our shortcomings. They can't fix theirs, but they're still a lethal fighting force. We can't lose sight of that."

Taking in Montgomery's neutral expression, Eisenhower paused and then resumed. "Look, Monty, your 1st Army did an excellent job of taking Antwerp. Liberating that harbor was always a key Allied objective, but the port is not yet operational, and until the Scheldt Estuary is cleared of the enemy, its facilities are useless to us, and it's up to you to do that.

"That being the case, I still like my broad-front strategy while we improve our supply lines and push toward the Rhine. Our next main objective is the industrial base in the Ruhr Valley. The factories there are having trouble meeting demand for weapons and ammunition."

He studied Montgomery's expressionless face and chuckled. "I want to hear your narrow-front approach. Did you see the two telegrams I sent you five days ago?"

"I did, sir," Montgomery replied tartly, "and they were nothing but balls, sheer balls, rubbish." As soon as the words had left his lips, he flushed red and stiffened.

Although a recognizable figure to anyone following the war's progress, he was under average height and spoke in a high-pitched voice. However, his force of personality, methodical planning, and aggressive execution had turned him into an icon that won him the loyalty of his soldiers and the love of his countrymen.

Controversy had followed him, however. Most recently, he had miscalculated in planning for Operation Goodwood in a failed attempt to break out of Caen after landing at Normandy. The catastrophe that resulted from the largest British tank battle to date caused staggering numbers of casualties and equipment losses, and it had almost cost Montgomery his job. Only Eisenhower's patience had saved him.

Startled at Montgomery's comment, Eisenhower raised his eyebrows. The other officers at the table opened their eyes wide but otherwise remained silent.

Eisenhower reached over and clasped the field marshal's knee. "Steady, Monty. You can't speak to me like that. I'm your boss."

Before Eisenhower had finished, Montgomery stood and bowed slightly at the waist. "Ike, I apologize." His voice shook, and he stuttered. "I've embarrassed myself. What I said was out of line." He took a breath. "The Siegfried—"

Eisenhower interrupted him with a gesture. "We're all just as frustrated as you about the supply situation. This might be the time to go over the points I made in those wires."

Montgomery acquiesced and took his seat. Eisenhower resumed. "Your main objective in the proposed operation is a drive on Berlin. As I stated in my telegrams, I agree with a powerful thrust to get there, but I don't see wisdom in attempting that now to the exclusion of all other operations.

"We have to breach the Siegfried Line, cross the Rhine on a wide front, and seize the Saar and the Ruhr. That'll cut off Germany's industrial capacity and its ability to replenish its weaponry. Our main thrust is north of the Ardennes Forest because the roads are better there than either south of those woods or on the northern German plain, which has a lot of marshland."

Eisenhower swept his hand over the map to indicate the area he spoke about. "While we continue our advance east, we'll open the ports in the west at Havre and Antwerp and the others in Brittany. If we hope to sustain the drive into Germany, that's imperative. Even if we diverted all of our resources to your plan, though, which I won't do, we couldn't sustain the drive to Berlin with supply lines extended that far, and particularly with the enemy on both flanks.

"I intend to continue with the current plan and occupy the Saar and the Ruhr. By then, Havre and Antwerp should be open to maintain a drive like yours across Germany. But right now, all our supplies come through Cherbourg. That's a chokepoint."

Eisenhower paused to gather his next thoughts. "Essentially, what you've asked me to do, Monty, is divert the bulk of our logistics to you—guns, ammo, and fuel—for a thrust north through Arnhem in the Netherlands—"

"That would get us past the Siegfried Line," the field marshal interrupted, "and then we'd turn east toward Berlin. The terrain is better for tanks in northern Germany."

"We can't dismiss the marshlands up there. They could bog you down," Eisenhower countered. "Your proposed operation is extremely risky. With my broad-front strategy, we have two army groups plus the 7th Army supporting each other and protecting each other's flanks as they assault the full length of the Siegfried Line, from southeast of Arnhem to the Swiss border.

"Your 'narrow-front' strategy would put large columns of soldiers sixty miles deep inside enemy lines with questionable ability to be reinforced and resupplied. If we've miscalculated German strength behind the Siegfried, the potential for a military calamity is enormous. We might not be able to recover from it."

Montgomery took a deep breath. "Sir, you know I'm a careful and meticulous planner and I execute aggressively. I understand fully what I'm proposing. It's almost the reverse of the way that the jerries invaded France at the beginning of the war. They went around the north end of the Maginot Line."

Eisenhower acknowledged the comment with a nod. "And the Maginot parallels the Siegfried near the French-German border. But the *Wehrmacht* had surprise and speed going for them."

"We'll have both speed and surprise," Montgomery insisted. "They see us continually attacking across your broad front, approaching the whole border. They won't expect a thrust northward in the west that gets in their rear."

Eisenhower shook his head in obvious doubt. "You're talking about dropping airborne troops in three places to seize key protected bridges. That will end surprise.

"Our ground infantry would be sent to reinforce, but to get there, they'd travel in armored convoys on a very narrow axis, and on the way, they'd have to cross a bunch of rivers and ditches, and three major canals."

"We've done this before," Montgomery cut in. "We sent in airborne and glider troops in advance at Normandy. That's the reason for having them. Then they're reinforced with ground troops."

"The distances were much shorter," Eisenhower countered, "and the time to transport reinforcements was much less."

"The risks were greater. If we had foundered on the beach, we would already have lost the war."

Eisenhower agreed with a nod. "The scale was different, but we had no chance without a beachhead on the Continent." He glanced up at Montgomery with a wry smile. "Unless you wanted to let the Russkies come in from the east and take over all of Europe."

Montgomery smacked his lips and shook his head, but did not reply.

Eisenhower mulled in silence while the other officers looked on. "Let's go over your plan again," he said at last.

Eagerness flashed in Montgomery's eyes. He stood and leaned over the map. "It's simple in concept. We'll need to capture these five bridges intact." He pointed them out on the map. "One at Eindhoven, one over the Wilhelmina Canal at Son, the one at Willems Canal near Veghel, then twenty miles north, the Waalbrug at Nijmegen, and the last one nine miles north of there, at Arnhem."

He then pointed out three towns in a line from south to north. "To accomplish that, I propose to drop the US 101st Airborne Division at Eindhoven, the 82nd at Nijmegen, and the British 1st Airborne Division at Arnhem. The bridges in those three towns are the most significant, and the ones we must capture."

Montgomery straightened up. "We've codenamed the operation 'Market—'"

Eisenhower grimaced. "You're proposing the largest airborne assault ever contemplated," he interrupted incredulously, "with three separate landings. And you'd be using my strategic reserve. We'd have to hope those troops aren't needed elsewhere—"

"Which they would not be," Montgomery broke in. "You've already paused other operations across France for the time being." Sensing Eisenhower's doubtful reception to his proposal, he ran his finger along a line on the map that delineated a road connecting the three towns. "Simultaneously," he continued, urgency mounting in his voice, "I'll deploy the British 2nd Army for a complementary maneuver, a road march on this route. I call that part of the plan 'Garden.' The ground forces would move rapidly to reinforce the airborne units at those bridges.

"Together with the airborne assaults, the whole maneuver is dubbed 'Operation Market Garden.'"

Eisenhower studied the map. "That's a long road plowing deep into enemy territory. What about your flanks?"

"I'd deploy the Canadian 1st Army to protect the left flank. You've already attached the US 9th Army to my command for the planned drive across northern France under your broad-front concept. Instead, I'd use it to protect my right flank as I push north.

"Once we're past Arnhem, we'd continue on to Ijssel Lake and turn east. We'd be behind the Siegfried Line, and poised to march across the German northern plain. That's tank country, and the marshlands are manageable."

He enunciated his next words distinctly. "Next stop, Berlin."

Catching some of Montgomery's excitement, Eisenhower stood and pored over the map. "For your plan to work, we'd need to divert most of our gas and ammo to you. You know Patton is pushing me for a quick thrust south of the Ardennes that would cross the Rhine and would, he argues, force a quick surrender. Of course to do that, we'd have to dedicate the same resources you're requesting, which would mean delaying plans to open Antwerp's port facilities."

He rubbed his chin and chuckled. "Your plan halts Patton at the Meuse River. Do you want to be the one to tell him that?"

"Gladly, sir," Montgomery replied with no hint of humor. The personal and professional rivalry between him and Patton was well known. "We've reached a stage where a powerful, full-blooded thrust to Berlin is likely to end the war."

Eisenhower met Monty's intense gaze momentarily and continued to mull. "What's the timetable?"

"From start to finish, four days. That is, we'd be north of the Siegfried Line in that timeframe and preparing to move toward Berlin."

"That's ambitious. We'd have a hard time resupplying you adequately, and I'd still have to delay opening the port at Antwerp, which we need, to help resolve our overall logistics problems. The fact is, without that harbor, I can't sustain a long drive by either you or Patton. And if storms over the Channel interfered with our supply coming through Cherbourg for even a week, we'd be in a real pickle. The airborne troops would have to fly from Britain too. The weather's good now, but that can change in an instant. Those combinations of factors make both plans very chancy.

"Besides that, we still have to consider the other three army groups: Bradley's 12th, Hodges' 1st, and Devers' 6th. If you get bogged down, we'd have to revert to the broad-front strategy. I wouldn't want to re-start operations along our whole front where soldiers had been idle while we wait to see if Market Garden works. We'd lose more momentum and see a plunge in morale. Starting the men back up might be difficult, and the logistics could be a nightmare."

"The current high morale rests on the rapid march across France after Normandy, culminating in liberating Paris," Montgomery interjected. "The fight ahead will be much more difficult."

"You've made my point," Eisenhower remarked with a lifted brow and a slight nod. He drummed the table with his fingers while he thought. "The soldiers are almost euphoric, and that's worrisome. The talk of victory and being home by Christmas is at fever pitch. But you're right about the effects of a standstill across the front. Euphoria will wane. Rapidly."

He stood again, and stretched in place. "On the other hand, we can't act on hubris. We could get a lot of good men killed and have nothing to show for it." He deliberately did not mention Operation Goodwood, but images flitted across his mind of Caen's bloody battlefield and the stern conversation that ensued with the field marshal in its aftermath. He had no doubt that Montgomery entertained similar recollections.

Montgomery also rose to his feet. "I know the risk, sir. General Browning, the deputy commander of the First Allied Airborne Army, told me that, by going for Arnhem, we might be going a bridge too far. But consider this: the Germans are fortifying both the Maginot and the Siegfried Lines. We're heading into autumn and winter, and with the broad-front approach, our troops will likely bog down in mountainous terrain before they even have to contend with those defenses. Improved resupply won't change that. We wouldn't have a prayer of entering Berlin before sometime next year.

"By taking my narrow-front approach, we'll outflank the Siegfried Line on the path the Germans least expect. We'd do that by capturing and holding the crossings over the canals and rivers on the 2nd Army's main axis of advance from Eindhoven to Arnhem." The field marshal warmed to his own argument, his enthusiasm raising his iconic high-pitched voice another octave. "We'll lay an airborne carpet, dropping thousands of paratroopers around key bridges with orders to ensure that they remain intact. And they'll be followed by thousands more soldiers, supplies, and equipment in gliders—"

Eisenhower interrupted. "I'll grant you, the route is within easy range for the transport planes if the weather holds up." He arched his brows. "That's a big if."

"Sir, we'd have a real chance of ending the war in Europe by Christmas."

Startled by Montgomery's comment, Eisenhower peered at him through narrowed eyes. "But if Operation Market Garden does not succeed," he countered, "we could have a whole army group cut off without support."

Eisenhower reflected quietly again, and when he continued, he seemed to be thinking out loud. "The fact is, we've built this enormous airborne capability, and it's sitting in Britain, constantly training, but not being used. The War Department is champing at the bit to see what the airborne can do as a strategic asset, but every time we identified a target, eighteen of them so far, our ground troops overran it before we could mount the mission."

He addressed Montgomery directly once more. "Frankly, General Bradley likes using air assets to resupply ground operations. He sees supporting our soldiers as the best use of air transport assets. He thinks that your plan is inspired, but he told me, 'Ike, it's foolhardy. You'll take a lot of casualties.'"

Montgomery grimaced. "We *will* take a lot of casualties," he admitted, "but we could take as many or more with the broad-front strategy." He let out a long breath. "I'm sorry to say that there is just no way around casualties."

Eisenhower acknowledged the comment with a nod, and sighed. "I need time to study your plan in detail and look at the ramifications across the theater. I'll need weather predictions and updated intel on enemy dispositions in the area."

Still standing next to him, Montgomery inhaled sharply and looked at the ceiling. "Sir, I assure you—"

Eisenhower raised a hand to interrupt him. "You make good points, Monty," he said pensively. "I might consider diverting *some* resources to Market Garden, but I won't pause or cripple other operations that are in the offing. The field commanders will make their plans based on the resources we're still able to get to them."

While Montgomery stood in expectant silence, Eisenhower bent over the map once more. Finally, he straightened, but sat in quiet reflection. "All right," he said slowly, "I can see the strategic objectives your Market Garden could achieve, and the joint chiefs have been pushing to test airborne assets as a strategic asset. So, I'll approve planning and coordination for the operation, but understand this: your final objective is the bridge at Arnhem. Intact. When that's accomplished, we'll take another look, but Market Garden will not include continuing on north to that lake or starting east to Berlin. Further, you'll execute only on my express order. Are we clear?"

Montgomery was already shoving his trademark beret with a Royal

Tank Regiment crest onto his head. "Yes. Thank you, sir. Is there anything else? If not, I'll get on it straightaway."

Eisenhower smiled distantly. "Monty, I have to say, for all your caution, you never lack for energy. I think we're done here. How soon can you be ready?"

"Within a week," the field marshal shot back as he headed for the exit.

Eisenhower turned to the other three generals. "Berlin by Christmas," he breathed, and added, "being done with this nasty business by then would be nice. For once, the politicians, the soldiers, and the people would be happy at the same time." He grunted. "If we do this thing, Monty will finally share the news limelight with Patton that he's been clamoring for and that Churchill mentioned to Roosevelt." He added in a tone barely above a growl, "If we do it, it had better work."

9

September 12, 1944
Guam, Mariana Islands, Pacific Ocean

Lieutenant Commander Josh Littlefield tested the ailerons of his F6F Hellcat fighter one more time, listened to the hum of its engine, and checked his flight instruments while he waited to lead his squadron into the skies. Adrenalin surging through his veins raised anticipation of confronting danger even as a tinge of fear roiled his gut. He forced his mind to focus on his aircraft, the readiness of the pilots awaiting his command, and the mission.

On receiving clearance from the tower, he keyed his mic and intoned, "Let's roll." Then he released his brakes, throttled up, and began his taxi. Minutes later, in flight, he set his trim, monitored as eighteen other Hellcats formed up behind him, and set a southeasterly course. Destination: Peleliu.

Be careful what you wish for... Josh had admonished himself with the time-worn adage over his persistence to be returned to flight status from the CIC, the combat information center aboard the USS *Lexington*. His request had been granted along with command of a Hellcat squadron, but the aircraft carrier had since deployed to support operations in General

MacArthur's Southwest Pacific Theater, and Josh's squadron had been transferred to a land base on Guam following the island's recapture.

Hence his admonition to himself about wishing. He had spent weeks of relative inactivity on Guam. No rolls of the ship on the waves, no screaming sirens, no mad-dash analyses of incoming intelligence, no commands over the PA system for all pilots to "report on the flight deck for duty aloft"—no tempo of combat. He also missed being intimately aware of the war's progress. Instead, he received news mainly from the *Stars and Stripes* and whatever information he could glean from meager intelligence reports.

The 77th Infantry Division provided a robust initial intelligence staff on Guam, but the information was mainly local and provided scant value in assessing enemy strength and movements, relying as it did on air reconnaissance, local intelligence from Guamanians, and infantry patrols over the island. Lacking for Josh was a sense of the larger picture, of how the war in the Pacific proceeded beyond Guam's shores or of what was happening in the European Theater. The meager amount of information was maddening to him.

Josh found himself missing his work within the CIC too. In his capacity there, he had supervised twenty-seven intelligence specialists who gained information from decoded enemy intercepts, air-reconnaissance and submarine spotter reports, and various other sources. They had analyzed, synthesized, drawn conclusions, and recommended actions that had significantly affected outcomes, including defeating Japan's last attempt in the Battle of the Philippine Sea to destroy Admiral Spruance's 5th Fleet, the largest ever assembled to date. The battle had resulted in Japan's withdrawal to the protective perimeter of islands closer to its own coast, leaving Admiral Nimitz's Central Pacific Theater clear of enemy threat or encroachment from Guam to California.

Despite that he had been assigned to the CIC unwillingly, Josh looked on his time there and his results with pride. The work had kept him occupied day and night and informed him up to the minute on what occurred in the 5th Fleet's battle space and its adjacent areas. However, he was a pilot at heart and insisted that his greatest contributions to the war were made in the cockpit of a fighter leading other pilots. His last aerial engagement had been over the Philippine Sea three months ago.

Ahead of that battle, USN Commander Joseph Rochefort, the cryptana-
lytical genius who, along with his team, had broken the Japanese code that
led to US victory at Midway, had once again intercepted and decoded
crucial Japanese messages that provided critical information on enemy
plans and movements. By the time the enemy launched the Philippine Sea
attack, Admiral Spruance had already taken countermeasures. Within two
days in mid-June, he had driven east the largest Japanese fleet ever assembled, having destroyed much of it.

Three weeks later, the 1st Marines and the Army's 79th Infantry Division
recaptured Guam, thus controlling the Marianas chain and relegating the
Japanese navy to defending from a perimeter of islands closer to home.

Additional US advantages came about in advanced radar that spotted
enemy aircraft at distances of three hundred miles. US fighters intercepted
and fought them off well away from the capital and support ships that were
their intended targets.

Meanwhile, the proficiency of Japanese pilots had waned resulting from
high casualties and insufficient training for replacement pilots. Their lack
of proficiency was demonstrated by hesitancy to act, overcaution when
executing tactics, and obvious errors in navigation. During the decisive
battle in the Philippine Sea, they had initially missed, by many miles, the
fleet they sought. In so doing, they burned up scarce fuel.

That particular assault was defeated handily, and became, as one pilot
exclaimed, "the Great Marianas Turkey Shoot." The losses on the Japanese
side had been great, with around four hundred planes downed. On the US
side, they had been minimal, only twenty-nine.

After the battle, the *Lexington* had anchored in the Eniwetok Atoll while
a new naval base was built there. Josh had found himself inactive with little
to do. He had written letters to his brother Zack, now fighting with the 36th
Infantry somewhere in France, and his sister Sherry, who, God bless her
soul, was one of the Flying Angels who tended to the most seriously
wounded soldiers aboard medical flights, ferrying them from combat zones
in Europe to hospitals in England.

He had not heard back from either of his siblings, but had resigned
himself to the notion that such would probably be the case. The same had
been true for his communication with his cousin, Paul Littlefield. He and

Paul had first met in New Jersey, and they had served together briefly in North Africa. Josh knew that Jeremy and Lance had escaped from Dunkirk and that Claire tended to an orphaned child whom Jeremy had rescued from a sinking ship, and that the entire family had been involved in the war in one way or another, but he had never met Paul's siblings or their parents. A burning desire had grown inside him to bring the entire family together after the war and to stay in close touch with them. Often, when the thought occurred, he shook his head. *If we all survive. The occasion could be a sad one.*

Boredom resulting in a mix of anticipation juxtaposed against melancholy had stirred him to press harder for a transfer, and it had finally come through. Then, five weeks ago, the US 3rd Marine Division, the 1st Provisional Marine Brigade, and the US Army's 77th Infantry Division had defeated General Takashina's troops on Guam, and re-captured that American island.

After-action analysis of recent naval battles, in particular the Battles of Saipan and the Philippine Sea, had led the navy to conclude that pre-invasion bombardments of Japanese defenses should be increased massively to give Marines the best chance of establishing a beachhead with the fewest casualties.

Japanese ground resistance had been so ferocious during the Saipan campaign that Admiral Nimitz determined that increasing invasion forces to overwhelming numbers was imperative. Enhancing the overall combat strength for the incursion at Guam by adding the US Army's 77th Infantry Division had produced a result that proved the wisdom of his mandate. Of Takashina's nineteen thousand combat defenders on Guam, fewer than a thousand survived three weeks of fighting against fifty-five thousand US Marines and soldiers who invaded the island. By contrast, US casualties were less than a third of Japanese.

Improvements in sophisticated air-to-ground coordination systems led to more effective close-air support for fighters in the thick of combat. Modified command and control procedures allowed for rapid adjustments to respond to rapidly changing ground conditions. Lessons learned from Tarawa, Saipan, Tinian, and Guam resulted in better anticipation of amphibious forces' immediate needs on hitting shore and logistics processes to deliver them most efficiently.

Josh understood and appreciated the changes. He well remembered his days on Edson's Ridge in Guadalcanal where he had lived in foxhole squalor and fought savagely, hand-to-hand, against crazed *banzai* assaults. The memory of a Japanese soldier leaping toward Josh with a fixed bayonet still woke him from nightmares in cold sweats. Josh had struck first with a bayonet just seized from a fallen Marine comrade. The image of the impaled soldier's face as all expression faded from it was one that Josh feared would be with him always.

The recapture of Guam marked a critical point in the Pacific Theater, providing protection for the right flank of MacArthur's Southwest Pacific Area as the general prepared to liberate the Philippine Islands. Guam also served as Nimitz's strategic base as the admiral prepared to attack Iwo Jima and Okinawa. All three islands represented critical steps in the final thrust to defeat the Land of the Rising Sun.

To that end, Guam represented an opportunity to build new airfields and expand existing ones from which to base and launch Boeing B-29 Superfortress bombers against the home island of Japan. To help maintain air superiority over the island, five weeks ago, two Hellcat squadrons, including Josh's, had been moved to Guam.

They had spent the past four weeks patrolling the skies, now empty of enemy aircraft in their sectors. When not flying, they attended tactical briefings, practiced communications procedures, and checked on aircraft maintenance. Essentially, they secured the local airspace and paid attention to details required to increase the odds of staying alive in combat but that bored fighter pilots to tears. When all that was done, they played horseshoes, pinochle, poker, and baseball, swam in Guam's gleaming waters, wrote letters, or dreamed of home—that is, they fought monotony.

The routine ended this morning. At the mission brief, Josh announced, "We're transferring again, this time to the USS *Essex*, commanded by Captain McClusky, to participate in Operation Stalemate II." As his pilots whooped, he held up his hands for quiet. "I'll simplify the situation."

He gestured toward a large map on an easel and used a pointer to indicate locations as he spoke. "The Japanese are dug in on an island, Peleliu, on the south end of the Palau Archipelago, the westernmost part of the Caroline Islands chain. Peleliu has an airfield that our leaders see as crucial both to support General MacArthur's thrust to re-take the Philippines and to Admiral Nimitz's intent to capture Iwo Jima and Okinawa. Those objectives are key to invading Japan itself."

"We're getting close," someone yelled. "Tell those Japs the Yanks are comin'!"

"I love the spirit," Josh cautioned in a commanding voice, "but this is no time to lowball the Japanese. The closer we get, the more fiercely they'll fight. Their air force is depleted, their best pilots are dead, but that doesn't mean they're out of the game.

"We can count on their Betty Bombers coming for our ships, and they've got quite a few Zeros stationed on the island. We don't know how many, and they've undoubtedly got 20 mm cannons and heavier artillery guns, 37 mm and 75 mm. None of those weapons systems are toys.

"Our mission is pretty simple. We're part of a pre-invasion bombardment to soften up defenses on Peleliu. Today, we'll drop bombs on designated targets, strafe anything we see that needs strafing, and then fly on to the *Essex*, re-arm, re-fuel, and run more missions over the island—"

"It's got a pretty name," another pilot joked.

"And yours will be Mudd if you interrupt me again with bullcrap," Josh mock-chided, his face screwed between a frown and a grin. "We'll camp out on the *Essex* and run missions until ordered to return here, probably three or four days into the invasion. It's not expected to last much longer than that. So, with four days of pre-invasion action, including D-Day, and roughly the same amount of time in ground support, we can expect to be away from this paradise for a little over a week.

"During pre-invasion bombing prep, our battleships and destroyers will let loose with everything they've got, non-stop. We'll make bombing runs and coordinate closely with them, 'cuz we don't want our friendlies shootin' us down." He chuckled, but then made eye contact with his pilots, and his expression turned decidedly serious. "That's no joke." He paused to let the admonition sink in.

"Once Peleliu is captured and secured," he went on, "we'll return here.

With the amount of ordnance we're throwing at them, that's not expected to take long—"

"That's what Intel told us about Tarawa—"

Josh shrugged, thinking of the dedicated analysts he had supervised in the *Lexington's* CIC. "Sometimes they get it right, sometimes they don't. Have you ever shot and missed?"

The pilot who had made the comment acknowledged Josh's response with a slight nod and a sheepish smile. "Point taken."

Three hours later, Josh led his squadron over Peleliu, dropped his bombs, fired his machine guns at anti-aircraft positions, and landed on the *Essex* without incident.

Peleliu, shaped like a lobster claw with its pincers protruding northeastward from a southern body of land suitable for an airfield, was situated just inside the Palau coral reef that had built up over millennia. Umurbrogol Mountain, composed of parallel coral ridges, dominated the western pincer.

Nicknamed the "Devil's Anvil" by naval strategists for its strategic position pertinent to this war, the island was so tiny, only five square miles, that it appeared as a speck on a map of the Pacific. Almost no one had ever heard its name. Its fate resulted from its ability to support a key airfield at the crux of conflict between two great naval powers, one intent on defending its homeland and eastern conquests with vital resources, the other determined to destroy its adversary's naval capacity and extricate the enemy's armies from everywhere, including the homeland itself.

Josh never would have predicted that bombing and strafing runs could become monotonous, but that was exactly the sense after the first three days of missions over Peleliu. Pounding the island continued all day and throughout the night by the navy's big 5 In. and 16 In. batteries, followed regularly and with close coordination by Hellcat and Marine F4U Corsair combat runs over the island to knock out anti-aircraft sites. Enemy resistance by air had been light and was quickly shot down on the first day, as were the Japanese Betty Bombers heading for the ships.

During an off moment between flights, Josh meandered along the flight deck to take in the vast array of warships spread out over the waters. Then he went into the *Essex's* operations center to gain a sense of the forces ranged against the island. Displayed on a large wall map, they were mind-boggling and included three large carriers, five light carriers, five battleships, five heavy cruisers, and three light cruisers.

Late in the afternoon on the third day of their mission, Josh and his squadron touched down on the *Essex* and, after on-deck post-flight duties, they made their way to the ready room they shared with another squadron. While his pilots relaxed and stowed their gear, Josh went to the operations room for an update.

He returned minutes later. "Listen up," he called, and his tone caught the pilots' immediate attention. "The 7th Fleet Commander, Admiral Oldenorf, reported to General MacArthur today that we've run out of targets on Peleliu." His news was greeted with silent stares. "The Marines hit the beach at 08:30 hours tomorrow morning."

The pilots exchanged grim looks. An invasion always meant much bloodshed, mostly spilled by Marines. With the changes in methods based on the lessons learned from the Battles of the Philippine Sea and Saipan and the resulting addition of US Army divisions to the mix, the hope was that the operation would go much faster, the objectives would be captured sooner, and less blood would be spilled.

"The 1st Marine Division gets to do the honors again—"

"Those poor bastards," someone muttered, and received affirming comments.

"The Army's 81st Infantry Division goes in to take Angaur Island just off of Peleliu's south coast. It'll base there and provide a reserve if the Marines need it."

Gloomy silence hung in the room.

"We've pounded that island for four days with hardly any resistance," another pilot broke in with a tone of optimism. "This'll be a piece of cake."

Josh scrutinized the faces of his men and muttered, "Remember Tarawa."

10

September 15, 1944
Peleliu Island, Palau, Western Pacific Ocean

Josh looked to his left for a visual check on nine of his Hellcats spread at an angle behind him. Then he checked for eight more spread out to his right at a complementary angle, the entire formation forming a "V" with himself at the fulcrum. He scanned across his instruments looking for anomalies, and finding everything normal, he searched ahead for the specks that would be the Marine F4U Corsair squadron that his own formation would follow.

The evening before, his pilots had groused at the mission briefing on learning that they would be following rather than leading the initial charge over the island. "The Marines say that those are their guys on the ground, so they get first dibs," Josh had explained. "Besides, between us, Marine air, and the Navy's big guns, we've dropped more tons of softening-up ordnance on Peleliu than on any island the US has ever invaded. And we've got eight carriers' worth of aircraft launching to that target, so the odds of our leading were pretty small. In fact, several squadrons will be ahead of us."

The light grumbling had continued. "Now look," Josh admonished sternly. "From our view, this might look like a cakewalk, but I assure you that those troops on the ground don't think of it that way."

Recollections of Tarawa flitted through his mind. That atoll was also supposed to have been lightly defended. Not only had that proven not to be the case, but a miscalculation in the tide levels had caused the Marines to be deposited on the coral reef in chest-high water a half-mile out from dry land.

Many had drowned, pulled underwater by the weight of their own equipment, but most of those killed in action died from struggling forward, with nowhere else to go, into unexpectedly heavy and blistering machine gun fire. The operation that the planners had thought would be over in a matter of hours had lasted more than three days. On the first day, only five thousand of an expected eighteen thousand Marines had managed to fight their way onshore at Betio, site of the main attack on the Tarawa Atoll. Of those Marines, several hundred were killed. After three days, the battle was won, but nearly a thousand Marines lay dead, and more than two thousand more were wounded.

Josh knew the battle intimately. He had flown close-air support there. It was where he had been shot down for the second time.

He snapped himself from his short, sad reflections. "Forty-five hundred Marines will lead the charge," he said, "and within twenty minutes, twenty-four thousand are supposed to be onshore to establish a beachhead, and the weather won't be their friend. Temperatures will range to a hundred and fifteen degrees, humidity will be high, and rain will hit intermittently. It'll be hell on earth before the firing starts."

He allowed a few moments for the severity of the gloomy images to form, and then continued. "Given the pounding we've delivered over the past four days, meeting their objective seems possible, but it's not a given. We'll see. From our perspective in the air, we're expecting an easy run, but be ready for anything."

He moved in front of a large map on the wall with the island detailed in large scale. "The landing force will come in from the west at these two beaches." He pointed them out. "The enemy navy is scant in the area, and we have submarine pickets out. We've also established air superiority, so circling around into position shouldn't present difficulty, and frankly, those two beaches are the only ones that offer much opportunity for the ground troops. The rest of the coast is too rugged.

"The naval bombardment will continue until the Marines are in close range. That's when the ships' barrage will halt and close air support—that's us—begins.

"We'll launch heading southeast and circle to come in over the Marines' heads from the west, so we'll have the sun in our eyes, and you'll need your goggles on and to be paying close attention. We don't want to be shooting our own guys.

"The lead squadrons will light up the beaches in front of the Marines and work north toward the opposite end of the island. If there's much anti-aircraft fire left there, those of us trailing should see it and take it out. Any questions?"

There had been a few, and Josh went over details of rally points, actions if hit whether over land or sea or over friendly or enemy territory, and other issues that the pilots had been over ad nauseum. They talked themselves through brief backs on mission details until Josh was satisfied that each and every one of his pilots was fully prepared, and then he ordered them to hit their racks. "You need to be rested."

Before the first rays of dawn lit the eastern sky, the pilots were up. They scarfed down a breakfast of steak and eggs, and then headed to the massive hangars just below the flight deck to pull pre-flight checks. The first planes to launch were already on deck, their engines pulsating as their pilots awaited the deck officer's flag signal at the forward end of the ship where he checked the rise and fall of the prow over the waves.

The flag waved, and the first Corsair sped to the right of the white stripe painted along the side of the flight deck. The bow rose, and the fighter dipped slightly as it cleared the front end of the massive carrier, leveled out, gained altitude, and then soared into the morning clouds, followed by another, and another, and another...

At last, with impatience building, Josh's squadron moved onto the huge elevators to transfer their planes above. With the deck crews, they unfolded their wings, locked them into place, set chock blocks, confirmed fuel levels, and cranked up their engines. Within minutes all eighteen Hellcats sat poised, their fuselages vibrating and their propellers spinning as the pilots checked gauges and systems.

When all were ready, Josh made eye contact with the air boss and saluted. He, in turn, signaled his own crew to pull the chock blocks away and relayed the squadrons' readiness to the deck officer.

Josh maneuvered his fighter into position, set his brakes, pulled his throttle to full open, and waited. His heart beat against his sternum as he concentrated all his attention on the tiny figure at the far end of the ship. The flag went up, held steady, and then dropped.

Josh roared down the deck as the front of the ship rose from a valley between waves, and just as the bow hit its peak, he zoomed over the edge, pulled his stick far back, leveled out, climbed to an altitude of twelve thousand feet, and then loitered while his squadron formed up behind him.

"Wannabe, Yellow Bird," Josh's executive officer called. "We're all here."

"Roger, this is Wannabe. Let's roll."

"Wannabe" had become Josh's tongue-in-cheek callsign after being in ground combat with the Marines on Guadalcanal. The joke was that he really wanted to be a Marine. The good-humored nickname became his callsign, and stuck.

As his squadron flew toward Peleliu, obscured by smoke clouds that hovered on the horizon, Josh scanned the ocean. Spread out below him, large troop ships disgorged hundreds of landing craft of various types, their occupants visible as massed bobbing helmets reflecting the sun.

Some of the landing craft were small, carrying as few as sixteen Marines. Others were large, carrying two hundred Marines and soldiers. Josh guessed that the tip of the spear rode in the smaller vessels, as they were far out front, their white wakes trailing behind them, transporting forty-five hundred Marines to assault both beaches.

The large landing vessels cruised behind them, expecting to deposit another nineteen thousand five hundred soldiers and Marines onshore within minutes of the initial onslaught. Among them were amphibious tracked carriers—amtracks—capable of cruising to shore and then driving well up onto the beach. Also present in the armada of mini-vessels were small boats with rocket launchers intended to cruise offshore and provide heavy, close-in fire support.

Even at this altitude and distance from the island, and with his helmet and earphones firmly in place, Josh heard muzzle blasts from the navy's big guns thunder in a ceaseless chorus and the dull, far-off whoomphs of their giant rounds striking the ground, and every now and then, for a split second, he caught sight of the lethal projectiles. The volume of ordnance delivered on the island over the past four days had laden the air with the pungent odor of spent ammo, and the island itself was covered by thick smoke clouds of every shade of white, gray, brown, and black.

The batteries ceased firing. Aside from the sound of his own aircraft in the wind, all was quiet.

Josh's gut tightened. He watched the hundreds of small vessels headed toward the speck of island. "This is Wannabe," he intoned into his mic. "Let's head south."

He banked left and set his course to a predetermined area where his squadron would orbit around a point in the air until they were either called to support an unexpected incursion by Japanese fighters or until it was their turn to attack. His squadron would be fourth behind three others of Marine Corsairs.

At last, Josh received the order to execute. "Let's roll," he called over his radio.

He turned onto his azimuth, dropped his nose slightly, increased to full throttle, and set his trim. For a few minutes, Peleliu, still miles away, seemed to come no closer. Then it gradually grew in his windshield, and suddenly he was nearly on top of it.

As he approached, Josh's nerves tightened. The water sparkled in spite of a light cloud cover. Plainly visible below its surface was a long stretch of coral extending out many hundreds of yards. He watched amtracks struggle across the rough, hard, spiky material. However, they did not appear to be taking fire from inland, nor did the squadrons ahead of Josh's appear to be drawing anti-aircraft fire.

Maybe the four days of softening up worked.

As had all his fellow commanders and subordinate pilots, Josh expected at least a modicum of opposition. Within a few seconds, his squadron had dropped its bombs on their target, flown the full length of the island, and were back out to sea.

Josh called his commander of the ad hoc air group to which his squadron had been assigned for Stalemate II. "First run complete," he reported. "Something strange. Saw amtracks thrashing over coral eight hundred yards out. Marines dropped from LVTs will struggle. Feels like Tarawa. Just waiting for Japs to shoot back."

"Roger. Hearing similar reports. Will advise higher."

"Maneuvering for second run. Strafing only. Wannabe out."

Josh veered west. His exec reported no losses, no casualties, nor had they seen evidence of downed US aircraft for the duration of their run.

By the time they had circled again, the full body of twenty-four thousand Marines had arrived. Some amtracks were on the beach, and Marines struggled over the walls of the older models or out the open ramps of the newer ones. Some lay still in bloody pools. Others were prone and shooting, evidenced by their jerking motions, the positions of their rifles, and the puffs of smoke rising from their chambers. Still others crawled across the sand or dared to rise to a crouch and scamper for cover.

Josh saw the source of enemy fire, a natural coral wall, at least twenty feet high and set back from the beach about two hundred yards. It spewed smoke and flame, and as he skimmed above it, he saw the mouths of dark tunnels with doors standing open and guns protruding. He opened up with bursts from his six M2 .50 Cal machine guns.

"They're in the coral wall," he called. "Open up with everything you've got."

Then, as he flew over the island, he was suddenly confronted with a gauntlet of anti-aircraft guns spewing flak into the air across the full length and breadth of Peleliu.

"They've changed tactics," he called to his air group commander. "Instead of meeting the Marines on the beach, they let them come ashore, and then opened en masse from dug-in positions in a coral wall. We saw heavy mortar and artillery fire too. And the Japs are defending in depth against air attacks across the whole island. The coral has been hard enough to withstand our naval barrages. The Japs are still on Peleliu in force and they're dug into the coral. No tellin' how many."

Keying to his squadron frequency, he asked for status. He had lost no planes, but two had been damaged and would limp back to the *Essex*.

"I saw three from another squadron go down in enemy territory," one of his pilots reported.

"Several ditched out at sea," another chimed in.

"Roger. Head for home to rearm and refuel," Josh ordered. "This is going to take longer than anyone thought."

11

Same Day

The explosive booms from heavy mortar tubes and artillery cannons, the earsplitting whistles arcing overhead, and the terrifying geysers erupting as rounds struck water in close proximity left Corporal Eugene Sledge shaking and ashen-faced. Worse was hearing the blasts of a direct hit on a nearby landing craft, Marines screaming in physical agony with some cries fading abruptly amid a rhythmic staccato of machine guns, the crackle of small-arms fire, and the whisper of bullets whizzing over the protective walls of the amtrack that carried him and a platoon of Marines to this hostile shore. He tried to quell his fear, sure that he must be the most cowardly of all Marines, but when he glanced at his comrades and attempted an encouraging smile, he found that his facial muscles had tightened into an inflexible mask and saw that they wore similar fixed expressions, but the terror in their eyes could not be hidden.

Sledge had hoped to go ashore via an amtrack and ride right up onto the shore. But two types of such a vehicle existed. The newer ones opened at the rear to provide its passengers with a modicum of shelter and the ability to enter the battle with guns blazing. The older ones had no such provision. Its cargo of combatants were obliged to climb over its sides and drop to the ground while fully exposed to enemy gunfire.

Early that morning, as he had joined the platoon that he supported in his role as assistant mortar gunner, he learned to his dismay that he would go ashore on the older type of amtrack. At five feet eight inches and one hundred and thirty-five pounds, his equipment outweighed him, particularly since, in addition to his MI Carbine and its ammunition, two full canteens of water, and the normal load a Marine lugged into combat, Sledge also carried the mortar's heavy bipod and twelve of its 60 mm rounds. Thus, pulling himself up and over the vehicle's side was no easy task, nor was letting himself down to the ground on the other side, irrespective of mortar or artillery detonations, or flying small-arms rounds.

As the flotilla of over four hundred landing craft closed the distance to the island and the intensity of clamoring battle sounds increased, Sledge did his best to ignore nausea brought on by fear and exacerbated by the motion of the amtrack through choppy water. The irony of his situation was not lost on him. Born to a surgeon's family in Mobile, Alabama, he had attended Marion Military Institute, intending to be an officer. However, concerned that the war would be over before he would have a chance to fight, he resigned from Marion and enlisted, even deliberately failing Officer Candidate School to get into combat faster. Then, after basic training, he had sought to be assigned as a mortarman, taking pains to appear too small to hump a seventy-pound flame thrower.

He swallowed hard to hold down his breakfast as some of his comrades vomited onto the vessel's floor, or worse, found themselves unable to control normal bodily functions, thus adding to the stench of war. Across from him, Sledge's boss, Snafu, the mortar gunner, sat quietly, eyes closed, leaning back against the steel side, a cigarette lolling from the corner of his mouth while smoke floated out from his nostrils, contributing a pleasant element to the mix of smells.

Sledge had no idea how the gunner had gained his nickname, but Snafu was universally respected, a member of the "old breed," those Marines who had survived countless battles with the Japanese and conducted themselves with courage, resilience, camaraderie, and the quiet confidence and authority of old men with "know-how." They were greatly outnumbered by Marines like Sledge.

This combat was Sledge's first. He felt fortunate to work directly with Snafu. If anyone could see to it that they both survived the war, Sledge was sure that his boss could do it.

As the landing craft closed the distance to Peleliu's beach, naval gunfire abated and moved to the flanks. Then another sound joined the discord as a squadron of Marine Corsairs roared overhead. It was followed by another squadron and another, and then a squadron of Navy F6F Hellcats, and more squadrons of both types in a seemingly endless stream, separated by regular intervals, all headed toward the beleaguered island.

Sledge knew exactly when the forward squadrons and the first landing craft converged on the beach because suddenly the sound of exploding bombs and hundreds of .50 Cal machine guns belching hot steel from their wings onto enemy targets rolled across the water. For a few minutes, his amtrack held still, and Sledge assumed that the other landing craft in his wave of troops had as well, waiting for the initial assault to land. The sounds of automatic and small-arms fire increased, his amtrack groaned forward again, and then the dissonance of sounds was joined by the most terrifying one yet, that of enemy mortars and artillery.

A heavy round splashed next to Sledge's amtrack.

His vehicle bumped against another one.

An explosion erupted. *Was that the amtrack next to us? Did it survive?*

He could not tell. The eyes of his comrades opened wider. More bullets whizzed above the steel sides.

Then the vehicle grated against the coral reef and the amtrack rose higher, ceased to be a waterborne vessel, and crept forward as a land vehicle. At moments its steel tracks ground against the coral. At other moments, the war machine slid sideways.

Snafu stood and peered over the edge. "Get ready," he shouted.

Sledge sucked in an involuntary deep breath and blew it out. He grabbed his backpack, threw it over his back and secured it, checked his carbine, his canteens, his other equipment, had a buddy double-check him, and did the same for those around him. Then he waited, his eyes locked on Snafu.

The amtrack halted.

"Everybody out," Snafu shouted. "Let's go. Over the side."

Sledge had practiced this dismount many times, but suddenly, his limbs seemed heavy, immovable. He forced his arm over the edge and pulled himself up. Next to him, a buddy took a bullet to his jaw and fell back into the well of the vehicle, screaming. Sledge stared at him.

"Keep moving, or there'll be more of you," Snafu yelled. "Get out, and get off the beach."

Spurred by adrenaline, Sledge yanked himself and his equipment up and over and dropped to the ground. When his feet were firmly planted, the abject terror that had gripped him suddenly disappeared. It immediately possessed him again when he took a single step forward and fell face-first into the soft sand under the weight of his load, and he was momentarily panicked that he had been knocked down by bullets.

He felt a hand on his shoulder and jerked his head up, expecting to see a Japanese soldier ready to cut his heart out, and he cursed himself for not having his Ka-Bar, his Marine-issued combat knife, in his hand ready for use.

The hand on his shoulder and the face that went with it belonged to one of his friends. "You all right? I saw you fall. I thought you'd been hit."

"Thanks," Sledge shouted back. "I'm fine. Let's get off this beach."

His buddy scampered away, heading inland. Sledge followed, but with his heavier burden, he went more slowly, crawling most of the way. At intervals, he paused, and while keeping his head next to the sand, he found slight refuge in a shallow bomb crater. Only then did he dare to view where he had been and the entire beachhead by peeping over the depression's edge. The sight appalled him.

Thousands of Marines swarmed across the waterline attempting to scramble up the short rise into the scant vegetation that provided the only concealment and no cover from the heavy machine gun and mortar fire that opened up as soon as the main body was firmly ashore. Scattered over the white bomb-cratered beach in both directions as far as he could see, his comrades struggled forward, or in many instances, lay still in ghastly reposes. Cries for aid rippled on the breeze as the sun rose higher and its rays bore down with sweltering heat, and still more vehicles arrived on shore or disgorged their human cargoes into the surf. More men fell in sprays of red blood, and yet the swarm continued up the beach into the knee-high grass.

Sledge expected to hear blood-curdling screams of "*banzai*," the chilling war cry that the old breed had warned about that preceded a mass charge of the enemy soldiers into American lines with grenades, bayonets, swords, and massive rifle and machine-gun fire, laying waste to anything in their path. Because he was laden with equipment relegated to an assistant mortarman, Sledge's access to his carbine and his Ka-Bar was awkward, his vulnerability plain, his ability to defend himself in close quarters questionable.

A "duck" drove out of the frothing surf onto the beach near Sledge. It was a six-wheeled vehicle with rubber tires capable of swimming ashore and driving inland with twenty-five troops and an array of weaponry including rocket launchers, machine guns, and even mortars.

He watched it from his scant cover in the well of the bomb crater, hoping it would come his way with its armaments blazing. Then, a flash and a bang exploded from it as it took a direct hit, and black smoke rose from its belly into the air. No one escaped.

Sledge pulled back into the crater, dropped his head, and sank into despair, momentarily wondering if he should halt in place and wait for the seeming inevitable or chance once more exposing himself completely. More chatter of small-arms fire and whoomphs of mortars rousted him to action. He peered over the inland lip of the crater and recognized several men from his platoon also painstakingly making their way up the beach. He searched all around. *Where's Snafu?*

Not seeing his mentor but sensing a break in the volume of gunfire, he kicked both legs to push himself over the uphill edge to continue his crawl up the rise. Just as he did, a rain of automatic fire from the coral wall zeroed in on him.

Josh already felt fatigue from hours of operating his Hellcat in stifling conditions. Flying at higher altitudes between runs gave some relief, as did the design capability of opening the canopy for fresh air, but with outside temperatures over a hundred degrees at sea level and with a limited ventilation system when the windshield was closed, the inside of the cockpit quickly became hellish. Perspiration streamed from his forehead in rivulets that were impossible to keep out of his mask. His eyes stung, his vision blurred.

This was his second sortie, the beginning of his fourth run over Peleliu. Re-arming and re-fueling had taken no time, and his pilots, battle-seasoned as they were, knew the rote. With very little communication, they flew back into the sky and sped toward the island, more wary now, since the discovery of how widely and heavily it was defended.

With no threat from the Japanese navy or its air arm impeding the attack, the American aircraft carriers were stationed closer to the beach-head than in past invasions, so closing the distance took only minutes. The wind, blowing from the east-northeast, had provided no help, contributing to a thick surf that added difficulty to the struggling Marines on the surface, and it obscured the pilots' clear sight of targets.

As the squadron approached, the filmy smoke of every dark tone thickened momentarily with the explosions of heavy rounds, regardless of whether they originated with friend or foe. Then, for brief moments, the smoke cleared in places, and the full drama of this inhuman struggle unfolded in grisly detail.

All across the white beach, men in green wormed their way to the thin grass beyond. When smoke cleared over spots briefly and the sun shone through, bright red splotches appeared on the white coral and faded to brown as smoke once again closed in. Smashed landing craft lay in disarray on and offshore, and near them, bodies lay or floated, some face down, others facing the heavens. Among the debris along the beach lay body parts and torsos.

Black whisps spiraling from a "duck" that had taken a direct hit caught Josh's attention, identifiable by the shape of its nose and three of the six rubber tires that had somehow survived the blast and still stood upright, affixed to their axles.

Josh had no time to dwell on the horror he witnessed. The unceasing thunder of heavy artillery and mortars mounted as the squadron closed in, and now he made out individual Marines as they struggled to a safe place from which to carry on the fight.

At Edson's Ridge on Guadalcanal, when all had seemed lost other than a final battle with the fierce and determined Japanese enemy, a Marine air squadron had roared in. Josh recalled the sense of exultation as they flew over his position and unleashed a hail of .50 Cal bullets streaming past him onto his attackers, and the whistle and whoosh as they dropped their bombs.

Now, concentrating on the present, he flew past the stricken duck and sighted on the coral ridge inland from the beach. He saw a nest of three enemy machine guns, identified by the profusion of smoke emanating in a line from their muzzles and glints of streaming sunlight reflections as their bullets flew toward their targets. He saw that their fire converged, evidenced by a cloud of coral and sand kicked up at the point of impact near a lone, prone Marine.

As Josh raced over the coral beach, he glimpsed the Marine struggling over the edge of a bomb crater. The side of the man's face was in the ground, and his feet kicked as he struggled over the lip of the crater to bring his carbine forward. He was impeded by the pack on his back and the long legs of a mortar tripod.

He was headed into the gunfire.

Josh keyed his mic. "Follow my lead. Get that machine gun nest," he ordered, and simultaneously pressed the trigger to fire all six of his machine guns, delivering one hundred and twenty rounds per second. Immediately, the eighteen fighters of his squadron also opened up, delivering equal doses of .50 Cal steel rounds in quick bursts onto the enemy nest.

"Yellowbird," Josh called on his radio, "you and Tomahawk drop a load on those machine guns."

"Roger. Tomahawk—"

"Got it," Tomahawk replied. "The one on the right is *mine*."

"Next three, go behind and make sure we finish 'em," Josh intoned.

Three squawks in his ear let him know that his order would be executed.

Sledge heard the roar of aircraft close to the ground, sensed that steel bullets ceased to fly over his head, and heard the bursts of one hundred and eight machine guns delivering hell on the Japanese who had targeted him. Without raising his head, he tilted it enough to see forward to the coral wall, saw it erupt in flying bits of debris as return-fire from the fighters struck the nest, and then watched as first three, and then three more bombs dropped from the planes' underbellies. Massive explosions erupted, and black clouds rolled into the sky. To the left and right of the destroyed enemy positions, more aircraft struck adjacent targets.

Sledge blew out a long breath of relief and gratitude. With effort, he rolled onto one side, extended an arm along the ground, and raised his thumb in the air. "Thanks, guys," he murmured. "I was a goner."

The battle still raged on both sides of him, but a corridor had been cut ahead of him that, at least for the moment, allowed him to rise to his feet and run in a crouch to safer ground.

He reached the first vegetation and flopped into the thin grass, out of breath. Someone called to him hoarsely from farther forward to his right, "Over here."

Panting uncontrollably, Sledge low-crawled toward the voice. Then he felt two strong hands grasp each of his shoulders and drag him through the grass and into the recesses of a natural depression. "We're out of the line of fire and in the shade here," one of his rescuers said, and added, "You look like you could use some water."

Sledge nodded gratefully. The men sat him up, removed the mortar tripod and his pack, detached a canteen from his belt, opened it, and brought it to Sledge's lips.

He took a sip. Only a sip. "Remember," Snafu had warned repeatedly, "conserve your water. We don't know when we'll get resupplied."

Sledge looked through bleary eyes into the faces of his rescuers. He had seen them around his company area, but he did not know them. But they were Marines. Brothers. That was all he needed to know.

"The Japs have been falling back somewhat on this right flank," one of them said. "The last round of close-air support drove them back farther.

Some of our officers made it to the top of this ridge. There's a plateau there, and they're organizing."

"Did Snafu come past here?" Sledge rasped. Everyone in the company knew Snafu for his steadiness and constant willingness to help out in almost any situation.

"Are you Sledgehammer?"

When Sledge affirmed with a quick nod, the Marine said, "He was looking for you. He said if you came by to send you on up. He'll watch for you up top."

A wave of relief swept over Sledge, both because Snafu was alive and because the man he trusted most in this war had been looking for him. He started to move out.

"Rest," one of the Marines said. "You're close to dehydration. You need to be out of the sun for a while, and it's shadier here than it is up there. We'll let Snafu know."

Sledge craned his neck and peered around through still blurry eyes. He saw that both men wore white armbands with red crosses emblazoned on them. As his vision cleared, he realized that they had established a holding point for the wounded.

He almost gagged when he saw the severity of some of the wounds: men missing limbs, others with massive bandages around their heads or abdomens. Most had been injected with morphine that had knocked them out. Some moaned in pain despite the drug, and some lay still, staring, sightless.

"How'd you get the name Sledgehammer," one of the medics asked. "That's a hell of a nickname, even for a Marine."

Sledge grunted and averted his eyes from the casualties. "Not anything I did," he said, still panting. "My last name's Sledge, and I'm a Marine. I guess it was natural, but I promise, I paid a high price for it in basic."

"Well, when you get up top, you set that mortar up, and you bring that hammer down on those Japs."

Sledge grinned in spite of himself. "Thanks, guys. Point me the way. I'll be ready in a few minutes."

12

September 16, 1944
Hyde Park, New York, USA

"Ah, Franklin, I do enjoy these trips to your family estate. It's an escape that neither of us enjoys very often of late."

President Franklin Roosevelt drew on his cigarette and glanced across at British Prime Minister Winston Churchill as the president drove his 1936 Ford Phaeton convertible along the tree-lined lanes leading from a nearby airfield to his home on a wide plateau overlooking the Hudson River in upstate New York. He then threw his head back and laughed, clearly enjoying the rush of wind on his face. "It's the least I could do for an old friend after another one of those war conferences. I like Quebec, and I like Prime Minister King, but I'll welcome the day when those confabs are history."

"Agreed," the prime minister returned, "but I referred to the sense of freedom when coming here. You're driving, no one else is in the car, the security detail keeps its distance, and people here are generally accustomed to your comings and goings, so we don't have huge crowds to maneuver through. For all intents, we're just two old codgers trying to enjoy life like everyone else."

"I'm glad you feel that way, Winnie. We've both found that having a rejuvenated mind leads to better decisions."

"And we still have a few of those to take before I leave in two days."

Roosevelt laughed again. "Let go of that worry for the moment. We have time to have some pleasure before getting back to business. There's a new restaurant in town I want to try out—the SBD Station. I hear it has a wonderful menu, the professionals love it, and popping in there will give our security fits. It'll be such great fun."

Churchill looked askance at him. "I hate to bring this up, Franklin, but what about your legs?"

Roosevelt chuckled jauntily. "The people here know about my polio, my wheelchair, and that my car has special hand controls so I can drive. They're discreet, and the eatery is a drive-in."

"A what?"

"A drive-in. The waitresses there—we call them carhops—bring the food to the car. We've had those places around in this country for at least a decade."

Churchill grunted and arched his eyebrows. "For most of that time in the United Kingdom, we've had food shortages and rationing, and that's still the case."

"Ahh, but with the Battle of the Atlantic all but won, the supply lines being better and more robust, and Great Britain already healing, before you know it, you'll have these drive-ins dotting your countryside."

Churchill snorted. "Heaven help us."

Comfortably ensconced in Roosevelt's study on the family estate with a view down to the Hudson, the president opened the conversation. "I initialed off on further study of the Morgenthau Plan, but I'm not sure I like it. Even the plan's author, Morgenthau, sees it possibly leading to starving the population. The idea of stripping Germany's industrial base away and turning the country into a purely agrarian economy smacks of what we did after World War I. Our side impoverished that nation and raised resentments, which brought about Hitler and the Nazis. The people are punished for the wars, but invariably, it's the leaders who start them, and this plan punishes the wrong parties."

"Well, I don't want that, of course, but removing Germany's war-making capabilities seems prudent. After all, they were the aggressor not just in this conflict, but also in the Franco-Prussian War and the First World War. For its own good and ours too, we have to defang Germany."

Roosevelt sighed. "There must be a better way," he said wearily. He dropped his head into his hands and took a moment to catch his breath. When he looked up again, he seemed to require effort to keep his eyes open, and his voice was laced with fatigue. "The matter needs more analysis. In any event, we're not yet at the time to implement."

Churchill regarded him worriedly. "Are you feeling all right, Franklin? You can tell me. I'm your friend as well as your partner in this conflict. I observed in Quebec that you appeared not well. Your skin has a pallor to it, even a blueish tint."

The president inhaled. "Your observation is as keen as ever. I'm getting old, Winnie, and so is the war. Your people are tired of it. Ours are too, and I expect you are. I am, and I'll admit that it's taken a toll on me physically. The blueish tint you noticed is from poor circulation, and my blood pressure has been dangerously high. My doctor is worried." He grunted. "But meanwhile, we've got a war to win, so let's get on with it. Next topic, how are we to carve up Europe after victory."

Churchill harrumphed. "I hate to put the matter in those terms, but before we go into that subject, I'm curious about this 442nd Regimental Combat Team—"

"You heard about them." The president chuckled. "The 'Go For Broke' regiment. It's all Japanese-Americans from platoon leaders on down, and I have to say that they're doing a bang-up job. I'm told that they are determined to prove that they're good Americans. I was against the idea initially, but public pressure built against the internment camps. Meanwhile, we still had a country to protect. This turned out to be a good compromise, and in Italy and France, the people are glad we brought them on board. Now, as to Europe—"

"I believe you know precisely what Comrade Stalin wants regarding post-war Europe," Churchill broke in, "with the Soviets controlling most or all of Eastern Europe, including Poland, Czechoslovakia, Hungary, Romania, the Balkan states down through Albania—"

"Not Greece?"

"He's been warned away on that score," the prime minister intoned with a shake of his head. "He knows how important it is to Britain's position in the Mediterranean. We wouldn't give it up without a fight.

"One reason why Operation Market Garden is so consequential is that, if Field Marshal Montgomery can pull it off, we'll have a direct path into Berlin and can end this war by Christmas. The further advantage is that Stalin's hand for post-war negotiations will be weakened because we'll already be in Berlin while he's far away, still fighting in the east." He grunted and added, "He'll push for a large chunk of Germany, and he'd have had France too, but for the actions General de Gaulle took to forestall a civil war and restore civil authority."

"I'll give de Gaulle that," Roosevelt said with a mixed note of reluctance and admiration. "I never supported him until that general of his, Philippe Leclerc, took Paris. Everyone knew I opposed de Gaulle, but he came through. Most of France is free now."

He raised his eyes to gaze at the view outside his window and cocked his head to one side. "You know, Winnie, I think I've told you before that I come to this study to think, reflect, read. Hopefully gain wisdom. The issues have become so complex. I'm not sure that wisdom is even available at this point. Regardless of what we do, thousands, if not millions, will be maimed, killed, starved, left homeless, penniless..." His voice trailed off.

Churchill reached across and patted the president's hand. "You've done a remarkable job, my friend, and whether by Christmas or sometime next year, we will win this war and the suffering will recede."

"I hope you're right," Roosevelt muttered. "I see the sense of Market Garden, but Eisenhower has his reservations, and frankly, so do I. Our logistics are already strained, and this venture will stretch them further, possibly to the breaking point if the operation doesn't succeed."

"I understand the concern," Churchill said soothingly, "and it's one that we should consider carefully. In his planning guidance to Montgomery, Eisenhower was clear that he was to go no farther north than Arnhem, which is a hundred miles short of the original objective at Lake IJssel. Once

Arnhem is captured, he and Monty will reassess. We can then determine whether to continue north to isolate the German forces in northwest Netherlands, or turn immediately and drive east to Berlin."

"Monty," Roosevelt said with a flat tone of implied doubt. "Are we forgetting Operation Goodwood? Monty lost it. The battle for Caen took much longer than expected as a result. He assured Ike that he had the resources for it, but he didn't."

Churchill drew back, obviously annoyed. "Sir, the Persians had their three hundred Spartans, Napoleon his Waterloo and his time on Elba. General Lee had his Gettysburg, Grant his bottle of whisky, MacArthur his embarrassment in the Philippines, and Eisenhower announced to the world that Italy had capitulated at the same time that our troops were heading to the beaches at Salerno. What was expected to be an easy landing turned into a massacre and the long slog up Italy's boot. And of course, I had my Gallipoli. Monty drove the Hun right out of North Africa—"

"With our help."

"Of course with your help, but he did it, and he's a brilliant field marshal, and frankly he deserves more positive mention in your national press than he's getting."

At the last comment, Roosevelt chuckled. "You *do* get prickly sometimes, Winnie. All right, Ike says he won't oppose the plan despite his concerns, and with your strong endorsement, I won't object."

Churchill stood and ambled across the room to gaze out at the Hudson. "Then it'll execute at first light tomorrow morning, God help us all." He heaved a sigh and turned. "But you know, we haven't discussed the most dangerous issue."

Roosevelt nodded. "The atomic bomb and Japan." He took a deep breath and let it out, long and slow. "As I said, perhaps there's no wisdom to be had to end this war."

"Well, preliminary to that subject," Churchill interjected, "let me inform you that orders have already gone out for major parts of our British navy to transfer to the Pacific. With only a smidgeon of German naval capability left in the seas north of the United Kingdom and a few U-boats still in the Atlantic—"

"You still have the *Tirpitz* lurking somewhere in the northern fjords of Norway—"

Churchill grimaced. "We do. We sent in another mission to bomb her again just yesterday. Unfortunately, it failed to sink her."

Roosevelt looked at him sharply. "What happened?"

Churchill shrugged. "The ship is deep in a fjord where it's difficult to bomb. The Germans covered it with a smoke screen. Our pilots dropped their bombs but we don't know yet if any struck or the extent of damage."

"Hmph. You've been after her for some time. That's critical—"

"She's formidable, to be sure," Churchill said firmly, "but our constant attacks, yesterday's being number thirty-two, have battered her and limited her effect. Our mini-sub attack on her last year kept her out of commission for seven months. We'll stay on her until the *Tirpitz* is no more."

Roosevelt nodded tiredly. "I know you will." He let his head fall backward and closed his eyes while he contemplated.

Churchill returned to his chair, took two cigars from his pocket, and held one out for the president. Roosevelt re-opened his eyes, declined the cigar, pulled out his own cigarette, and lit it. "This issue of the atomic bomb weighs heavily on me, Winnie, as I'm sure it does on you."

"The thought of atomic power should chill any sane person," Churchill replied matter-of-factly, "but the casualty estimates for Allied troops, if we do an amphibious invasion of Japan, is between a quarter of a million to a million men. And before we get to the main island, we have to go through the Philippines and Okinawa, not to mention Peleliu. Look at what's happening there right now."

"The Marines went ashore yesterday, and the reports are horrendous," Roosevelt said, frowning grimly. "The first day's casualties rivaled those of Tarawa, which had been our bloodiest battle across the Pacific to date."

"And that's just Day 1 on an island seventeen hundred miles from Japan," Churchill said. "Can you imagine how fiercely they'll fight on the main island?"

Roosevelt nodded solemnly. "Well, when we're done with Peleliu, the Philippines are next. General MacArthur briefed me two months ago on his plans to return there. The thought then was to invade at Mindanao, but per reconnaissance reports ordered by Admiral Halsey and forwarded by

Admiral Nimitz during our Quebec conference, Leyte is especially weak. Halsey and Nimitz recommend that we invade there first and bypass Mindanao for the moment. MacArthur agrees, and the joint chiefs concur."

"That's remarkable," Churchill said. "A meeting of the minds between the principals without you or me tipping the scales." He chuckled. "I can't claim to be an expert on the region, but your Admiral Halsey certainly is, and he took the war to the Japanese—"

"Within a day of Pearl Harbor," Roosevelt enthused, "and he just destroyed around five hundred of their aircraft in a day in the Philippines, most of them on the ground. Halsey thinks we can go in at Leyte with light resistance."

"MacArthur doesn't seem to expect any large-scale naval opposition to an Allied offensive in the Philippines," Churchill said.

Roosevelt agreed. "That'd be risky for them. They're down to a fraction of their former naval power. They'd have to put everything they've got left into a single massive offensive against our navy, hoping to cripple it." He shifted in his wheelchair. "Three months ago, they replaced Prime Minister Tojo. The new one is former governor-general of Korea, Kuniaki Koiso. He's intent on building defenses on the home island. That's a signal that he expects Japan to be invaded, a hint that they know they're losing. His military will pick up on that. They're preparing for our invasion."

Churchill leaned forward, his expression intense. "Which is why we must consider the atomic option," he said gravely.

"I know," Roosevelt groused. "I just don't like it."

Churchill breathed out hard. "And I don't either, but the probability of widespread death and destruction is even more horrendous the conventional way."

Roosevelt nodded somberly. "I don't disagree, but the destructive power of just one of these bombs is unfathomable, and when knowledge of them is released, which it will be the day we drop them, every two-bit wannabe dictator will want one. We kept Hitler from getting them by a hair's breadth. If we do this thing, we'll enter an age so dark, I can't imagine..." His voice trailed off.

Churchill sat quietly listening. Then he reached into his jacket pocket. "I have the draft of the so-called Hyde Park Aide-Mémoire here, recording what we've agreed to. I've scratched a few notes on it for clarity, but it is otherwise as we discussed. We've agreed that we should not inform the world of the bombs' existence prior to deploying them, that we should give Japan warning a few days prior to dropping them, and advise them that we'll drop more until unconditional surrender.

"The mémoire includes that the US and the UK will continue collaboration between our two countries, with full sharing of atomic research breakthroughs and developments, and that Stalin must be kept in the dark about the project prior to releasing the bombs.

"Finally, we've agreed that the main scientist in atomic development, Neils Bohr, must be monitored to ensure that he doesn't let the cat out of the bag. He has idealistic notions about sharing any science for the good of all mankind. We had to nab him out of Denmark to stop his development of the technology on Hitler's behalf. He came willingly and at great personal risk, but only after he had personally witnessed the cruelty and ambitions of the Nazi regime. This weapon would have handed Hitler world domination."

"I remember," Roosevelt said. "As I recall, a young lady, the first cousin to your King George, was lost on the mission to rescue Bohr, and she is presumed dead. You have my deepest regrets."

"Thank you, sir. I passed them along to His Majesty when you first expressed them right after the incident occurred."

Roosevelt took a long drag on his cigarette and blew the smoke out in rings. "Is there anything else we should discuss now?"

Churchill took a similar time with his cigar, and then, amid the ghostly swirl, he shook his head. "I think that does it for now."

"In that case, I think I will retire. I am a bit tired this evening."

"Very good, sir," the prime minister responded. Then, as he had at every location where they had met for war conferences in far-flung corners of the earth, and out of respect, he pushed Roosevelt in his wheelchair through the Hyde Park mansion to the president's bedroom before retiring to his own guest quarters.

13

_____

September 17, 1944
Groesbeek, Netherlands

Bone-jarring vibrations generated by a C-47 Skytrain's engines pulsed through Lieutenant Lance Littlefield's feet and legs as he stood up in the plane's narrow aisle running between wooden benches affixed to it sides. Similar sensations ran through his left hand and arm as he reached up and hooked his static line to a cable strung the length of the cargo bay along the airframe's ceiling.

Looking out one of the rectangular windows, he gulped as dirty gray puffs exploded all around. They looked harmless, visible indications of Flak antiaircraft rounds, but just one of them could knock the plane out of the sky. What Lance hated most about them was that there was no way to fight back against them. Fortunately, the Skytrain flew safely past the ground batteries that launched the explosive rounds.

The flight from Wollaton Park in Nottinghamshire, England, lasted only ninety minutes, but it was arduous. The fuselage reeked of vomit from those reacting badly to air turbulence and urine from those unable to hold their bladders. After crossing the North Sea, Lance had watched the passing landscape below, noting the many rivers and the wide fields now turning brown. The paratroopers would drop south of the Waal River to capture and hold the Waalbrug bridge, spanning over nineteen hundred feet.

Early that morning, word had come through channels that General Eisenhower had ordered the execution of Operation Market Garden. Hence, as executive officer of Jedburgh Team Clarence that was attached to the 82nd Airborne Division, Lance would jump into the Netherlands at Groesbeek with one of the major subordinate units, the 508th Parachute Infantry Regiment. Their designated landing was at drop zone Nan on a wide field roughly four miles to the northwest of and overlooking Nijmegen. The team would link up with its commander, Dutch Captain Arie "Harry" Bestebreurtje, who rode in another C-47 to jump with Major General James Gavin. The team was there to provide liaison to Dutch Resistance groups.

Due to Harry's native familiarity with the language and the region, and because of his tenacity, Team Clarence had been assigned to the general's staff as liaison to local Resistance groups. Harry had personally requested that Lance join his team.

Having escaped from Colditz POW camp several months earlier, Lance had been on Brittany's coast the night before Normandy's D-Day, working with a French Resistance group and an advance team of British-trained French commandos at Saint-Brieuc. The town was a major rail and road intersection. The combined teams conducted widespread sabotage against a railroad terminal and several locomotives parked there, as well as key bridges and roads in the area. Then, in the last hours before the invasion began, they cleared fields to receive a battalion of British paratroopers who dropped in to support the main Allied assault force on its right flank.

Subsequent to action at Saint-Brieuc, Lance had been absorbed into one of two Jedburgh teams that had also jumped in to operate behind Normandy's enemy lines. One of the Jedburghs, an executive officer, had broken a leg on landing and was evacuated back to the UK. Since Lance was already in situ and had the equivalent training and experience, he had replaced the officer.

The full Jedburgh organization consisted of ninety-three such three-man teams whose missions were to infiltrate into France, Belgium, and the

Netherlands at strategic times and places and train local Resistance groups to destroy the *Wehrmacht's* ability to move and resupply itself by sabotaging its transportation and communications lines and major terminals. They were known surreptitiously as Eisenhower's secret army, a special operations cooperative between the US Office of Strategic Services, aka the OSS, and the British Special Operations Executive, aka the SOE.

Shortly before the liberation of Paris, Lance and another Jedburgh team helped liberate the town of Dinan, France, after which they were recalled to headquarters at Milton Hall near Petersborough, England. Because of Lance's fluency in German and French, his training and experience as a commando, and his proven abilities to evade Germans and work with Resistance groups, Harry chose him to replace the injured executive officer.

Lance regarded the invitation as an honor. Harry, so nicknamed because Americans and Brits found his last name, Bestebreurtje, difficult to pronounce, had been a champion speed skater before the war, participating in the 1936 Olympics in Garmisch-Partenkirchen as an alternate. Unfortunately for him, he did not compete.

Lean, thoroughly professional, with friendly eyes over a mustache and a warm smile, Harry was known for leadership qualities, courage, and resourcefulness. Earlier in the year, he had participated with Dutch commandos and British paratroopers in several covert operations in the Netherlands behind enemy lines.

Lance had accepted Harry's offer. "I have one request," he said. "I'd like to visit my sister before deploying again."

Harry had agreed.

In retrospect, because of the emotional toll, Lance almost regretted the trip.

Claire Littlefield had been playing with Timmy in the back garden of her rented home on the estate in Stony Stratford, where she had lived almost since the inception of the war, when Elsie, her nanny, called frantically to her. Rushing into the house, she saw Elsie pointing out the window. A government car had pulled in front of the garden path and a uniformed man emerged.

Blood drained from Claire's face and she found herself breathing in short gasps. Then the man straightened and she recognized his face.

"Lance?" She rushed to the door and threw it open. "Lance, is that really you?"

He grinned and threw his arms wide open as she rushed to embrace him.

"I didn't know if you were alive or dead," Claire cried. "I'd heard of your latest escape but that was at least five months ago. I can't believe you're here." She buried her face in his chest. "When I saw the car, I thought you were someone coming to tell me that one of my brothers was dead."

Lance held her until her joyful sobs subsided. Then he stepped back and grinned. "I'm here, Sis. Intact and healthy. The jerries haven't made the bullet intended for me."

She embraced him again. "Let's hope they never do."

Timmy had run out of the house after Claire, and now he stood back, looking up in awe at this thin, weathered version of Jeremy and Uncle Paul who exuded physical prowess. Lance stooped and extended a hand.

"You probably don't remember me," he said. "It's been some time."

Timmy looked up uncertainly at Claire, who nodded reassuringly. "This is your Uncle Lance, my brother," she said. "We talk about him all the time."

The little boy gazed back at Lance, took a step forward, and grasped his hand. Lance pulled him gently forward and held the child close to his chest.

Now, as Lance stood awaiting the signal to start the parachute drop, visions of the overnight stay with Claire played in his mind. As happy as she was to see him, when she learned that he would leave again the next morning to places unknown, she wept. The constant worry for the health and where-abouts of her family had gnawed at her such that her natural enthusiasm for life had dissipated to forced optimism. When Lance left her the following morning, she stood at the bottom of the garden path with Timmy and Elsie at her side, waving forlornly as he drove away.

That had been a week ago. Meanwhile, he had been at Milton Hall training and waiting with Harry, his Jedburgh teammates, and the 82nd Airborne Division for an upcoming mission, Operation Market Garden.

The emotions that had flooded his senses when he picked up Timmy threatened to overwhelm him again. Lance had always been an adventurer and had all but welcomed the war at its outset. Against his parents' wishes and prior to hostilities, he had enlisted in the army for the excitement. Now, having witnessed the torn lives, the destroyed towns and countrysides, and lived the depravities of POW camps, in that instant of holding Timmy, the sense of a greater responsibility overcame him, that of fighting evil for the benefit of younger generations.

Behind Lance on the Skytrain, the team's wireless operator, Technical Sergeant Willard "Bud" Beynon, jostled Lance back to the present by pulling and prodding on Lance's gear to ensure that it was all soundly packed, that nothing had come loose since leaving the ground, and that the static line would not snag. Lance proceeded to perform the same checks on the paratrooper to his immediate front, and then, since Bud was the last jumper in the stick, Lance inspected the sergeant's equipment as well. Ahead of them, each of the twenty-five paratroopers from A/508th checked the gear of the soldier in front of him. That done, all waited pensively to shuffle to the open cargo door near the rear of the aircraft on the port side.

Lance's heart beat furiously. Sweat streamed down his temples. The weight of his equipment, including his parachute, bore down on him. Beyond his Sten gun and ammunition were sundry items, including maps, compass, first-aid kit, rations, flares, and a survival kit, over one hundred pounds of war-fighting gear.

Wind whistled through the plane's interior. Lance jockeyed to see the door over the shoulders of those in front of him who did the same thing. Everyone's eyes, set in hardened faces, alternated between the red light over the door and the bright sunshine streaming beyond its frame.

A jumpmaster crouched at the opening, keeping a steady eye on the red light.

It flashed to green.

The first jumper trundled forward and stood in the door. The jump-master clapped his shoulder. The paratrooper hopped out. The line moved forward as one man after the other dropped out of the plane in a continuous stream.

Seconds later, Lance stepped into the wide blue sky. Thrill tinged by panic engulfed him, but then the comforting jolt of the static line interrupted any conscious thought as it jerked the parachute from its casing.

Lance looked skyward, saw the canopy spreading wide, and grasped his risers. Then, gazing around on a perfect day with clear skies, he saw thousands of other parachutes floating gently to the ground. In the distance, the sight and roar of hundreds of the C-47 transport planes receded toward the horizon while those of hundreds more increased from the direction he had come and dropped thousands more soldiers.

A spectacular view of wide-open fields around Groesbeek greeted Lance. Forested slopes descended gently to Nijmegen several miles to the northwest where the Waalbrug bridge, the division's main objective, was clearly visible.

Adding to the panorama, thousands of people lined the roads waving jubilantly and shouting welcomes to their descending liberators. Meanwhile, far-off booms of field artillery near Nijmegen caught his attention as well as the rat-tat-tat of machine guns and small-arms fire. Flak bursts dotted the sky over the town. Intermingled with them, Allied fighters strafed with machine gun and cannon fire, their added noise muffled by distance.

His nerves fully active, Lance scanned to the east and caught his breath. There, so close, was Reichswald Forest, Germany, and nothing delineating a boundary between the two countries.

Another detail caught Lance's attention. The interval space his probable landing point and the 508th's main body seemed wide, maybe by more than a mile.

The sound of a sputtering engine caught his attention. He turned, horrified to see a C-47 in a downward slant headed straight toward him. Both tri-bladed propellers had stopped spinning. Smoke trailed out of each engine. It had already struck other paratroopers floating to the ground, their blood flying from the wings' leading edges, their bodies falling in pieces to the ground, and their deflated parachutes following them.

Horrified but helpless to maneuver, Lance watched, grateful to the pilot for the obvious effort to avoid more troops suspended in air.

Colliding with Lance looked unavoidable. Accepting the inevitable while fighting fear and overcome by sudden nausea at the terrible sight, he tensed in his harness and prepared for the worst.

The aircraft bore down. Lance could not see if its stick of paratroopers had jumped or if the supply bundles on the plane's belly had been dropped.

His gut seized. Sweat poured from his brow, stinging his eyes.

The aircraft's nose suddenly dipped further, heading on a path below him. With his eyes wide and locked on its silver roof, he watched the cockpit pass beneath him, barely making out the pilot and co-pilot struggling with the controls. The tail swept by only inches below his feet. Air turbulence rocked his parachute, leaving him swinging like a pendulum.

The aircraft continued on, skimming above the fields dotted with men in various stages of activity who suddenly looked up at the iron apparition and either flattened themselves on the ground or ran for cover. For some, warning came too late as the plane flared, and then plowed into the ground and slid along its surface.

Lance had no time to see where it halted or wonder about more casualties. Fewer than ten seconds had elapsed since he jumped. The ground rushed up to meet him, and he prepared for landing. Holding his legs together and looking out across the horizon, he waited. When his feet hit the surface, he rolled to dissipate the shock and immediately pushed the quick-release knob in the middle of his chest.

The canopy fell away.

Lance crouched, but with the aerial carnage he had just seen and despite his best effort, he puked into the dirt. Then, forcing composure, he scanned the field to detect signs of close enemy activity, searched for available cover, and looked for his teammates. He glanced at his watch. 13:30 hours.

Bullets pounded only inches away, fired from the forest. Lance hugged the ground and pressed his head into the dirt. Nearby, an American soldier called for a medic. From a tree line, more enemy small-arms fire erupted. It was returned by other paratroopers.

Keeping low, Lance scanned his map and shot azimuths to Nijmegen, Groesbeek, and the middle of the Reichswald and checked where the back azimuths crossed. Realization dawned that somehow, his stick had dropped off course. He was inside the German border. The stick he had jumped with and one other from A/508th had dropped in the same vicinity. Gunfire from the Reichswald grazed the field. More wounded men called for medics.

Late That Night
Groesbeek, the Netherlands

"Harry, you didn't tell me that the Germans got slaughtered when they tried to capture the Nijmegen bridge back in '40." General Gavin shot a mock accusatory glare at the Dutch captain. "As my Dutch advisor, I'd have expected you to let me know that detail."

They stood in the principal's office of a school that had been requisitioned to serve as the 82nd Airborne's field headquarters for the operation. It was situated on the eastern edge of town.

Harry replied to Gavin's comment with a similar expression. "Sorry, sir. My omniscience expired before we spoke about it. I thought you knew. I'll try to do better."

Lance observed the exchange with a controlled sense of awe for America's youngest army general. Tall and lean with full, dark hair and brown eyes, Gavin was known as a man of action, a stickler for intense training, forthrightness, and leading from the front like George Patton, and thus adored by his men. They dubbed him "Jumpin' General" among other sobriquets, for entering combat the same way they did, by parachute. His reputation was that he picked his subordinates carefully, and entrusted them with full authority to carry out their assigned missions without higher interference.

Lance was captivated by Gavin's background. Orphaned at two and adopted by impoverished coal-mining parents, he dropped out of school after the eighth grade to work and help support his family. Then, at seventeen, he joined the army. Stationed in Panama, he self-studied sufficiently during his off time to pass the West Point entrance exam and graduated from the Academy in 1929. And now, only fifteen years later and with two stars on each shoulder, he commanded one of the most lauded and audacious units in the US Army.

An apparent affinity had grown between Gavin and Harry at the general's headquarters camp at Mourmelon-le-Grand, a hundred miles northeast of Paris. After observing Harry's leadership effectiveness, Gavin had selected him to be his advisor on all things Dutch. Gavin's regard had deepened earlier today when, as the two men trudged their way from their landing to the field headquarters, Harry spotted an enemy soldier just as the German also spotted and aimed his machine gun at Gavin.

Harry shot first, killing the German, and thus saving the general's life.

Gavin grunted at Harry's reply regarding omniscience. Then he turned to Lance. "You're the guy who keeps getting captured and escaping from the Germans," he joshed. "How many times have you wound up in Colditz?"

"Three, sir."

Gavin grunted again. "You must like the place. Tell me about what went on with those two Alpha Company sticks on the jump this morning. Sounds like you escaped the krauts again without taking them up on lodging this time. Let's hear the story."

"All the credit goes to Captain Rex Combs, General—"

"I'm not surprised," Gavin broke in. "He was a hero at Normandy on D-Day too. He parachuted in under fire, immediately organized his men, and counterattacked into the enemy. What'd he do this time?"

"The same thing. I was still getting my bearings, and he had rallied his men, attacked into enemy positions, and routed them. I have to say, he was marvelous—probably saved my skin. He had roughly fifty men against over a hundred and twenty, but his group killed twenty-nine of theirs and took over fifty prisoners."

Gavin inhaled. "I'm glad we got our guys out."

"It was all Captain Combs' show," Lance continued. "He did the rallying. His men responded. I was just another grunt taking orders and pulling a trigger."

Gavin regarded him a moment. "All right. Let's get into the staff meeting."

"One question, sir," Harry interjected. "Is it now on to the bridge at Nijmegen?"

Gavin arched his brows. "Don't know yet. I was in conversation about that with my boss, General Browning, shortly before takeoff. We have several other objectives to secure before tackling that one.

"Since landing, we've had intel about large armored elements in the Reichswald Forest where Littlefield and Combs were. The 508th is supposed to secure that area, but its troops are green. When we landed, its main body was just milling around. You saw, I had to go in personally to get it organized. By contrast, the 504th and 505th were busy digging in and securing their perimeters. But the fighting was fierce in 504th's area."

He frowned. "More training indicated for the 508th," he growled as he headed for a classroom that served as a conference room.

"Before we get the formal meeting started," Gavin's chief of staff said, "let me tell a couple of quick anecdotes from today's actions. I gotta say, our guys are magnificent."

Gavin nodded, and the colonel continued. "The drop had its successes and failures, and its comic relief. Over in the 504th's area, the troops dropped near Grave to seize and hold the bridge over the Maas River. Lieutenant John Thompson was watching for the green light to jump. When it flashed on, he saw that the aircraft was over buildings, so he waited a few seconds and then led his platoon out the door.

"They landed only three hundred yards from the bridge over the Maas. His platoon had lost contact with the company, but they went for the bridge anyway. They found themselves in shoulder-deep drainage ditches full of water. That didn't stop 'em, though."

Lance saw that the colonel was enjoying his storytelling and that he was proud of his soldiers. And Lance enjoyed listening.

"Thompson noticed some kraut soldiers darting around by a generator on our end of the bridge, so he ordered his men to open up with machine guns. More krauts showed up in two trucks, but he could tell that these were rear-echelon guys. They had awful tactics, and Thompson's men finished them off real quick. Then Thompson spotted a 20mm anti-aircraft gun in a concrete tower. His soldiers finished that one off too. Long story short, they took that bridge in short order."

Among whoops and applause, the colonel held up his hands for quiet. "I've got two more quick ones," he said. "A lot of you know Captain Briand Beaudin, the surgeon over in 508th."

Lance's ears perked up. He knew the captain.

"You might recall that he was captured at Normandy and we liberated him. This time, as he was coming down, he saw that he was heading straight into an anti-aircraft position with nothing he could do to avoid it. He wanted a fighting chance, so he pulled his pistol and started shootin'. When he got to the ground, he captured the gun and the crew!"

Amid cheering and laughter, the colonel went on. "Wait, I got one more, and then we need to get to business. And don't forget, we've got our own hero in here. Harry saved the ol' man from getting shot up by a kraut with a machine gun."

After once again quelling raucous approbation, he continued. "So, here's the last story. It's similar to Beaudin's. This one's about Private Edwin Raub of the 505th. I think we need to promote him. He was also heading into a 20 mm flak tower, and they were shootin' at him. He yanked on his risers and side-slipped to land near the gun position. Without even trying to release his parachute, he charged the krauts while spraying them with submachine gun bursts, an' he captured the whole bunch."

The room erupted into cheering and applause again. The colonel glanced at Gavin. The general had listened while scanning several pages in his hands. By the time the chief of staff had finished, Gavin's face had become grim.

The colonel called for quiet. Gavin faced his staff. "I've been reading the battle reports," he said. "They're sobering."

In the north at Arnhem, the British 1st Airborne Division under General Roy Urquhart had been tasked with securing the main bridge and other key crossings. The force had landed seven miles from its objectives in order to avoid anti-aircraft fire as the paratroopers dropped. Once on the ground, assembled, and heading toward its objective, it had encountered unexpectedly high resistance from elements of the 9th and 10th SS *Panzer* Divisions, both crack combat units.

The British division's 2nd Parachute Battalion, commanded by Lieutenant Colonel John Frost, had secured a foothold on the north end of the bridge over the Nederrijn, but it had fought fiercely to get there and had taken many casualties. Furthermore, it was cut off from reinforcements and faced frequent and furious German counterattacks.

Meanwhile, the division's 1st Parachute Battalion under Lieutenant Colonel David Dobie was supposed to have secured the high ground north and west of Arnhem. It had met other elements of the SS *panzer* divisions. The battalion was encircled and forced into a pocket in the town of Oosterbeek, four miles west of Arnhem. It was thus unable to support Frost's battalion.

The plan had called for the two battalions to establish a firm bridgehead and hold for two days while XXX Corps drove its three divisions north from Geel, Belgium, to relieve them. The airborne battalions were expected to hold for two days or a maximum of four. Now that looked extremely optimistic.

The XXX Corps had, indeed, started north on schedule. However, on entering the Netherlands, the two-lane road was suddenly crowded with Dutch residents thrilled with their liberation. So effusive were they in showing appreciation that their throngs filled the narrow passage. The resulting traffic jams were exacerbated by a force of fifty thousand men and their transport trucks, tanks, artillery pieces, and all manner of support vehicles pushing north and forced to a crawl.

Fortunately, the 101st Airborne Division had captured its main objective in the south, the bridge at Eindhoven as well as three lesser bridges. All had not gone well, however. The Germans had blown a bridge that had been an objective to capture intact. Further, the lead elements of the XXX Corps came under anti-tank ambushes from the flanks, causing casualties and destroying equipment along the narrow road that created even more obstacles.

"We have a problem," Gavin said, facing his staff. "The British airborne is fighting for its life north of Arnhem, and the XXX Corps is moving up at a snail's pace in the south. It hasn't even reached the 101st's positions at Eindhoven. Meanwhile, we're encountering heavy fighting to our rear out of the Reichswald Forest, and we still have to take the bridge at Nijmegen." He paused. "This operation relied on speed and surprise. We got neither."

"Sir," the chief of staff broke in, "the 508th's commander, Colonel Mendez, reports that his element has been in position with a clear path to the main bridge at Nijmegen, the Waalbrug, almost since we set foot on the ground. His 3rd Battalion's G-Company reported that it's at Berg-en-Dal and prepared to attack. That's only four miles southeast of the Waalbrug, and they've encountered hardly any resistance.

"Better yet, a few minutes ago, I-Company's night patrol on the town's eastern outskirts just reported that it's within a mile of the bridge. They've also met very little opposition. And Dutch partisans report that the Germans deserted Nijmegen, pulled back the guards, and that the bridge is only lightly defended. Mendez says all he needs is the order to execute."

Gavin listened carefully and deliberated silently with his chin resting on his interlocked fingers. Then he shook his head. "My orders are clear. I'm to take the bridge only after securing our other objectives. Groesbeek Heights is not secure, and if we believe our intelligence, major armored units are massing in those woods east of there, preparing to strike our rear. If we attack the bridge prematurely, we could blow the whole operation."

He called to Harry, who sat with Lance among the secondary staff. "Captain, while we get ready to assault that bridge, I'd like your team to go into Nijmegen to assess enemy strength there. Contact the Dutch Underground too. I want to know its strength and capabilities."

Harry assented with a quick nod.

"Sir, may I—" Lance cut in on impulse.

Harry nudged him sharply.

Gavin noticed. "Let him speak," he said with a wave of his hand. "I know his background."

Lance stood with a sidelong glance at Harry, who nodded, slightly peeved. "Sir, our team's primary mission is to train local partisans to fight effectively, usually by carrying out sabotage."

Gavin nodded. "Go on."

"We're already in the fight, sir, with Germans all around us. We won't have time or a place to train. I'd suggest that we split the Jedburgh team for the moment. While Captain Harry goes into Nijmegen with Bud, I could go back out on the 508th's periphery. You said many of those troops in the Heights were green replacements, their first time in combat. I'm sure Resistance chaps are monitoring the enemy there.

"I might be able to help out with contacting Resistance people in the Heights and gaining more intel about whatever armored threat is massing in the Reichswald Forest."

Gavin gazed at Lance in thought. Finally, he said, "I like the idea, but Captain Harry is your boss." He turned to the Dutch officer. "What do you say?"

Lance's cheeks suddenly flushed red as he recognized that he had just broken protocol and had probably embarrassed his boss. He felt all eyes on him.

Harry glanced up with an accepting nod. "That makes sense, General. I have no objection."

When the meeting had adjourned, and as Harry and Lance left the schoolhouse together, Lance apologized anxiously. "I'm sorry, sir. I spoke out of turn, on impulse. No excuse. It won't happen again."

"I'm glad to hear that, Lieutenant," Harry replied. "Your suggestion was good."

14

September 18, 1944
Nijmegen, the Netherlands

Captain Harry and Bud stayed close to a row of buildings and within shadows as they observed the sleeping city in the early morning hours. They had been surprised to find Nijmegen fairly empty of Germans until they drew near to the Waalbrug. Seizing that bridge in very short order was the 82nd's main objective, to pave the way for XXX Corps to drive over it and press on to Arnhem.

Burned-out collapsing buildings manifested the war's cruelty. Seven months earlier, in February, an Allied bombing run had hit Nijmegen by accident. Eight hundred civilians had paid for the error with their lives, and the cityscape remained blighted. Harry and Bud took in the devastation, wondering how the population would react to soldiers of the Allies who had brought such destruction.

Despite their caution and the low light, German soldiers detected them and fired, wounding Harry's arm in three places. As dawn turned to early morning half-light, Harry and Bud observed a reinforced blocking position on the southside of the bridge and rumblings of heavy military traffic on the opposite end. The two Jedburghs evaded capture and headed back toward headquarters, stopping in a safe place to bandage Harry's injured arm. Bud also called in their observations to headquarters. A short time later, American infantry soldiers filed past them to infiltrate the town.

As Harry and Bud watched the troops, they heard a low whistle from deeper shadows by a barn. A young civilian in his early thirties appeared and beckoned to them. He was tall, with thick hair, and an expression of fatigue reinvigorated by the excitement of nearby combat. Oddly, he was well-dressed in business attire with a pullover sweater under his wool jacket.

Weapons ready, Harry and Bud approached him. "I am Jan Van Hoof," he said in Dutch.

"Do you speak English?" Harry cut in.

Jan nodded. "Quite well."

"Then for the benefit of my British friend," Harry said, "let's continue in his language."

"Of course," Jan said brusquely in English. "I must tell you about this bridge over the Waal. Everyone knows why you're here, that you dropped from the skies, and that a huge force is coming up the road from Eindhoven intending to drive on to Arnhem and perhaps beyond. But the Waalbrug is set with explosives. When your lead tank reaches the north end, the Germans will blow the bridge. You'll lose every man and every piece of equipment on it."

"We know that, and that the detonation mechanism is in the post office here in town. We just have to get to it."

Jan shook his head. "It is not there. It's on the other side of the river. Someone will have to sneak inside the German perimeter and crawl the entire length underneath the bridge and cut the lines. Let me tell you how we're organized."

He explained that a major Underground group, *Krijgsraad Partizanen*, operated around Nijmegen. It was led by Jules Jansen, an engineering professor at the Saint Canisius College. "He runs a demolitions factory inside his house and a shooting range in his cellar. He vets and trains our recruits, and oversees sabotage operations. We call it the KP. He also sets up cells in other towns and villages.

"Another major organization is the *Ordedienst*. That means 'order of service.' It's primarily concerned with preparing to re-establish our government and Dutch civil authority.

"Then we have the Council of Resistance. We call it the *Raad Van Verzet.* It primarily sabotages German communications—"

"I'm familiar with it," Harry interrupted. "It also protects members of the *Ordedienst,* who are prominent citizens and former military officers, essentially people in hiding from the Nazis."

"That's almost correct," Jan replied. "The most important of the organizations is the *Landelijke Organisatie Voor Hulp Aan Onderduikers,* or the LO." He turned to Bud. "In English, that means the Central Government Organizations For Help To People In Hiding. It has primary responsibility to protect and exfiltrate anyone needing it. They also get food coupons, either stolen from government offices or counterfeit, so we can feed those in hiding."

Harry looked on Jan with increased admiration and respect. "I knew the Resistance here was well organized, but I had no idea—"

"We're decentralized," Jan went on. "No group informs or needs permission from any centralized authority in some hierarchical scheme to carry out an act of sabotage. But, for instance, if an LO group decides to conduct a sabotage operation, it automatically falls under KP, but only for coordination and training, not for approval."

"That's remarkable."

Jan pursed his lips. "Our system works well most of the time. I can't think of any time that it hasn't, but Market Garden is putting it to the test. General Eisenhower ordered that most of the Resistance stays underground through most of the operation. He doesn't want people to be subjected to mass retribution if it fails.

"The exception is that he wants us to sabotage the trains and railroads, particularly between Eindhoven and Nijmegen, to deny the Germans quick movement of its troops along the corridor between Eindhoven and Arnhem.

"The Grave bridge over the Maas just west of Nijmegen is also a Market Garden target, and an LO group there was activated to sabotage and provide intelligence support, so of course, it becomes a PK group. That's how it all works."

"It's amazing, really," Bud broke in. "I'm floored."

"Are you using that special telephone number?" Harry asked. "You must be, to know so much about the German status and our own."

Jan shrugged impatiently. "Of course. It's how we keep each other informed all over the Netherlands. Do you have it?"

Harry nodded. He had used it on previous covert missions. Near the beginning of the war, a brilliant Dutch communications engineer had set up a special telephone number. Dialing it would take the user to a new dial tone from which a call could be placed to any number inside the country. The number's existence was among the most protected of the Dutch Resistance's secrets.

"You should come with me," Jan said. "I'm an *Ordedienst* member. Last night, I met with Captain Walter Silver, the regimental intelligence officer at the command post of the 508th PIR in Western Moerdijk. He told me about you. I gave him a lot of good information about German units, dispositions, and strength in the area.

"I can take you to the leaders at our headquarters. It's in a café, the Bonte Os, just off the city square, Keizer Lodewijkplein. You can confirm what I've told you and get the latest information there."

Bud arched his brows and looked at Harry. "You should get that arm seen to. How is it now?"

Harry winced. "Holding up. The bleeding stopped. I should get it treated fairly soon."

"Our doctors can do that for you," Jan said firmly. "We don't have much time." He shifted his eyes between Harry and Bud. "Your ground forces moved past Eindhoven during the night. They'll be here today or tomorrow. The Waalbrug must be disarmed, and that will take several hours."

Harry studied the man a moment. "All right. Let's go," he said brusquely.

Jan led them through back streets and alleyways, going farther into the city's center and drawing closer to the huge arches of the Waalbrug. As they went, morning traffic grew, and when people saw Harry and Bud in their uniforms, they called to them, thanking them for being in the fight and wanting to stop to chat.

Jan explained multiple times that the war was still on, that Nijmegen was not yet liberated, and that he and the two soldiers must push on. He also pressed the good citizens to be cautious lest they reveal to the enemy the presence of the Allied captain and sergeant in the city. Invariably, on being so warned, the people's eyes opened wide, they placed a finger to their lips to signify silence, and went on their ways, albeit with jauntiness in their strides and smiles on their faces that had been absent prior to their encounters.

Before reaching the plaza, the trio walked up a rise overlooking rows and rows of dwellings that had been almost leveled by the February bombing. Rising up to their left were the remains of Saint Stephen's Church, locally called the *Stevenskerk*. Its massive tower, previously the tallest building in the city, had been halved, its roof caved in. Off to the right of where the men now stood was the Waalbrug, its elegant, dark green arches and upright supports rising over two hundred feet above the Waal River and supplanting the church tower as the tallest man-made structure in the area.

Contemplating that fact and the rubble where thriving neighborhoods had been, Harry's throat constricted. His birthplace in Rotterdam was only fifty miles away. This was his country. These were his countrymen. He sniffed and wiped his nose.

Squinting for a better view, he saw signs of current *Wehrmacht* activity at both ends of the bridge. *Preparing for battle.*

"Let's press on," Harry said, ignoring the sharp pain that mounted in his arm. He turned and found Jan speaking with local residents.

Jan's face had turned grim and an expression of resoluteness had formed in his eyes. "I cannot continue with you," he said. "It will take too long. The Germans widened their perimeter near the bridge. Their security area now includes the café where our headquarters is, and they're centering their defenses on Keizer Lodewijkplein and Keizer Karelplein. The bridge is another mile inside there, through neighborhoods and commercial areas. Guards are stopping people who try to enter."

He introduced two men his own age. "Go with them. I trust them. They will take you to an alternate location where the *Ordedienst* leaders will meet. The members will be happy to receive you, and they will get you safely back to your headquarters." He inhaled sharply. "I'm sorry to say, I must go home."

As Jan indicated, the *Ordedienst* members, and particularly the leaders, met at a farmhouse that served as the alternate headquarters. They were overjoyed at receiving direct Allied participation with their organization. They were particularly fascinated by Harry's position with direct access to Gavin. "Tell the general that we'll do whatever he says," they told him. "We know that our day of deliverance is near, but getting your army across that river will be difficult, and we won't be free until the other side is clear, and then there's Arnhem still to go."

Before escorting him by car to Groesbeek, a doctor tended to Harry's arm, cleaning and bandaging it. "We're out of supplies," the physician said with regret. "I have no pain medicine or antibiotics to give you."

"Not to worry, Doctor," Harry said, knowing the 82nd's aid station at Groesbeek would have plenty. "I'll live."

Many hours after having left General Gavin's headquarters in Groesbeek, Harry and Bud returned. "The bridge is currently lightly defended," he reported to the general, "but the situation is changing rapidly. While we were in the town, the 9th and 10th SS *Panzer* Divisions were re-establishing the German positions on this side of the bridge. They pushed their perimeter south into Nijmegen by at least a mile. We could still overwhelm them if we move now, but that window is rapidly closing."

Gavin shook his head grimly. "Can't do it. Groesbeek is still being attacked from the Reichswald. If we capture Waalbrug without securing the other objectives, we won't be able to hold our positions, and this whole escapade will have been useless."

He reached for a cup of coffee on his desk. "What did you find out about the local Resistance?"

"It's well organized. I can't call their fighters professional soldiers though. They need training, but they're eager to be in the fight."

Harry had brought back with him a dozen young members of the Underground. After briefing Gavin on everything he had learned and who the men were, he received permission to arm them and integrate them among front line units.

"Take six out to the 508th," Harry instructed Bud, "and take the rest to the 504th."

15

After having left Harry and Bud that morning, Jan Van Hoof hurried home through Nijmegen's streets as fast as he could without drawing unwanted attention. Once there, he took off his suit, put on overalls, scruffed up his hair, and grabbed his toolbox. When he emerged onto the streets again, he looked like a repairman.

He made his way across town for the third time that day, and approached the Waalbrug. Carefully, he skirted around the southern end of the bridge, observing all the approaches to its base and the German encampment with its recent reinforcements. Jan recognized the insignia of a company from an SS-*Panzer* engineer unit and a battalion from the 19th SS-*Panzergrenadier* Regiment. Obviously, the *Wehrmacht* did not intend to give up the Waalbrug easily.

While contemplating his next actions, he admitted to himself surprise that the 82nd had chosen not to attack immediately after landing the day before. The bridge had not been heavily defended then. The German defenses had mainly consisted of anti-aircraft batteries with a light ground force to protect it.

Jan had seen that, almost as soon as the paratroopers descended from the sky, the *Wehrmacht* began pouring troops into the areas at both ends of the Waalbrug in Nijmegen and to the north of Arnhem. He was sure that German Field Marshal Model must have deduced the intent of Operation Market Garden, to punch through German western defenses and circumvent the Siegfried Line. German intelligence officers would have estimated that, to accomplish its objective, the force would drive northward on a narrow avenue with possibly the largest army group ever assembled, consisting of three armies, each composed of three corps and supporting elements.

What rankled Jan more than a little was that the *Ordedienst* and other Dutch Underground groups had been monitoring German movements since the beginning of the war. With their telecommunications system intact and the brilliance of the engineer who had thought to develop the workaround telephone number, the groups had virtually unfettered ability to gather and disseminate intelligence across the Netherlands.

They knew that the 9th and 10th SS-*Panzer* Divisions had moved into the area for rest and refitting. They reported such to the Allies, but saw no evidence that their intel had been considered. Even now, in the latter half of the second day of the operation, Jan had seen no sign that the 82nd intended to move in force to take the bridge today.

Phone conversations with compatriots confirmed Jan's sense. Some fighting had taken place along the northeastern ridge of the Groesbeek Heights above the Reichswald Forest, his comrades told him, but that was with only light weapons. They had heard reports of heavy armor massing in the woods, but because the forest was so dense, they believed that ensconcing armor there made no sense, and they had seen no evidence that such had taken place.

Jan inferred that the Waalbrug must be saved. Intact. Failure to do so would stop the Allied advance cold, destroy a large part of its army, isolate the 1st Airborne Division north of Arnhem to be killed or captured, and relegate his family, his people, and the city and country he loved to more tyranny with no end in sight. Further, it could lead to defeat of the Allies in Western Europe.

Carefully, Jan picked his entry point into the German security area. Two guards at one of the checkpoints appeared tired, and bored, and they joked and slouched at their post when they thought no one was looking. When activity had slowed and shortly before the guards' shift change, Jan approached them.

He carried with him beautifully forged ID papers purporting to show that he was employed by the German company Siemens & Halske AG to maintain and repair *Wehrmacht* equipment beyond the abilities of its operators and normal maintenance crews. The ID had been aged to indicate long and frequent use.

The two guards allowed him through with only a cursory glance at his papers. One of them asked, "What's your business?"

Jan shrugged and replied in the manner of a dull workman who had already seen the best of life go by. "I have to fix several generators. The boss said it was urgent." He looked about anxiously. "He's worried about the enemy attacks."

The guards hurried him through.

On entering, Jan made his way slowly and methodically through back streets toward the foot of the bridge. German soldiers were all around him. Twice more, he had to show his papers.

Finally within the area abutting the foot of the Waalbrug, he found, as he had expected, a profusion of soldiers and equipment. Despite four years of practice at sublimating fear and showing only a blank face, he took a deep breath as his heart raced. Two more times, he endured close examinations of his papers, but then he was inside the innermost defensive circle at the base of a massive concrete pylon.

He looked over various pieces of equipment as if to examine them, and then appeared to make repairs. In reality, he only took parts out and put them right back, in proper working order, not caring to sabotage his real mission by causing an implement to malfunction after he had just been seen "repairing" it.

When he felt that nearby soldiers had become sufficiently accustomed to his presence that they no longer paid attention to him, he moved to the upstream side of the bridge. The sun had already moved beyond its zenith, creating dark pockets of shade under this side of its span. There, he moved swiftly.

He pocketed two pairs of wire cutters and hid his tool box under a bush. Checking to make sure that no one lingered nearby or was in a position to observe his next moves, he stared up at the underside of the bridge.

The Waalbrug, a two-hinged arched bridge that opened only eight years ago, had been an engineering innovation. Using steel to push technological boundaries, it had been built in five sections. The first two and the last two were almost identical to each other, each consisting of an arched, steel understructure secured at each end by massive concrete pylons that absorbed and distributed the weight of its load, including passing traffic.

The center arch was the main structural component. Also constructed of steel, it spanned eight hundred feet, rose two hundred feet into the air, and absorbed the load of traffic and its own weight through upright struts that dispersed into concrete pylons at either end.

Jan found that he could easily lift himself from the ground onto a crook between the first pylon and nearest arch. From there, he could shimmy up the curved steel and then assess what to do next.

Salty sweat poured into his eyes, and his heart pounded as he mounted the structure and began to pull and push himself up the curve of the arch. As he worked his way up, he watched for anyone coming his way. However, no German soldiers came to check on him.

He wiped away the sweat and kept going.

Reaching the top of the first arch, Jan took time for a breather and to consider the situation. He had thus far encountered no sign of demolitions. The thought occurred to him that to meet their own objectives of halting the northward trek of the Allied armies, the Germans would need to destroy only a single major section anywhere along the bridge. They could have rigged just the ends of the main arch. Dynamiting there would bring down the center span.

Then Jan recalled that somewhere on the opposite end of the Waalbrug was a main line that ran to the detonator. He would have to cut that too, to ensure that no power went to any lines he might miss.

He took a deep breath and let it out slowly as he contemplated his task. To complete it, he must crawl under the bridge for its entire eighteen-hundred-foot length, cut whatever wires he encountered, and crawl back, all without being seen.

From his perch, he observed the four junctures of the arch he was currently on. They were empty. No suspicious objects. No wires. He could move on to the next section.

He faced a new challenge. The pylon was too long and wide to climb, and even if he could, he would be exposed to the enemy and likely spotted.

Seeking an alternate route, Jan saw a steel shelf-like structure beneath the road's surface. It was just wide enough to hold him. Taking a deep breath, he pulled onto it and began to belly-crawl.

Jan stared down at the center arch where the steel joined with the pylons. He had easily crawled through the small spaces at the top of the concrete structures, and he found the second section, like the first, to be empty of anything ominous.

The same was not true for the main arch. Dynamite charges with protruding wires had been placed immediately under the roadway wedged between the pylon and the end of the steel structure.

Jan had been trained enough on demolitions to determine that if detonation occurred, the amount of dynamite was sufficient to slice through the road's surface and the arch. Further, he had to assume that an identical charge was placed at the opposite end of the span, eight hundred feet away, and that the charges might be booby-trapped.

The first of the wires were just feet away, within easy reach. Seeing no sign of safeguards, he pulled a pair of wire cutters from his pocket, extended his hands, and slipped the opposing blades over the nearest lines. Then he closed his eyes and held his breath.

Jan had told no one of his intentions. Saving the bridge was critical to saving everything he held dear. Images of his mother, father, and sister flitted across his mind.

With the next movement of his hand, he might start the process of dismantling the threat to the bridge. Conversely, he might set off an explosion that could warn the Germans at best, or at worst set off a series of detonations that would bring down the massive arches. He would go down with them.

Still holding his breath, he opened his eyes, ensured that the sharp edges of the blades still held the wires firmly, squeezed, and heard the slight sound of wires being clipped.

Then, nothing.

Jan breathed out with a brief sense of exultation. Then he looked down, spotted another explosive packet at the lower end of the pylon, and let his eyes trail up to study as much of the bridge as far as he could from his limited vantage. Looking back at the wires to his immediate front, he continued cutting.

Late that evening, Jan's sister paced in her family's small living room. She had placed calls to friends, but no one had seen her brother during the afternoon or knew anything about his whereabouts. Meanwhile, far-off explosions had raised fear that the battle for the Waalbrug would soon be joined. She knew of Jan's involvement with the Underground, and terror gripped her that she might never see him again.

Six years younger than Jan, she had looked at him as a hero, particularly during the war. He had always called her "Schatje," for "Little Treasure."

Wearily, Schatje sat on her sofa. Her mother was napping in the large bedroom and had not been apprised of Jan's disappearance. Soon, she would be up and asking about him, and when Father returned from work, he would be equally concerned. He was due home at any moment and always looked for Jan. He knew about his son's activities, but not the details, and he always worried that Jan might not come home alive or in one piece.

The front door opened softly. Schatje looked up, expecting to see her father. Instead, Jan stepped in, looking as bedraggled as she had ever seen him. His hair was matted, his shoulders drooped, his overalls were filthy, and the odor of sweat from his underarms was piercing. He trudged in and stood on unsteady legs looking at Schatje through eyes sunken into deep sockets.

Alarmed, Schatje ran to him. "Are you all right?" She flung her arms around his shoulders.

"I stink," he croaked, barely above a whisper.

"I don't care. No one knew where you'd gone, and with the fighting going on—" She shook her head. "I was so scared that we'd lost you."

Jan smiled tiredly and wrapped his arms around her. "I'm all right," he said. "The explosions you heard were by Groesbeek. The Germans are too busy dealing with the Allies to pay any attention to me. But I can tell you this, Schatje." He reached down and lifted her chin so that her eyes met his. "The bridge is safe."

Same Day
Groesbeek Heights, the Netherlands

Lance wondered if he had made a mistake by choosing to help secure the 508th's right flank on the high ground overlooking Nijmegen rather than go on into the city with Harry. From his perspective, General Gavin did not seem on the verge of launching the assault, and the fighting along the Heights had been fierce, although so far with light weapons. However, given that the routes to Nijmegen from Groesbeek were limited, and if reports were correct about armor massing in the Reichswald Forest, then a reasonable expectation was that the 508th would be attacked in force on its left flank.

Lance's thought had been that he might be more useful with the 508th, but now he wondered if he had miscalculated. Captain Combs had been friendly enough on receiving him but then seemed at a loss for what to do with him. Lance volunteered to help out with planning or reconnaissance and suggested ideas about recruiting partisans, gaining whatever intelligence they had, and preparing them to be in the fight.

"That sounds good," Combs said, "but I ain't seen any Resistance people around here. Have you?"

Lance had to agree that he had not. "But we know that they have a strong organization in the area. I think the problem is that we're away from the villages and already in the fight. They'd be concerned about coming on us unexpectedly when a firefight could erupt at any moment."

"No dispute on that, LT. I'm glad to have you. Having another trigger-puller is a good thing. Hang tight. We'll figure a way to get you in the fight."

Then, late in the afternoon, Bud showed up with a dozen Resistance members from the *Ordedienst,* all dressed in civilian clothes. Some had bits of military paraphernalia they had scavenged over the years. All wore Resistance armbands with orange horizontal stripes in the middle representing the Dutch Royal House of Orange-Nassau, and thin white stripes on the borders.

"These chaps are fighters," Bud told Lance. "Captain Harry recruited them out of Nijmegen this morning. They have a lot of useful intelligence. They'll be good for infiltrating and getting fresh information from civilians behind enemy lines. I've just come from 508th HQ. The commander asked that I leave one with you and drop five at the most vulnerable places along the front. The others will go to the 504th. General Gavin says to make good use of them."

"I'll do that," Lance said as Bud headed out.

Lance turned to regard the man left behind, noticing that he carried a helmet. He had waited with the others near Combs' headquarters tent, observing while Lance and Bud conversed. Now he watched as the group followed Bud away.

He came to attention as Lance approached. "Do you speak English?"

"We all do, to varying degrees," the man said, gesturing toward those departing. "I've had the most exposure. Some also speak French, and some speak German."

He turned to face Lance directly. "We're all ready to fight. I'm Agardus Marinus Leegsma, Jr."

Lance raised his eyebrows in appreciation. "Pleased to meet you."

"You can call me Leegsma, if you like. It might be easier for you—"

Lance chuckled. "'Agardus' is fine. I can see that we'll get on splendidly."

"My comrades are good men. We've been active in the Underground since the beginning. We were so happy that you came."

Tall and slender with dark hair and round-rimmed glasses, Agardus wore a friendly smile. He carried himself with quiet ease and subtle authority. "One other thing, Lieutenant. My home is not far from here and we've managed to store a good supply of food. We know soldiers in the field do not always have the best meals. My mother and several families in the area would consider it an honor if they could cook for some of your soldiers."

Lance's mouth gaped open. "Seriously?" He grinned. "They'll welcome you with open arms."

16

September 19, 1944
Bourg-Léopold, Belgium

Lieutenant Derek Horton rolled over in his sleeping bag, luxuriating in its warmth and comfort despite the hardness of the ground on which he had slept. His next sense was of unfathomable fatigue that pressed into the bone. Then came the inexorable horror in the pit of his stomach that had become axiomatic with being awake, the unwelcome images of blood-spattered faces and bodies of mates lost; of explosions and smoke and desperate cries for medics; of rapid gunfire and unrelenting field artillery reports; of smoldering tanks, destroyed trucks; of muddy roads or blindingly dusty ones lined with exhausted infantrymen plodding to the next battle. Dread followed for what lay ahead and his responsibility to clamber up from his bed, such as it was, refresh his own spirits, prepare to lift those of the soldiers in his charge, and be ready for the mission ahead.

To that end, he deliberately focused his mind on the conjured image of a young girl, a woman now, Chantal Boulier. He had been at war the entire time he had known her, four years now. She had been fourteen years of age at the time they met and she was besotted with him. Being three years and six months older than she, he had not been interested, tolerating her juvenile approaches with annoyance. But she had settled her heart on him, and she never let go.

Fate had thrown them into the same Resistance group in Marseille where he had been an adviser. Despite Chantal's young age, she had sought out critical missions irrespective of danger and completed them with remarkable success. Her intelligence coups included garnering important information about a German radar site and helping provide details of ground forces, shore-gun locations, and enemy supply routes along eighty miles of Normandy's coastline, ahead of the Allied invasion.

Separated for a time, when Horton had seen her again, she had just finished SOE spy training in the UK, and she had matured into a beautiful young woman with a slight frame, auburn hair, and honey-colored eyes, like her sister Amélie. Her affection for Horton had burned as deeply as ever, and her persistence finally bore fruit. When Horton last saw her—at Christmastime nine months ago in London, just prior to his departure for combat in Italy—he was transfixed by her charms. She kissed him then, and his heart melted.

Memories of Chantal became Horton's escape from the ravages of war. Between furious times in action, thoughts of her returned a smile to his face. Her image in his mind caused the apprehension of yet more heated battle to recede, and he could regard himself as something approaching a human being.

Through Resistance channels, Horton had been able to get a short letter to her in which he stated his intent to marry her, if she would have him, writing that he would get down on one knee to propose properly. After many weeks, he had received her response: "I'll ask you to please get off your knee and kiss me, because I'll accept."

His heart had pounded against his chest as he read, and he conjured her lovely visage in his mind at every spare moment, often involuntarily. But he worried about her and the dangers she faced. He had hoped that, with the liberation of Paris, Chantal would remain in the city in safety and security, but her note had cryptically included the information that she would be traveling with Hérisson. That was the code name for Madame Fourcade, the leader of Alliance, the largest and most effective Resistance network in France.

Horton loved Chantal's high spirits and daring, but to his mind, traveling with Fourcade necessarily meant that Chantal would be carrying out dangerous missions. She had come close to capture once while transporting the sketch map of Normandy. When two German soldiers attempted to detain Chantal, they were killed by Resistance fighters watching over her. On another occasion, she had been arrested by Vichy *gendarmes* and managed to escape.

With thoughts of her lacing Horton's consciousness, he rolled over and prepared to face the day. Crushing fatigue slowed him as he opened his sleeping bag and clambered to his feet. His joints and muscles ached, his brain functioned sluggishly, and he contended with lack of adequate hygiene facilities. His steel helmet served as his wash basin.

At least breakfast would be hot. That was generally the case when a unit had been at rest and was about to go back into the front lines.

Horton's armored reconnaissance troop had come to Leopoldsburg for respite after four days of battle at Geel. That had been the most intense combat he had experienced during the whole war. Considering that he had been at Dunkirk and was abandoned there during the evacuation, worked with the French Resistance as part of Britain's MI-9, fought in Italy after landing at Anzio, and battled across France with the Sherwood Rangers Yeomanry since landing at Normandy, characterizing the combat at Geel as the most violent he had seen was no small matter. And today, the Sherwoods would once again deploy into the thick of combat attached to the 43rd Wessex Division to protect the British 2nd Army's right flank as it thrust north into the Netherlands to reinforce the 1st Airborne Division at Arnhem's bridge.

After cleaning up and shaving, Horton made his way to the mess tent, calling jocular greetings to his soldiers as he encountered them. Feeling inauthentic, he injected forced enthusiasm. "G' mornin', Tom." "Hello, Harry." "Ready for breakfast, Charlie?"

Despite his successes, he questioned his own ability to lead men in battle. At the outset of hostilities, he had been a corporal. During successive battles, as leaders had fallen, he had been elevated, and now, not yet twenty-two, he found himself leading a cavalry troop. "Rally the men right after breakfast, Sully," he called to his troop sergeant. "We'll start our pre-combat inspections straightaway."

Sully had thus far been competent, but he had joined the troop at Leopoldsburg, coming from another troop that had been all but annihilated. He came to replace Horton's troop sergeant, who had caught a bullet in the forehead at Geel. Horton and Sully had spent time together during the rest period, but they had not fought together in combat. The sense of relying on each other unquestionably in battle had not yet formed. The best that each knew of the other at this point was that both had been with the regiment since Normandy. That alone counted for much in reciprocal respect.

Horton had joined the Sherwoods shortly before the regiment landed on Gold Beach at Normandy, the first British unit to do so. It had a proud, aristocratic history as a lauded horse cavalry outfit dating back to 1794 in the area of the Sherwood Forest of legendary Robin Hood fame. Its members, voluntary weekenders during peacetime, had fought in the Boer War in the early nineteenth century and in the Middle Eastern countries during the Great War two decades ago.

At the outset of the current conflict, the regiment was still a horse cavalry unit and shipped out to Palestine with their mounts, even charging insurrectionists in the desert on horseback. Quickly realizing their foolhardiness, the unit reorganized as an armored reconnaissance regiment. Stumbling at first, its composure changed significantly when Lieutenant Colonel Flash Callas became the commander. He recruited highly competent officers from across the British military and developed effective tactics that carried them well through the campaigns in North Africa and Italy. By the time they landed in Normandy, the Sherwoods' reputation as a fighting machine had spread. Typically, its job was to lead an assault on the enemy and breach its defenses.

As the war progressed, high casualties reduced the number of members who had been with the regiment at the outset. That had been particularly true at Normandy prior to breaking out of *bocage* country.

The battle at Geel had resulted in a high casualty count. The Albert Canal ran just north of the town. The 50th Northumbrian Infantry Division had established a foothold on the far side more than a week ago, but it was tenuous and subject to numerous counterattacks. Securing and expanding it was imperative to opening a route to Market Garden's departure line along the Belgian-Dutch border. Doing so had required capturing Geel. Eight days ago, the Sherwoods had spearheaded the drive.

Over four days of ferocious combat, the weary regiment battled through forests, sunken roads, and unceasing field artillery and mortar fire amid dirt, mud, poor visibility, and depleting supplies. Tanks burned and exploded. Men fell on all sides, veterans and replacements alike. A new troop leader arrived to replace one just fallen, and he crumpled under gunfire fifteen minutes later. Despite the conditions, the troops fought on, and after four days of bloodshed, the Albert Canal had been crossed, and the Sherwood Rangers had moved to Leopoldsburg to rest and replenish.

Soldiers who had been with the regiment when it landed at Normandy, Horton among them, had seen the numbers depleted by death and gaping wounds beyond imagining. As a curious result, an oxymoronic sense of distant camaraderie set in. Each man knew that his continued existence in a firefight depended on the men to his left and right. Simultaneously, each knew the pain of losing a treasured comrade. Hence, a common practice rose of allowing no one to get too close.

Horton knew his own odds. A troop commander lasted two weeks on average. He had landed in Normandy three months ago and had engaged in combat more times than he could remember, yet he lived, and no bullet or shrapnel had touched him.

He was of stocky build and hardened by the constant physical demands of war. His natural demeanor was one of humor, but with the weight of responsibility for a Sherman Firefly, three regular Sherman tanks, and a crew of five in each one, his natural wit had waned. His instinct to manage his own morale for the sake of lifting that of his men bore down on him constantly, but failure to do so could result in preventable fatalities, including his own.

Horton emerged from the mess tent, field kit in hand with steam rising off his porridge. He had been pleased that this morning, the breakfast meal included two slices of bread and two carrots. As he made his way to a seating area, another troop leader, Lieutenant David Render, called out to him. "Horton, over here."

Horton caught Render's eye, waved his free hand, and ambled over. "We're in for it again today," he said as he lowered himself to sit cross-legged on the ground next to him. "I hope our blokes haven't lost their edge during these past four days."

Render cocked his head and studied Horton. "With you as their leader, they'll do marvelously," he said.

Horton smirked slightly. "Oh, I don't know about that, sir. I've been lucky. Some of my men not so..." His voice trailed off. "I lost half of them in Geel."

Render cast him a somber glance. "Still calling your peers 'sir,' are you?"

Horton chuckled in spite of himself. "Force of habit, from coming through the enlisted ranks." He regarded Render seriously. "You don't feel like a peer to me, David. You're several classes above me. I've watched you. I admire and respect you deeply. A Sandhurst graduate, thrown into the fray at Normandy as a troop leader at nineteen years of age. But you always seem to know what you're doing. You're so confident—"

"If that's the way you perceive me, then my act is working," Render replied, laughing. "Most of the time, I'm as terrified as anyone. But let's get one notion out of your head. I am certainly not above you, and you are a worthy peer, a colleague. Your promotions came from your actions in the field."

"Leaving me terrified that I'll get someone killed," Horton muttered. "But thanks for your kind words. I'm not sure I belong as troop leader, though. I didn't train for it. I haven't studied leadership or tactics. My education—" He glanced at Render. "It isn't Sandhurst quality. I was just the most senior man still alive after an engagement—"

"But you took charge, completed the mission, and saved your men. I've heard about what you did at Anzio, subduing and capturing a much larger German unit. And you've proven yourself over and over again since then. You came up in the most effective military classroom in existence, the battlefield.

"I've learned from you too. Your tactics are the best kind, instinctual, gained by experience. You were a non-com. Every army in the world is run by non-coms. You learned to survive on the ground and keep yourself and your men alive while winning."

Horton grunted. "I didn't do such a great job of that at Geel."

Render swung around to face him. "Stop it," he said severely. "Your casualty rate was in line with the regiment's and mine. Your men trust that you'll bring them through alive. These moments of self-doubt will pass. We all have them."

They lapsed into silence while they spooned their porridge. "Thank you for that, David," Horton said at last. "This can't be a day of chasing blues away." He took a sip of tea. "What are you hearing about what lies ahead?"

Render grimaced. "It doesn't look good. I stopped off at operations. Our chaps took all three major towns on the first day as planned, but surprise had been blown. From what I gather, and this might be inaccurate, the paratroopers at Arnhem captured the north end of their bridge, but they met stiff resistance and took high casualties. It's taken three days to get all the airborne troops in. The last ones will drop today—the 1st Polish Parachute Brigade. The fighting's been heavy. On the first day, after the first drop, the Germans moved in reinforcements on the north side of the river to counter our forces at Oosterbeek and counterattacked our chaps who made it to the bridge.

"On the south end of the operation, the ground battle started on schedule on the first day. The 5th Guards Armored Brigade attacked over the Escaut canal and captured Valkenswaard inside the Dutch border. They were supported by heavy artillery and Typhoons from the 83rd RAF Group.

"On the second day, yesterday, they took Eindhoven, but it was forcefully defended and the weather was awful. Heavy rain. It took a triple attack by the 101st Airborne from the north, the 32nd Guards Infantry from the east, and the 5th Guards Brigade from the west to subdue the area, and they still needed the Grenadier Guards group from the south to finish the job.

"Most of the route is passable beyond Eindhoven. Reports are coming in that XXX Corps encountered major obstacles to forward movement inside the Netherlands' border caused by the people themselves. They're welcoming our chaps as liberators. Their celebrations are so thick in the streets that our units can sometimes barely move."

"I've seen celebrations like that," Horton broke in. "The people are so happy to be free. They don't realize how they get in the way of finishing off this damned war."

"The crowds have eased up a bit since the first day," Render went on, "but the convoys have been hit from the flanks by enemy anti-tank squads. Damaged vehicles and ambulances are now impeding traffic toward the battlefield."

He took a sip of tea. "VIII Corps is protecting the right flank. As part of that, we, the Sherwoods, will link up with the 82nd Airborne Division late today in an area called Groesbeek Heights near the German border. We'll pull picket duty on the 82nd's eastern flank, between them and the German border."

"The All-American Division," Horton exclaimed. "That should be interesting. And picket duty will be a nice change from leading the charge." He laughed. "I can man a checkpoint."

17

Two Days Earlier, September 17, 1944
Bletchley Park, Bletchley, Milton Keynes, Buckinghamshire, England

Late in the afternoon, Claire Littlefield barged into Travis' office without knocking. "Sir, I don't mean to be impertinent, but I not only analyze decoded enemy transmissions, I also read the newspapers. I know a disparity when I see one."

Startled, Commander Edward Travis, affectionately called "Jumbo" within Bletchley for his large size, looked up from his desk into Claire's distraught face. Gone was her usual beaming smile below her large brown eyes and dirty-blonde hair.

"This is a rare attitude for you, Miss Littlefield. Whatever brought this on?"

Claire placed several newspapers down on his desk before taking her accustomed seat in front of him. "See the headlines, sir."

Travis picked up the papers and scanned them. "Well, London appears to have been hit by V-2 rockets again last night. We've been hit almost every night for the past week. I imagine they might intensify because of that operation we have going on with our armies headed toward Arnhem. But we'll be pushing the jerries off their launch sites so maybe we'll see that alleviated soon. Our chaps in that operation are having a rough go of it, though."

"That's my point exactly, sir. I see the enemy's coded and decrypted messages, and the analysis. You elevated me to my position, and that's very much appreciated. But I can't be expected to see what the enemy is reporting in its own networks without recognizing that news reports to the public don't meet reality as I know it. In this case, I'm seeing a catastrophe developing that could have been averted while the public is painted a rosy picture."

"I thought you were concerned over the V-2s. What are you talking about? Be more specific."

"Operation Market Garden. It was hailed by the *Guardian* this morning as Monty's brilliant maneuver to outflank the Germans' Siegfried Line. America's Walter Cronkite gave it a glowing report on the wireless as it launched. Of course, our analysis sections didn't know about the operation before then, but we did know about German moves in the area and provided relevant intelligence. Now men are dying because that intel was apparently ignored."

She took a deep breath to calm herself. "The rockets dropping here are terrible, and they're causing so much fear and injury, but meanwhile we work around the clock to gain information that's already shortened the war, at least that's what we're told, and now it's not being used. Soldiers in the Netherlands are dying needlessly."

Known for a brusque manner, Travis was also known for his care of the people at Bletchley who guarded the nation's most precious wartime secret: the ability and mechanisms to intercept, decode, translate, and analyze enemy transmissions almost as fast as the intended recipients could do so. Since the beginning of the war, his army of men and women had worked under threat of death if they revealed anything proscribed by regulation.

Claire had been part of the organization almost since its inception, starting as a decoder, then having been elevated into one of the analysis teams, and then placed in a supervisory capacity over several teams. As such, one of her primary functions was determining the priority of intelligence and personally handling that which rose to the level of "Ultra," the highest classification. Such information was deemed to be of such importance that it was required to be expedited to Winston Churchill himself as well as other political and military leaders, and in particular, to pertinent senior commanders. Field Marshal Montgomery had credited much of his success in North Africa to timely Ultra communiques that detailed when and where to expect General Rommel and the disposition of his forces.

Because of unique talents musicians shared for cryptography, Claire had been recruited to Bletchley on a patriotic basis from playing piano with the London Philharmonic Orchestra. As a decoder and analyst, she had personally realized several intelligence coups, including ferreting out a friendly spy inside a *Wehrmacht* headquarters specifically established to plan the German invasion of the British Isles. Also, by careful analysis of intercepted *Kriegsmarine* communications, she provided the bases to locate and destroy the battleship *Bismarck* on the Atlantic's high seas. Her effectiveness and fluency in German and French had brought further attention from her superiors and resulted in significant promotions.

"Sir, as you know," Claire went on, having collected her composure, "because the Germans' retreating armies are in disarray, their communications are almost exclusively by wireless. Their landlines have been blown up or otherwise destroyed. The disruption is massive between major headquarters and their high command in Berlin. One result is that Hut 6 is overwhelmed with intercepted and decoded messages.

"We've been able to piece together communications coming down from Berlin by forming teams that look for message fragments and putting them together like jigsaw puzzles. The fact is, we reported that the *Wehrmacht* is fortifying behind the Siegfried. Everyone expected that, and the Germans anticipated that we would make a move on Antwerp, which we did, and Montgomery just liberated it. But our forces cleared neither the Scheldt Estuary that provides passage to the port from the North Sea, nor Walcheren Island at its mouth. Sixty-five thousand German soldiers slipped away. Since Market Garden began this morning, the *Wehrmacht* started reinforcing Walcheren, and it doesn't intend to let us have it without a major fight. It was ours for the taking, and now men will have to die to secure it.

"More to the point concerning our operation, the *Wehrmacht* guessed that we might try to flank them at Arnhem, so they reinforced along our axis of advance *before* we started. The *Waffen*-SS positioned the 9th and 10th SS-*Panzer* divisions to be deployed against that eventuality. They were reinforced with six parachute regiments and ten thousand of Göring's *Luftwaffe* infantry, and those are experienced fighting troops now. Together, those units formed the 1st Parachute Army.

"My teams reported all of that and the situation on Walcheren, and no one acted on any of that intelligence. Of course our teams knew nothing of Market Garden before it was reported in the newspapers, but that's beside the point. The failure to act on our reports cost our chaps dearly."

Claire took a deep breath. "What we know now through German transmissions is that things are going horribly for our soldiers. Today, on the very first day, the enemy captured a copy of the entire Operation Market Garden plan from a crashed glider. Even without it, though, when the first paratroopers landed seven miles west of Arnhem, the Germans figured out the objective and how it was to be reached. Surprise was blown.

"In fact, Field Marshal Model was eating dinner at a hotel just two miles from the drop zone and watched the whole landing. He was puzzled over why we would drop so far from the objective. Regardless, he set about immediately moving assets and reinforcing the key bridges, which I determined were at Eindhoven, Nijmegen, and Arnhem. The result is that our soldiers are caught in a deadly debacle."

She took a deep breath. "I am furious, sir. I'm no military person, but I've been here long enough to know a few fundamentals, and anyone could have seen that surprise would be lost when the first men were dropped, in broad daylight no less."

Claire took a deep breath, leaned over Travis' desk to look directly into his eyes, and lowered her voice. "Sir, our teams here at Bletchley delivered intelligence that could have led to better planning, but it seems to have been ignored. Meanwhile, our men are maimed and dying, and the public is being fed rosy reports."

Travis had listened intently. When Claire stopped talking, he regarded her somberly. "Have you spoken with anyone else about any of this," he asked.

Claire shook her head. "Of course not, sir, not outside the confines of my analysis team. But I'll tell you this: the decoders and translators have figured it out. I can see it on their faces. They read the newspapers and listen to radio reports. It doesn't take a genius. The news is demoralizing."

"Yes, I suppose that's true."

"Honestly, sir, at this moment, I would rather be a member of the public blithely believing that our brave soldiers are pushing the Hun north and that all will be over by Christmas. That would be a sight better than knowing what I know and being helpless to do anything about it."

"You are hardly that, Miss Littlefield. You're here now, in front—"

Claire went on as if Travis had not spoken. "The public will figure out the situation when the death notices and the wounded start arriving, their stories are told, and finger-pointing begins among senior leaders."

Dismayed, Travis leaned forward. "You're not thinking of leaving, are you? Your work is highly valued—"

"Is it?" Claire retorted uncharacteristically, her eyes flashing. "Then why is my team's work disregarded. We gave details down to specific units, types, their locations, and strengths." She rubbed her eyes while shaking her head. "Sorry, sir. No, I'm not resigning." Her voice caught. "For all I know, one or more of my brothers might be in that mess. Until this damnable war is over, I must do my bit."

"I can tell you this," Travis said gently, "I don't filter what you designate as Ultra. What you've sent through went forward with that classification. I will commit to you to raise hell upstairs as to why those reports weren't acted upon. I won't be able to provide feedback. You know that. As far as we're concerned at this level, what's done is done."

Claire sighed. "I know, sir. If nothing comes out of my rant other than leaders paying attention to actionable intelligence..." She left the sentence unfinished.

Travis regarded her compassionately. "You're a good soldier, Claire. I promise to follow through. While you're here, I need to ask about something else.

"Our RAF bombers launched a mission into Norway two days ago against a battleship, the *Tirpitz*. It was anchored in one of the fjords. Have you heard anything about it? That's out of your area, but Hitler has a personal interest in that ship, so covering Berlin as you do, I thought perhaps—"

"In fact, I've seen scattered messages," Claire interrupted, glad for the chance to recover composure. She took a deep breath as she pulled her thoughts together. "No one in my section was covering the *Tirpitz* or that war zone specifically, but we did hear rumblings out of Berlin. Naturally, Hitler was infuriated, but the ship seems to have survived. Some communiques say that it was untouched, that bombs only landed nearby. Others say that one bomb hit and tore a large hole in its bow. We haven't heard anything definitive on damage.

"There were some messages about it being moved. Let me think—" She cocked her head to one side. "Yes, it was sailing under its own power assisted by tugboats to another fjord."

Travis sat bolt upright. "Are you certain?"

"I'm quite certain. The matter registered in my mind because the information was off our beaten path, so to speak. We passed it along to the Norway section that normally monitors the *Kreigsmarine's* communications up there."

Travis grabbed his phone off the hook and dialed. "Please tell the head of the Norway section to come to my office," he said into the mic. "Immediately."

On hanging up, he turned to Claire with bulging eyes. "We need to confirm what you've just told me. This could be a crucial event." He fidgeted. Then his expression softened, and he asked her gently, "While we wait, may I ask about your family? I don't mean to intrude. I just want you to know—"

"That you care. I know, sir. So do we all here. You're always kind that way." Claire took a deep breath. "My family is difficult to talk about because I have no clue about a single one of them. Since the Germans cut off Red Cross messages from Sark, I have no idea about my mother. The same for my father in that detainment camp in Germany. I heard from Paul while he was in Paris, but now he's off to battle. He told me that Jeremy was waiting for his next SOE assignment."

She sighed. "Are you sure you want to hear all this, sir?"

Travis smiled. "Only if it helps."

"It does. I have no one else to talk to about the whole mess. My brother, Lance, came by two weeks ago. He had escaped from Colditz POW camp some months back, made his way to Brittany, and fought with the French Resistance there. He said everyone knew the invasion was coming so he stayed to help out. He somehow became involved with an Allied group called the Jedburghs, but I don't know who they are or what they do, and he couldn't tell me. They brought him back to England after an operation supporting the Normandy invasion, I think."

Claire sat quietly while her face showed the effort of holding back emotional turmoil. "I loved seeing him, but he only stayed overnight. He said he was going back in. That's all I know about him. Then there's Lieutenant Horton, who's become like another brother, and the Boulier sisters —" Her voice caught, and she stopped talking.

"Tell me about Timmy," Travis said in a deliberately jovial tone.

Claire's face lit up, and she broke into something approaching her usual broad smile, tinged with weariness. "He makes my life worthwhile," was all she could manage.

A knock on the door interrupted the conversation, and Claire's counterpart for the Norway section entered. In a quick conversation, she confirmed Claire's intelligence and added, "The *Tirpitz* was headed to a place called Tromsø. We're not sure if it's arrived."

Travis spun to his phone and dialed furiously. Moments later, as Claire and her colleague listened, he said stridently, "We need to order up a reconnaissance flight over Tromsø, Norway. It's urgent."

Stony Stratford, England

Claire walked tiredly up her garden path at the end of her gravel driveway. She smiled as the front door flew open and Timmy bounded down a short flight of stairs and ran to her. He threw his arms around her legs.

"Ah, Timmy," she greeted him, "you're growing too big to pick up."

"That's all right, Gigi," he replied in his little boy's voice. "I'm going to grow bigger and stronger, and I'll be a soldier, like Jermy and Uncle Paul and Uncle Lance."

Claire sucked in her breath, and she stooped to clutch Timmy to her chest. "Maybe we won't need soldiers when you grow up."

He stood back and looked at her, puzzled. "But all the men are soldiers."

Claire gazed at him, her heart heavy. She smiled and forced a laugh. "Things will be better then. You'll see. Maybe you'll be a doctor."

"A doctor? What's that?" He grabbed her hand and led her into the house.

Neglecting to reply, Claire greeted Elsie, her nanny, who stood by the door. "You've had a telephone call, mum," Elsie said, "from a Mr. Davis. He sounded elderly. He wanted to inquire about Timmy. I told him he'd have to speak with you."

Claire's heart leaped into her throat. Aside from the war, her biggest fear was that one day a blood relative of Timmy's would appear and establish legal claim to his guardianship. When Jeremy had evaded capture at Dunkirk, he had made his way to Saint-Nazaire where thousands of other British and French soldiers in the same circumstance had gathered to be rescued by a flotilla of warships and other vessels, including the *Lancastria*, a luxury liner converted for wartime service.

Jeremy had gained passage, but no sooner had he boarded than the ship was bombed by a German Stuka and began to sink. Among the passengers were civilian members of the British diplomatic mission to Paris and their families escaping to Britain, Timmy and his parents among them. Jeremy rescued Timmy, who was then a toddler, but his mother and father were lost.

On arriving in England, Jeremy managed to have himself appointed as Timmy's guardian, but Claire had cared for him for the past four years while Jeremy was away fighting in the war. She had become inseparably attached to the boy, and she dreaded the day that a relative might appear to claim him. Early on, Timmy's maternal grandparents had been located in India, but thus far they had not journeyed to England. *Then again, we've been at war the whole time.*

"Did Mr. Davis leave a message?" Claire asked.

"Only that he would call back this evening."

18

September 19, 1944
Groesbeek, the Netherlands

The sound of distant guns brought Horton to full alert. The going had been fairly easy, the way cleared over the past two days by other combat units of VIII Corps that had gone ahead of the 8th Armored Division to which the 43rd Wessex Division and the Sherwood Rangers Yeomanry were attached. All day, German units on the eastern flank had fired off anti-tank weapons as they progressed. Casualties were taken, not major in numbers, and not enough to slow the convoy, but even the loss of a single soldier reminded those who trudged on of their own mortality and lowered a cloak of solemnity among those who continued marching toward the battles raging at Nijmegen and Arnhem.

The soldiers sensed that Market Garden had gone awry. The evidence manifested in the tense faces of their leaders, in their squinted eyes, tight lips, and impatience with normal warrior chatter as they approached their objectives. It was buttressed along the way by increasing numbers of burned-out war machines. As the men passed smoldering hulks and recognized vehicle numbers associated with friends and acquaintances, chatter ceased. The numbing quiet was punctuated by sounds of battle as pessimistic conjecturing set in of what had happened to the occupants. A common thought predominated. *Will I meet the same fate?*

Riding in the turret of his M4A4 Sherman VC Firefly, Horton took it all in, realizing that there was little he could do or say to bolster spirits. Once, when his unit passed a wrecked vehicular carcass, he saw his men staring at it too long. "Keep moving," he admonished them gruffly. "We've got a job to do."

Little prepared them, however, for the sight that met them at Groesbeek. Hundreds of Waco CG-4A and CG-4B gliders littered the ground. Some lay on their backs, some toppled on one side or the other with broken wings. Many had dug their noses into the ground on landing, hoisting their tails high in the air. Some were clustered, and others isolated. Most had landed smoothly. They sat poised, as if ready for the next haul.

Most of the gliders, carrying as many as thirteen soldiers each, had been towed behind C-47s, their cargoes of soldiers augmenting the twenty thousand paratroopers who had already landed near Eindhoven, Nijmegen, and Arnhem. Some of the rickety, wooden, motorless aircraft transported jeeps, light field guns, or tons of supplies.

As Horton's four Shermans approached Groesbeek from the south at the spearhead of the 8th Armored Division and its attachments, he steered them through the 504th/82nd's sector to the 508th/82nd's on the northeastern side of the gently sloping high ground overlooking Nijmegen. The units following behind veered off to their own assigned destinations.

Horton's troop came to a checkpoint between the two 82nd Airborne regiments, and he ordered his driver to halt. As he dismounted, a sentry hurried to meet him.

"We're glad to see you, sir," the soldier said. "We can sure use the reinforcements." He stood straight and saluted. "I'm Private Lohan of Company A of the 508th Paratroop Regiment," he said. "I was ordered to bring you straight to Captain Combs as soon as you arrived. He's at his command post. I'll show you where to park your vehicles. You won't be there long. The krauts keep counterattacking. The CO will want to get you guys out on the line as fast as possible."

Horton grinned. "Slow down, Lohan. I don't mind going to see your CO, but I still take orders from my own. I'll call up and see what he wants me to do." He extended his hand. "I'm Lieutenant Horton of the Sherwood Rangers Yeomanry."

Lohan stared at him in awe as they shook hands. "I never spoke with a British *ranger* before." He looked back along the line of Shermans. "Are all of you Brits rangers?" He stared at Horton's Firefly. "And the main guns on your tank. It's big. Most Shermans don't have 'em that big."

Somewhat bemused, Horton nodded. "Yes, we're all Sherwood Rangers. And the gun *is* bigger than usual. That's an upgraded version of the Sherman. It's big gun is a 17-pounder anti-tank gun. It's better suited than the regular Sherman to hit a German Tiger tank straight on."

He called to his driver. "Smitty, ring up the boss. Tell him I'm in contact with the component we're here to support. The guard wants me to go to his company CP. I'll await our CO's response."

When he returned his attention to Lohan, the soldier's eyes were still round with amazement. "I can't believe it. An honest to goodness outfit of British rangers, and in tanks too."

Horton had to smile. He did not grasp why he had generated so much enthusiasm, but it was a nice diversion.

Smitty called back, "The CO says to go on. He's in touch with the higher element's headquarters. He said we're likely to be thrown into the fight straightaway, so stay in close contact."

"Roger. Follow me." Horton turned to Lohan. "Lead on."

Horton's troop of Shermans followed behind while he and Lohan trudged ahead of them to the company headquarters. On the way, they traversed below the crest of the gentle hillside across fields with a stubble of crops that remained unharvested as autumn approached.

"Do you know what was grown here?" Horton asked.

"Some of our guys came from farms back home. They think the farmers here had rye, beans, and potatoes growing, but the crop was lean." Lohan laughed. "Come to think of it, I'd sure like to see some supply drops or a convoy get in here. We've about run out of rations and we're ready to eat whatever we find in these fields."

Horton made a mental note. "Where are the jerries?" he asked.

Lohan laughed again. "The *jerries*," he imitated. "I like that. We call 'em krauts." He pointed up the gentle rise. "They're on the other side of that ridge and down a ways, in the woods. They keep counterattacking us, but they don't seem to have any big guns. They say there's heavy armor in the forest, but we ain't seen any sign of 'em."

"Who says?"

"Rumor mostly. I ain't heard nothin' official, but then again, I ain't seen nothin' big in three days of fightin'."

They arrived at a low tent set up behind a stand of trees. Captain Combs came out to meet Horton. "Glad to see you, Lieutenant," he said, extending his hand. "We received word you were on your way in." He tossed his head toward Lohan and grinned. "He got all excited about the 'British rangers' joining us, and radioed in. By now, word has spread all over the 82nd."

Horton liked Combs at once. He was medium height, blond, and carried himself with total ease. His eyes were serious, but his affability was obvious in his handshake. "Come on in," the captain said. "It's quiet right now. Sorry we don't have tea, but we've still got some coffee. I'll bring you up to speed and assign your positions."

"Sir," Horton replied, "Lohan said you were short of supplies, that your troops were about to go hungry."

Combs flashed a scolding glance Lohan's way. "He's got a big mouth."

Horton responded to the good-natured jibe. "Meanwhile, you've got to fight, sir," he said, "and that's hard to do on an empty stomach."

"We can handle it. I'm sure we'll get regular supplies in here soon," Combs said. "Airborne always goes in light, behind the lines." He grinned. "Then our ground force types bring us whatever we need. Sometimes, it gets to us a little late. We make do."

"We carry several days' worth of rations in our vehicles," Horton broke in. "We're attached to the 43rd Wessex. That's a whole division. I think we can spare enough food to keep everyone fed until regular supplies start coming through. I'll spread the word to our higher command. I'm sure everyone will want to help out."

Combs scrutinized Horton. "Thanks, Lieutenant. That's mighty neighborly."

At that moment, a dispatch motorcycle roared up. The rider

dismounted, approached the captain, and handed Combs a slip of paper and his ID.

Combs took and examined both. "Wait here," he told the messenger. "I'll get the overlays." Turning to Horton, he said, "Excuse me a moment."

While Combs entered his tent, Lohan ambled over to gawk at the motorcycle and converse with the rider, who kicked the engine into life and idled it at a low roar. Lohan looked on admiringly. Meanwhile, Horton walked over to speak by wireless with his commander concerning sharing food supplies.

The captain re-emerged from the tent. "Littlefield," he called loudly.

Startled, Horton swung his head around and stared at the rider, unsure of the name he thought Combs had shouted.

The captain hurried over to the bike. "Get this back asap," he said, and handed the corporal a batch of papers.

Horton started their way, but the rider crammed the papers into a satchel strapped over his shoulder, jammed the motorcycle into gear, and rode off. "Did you call that man 'Littlefield?'" Horton asked excitedly. "What's his first name?"

"Leonard. That's what's on his ID. He's one of yours, a lance corporal in the Wessex division. He came for updated copies of our map overlays. Do you know him?"

Horton shook his head. "No. Littlefield is an uncommon name, though. I've known some in my past."

Combs laughed. "Maybe they're having a reunion here. One jumped in with us the other day. A lieutenant. I didn't get his first name."

"With the 82nd?"

Combs nodded. "He's a good man. Works well with the Dutch Resistance. He's out on the lines moving between six of their positions right now."

Horton shook his head. "I don't know any Littlefields with the 82nd. I suppose he'd be American anyway." Before Combs could reply, Horton added, "You'll be glad to know that I spoke with my CO. He said to say that we'd be happy to share our food, and he'd get word out to the other units to keep your chaps fed."

Combs broke into a wide smile. "Well bless my soul." He headed toward the tent. "You've already been a big help, and you just got here." He pushed aside the flap at the entrance and held it open for Horton. "Are you guys really rangers?"

"We are, sir." He let the issue lie, submerging a smile. He now recalled hearing about the American rangers, elite US Army infantry soldiers who operated in small and large units behind enemy lines. One such unit, the 2nd Ranger Battalion, had scaled the cliffs of Pointe du Hoc at Normandy, a heroic feat already ensconced in legend.

Horton also knew the history of the Sherwood Rangers. It was illustrious and one to be proud of. Its name, however, had nothing to do with "rangers" as the Americans knew them. In the days when the fictional hero Robin Hood roamed Sherwood Forest in Nottinghamshire of merry ol' England, "rangers" was the word used for "outlaws."

"Ah well," Horton muttered, chuckling to himself. "No need to disabuse them."

He followed Combs into the tent. A large sector map had been placed upright on an easel. Combs pointed out various points to orient Horton with the local geography.

"We're here at Beek-Ubbergen in the north end of 508th's sector. Nijmegen is a little over three miles thataway." He pointed northwest. "That's why we've got your whole squadron with us, to reinforce that flank and the front facing the Reichswald. You came through Mook to get here?"

Horton nodded.

"That's on the regiment's south end," Combs went on. "We're on the regiment's left flank and our front faces northeast, with Mook on the right flank. We're on a three-day rotation. Another company secures the other end now and has a troop of your Sherwood Rangers supporting it. A third company is held in reserve near regimental headquarters. So, we'll move southeast along the front tomorrow, the reserve will take over here, and the company at Mook will move into reserve. I'm unclear on whether you stay here or go with us. That's still being worked out."

"How's the fightin' been?"

Combs raised his eyebrows. "Hot and heavy. The trouble is that most of 508th's troops are replacements. They weren't battle-tested before they got here. The krauts keep coming at us all along the front. Their

'Screamin' Mimis' terrify our troops with their wicked high-pitched shrieks."

"I know that weapon, the *Nebelwerfers*," Horton interjected. "I faced them in North Africa, Sicily, and Italy. They're really glorified smoke generators. They're not nearly as lethal as field artillery."

"Right. But their rounds are shaped and delivered like rockets, and if you're a green private and you see a whole line of launchers along the entire front, each firing six of them your way, one right after the other with that horrendous screech and clouds of white and dark gray smoke suddenly cloaking you, it can scare the crap out of you.

"And you know that the enemy is creating that smoke screen 'cuz he's about to come after you in a mass assault with intent to kill you." He shook his head and sighed. "We have good troops. They've held steady. The veterans worked overtime to keep the newbies from breaking ranks and running." He straightened, and pride filled his voice. "No draftees in the 82nd. This is an all-volunteer outfit."

Combs cocked his head, obviously with a thought darting across his mind. "The funny thing is, those Screamin' Mimis are the biggest weapons they've thrown at us. We keep getting intel informing us that large armored units are mustering in the Reichswald. That's only two miles southeast of here, and that's where the ground assaults come from. But we've seen no sign of armor. No field artillery, no air, no rumblings of large armored movements. Just infantry with light weapons and their Screamin' Mimis."

He paused to ruminate. "This is the 82nd's third day in the area. When we arrived, German defenses around the bridge were light. Since then, they've reinforced there with huge numbers of heavy units, tanks, and artillery.

"And they're SS troops, seasoned veterans. Our soldiers know it. You can't keep information like that from 'em. Couriers crisscross the battlefield, liaison guys move about, soldiers pass information along, whether confirmed or rumored. The fog of war."

Combs shook his head in obvious frustration. "I promise you, the boys in the foxholes are askin', why didn't we seize that damned bridge when we got here? It would have been easy then. And if somethin' big was buildin' in the woods, you'd think we'd have seen or heard *somethin'* by now. But we ain't. Nothing. Nada. Zip."

Combs' face took on a haunted expression. "What our guys know is that we *are* going to take the Waalbrug. That's written in concrete. But a lot of them will die that didn't have to, and they know that too."

The captain let out a long breath. "If you ask me, the Germans played us. They're *not* assembling heavy armor in the Reichswald. They know what we know, that if we take the bridge, we'll be vulnerable to counterattack from this direction, so we need to keep this high ground. And if the krauts attacked our flank, they'd do it right here where we're standing. So they hold us in place with a rumor they generated, and somehow spread it on our side of the front. That's what I think."

Blood rose in his cheeks, and he looked suddenly angry. Passion laced his tone when he spoke again. "And we could have taken that bridge *and* held this high ground if we had just attacked two days ago."

He and Horton stood quietly contemplating the map. Then Combs tossed his head and displayed a crooked grin. "Oh well, ours is not to reason why..."

He gestured toward the map. "Let's go over where we're positionin' you."

19

No sooner had Horton set his four tanks into position than he received an urgent message to return to Combs' headquarters tent. "There's a commotion brewing in Nijmegen," the captain said. He placed his hand over a large area of the map. "As I showed you earlier, from a few miles east of the bridge there, we're working this area around Beek-Ubbergen. Our sector extends south along the Dutch-German border and crosses into the Reichswald Forest, the whole thing being on the kraut side.

"The enemy just put in a *Hetzer Jagdpanzer* self-propelled tank destroyer with a 75mm gun, essentially another tank. It's facing downhill toward us on a road at the top overlooking a dike. It's clearly visible on the edge of a tree line along our northeastern boundary. That's the first and only indication we've had of heavy weaponry coming from the vicinity of the Reichswald Forest.

"That German infantry's been there at the dike the whole time we've been here. So far, all it's done is skirmish with our guys, but that gun could do some damage.

"I have a platoon blocking that avenue. It's dug in on a bend farther west overlooking the bank of the dike. The *Jagdpanzer* is in a wood line three hundred yards farther on blocking the road to the border. I've held a platoon in reserve that I can send to support if the Germans come there in greater force.

"I need you to help consolidate our position and blunt any attacks. Avoid heavy engagements other than taking out that gun. If there's more behind it, we'll need to send in a larger force."

"So you want me to destroy that tank destroyer, find out what else of a heavy nature is hiding among the trees, and reinforce the blocking position?"

"Exactly. We need to know how trigger-happy the enemy is there, and how many triggers they've got. They moved troops out of Nijmegen when our division showed up, but those appear to have been second- and third-rate soldiers. Now they're being replaced in force with battle-hardened veterans, at least around the Waalbrug bridgehead. I want to know what we're facing on our own left flank."

"Roger. I understand."

"We're close to the bridge, which is in 504th's area. As soon as it gets the order, it'll assault the bridge, so watch that you're not getting in each other's way. Don't get caught up in anything they're doing. We can't open a hole that lets the enemy surge through there unopposed." He rolled his eyes. "Who knows, maybe the Germans do have armor and artillery in those woods."

"I heard that regimental headquarters sent down a Dutchman who knows the area," Horton said. "Did you learn anything from him about the enemy?"

"Agardus Leegsma," Combs replied. "You're taking him with you. He gave us a lot of good information, but the situation is fluid." He sighed. "I'm not sure how much to rely on the Dutch Resistance. They're not soldiers. They might not know what to look for or how to observe effectively."

"Sir, I found the French Resistance to be a dedicated lot, and their information was usually good—"

"This isn't France," Combs replied tersely. "These guys are new to working with us. We don't have time for a deep debriefing now. We need solid intel asap, and we need an armored force there that can slow the enemy down when it comes that way."

Surprised by Combs' impatience and attributing it to the stress of combat and a jumble of activity to manage, Horton nodded. "Got it, sir."

Agardus was more than pleased to accompany Horton on the reconnaissance patrol. "I've never ridden in a Sherman," he said as the two of them crowded in the commander's cupola, and he clipped the chinstrap of his helmet. "This is exciting."

"Blimey, let's hope it doesn't get too exciting," Horton replied. "I'm glad to have you along." He saw Agardus studying the main gun. "This tank is a Firefly, a modification of the Sherman," Horton informed him. "It's the only tank we have that the Germans fear. That cannon makes the difference. It can take out a Tiger."

"That's good to know," Agardus replied enthusiastically. He glanced at Horton. "You're only the second Brit I've met in this war. The other one is some kind of liaison officer with a unit called the Jedburghs."

Horton shook his head. "I haven't heard of them. What do they do?"

"I'm not sure, but two of them went into Nijmegen and recruited several of us to work with the paratroopers. That happened just before the Germans started reinforcing. I was turned over to the Brit who sent me to G-Company in the 3rd battalion of the 504th Regiment. I was sent to you on loan for your mission. I'm supposed to go back to G-Company when it's done."

Horton grimaced. "Hmph. I hear you're from this area and can keep me out of trouble," he replied. "If this works out, I'm not sure I'll want to give you up. I'll show you on a map where we're going, and you figure out the best way of getting us there. Your 504th chaps are on our left. Anyone popping up on our right is probably enemy, but it could be one of our own who's lost his way."

Agardus chuckled. "You call the Germans 'jerries.' We call them '*moffen*.' It doesn't mean anything. Some people think it means 'people without friends.' The description fits, but the word has no definition. It's just the most derogatory term we can use on them."

"*Moffen*. I like that," Horton said.

Agardus took out a map and studied it, penciling in the known friendly and enemy positions. "I know that road," he told Horton. "We have to be careful. The ground to the right of it is marshy, but before the bend, there's a trail over the top of the dike that goes down to the hard ground by the canal and comes out in a field across from the German position. We can use it to get close with two of your tanks while the other two cover from here." He pointed out the positions. "We can coordinate with the infantry platoon defending there for additional covering fire."

Horton regarded Agardus with increased respect. "You seem to know what you're doing."

Agardus shrugged. "This has been a long war. We've trained as we could, and we've learned some things."

Horton nodded. "It shows." He made a mental note to inform Combs of the valuable asset that had joined his company. "Let's go get some *moffen*," he told Agardus. Then he called down to his driver. "Smitty, put this machine in gear and get this party started."

Agardus showed Horton where to halt. "Our airborne infantry is just this side of the bend in the road at the end of the dike's near wall. The German gun is to the right of the road around the curve and a couple of hundred meters farther on."

Standing in his cupola, Horton observed the dike's wall. Essentially, it was a long mound of earth, probably over a rock bed, wide at its base, covered in vegetation, and narrow at its top with a rounded crest. It paralleled the side of a waterway, obviously intended for flood control, and though he could not see another wall from his current vantage, Horton guessed there must one on the opposite bank of a canal. He had never seen dikes before and was uncertain of their composition, but Agardus had recommended driving the tanks on them, so Horton thought they must be firm enough to carry the weight.

"Why are they called 'walls?'" he asked. "They're not walls at all. They're extended mounds of earth."

Agardus shrugged. "We've got to call them something." He laughed.

"Maybe you want to say 'extended mounds of earth' every time you mention them."

"Good point," Horton admitted with a wry grin.

"The trail over the wall is off to our left," Agardus went on. "Maintenance people use it. On the other side is flat ground running alongside the waterway. It comes out on that field I mentioned earlier. Your gunner should have a clear shot from there, and that will signal the vehicles left in this position to pull forward and reinforce."

"Sounds good. I'm going forward on foot to coordinate with the infantry platoon leader in the blocking position."

"While you do that," Agardus replied, "I'll scout around to the left of and behind the enemy position to see what's there." He gestured toward the right of the road. "We've got nothing but marsh on that side."

Horton agreed. He clambered off the Firefly and watched Agardus disappear into a stand of trees, silently sending up a prayer for his safe return. Then he started forward to contact the infantry platoon leader.

"The enemy is right there," Horton said, struggling to control his anger. He had reached the blocking position with no difficulty, but was surprised to find the platoon in a fairly relaxed state. "I can see it clearly, which means it can see us. Why aren't you engaging?"

The platoon leader regarded him languidly. "We've settled into a live-and-let-live mode. They don't bother us, and we don't bother them. I think both sides like it that way." Sensing Horton's annoyance, the lieutenant added, "We've both been here for three days. We haven't bothered each other."

"They've got a bloomin' anti-tank gun—"

"But it's been there a while with no hostile activity."

"They'll probably bring in more. Crack troops are deploying across the river. The *Wehrmacht* is trying to take back the ground they've lost. In particular, they aim to keep that bridge, and they'll need this ground to protect the south end."

The lieutenant smirked. "We'll cross that bridge when we come to it," he said, grinning at his own wit and leaving Horton smoldering and wondering if this officer really belonged to the 82nd Airborne Division.

"I have four tanks," Horton said, gesturing back along the road. "I suggest that we mount a joint attack and overrun that position. It shouldn't be difficult or take long. I've got a man out now assessing their strength. We'll wait until he gets back before we launch, and if there's more there than we can see, we'll adjust our plan."

The lieutenant shook his head. "Nope. You go ahead if you want to. Our mission is to maintain this blocking position and engage if they come this way."

Horton stared at him, aghast. "But that gun will make short work of you, and it'll hit before you even know it's coming."

The lieutenant grinned indolently. "That won't happen, 'cuz you're gonna take care of it."

A sergeant first class stepped toward the lieutenant. "Sir," he began, but the platoon leader cut him off.

"I'm runnin' this outfit," he said harshly, "an' I said no."

The sergeant tried to argue further, but the officer shut him down with a terse command. "Stand at ease, Sergeant." He turned to Horton. "You want to attack, be my guest," he said with a sweep of his hand toward the Germans.

Disgusted, Horton retraced his steps a ways to a covered position and there observed the Germans through his binoculars. The soldiers sat around, relaxed, much as the American platoon had been doing. He detected what must have been the gun's position from the built-up branches and leaves on either side of it, but the effort to camouflage it appeared decidedly weak. And they, no doubt, had an equally plain view of the American position.

He made out the mouth of the cannon. "I've got my orders," he muttered to himself. "John Semken would not approve of sitting around doing nothing when we could attack, probably with the element of surprise."

Major Semken, the Sherwood Rangers A Squadron commander, was a legend among his men. It was he who developed the tactics that carried them across North Africa, and he modified them successively for the battlefields of Sicily and Italy, and most recently for the landing at Normandy and the campaign in France. No one among his subordinates cared to be seen shirking duty, particularly not when it involved combat.

Horton scouted around on his own. Checking on the backside of the dike wall, he found the flat ground Agardus had mentioned and followed it to the field. Careful not to expose himself, he peered through shrubs and spotted the *Jagdpanzer's* position. From this angle, the large barrel protruded and even glinted dully in the sun.

Keeping an eye out for enemy activity, Horton peered over the top of the dike. Across a road at its base, water gleamed on the surface of a marsh that extended far out to his front and around the bend toward the enemy position. Wondering if anything could be stationed inside the swamp, he scrutinized as far back as he could see into thick vegetation on the enemy's left flank, but saw nothing worrisome.

Satisfied that he knew the lay of the land, he returned to the tanks and met with his commanders to sketch out his plan of attack while he awaited Agardus' return. "I think we could take out that *Jagdpanzer* with a single shot. One armor-piercing round might do the trick. We'll use two and be ready for more just in case."

He pointed to one of the commanders. "Skip, you've got the best gunner. You take the lead. You and Brett travel on the flat ground on the other side of the near dike wall. When you come to the curve, drive up the bank. You'll be able to see the target when you crest, but he'll be able to see you too, so be ready. Put a spotter out front, and have your main gun loaded and cocked. As soon as your reticles cross the target, let loose."

He turned to Brett. "You follow closely, and fire as soon as you have the gun in your sights. Then both of you get off the dike so you won't be skylined. Go downhill to your left. Follow the flat ground along the dike wall. It'll open to a wide field. From there, the Germans will be straight across from you.

"When Sandy and I hear your first round, we'll race up on this side of the embankment ready to fire high explosive rounds as soon as the target comes into view. We'll join you in that field, and then all four tanks will advance in line abreast firing round after round of HE and our machine guns."

Sandy spoke up. "What if there are more of them than we expect."

As if on cue, Agardus walked out of the trees where he had disappeared earlier and joined the group. "Good news," he said, smiling. "I scouted well off to their right flank and at least a quarter of a mile across their rear. There's nothing there. Either the Germans are bluffing, trying to make us think they're building up reinforcements in the forest, or they're stretched thin. Very thin. And those are not crack troops."

"Good. Let's do a few brief backs, some rehearsals, and we'll be off."

One of the crew members broke in. "What about that platoon of paratroopers? Will they be joining in?"

Horton had anticipated the question and considered relating his encounter with the platoon leader, but thought better of it. His men needed to concentrate on their mission and not harbor bad feelings against the paratroopers, particularly when only their leader had ducked his mission. "They'll hold down the center and join in when the shooting starts."

The assault was short and merciless, and the plan went off like clockwork. As Skip and Brett maneuvered their tanks onto the top of the dike toward the objective, Horton and Sandy inched their two tanks along the lower road between the long embankment and the marsh and halted on the blind side of the curve. No sooner had they stopped than they heard the boom from the cannon of one of the Shermans. The gun of the second one immediately followed.

"Let's go, Smitty," Horton shouted. "Jam the pedal down." When his tank rounded the curve, he saw sheets of fire shooting into the sky from the German gun, now in plain view, followed by more explosions and flame. No survivors leaped from the burning enemy hulk.

To the left and right of the destroyed vehicle, the distinct staccato of Mauser MG machine gun and rifle fire erupted. "Light 'em up with HE," Horton yelled into his mic.

Instantly, four high explosive rounds swooshed downrange. They struck to the left and right of the flaming *Jagdpanzer* and erupted, spreading fire wide with more flame and smoke shooting into the air. They were followed at once by another salvo, and then a third.

"Cease fire," Horton called, but as soon as he did, he caught movement in his right peripheral vision and sucked in his breath while cursing his oversight. In the next moment he felt the air compress over his head as an 88mm round whizzed by and he heard the loud report and a subsequent explosion behind the tank.

"Hard left. Now!" he shouted to Smitty. "We got an anti-tank gun to our right front," he called over the radio to the other tanks. "Evade and kill it."

He realized his error instantly. He had thought the marsh too sodden to support ground combat.

Apparently, the German commander had anticipated that such an attack might occur. He had found hard ground within the marsh to set a second gun and aimed it down the avenue that Horton's Firefly had just traversed. The saving grace had been that Skip and Brett fired first.

Horton's tank roared to life, spun left, and started toward safety. With the rim of the cupola biting into his waist, Horton rotated the main gun toward the German position.

Another 88mm round plowed into the ground within feet of the Firefly, throwing mud all over Horton, and he realized that the tank's track was spinning in high gear but the war machine was not moving.

"Get us outta here, Smitty," Horton bellowed into the intercom.

"I'm trying," Smitty yelled back with choice expletives. "The ground is soggy."

A third German round flew in and glanced off the Firefly's sloped turret at supersonic speed. The explosion rocked the heavy tank.

Intense heat seared Horton's face.

He screamed in pain, and everything went dark.

He heard two more explosions but had no idea of direction.

Then, over the radio, he heard cheering. "We got him!" Skip called exuberantly. "We got the jerry bastard! He's dead."

"I can't see," Horton yelled. He brought his hands to his face, but his own touch was excruciating. "I can't see," he shouted again in agony. "My face—"

Agardus had sat out of the way in the belly of Horton's tank while the attack was on. He had felt the jolt when the 88mm round had glanced off the tank's side. Now he clambered up to help Horton, who stood in the cupola attempting to stop shaking while not daring to touch his face again.

Horton refused to cry out further in agony.

"Let me look," Agardus said. He gently pulled Horton's hands away from his face. "You'll be red for a few days," he said. "But I think you'll be all right. You got a flash burn, but it's not deep. How are your eyes?"

"Vision is coming back. You're a blur right now."

Agardus shook his head. "That was my fault," he said. "I'm sorry. I should have spotted that gun."

"I made...same mistake," Horton gasped in a broken sentence. "No sense...for jerries...to use only one gun there. My fault...marsh...should'a checked better." He groaned as sharp pain crossed his burned face. Then he let out a short guffaw. "Supposed to marry...after war. Hope Chantal... not scared away...by face."

"Let's get you to an aid station."

Horton's vision became clearer. He reached for his mic and called Skip. "Take charge," he rasped barely above a whisper. "Get my tank unstuck. Set the troop in defensive positions. Seek CO guidance. I'll be back."

"You look awful," Combs said as he entered the aid station and looked down at Horton, who was lying on a cot with his whole face wrapped in gauze aside from two peepholes and openings for his nose and mouth. "How're the eyes?"

"Working," Horton croaked. He was under a blanket, still recovering from shock. "Still fuzzy."

"Good job taking out that kraut position."

Horton's voice was hoarse and weak. "*My* men...magnificent."

Between bouts of unspeakable pain and weakness, brief thoughts had flashed through Horton's mind about the unhelpful lieutenant. The officer's refusal to act could have led to friendly casualties; his lackadaisical attitude had left the regiment's left flank wide open as an avenue for enemy forces intent on defending the Waalbrug.

Hell, he nearly got me killed!

Combs regarded him somberly. "My top sergeant told me about a report he received from the platoon sergeant out there. It's damning. I'd like to hear about what happened from your end. The platoon sergeant says that he and the whole unit have lost confidence in their leader. The actions described are not what's expected of an officer or any soldier in the 82nd Airborne Division or in the rest of the US Army. I'm sorry to bother you, but if the report is accurate, we need to replace that leader immediately. Are you up to it?"

Horton sighed deeply and nodded. The captain pulled a stool next to the cot and sat down. Then, between fog brought on by morphine, bouts of pain, and brief moments of lucidity, Horton related in whispers what had taken place between him and the lieutenant, and the actions that followed.

When he had finished, Combs said, "I'll hear the lieutenant out, but odds are that he'll be relieved in the next hour. He's waiting at my tent." He added dryly, "I doubt he'll be an officer much longer."

Horton nodded slightly and groaned. "Good call."

"Get some sleep." Combs rose from his seat to go.

Horton called to him in an elevated whisper, "Wait."

Combs sat back down.

"Agardus... Good man. I followed...his plan. Competent."

Combs' expression softened. "I know. Your troop sergeant told me. Agardus and his brother volunteered to guide an assault by one of the 504th's battalions. That'll execute..."

Horton was not listening. He had fallen asleep.

Combs stood and nudged Horton's shoulder. "Rest easy, Soldier. You've earned it. I'll check back on you."

20

September 20, 1944
Berg-en-Dal, Netherlands

Agardus had regretted leaving Horton at the aid station the previous night. In the few hours they had been together, he had come to like the lieutenant's blunt humor, his camaraderie with his men, his openness to suggestion, and his competence. That he, Agardus, had not spotted the anti-tank gun in the marsh rankled the Dutchman. He came back to visit the next morning.

Horton was asleep, and Agardus was sitting next to him when Lance Littlefield entered. He looked down at Horton's bandaged face. "Whew, he looks bad," he said. "Who is he?"

Agardus let out a heavy sigh and replied, "He's the troop leader in one of the British ranger troops."

Lance drew a long breath. "A ranger? That's impressive. I hope he pulls through. What's his name?"

"Lieutenant Horton. I didn't get his first name."

Lance gazed at the still figure. "I know a Sergeant Horton. He's a great fighter too, if he's still alive. Like a brother to me. We escaped from Dunkirk together. Last I heard of him, he was fighting in Italy. I wonder where he is now."

He sighed. "I came to bring you back to the 504th. G-Company is preparing for a mission this afternoon. Captain Wilde needs guides, and requested you by name. Your brother said you might want to be part of the operation. The company plans to cross the Waal and assault Lent, the town on the north end of the Waalbrug. The commander spoke highly of you. He said you and Frits are 'living intelligence.'"

"We try." Agardus stood and took a moment to grasp Horton's shoulder. "Stay strong, my friend," he murmured. "I hope we meet again."

Agardus and his brother, Frits, glanced at each other, and then turned back to Captain Wilde, commanding officer of G/3/504th PIR. "We've dreamed of this," Frits said.

"Are you sure you're up to it?" Wilde asked Agardus. "That was some fight you were in on the 508th's flank, but if I'd known that's what you'd done, I wouldn't have sent for you. This river crossing will make that skirmish look easy."

"Use us as you need to," Agardus replied. "Aside from the operation with Lieutenant Horton yesterday, I've been with your company for three days. One of your wounded men gave me his rifle during fighting for the bridge two days ago. I watched him die, and then shot my first German with his weapon. I was sad for your lost soldier, but I was thrilled about taking down the German." His eyes fell and he added, "I was sorry for the German too. The three of us were strangers to each other, but we were all out there to kill other men. I was luckier than they were."

Frits, looking very much like his older brother, interjected, "Our country lived for four long years under German occupation, and we remember the invasion. It was bloody, it killed a lot of friends and family members, and terrified the survivors. Agardus and I will fight every minute to drive the last *mof* out. Being a little tired doesn't matter. And I promise that a lot of our people, men and women, feel the same way."

Peering through slits for eyes, Agardus nodded in agreement. "You need guides. No one knows the Waal River better than me or my brother."

"We're going to assault the north end of the Waalbrug through Lent, and we'll cross the river to do it," Wilde said in a somber tenor. "We'll be exposed. The enemy will probably detect us while we're in the water. Their machine guns are deadly. Just the sound of them is terrifying, and we'll have nowhere to run for cover until we're on the other side. Bullets don't care that you're not soldiers. They'll rip into your skin same as mine. And if we're lucky enough to get to the other side, we'll face the 10th SS *Panzer* Division. That's a crack outfit, much better than what was here when we arrived."

Frits took a deep breath. "Sir, we told you we'd do whatever it takes. Tell us what you want us to do." He paused. "If you're going to cross the river to assault Lent, you'll need us. The river is wide and the current strong. And after you land, you can't go to your objective in a straight line. It'll be too marshy. You'll have to go north a ways, and attack from the northeast. Our Resistance group can have the route prepared for you."

Agardus lifted his helmet from his knee and held it out. "You see this, Captain. I've been saving it all these years for the chance to fight for the Netherlands. I'm a combat veteran now." He indicated Frits. "We both are."

Wilde locked his eyes on the brothers' faces. Then he let out a long breath and called to his first sergeant, who had sat quietly observing the discussion. "Scare up some combat uniforms and gear for these two soldiers. If they get captured, I want them treated like POWs, not shot as civilian terrorists."

Under a clear and sunny sky, the Leegsma brothers led G-Company to a place a few miles up the Waal from Nijmegen. "The Germans never put security out this far, on either side of the river," Agardus told Wilde. "It's narrower here than in most places, but the current is stronger. Put me in the first boat. Friends will meet us on the opposite bank. They've been watching and haven't seen any *Wehrmacht* activity that far out from the town, and none was reported on this side. Our group has men staked along the best route into Lent."

While he waited for the operation to commence, Agardus shook off accumulated fatigue and reflected on the encounter that had brought him to this point.

On that morning, three days earlier, while sleeping in his family's home on the south edge of Nijmegen, Agardus awoke abruptly to loud cheers. Rushing to his window, he saw four men in combat uniforms sauntering along his street. Local residents had surrounded them and celebrated their arrival.

They walked confidently, calmly, unhurried but obviously alert, their eyes roaming in every direction. All four chomped on chewing gum, and they held their rifles ready to cover any direction, with their fingers along their trigger guards.

They were the first Americans Agardus had seen, easily recognized by their distinctive helmets. Before he could come to grips with what he saw, the salvation of the Netherlands right before his eyes, he heard the engine of a despised *kübelwagen*, and then one raced down the street with four staff officers and a driver.

The Americans dropped to the ground as one and fired, fired again, and kept firing until the staff car had crashed into a fence at the side of the road. None of its four passengers stirred.

Another engine roared, that of a half-track. The Americans rolled to the side of the road and ducked behind a concrete wall, their rifles aimed and ready. The half-track roared by the wreckage and its casualties without slowing down, in obvious flight.

Around them, the townspeople had also dropped in place or rushed to shelter. Now they clambered to their feet, stunned at first and then smiling, bursting into laughter, hugging each other, and profusely thanking the paratroopers.

Agardus watched the event in wonder. For four years he had dreamed of such a scene. At the beginning of the war, he and other intrepid comrades had undertaken sabotage against the *Wehrmacht*. Invariably, however, the Germans had retaliated by rounding up villagers, torturing some innocents and executing others, men and women. For the health of their friends and neighbors, the Resistance had refrained from additional aggressive actions and concentrated on gathering information and making plans for the day of their liberation.

It had arrived. The mighty *Wehrmacht's* soldiers in a heavily armed war machine had scurried like terrified hares past the site of an obvious fire-fight with no apparent thought of exacting retribution against the population.

More people poured into the streets, cheering, laughing, and hugging one another. They ran to friends' and neighbors' houses, pounding on the doors, and shouting for them to join in celebrating that the Americans had arrived and the hated *moffen* were on the run.

The entire event had played out before Agardus' eyes within minutes, and then the townspeople had encircled the four soldiers, crying tears of joy while plying them with food, pastries, and wine, and tossing bouquets of flowers on them.

Agardus ran into another room where his younger brother slept. "Frits," he shouted, "come see this. Frits, wake up. The Americans are here."

Frits stirred and yawned.

"Frits, the Americans are here," Agardus repeated. "Come see." He ran back to the window in the front room and watched as the celebration continued.

People pressed around them, reaching over shoulders, trying to touch their saviors. Young girls and mothers pushed through to take them in their arms and kiss them. The soldiers absorbed the spontaneous affection with good humor, relishing the female attention.

Agardus took it all in. Moments later, Frits ambled up beside him, still half-asleep.

"Look," Agardus exclaimed, "those are American soldiers. They just killed the *moffen* in that *kübelwagen*, and a *Wehrmacht* half-track fled town in a big hurry. We're free." He had grabbed his brother's shoulders in exultation. "And now, I know what I will do with my life. I will join that army."

On that first morning, after the celebrations had died down, Agardus and Frits managed to speak with the soldiers, telling them of their Resistance activities and offering their services to the US Army. On their return to their headquarters, the Americans had taken them to see Captain Wilde, who treated them with great respect. To their amazement, they had found themselves almost immediately in the thick of an assault on the Nijmegen bridge, joining as guides.

The fighting had been fierce. G-Company had entered Nijmegen without opposition, heading to the Waalbrug, but when they reached Keizer Lodewijkplein, the spacious plaza with its gardens and traffic circle, Agardus encountered the dull thuds and fierce explosions of mortars and the frightening power of an 88mm anti-tank gun, all amid the chaos and terror of ceaseless rifle and machine gun fire.

A soldier next to Agardus cried out in pain. As he had seen others do, Agardus immediately called for a medic and dragged the soldier out of the line of fire. The paratrooper grabbed Agardus' arm in grateful desperation. "Take my rifle," he gasped. "I won't need it." Seconds later, the light of life in the soldier's eyes extinguished.

Agardus stared at the dead American and then leaned over him. "Thank you," he whispered grimly. "I'll fight hard so that your life will always have had meaning."

He grabbed the rifle and ammunition, looked for a target, and fired, striking a German soldier running across his path at a hundred meters. The man went down.

Momentarily elated, Agardus looked for the next target. His roaming eyes once again landed on the American whose rifle he had just used to kill a German, and somberness replaced euphoria.

He glanced back at the dead enemy. *I didn't even know him.* His jaw set as another thought took primacy. *I didn't invite him to invade my country, threaten my family, and kill my countrymen.*

Numbing himself to his task, he sought the next target.

The battle spread around the plaza. Everywhere, soldiers ran from cover to cover. Smoke rose. Men cried out. Medics tended to wounded. Mortars dropped with dull thuds followed by thunderous explosions. Machine guns chattered.

The battle turned.

Agardus gravitated to the café, Bonte Os, the place where he, Frits, and their father had spent so many hours with other men and women of the Resistance planning operations for the safe return of their national government. During a lull in firing, Agardus glanced toward the café. The door had been barred. He maneuvered closer and, keeping low, dashed to its front and rapped in a specific rhythm on a glass pane.

The door opened. Agardus darted inside. A familiar face stared out in stark fear. "Get out of here. Now," Agardus blurted. "The battle goes against us. The Americans are falling back."

The young man, a boy really, trembled. "Your father is here," he managed to say.

Startled, Agardus called out, "Papa. Papa, are you in here." He turned to the boy. "Go. Now. Go out to the right and away from the river. Don't stop until you're home. We're going for reinforcements, and we'll be back."

He heard a noise, and through the low light, he saw the familiar form of his father. "Papa, go home. The battle goes badly for us, but we'll be back with more and bigger guns."

The middle-aged man with scraggly hair looked over his son, and noticed the rifle. "Let's go," he said.

Agardus shook his head. "I can't go with you, Papa. I've joined the Americans. They're relying on me. I came in to warn whoever was here."

Outside, the firefight intensified. The pulsating sound of Mauser machine guns moved closer.

"Get out, Papa. Go protect Mama."

"Come with me, please," the elder Leegsma implored. He grasped his son's shoulders and gazed into his eyes. "We need you there."

Agardus' throat tightened. "Americans are dying in our streets for us," he said. "You always taught me to do the task that must be done. I can't leave them now."

Sadly, his father nodded, his eyes full of pride for his son. "I'll wait for you at home," he said, and then he was gone.

Agardus stayed patiently with Frits as the men from the 82nd Airborne Division's 508th Parachute Infantry Regiment made their way into the assembly area and awaited the order to execute. He dismissed thoughts of those happy first moments of seeing the four American soldiers entering Nijmegen, his first firefight, and then his father's sad farewell, but he found himself thinking about Horton.

Agardus had accompanied Horton in the ambulance from the battlefield and watched in dismay as blisters appeared on the lieutenant's face and his breathing became labored. The medic injected him with morphine, and that seemed to have eased Horton's pain.

Agardus had stayed with him at the aid station until Lance had come by and informed him that Captain Wilde requested the Leegsma brothers' services. Agardus left reluctantly, torn between a sense that he should remain with his wounded brother-in-arms and a conflicting duty to re-enter the battle, particularly since Wilde had asked for him.

An age seemed to have passed since he had left the aid station, but in fact only an hour or two had gone by. Despite the danger, he was thrilled to wear the US Army uniform, He was also sobered by the thought of embarking on his third intense combat mission in three days.

Because Captain Wilde had treated him and Frits with welcome respect and accepted their offer of help, the brothers took pains not to disappoint. In consultation with Wilde, they had selected the fording site. It was around a bend where the crossing would be screened, and the current had slowed.

Agardus marveled that so many men could move so quietly, but he had watched the soldiers prepare by leaving behind nonessentials and securing their carried equipment with tie-downs and tape to reduce rattle. He mimicked their actions and sought their advice.

His growing sense of a smooth operation ended on the shore of the Waal. As they started boarding the tiny canvas boats, which gave no confidence that they could float the wide expanse to the other side of the river, chaos broke out. The water was shallow in places and deep in others. Men got stuck in the mud or fell into deep water with their full combat kit and drowned, even before shoving off from shore.

Agardus watched, aghast, and then realized that not only were the boats flimsy and needed to be paddled, but also that not enough of them were present. Several trips would be required to transfer the entire company of one hundred and fifty men, increasing their vulnerability as some waited on the opposite shore while others traversed the water. The remainder, waiting their turn to cross the Waal, would be even further exposed if the enemy was alerted before the crossing was complete.

When the first boats launched, some soldiers used the broad butts of their rifles to help paddle or steer. Agardus joined in, wondering at their tenacity and inventiveness. He studied their faces, fixing in his memory their expressions of determination and fear. As his eyes moved from one to the next, gratitude overwhelmed him, as did a growing sense of belonging.

They were men hardened by combat, yet he had seen them treat the townspeople with compassion, sharing their food, helping clear streets of debris or making repairs. He had watched them bringing candy to children, riding them on their shoulders, and kicking balls around with them in the streets. And now, some were gone, drowned, just as the operation started. Far from home and family, having seen comrades killed or maimed, yet again they went into harm's way to liberate the Netherlands.

More would die, and some would be mutilated, that was certain, particularly given this mission. If they made it across the river, they would approach Lent by stealth and launch a surprise attack against the 10th SS *Panzers*. At least that was the intent. Agardus wondered how long surprise could be maintained.

Assuming sufficient numbers arrived on the far shore, they would battle to capture the north end of the Waalbrug. Meanwhile a simultaneous operation would commence on the south side of the river to capture that end of the same bridge.

The first flotilla moved out into the current. Agardus watched the far riverbank for signs of the enemy, but so far none appeared.

Suddenly, small geysers splashed into the air followed by the deep rat-tat-tat of heavy machine guns that quickly ranged the small boats and fired just above water level. Wounded men cried out in pain. Some fell into the water, beyond help. The boats dispersed. The men paddled harder.

The German MG 4 guns continued in such great volume that spray fell like rain, and Agardus found himself questioning his sanity in volunteering for this mission. He looked around for Frits but saw him nowhere.

Miraculously, the boat Agardus was in reached the far shore. He scrambled out to waiting Underground members as soon as it touched shore. Captain Wilde followed.

They had landed on the east side of a dormant brick factory at a point just past where the river curved eastward. Out of sight behind solid cover, they watched as the remaining flotilla of boats returned to the south shore and brought more soldiers across, and then made one more roundtrip. They were followed both ways by sporadic machine gun fire, which waned as a diversionary battle raged on the opposite side of town.

Agardus found Frits, to his great relief, and together, they searched for and found Ruud, the leader of the Resistance group north of the river. He had been watching for them from behind the abandoned factory.

When no more soldiers remained to be brought over, Captain Wilde took final stock of his situation. His face was now a mask of anger and resolve. He had sufficient men to complete the mission, but surprise was no longer an element in their favor.

Heated battle sounds from beyond the west side of the bridge and the lack of more ground resistance gave evidence that at least one part of the overall plan was working. A diversion had been executed there to draw the 10th SS *Panzer* units away from the abandoned factory and the troops landing there.

Wilde, the two brothers, and Ruud conferred in a vacant hut on the factory's grounds. Ruud pulled out a map. He was all business, friendly enough, and dazzled to be working with American paratroopers he had watched descend from the sky, and he was competent and ready to set a plan in motion. Dark-haired, burly, and whiskered, he had already set his men out for security.

"We should travel north from here to Kommerdijk, about two and a half kilometers away," he said after brusque greetings. He spoke no English, so Agardus translated. "The road is good, it has drainage ditches on each side that the soldiers can dive into if attacked, and farther along, there are woods we can get into if we need to."

He pointed out the locations already marked on his map. "From

Kommerdijk, we'll head northwest to Bemmel. That's another eight kilometers." He raised his eyebrows and gestured for caution. "There, we'll be getting into an area that's been thick with Germans, but they've gone farther north, and the 10th *Panzers* moved south to defend close to the bridge. To bring in supplies and reinforcements, they use a north-south main road a few kilometers beyond Bemmel. That one goes on to Arnhem. We've got men out watching their movements. They won't expect us there, but we'll still need to exercise caution or we'll blow surprise."

"More than it's already blown," Wilde muttered.

Ruud glanced at him sharply but did not respond.

"From Bemmel, we turn southeast?" Wilde asked. "What's the distance to the Waalbrug?"

Ruud nodded. "About eight kilometers."

Wilde did a quick mental calculation. "So we have about an eleven-mile road march, and then we attack." He indicated the map. "Do you know how the Germans are deployed, where their positions are?"

After Agardus translated, Ruud pointed out several locations by type.

Wilde extended his hand. "You chaps are doing a marvelous job." He glanced down the road toward their objective. "Let's get going."

21

September 22, 1944
Hôtel Trianon Palace, Versailles, France

"I gather Monty won't be attending?" General Eisenhower addressed Major-General "Freddie" de Guingand, Field Marshal Montgomery's chief of staff.

The British general nodded grimly and cleared his throat. "I'm afraid he's—"

"I expect that Market Garden occupies his attention, and particularly Arnhem," Eisenhower cut in without his customary smile. "We'll talk about that. Be ready to provide a status."

Guingand stood aside and then followed as Eisenhower entered a large, stately ballroom, decorated in French Louis XIV style and showing signs of neglect and disrepair. An adjutant called attention, and twenty-one American, British, French, Canadian, and Soviet admirals and generals, members of the Allied command, stood straight. Eisenhower immediately bade them to take their seats.

The room had been arranged with tables positioned facing each other along its length for the attendees. A head table at the front accommodated the most senior Allied commanders and staff, including Generals Eisenhower, Omar Bradley, Courtney Hodge, George Patton, Miles Dempsey, Harry Crerar, and Guingand.

The Hôtel Trianon, situated within a few miles of Versailles Palace and built to reflect the elegance and opulence of King Louis XIV's lavish court, had been through much in its thirty-seven-year history. During the Great War, it had served as a British hospital, then as the headquarters for the Supreme Allied Council, and it was the place where the Treaty of Versailles had been drafted. Restored to its glory during the inter-war years, it then caught the eye of Field Marshal Göring, who established his *Luftwaffe* headquarters there as the German military swept through France in 1940.

Göring and his headquarters had vacated the premises ahead of the rapid Allied advance across France, and the hotel had become an Allied HQ not only to plan future operations, but also to become a conservator of culture. To that end, it hosted an army unit whose mission was to preserve historic monuments across Europe against theft and desecration.

Fine china and crystal with polished silverware on crisp white linen had previously adorned the tables under exquisite chandeliers, and large paintings of once famous personages and tapestries of distant landscapes had at one time hung from the walls. Today, although bouquets of flowers around the chamber spread a pleasant scent, the walls had been stripped of their artwork, and bare wires hung where chandeliers had been. The linen was faded to yellow, the china, crystal, and silverware had been replaced with non-matching everyday dishware and flatware. The absence of draperies added a dismal sense to the room, appropriate to the somber topics to be discussed.

Eisenhower opened the meeting. "I want to get straight into business, but first, I'll mention the fighting in the Pacific at an island called Peleliu. If you haven't heard of it, don't feel bad. I hadn't either, but from the reports I'm seeing, the fighting there is at a level of viciousness several levels beyond what we experience in Europe.

"That operation was one that was supposed to be over in a few days too, but it's not turning out that way. So today, while we confer in this"—he glanced around the room—"luxurious place, keep in mind what's happening on the other side of the planet with our brothers-in-arms as well as with our soldiers here who live in foxholes."

He cocked his head to one side and sighed heavily. "So now, to the Market Garden mess." He strode over to a large map positioned vertically on an easel beside the head table. "It's not going well, and we've got to address it before getting on with other plans. The operation kicked off five days ago. The Polish Airborne Brigade dropped in on the fourth day after several weather delays. The operation was supposed to take four days. We're in the fifth, and the battle at Arnhem still rages. We're headed into a significant defeat."

Gesturing to indicate Guingand, he went on, "Monty's chief of staff will bring us up to date, but first, to be fair, I must point out that the German units in that area now are not the same ones that were there when I approved the planning for this operation. At that time, the enemy had just the XV Corps deployed in the area. Now it's replaced with a major airborne light infantry unit, the 1st *Fallschirmjäger* Army, to defend at Arnhem.

"The *Wehrmacht* also stitched together another whole corps, including the *Landesschützen* Division. It's assigned to protect the German border along the Reichswald Forest from high ground overlooking Nijmegen."

Eisenhower shook his head, obviously dismayed. "We'll have to examine at some point why the 82nd initially concentrated on Reichswald Forest instead of assaulting the Nijmegen bridge on the first evening." On the map, he pointed out the 82nd Airborne's position around Groesbeek Heights. "Setting priority on securing this high ground southeast of Nijmegen postponed capturing the bridge for three days. That now looks like a colossal blunder. Market Garden might have succeeded but for that delay. We'll also need to look at how and why that happened."

He let out a long breath and traced his hand up the map. "The main objective of the entire operation was to capture the bridge at Arnhem, eight miles north of Nijmegen." He jabbed at the point on the map. "The British 1st Airborne Division landed here near Oosterbeek." He indicated the area. "Their landing zone is on high ground west of and overlooking the bridge. We should have secured that ground. We're paying a high price because we didn't."

Eisenhower stopped talking and stared distantly. A sense of gloom hung in the air. Finally, he turned to Guingand. "Freddie, the floor is yours. Bring us up to date."

Guingand was a thin man with a serious countenance, perceptive eyes, and a trimmed mustache. A respected and consummate professional, particularly in organizational and intelligence matters, he had been Montgomery's protégé for the past twenty years, and had been a significant contributor to British Army successes in North Africa as well as in planning Operation Overlord, the invasion of France.

"You rightfully called it a mess," he said, taking to his feet and glancing toward Eisenhower. "There's no room to represent it otherwise. That said, regarding what took place at Nijmegen and in defense of my commander, I'll point out that the subordinate objectives had to be achieved, or seizing the bridge there would have been pointless. We could not have held it with the forces we had. I'll also point out that the weather across the North Sea did not cooperate. That delayed the Polish airborne, which landed only yesterday, too late to reinforce the British forces already under siege."

"The weather is always uncertain," Eisenhower broke in, "but taking four days to land the paratroopers—"

Guingand anticipated the question in the supreme commander's voice. "The other driving factor was logistics, sir. We delivered the airborne troops as soon as we could, but we were also limited by air assets, irrespective of weather."

He started to go on, but Eisenhower held up a hand to pause discussion while he contemplated. "Airborne goes in light to seize objectives while reinforcements fight their way to them on the ground. A basic assumption is that the airborne units arrive in sufficient force to hold its ground until support arrives. Did that calculation not take place in the planning for Market Garden?"

Guingand stood straight and took a breath. "Sir, I can assure that it was considered in detail, but obviously we could have done better."

"We will definitely study that," Eisenhower said, "but do I understand correctly that the bridge at Nijmegen, the Waalbrug, is now ours?"

"Yes, General. The 508th captured it yesterday. It sent its G-Company across the river to attack from Lent, in the German rear. British tanks simultaneously assaulted across the bridge. The battle was bloody and long, but at its end, we owned that damned bridge.

"So," Guingand continued, "the Guards Armored Division, with the 8th

Armored Division of the XXX Corps, is fighting north along the last eight miles to Arnhem. And with respect to the bridge over the Nederrijn River there, the British 1st Airborne Division still holds out on the northeast side of it."

Guingand paused as his face knotted with emotion. When he spoke again, his voice had dropped, and it shook. "Unfortunately, at this point, the operation has become a rescue mission."

He sniffed and took a deep breath. "We're trying to get as many of our chaps out as we can and secure the ground south of the river. The casualties at Arnhem who are too badly wounded to move will create a diversion by providing radio traffic and return fire to keep up the appearance that we're still fighting to capture the bridge. Doing so might allow time for able-bodied soldiers to escape."

He paused, fighting to stem raw emotion. "I won't pussyfoot around. Of ten thousand men who went into Arnhem, we'll be lucky if we get twenty-five hundred out. A huge number will be taken prisoner. And the casualties coming from the rest of Market Garden, around Eindhoven and Nijmegen, were high, estimated between fifteen and seventeen thousand men." He looked into the eyes of the glum assembly of generals. "Unfortunately, that figure does not include roughly five hundred civilians killed."

Quiet descended on the room. Moments passed before anyone spoke. Guingand stood still under the steady gazes of so many eyes. Finally, he said, "Comments?"

"So General Guingand," someone asked, "was Operation Market Garden a success or not?"

"History will have to judge that," Eisenhower interjected, rising to his feet with a nod to Guingand. "We won't succeed in capturing Arnhem and its bridge now, although we'll have to do that at some point. In that respect, the operation is a failure. On the other hand, we have a sixty-mile salient into enemy territory not far from Antwerp, and we've isolated a sizeable enemy force along the Belgian and Dutch coasts. How we capitalize on that will be part of today's discussion."

He turned to Guingand, who had continued to stand. "General, while we were still planning Market Garden, didn't we have intelligence that, in addition to the new corps forming from fragments of units escaping back to

Germany, the 9th and 10th SS *Panzer* divisions had moved into the vicinity of Arnhem and Nijmegen?"

Shamefaced, Guingand acknowledged the question with a slight nod. "We had received Ultra reports that those divisions had moved there for rest and refit. I was in charge of planning. I am responsible for the oversight."

He took a breath and returned his attention to the audience. "The *Wehrmacht* anticipated that we might push to the bridge at Arnhem. When our airborne troops landed at Oosterbeek, the Germans deployed the 9th SS *Panzer* Division to drive them out of town and pin them on the western riverbank while elements of the new German corps plugged gaps in the *Wehrmacht's* defenses, particularly along the Albert Canal. That waterway runs from Antwerp southeast to just north of Geel. Meanwhile, the 10th SS *Panzers* drove south to counterattack at Nijmegen and set up a blocking position to hold back our ground force from using the main road to Arnhem.

"I can safely say that the salient is secured north past Nijmegen. Our objective now is to capture and hold the south end of the bridge at Arnhem to deny it to the enemy for resupply of troops along the coast or as an avenue for a counterattack."

He took another deep breath. "I must say that our soldiers fought magnificently. When Market Garden terminates, we will have suffered a heroic defeat. Any blame to be had lies above their level." He paused and went on in a taut voice, "It appears that General Browning was correct when he observed at the outset of the operation that perhaps we were attempting a bridge too far."

Eisenhower stood and faced the gathering. "I approved the plan. I bear full responsibility. We'll be studying Market Garden for decades, and we certainly want to determine and apply immediate lessons learned. But for now, we must move on.

"We've been happy with the German retreat across the rest of France," he continued sternly, "but we miscalculated its strength and will to fight." He leaned forward and peered into his audience. "During the pursuit of the *Wehrmacht*, we faced a worn-out army with lots of conscripts. But the game has changed."

He paused a moment to let the thought sink in. "No one should under-estimate the skill and tenacity of *Waffen*-SS combat troops," he went on, "and it's early to think that the regular *Wehrmacht* is done. Obviously, *Herr* Hitler recognized that he could not win in France, and he beat feet back to Germany to defend at the border.

"And one more point before we open discussion. Never should anyone discount intelligence reports that come through Ultra. We unquestionably did that in planning for Market Garden. We also had reports from local sources that proved very accurate. They confirmed the presence of the *panzer* divisions, and we neglected—. Well, I won't belabor the point."

He turned to Guingand. "We'll discuss what went wrong and look for recommendations so we don't make the same mistakes." Returning his attention to his full audience, he went on. "Our logistics problems are now driving this war. We have no choice but to resolve them, or no strategy will work. I'll tell you now that I won't entertain any proposals that don't address the supply issues up front—"

"General," a voice interrupted, "I suppose that means that my quick push across the Rhine is nixed?"

Eisenhower regarded the speaker, George Patton, with slightly patron-izing humor. "It is," he replied.

The legendary general sat back with his cigar protruding through his characteristic grin. "Thought so."

"One glaring conclusion," Eisenhower said, "is that opening the port at Antwerp is imperative, and right behind that in priority are the other ports on Brittany's coast. We can't expect Cherbourg to keep up with the supply needs of thirty-nine divisions that will grow to over six hundred thousand men. Saint-Malo just fell to us, but we need the other ports too."

He suddenly chuckled. "Let's take moments of levity where we can find them," he said. "That's how we keep our sanity. A story I heard just flitted across my mind. I can't confirm it yet, but the rumor is that three Brooklyn boys of German extraction who came over to fight for their fatherland brought about the surrender of Saint-Malo. They did it by poking a hole in the city's water tower. A white flag soon followed."

Amid a smattering of chuckles and lowered tension, Eisenhower and Guingand took their seats, and discussion commenced. After a break for lunch and time for side conversations, the conference continued through the afternoon. By its end, the participants had synthesized the issues to several top priorities, which Eisenhower addressed with firm decisions before adjourning.

"We're not giving up the ground south of Arnhem that our troops fought so hard to take. That salient is valuable for future operations. Until relieved, the 82nd and its attachments, as well as the Armored Guards and the 8th Armored Divisions with the 43rd Wessex and all attachments, will continue holding the area south of the Waal and east of Nijmegen right up to the German border.

"Clearly, launching Market Garden cost us an opportunity to open Antwerp's port facilities against limited resistance. We need that harbor. We've created the salient all the way to Nijmegen and we have no intention of giving it up. That's the good news. The further bad news is that we won't win this war by Christmas.

"Clearing out the Scheldt Estuary is a must, and that is Montgomery and his 21st Army Group's mission, and now its highest priority. That means capturing Walcheren. For those not familiar with that island, it's about thirty miles long and fifteen miles wide, and the ground is wet and soggy. Those operations belong to the 1st Canadian Army under Monty's army group. To fully make use of Antwerp, we must clear the Scheldt and take Walcheren." He sighed. "That will be one bloody fight."

The general stood silently a moment in sober reflection on the words he had just spoken. Then he took on an expression of renewed determination. "Also of immediate concern is taking and securing the other port facilities in Normandy and Brittany. Until that's done, all other operations are secondary, to be undertaken only when they can be sustained logistically. We won't launch another major initiative going east until that's the case across the board.

"When we've corrected our logistics situation, the next major objective is breaching the Siegfried Line and occupying the Ruhr. We'll do it on my broad-front strategy, and we won't pursue any more narrow-front maneuvers. We have to get to the other side of the Siegfried in force and envelope the Ruhr Valley's industrial complex, thus removing the enemy's resupply capability. Meanwhile, we can't outrun our own logistics, and we must protect our flanks."

He paused and looked around the room of grim faces. "Now look, from north to south inside France, we have the British 21st Army Group and the US 1st, 12th, and 6th Army Groups all moving east. For most of the time since we broke out of Normandy, the Germans have been intent on escaping France into their own borders.

"We're knocking on their door, threatening their home turf. They'll put up a hell of a fight, and we'd better be ready. I expect you commanders to coordinate closely with units on your flanks. Victory will require a unified effort all the way to Berlin."

He stopped and perused his notes. Then he looked up and focused his attention on General Omar Bradley, the amiable "soldier's soldier" on whom fortune had bestowed the challenge of being General George Patton's direct boss after being subordinate to the legend. Bradley was also one of Eisenhower's closest confidantes. "Brad, please communicate my decisions personally and directly to Field Marshal Montgomery. This conference is adjourned."

22

Same Day, September 22, 1944
Nijmegen, Netherlands

Agardus disliked his new task, but he knew it was necessary, so he accepted the assignment without protest. The ongoing battle still raged north of the city on the main road to Arnhem, but at this point, capturing the ground between the two towns was all but assured. After more days of combat than he cared to track, and after most of XXX Corps had poured over the Waal-brug on its way to Arnhem, G-Company had been relieved by fresh units and had re-deployed to its original position around Dal-en-Berg for a well-deserved rest and refit.

Agardus had been asked to help screen for infiltrators and collaborators among a steady stream of refugees migrating south. He translated for soldiers at a checkpoint at the south end of the bridge. Most people came on foot, pushing carts heaped with clothing and precious possessions. Those fortunate enough to have horse-drawn carriages or farm wagons rode or walked beside them while jumbles of bedding, household goods, and even chickens were loaded on top. Many had livestock pulled behind them. A few had automobiles, similarly burdened.

The migrants were exhausted, hungry, and their numbers so large and unwashed as to raise a foul smell. Old people trudged among them. Mothers and fathers with long, resigned faces, their backs bowed and their feet dragging along the ground, carried exhausted and shell-shocked children. Boys and girls staggered along with blank expressions, carrying water jugs, dirty stuffed animals, and other sundry items.

Agardus watched them in dismay, wondering when the lines would end and the suffering would cease. He heard a voice behind him.

"I've seen worse."

He turned to find Lieutenant Lance Littlefield sauntering up to him. "I was at Dunkirk during the evacuation and was left behind," Lance said quietly. "I escaped south across France. Nearly got away, but I was captured in the vicinity of Saint-Nazaire."

Agardus studied him. "You got away again. And you're back in the fight?"

Lance grunted. "When I was younger, I craved adventure. I think I've had my fill."

"But you're still here."

Lance shrugged. "The war's still on."

They stood quietly watching the crowd file by. "You said you'd seen worse?"

Lance nodded. "I was traveling southeast of Paris when the Germans came into the city from the north. Six million people hit the road." He indicated the trudging crowd. "It was like this multiplied many times."

Agardus shook his head. "I can't imagine." He glanced at Lance. "Did you come looking for me?"

Lance shook his head. "I came to observe the refugees. Out of curiosity. Pity too, I suppose. I saw you working the checkpoint and came to say hello. Your name is circulating. Captain Wilde is very happy with you and your brother on the battle at Lent."

"He wants me to be his cultural advisor. I declined. I want to be a front-line soldier. I like being part of a brotherhood that fights to do good. The men of the 82nd are hard, but they're good men."

"It's a good unit," Lance agreed. "How's your brother and your wounded friend, Horton?"

"Your countryman, the Brit? I hope he's all right. I haven't had a chance to see him or his men or my brother since the river crossing. Frits and I became separated." He sighed. "I'm no doctor, and Horton looked horrific, but I think he only suffered surface burns. We aren't close. I met him just before we started on that mission."

The sound of a motorcycle caught their ears. They both searched about for its source and spotted a trail of dust heading their way. Seconds later, a British dispatch rider pulled in front of them. His insignia denoted him as a lance corporal.

"Are you Lieutenant Littlefield," the rider asked, addressing Lance.

"I am."

"You're needed at division headquarters straightaway. Captain Harry sent for you."

"I'll head right over."

"Sir," the rider said, "do you mind if I ask where you're from? You see, my surname is also Littlefield, and that's not a common name."

"By Jove, you don't say," Lance enthused. He held out his hand. "I'm Lance Littlefield from Sark in the Channel Islands. What about you? Where are you from? What's your given name?"

The corporal grasped Lance's hand firmly, but a disappointed look crossed his face. "I'm Lance Corporal Leonard Littlefield at your service, sir, from up Bristol way." He was a good-looking young man with a square jaw and wide green eyes. "I was hoping to find a cousin, or an uncle perhaps."

Lance took to him immediately. "We're all family on this side of the war," he replied. "I'd be proud to have you for a cousin or a nephew. Which unit are you with?"

"The 43rd Wessex Division. We came over to France through Remparts at Normandy."

"Hmph. I can't say I know anyone in your division. Who's attached to you? I like to ask to see if any old friends might be around."

"I think we all do the same, sir. Let's see, we've got the 214th Infantry Brigade, which includes battalions from the Worcestershire Regiment, the Somerset Light Infantry, the Duke of Cornwall's Light Infantry..."

Leonard rattled off several more units, but when he mentioned the Sherwood Rangers Yeomanry, Lance stopped him, stunned. "Did you say Sherwood Rangers?"

"I did, sir."

Lance whirled around to Agardus. "What was the unit you supported on 504th's flank two days ago? Before the river crossing. Was that the Sherwood Rangers?"

"I think so. Everyone was so enamored with having British rangers around that we only referred to them as rangers. But I'm sure I heard some enthusiasm about the unit having something to do with Robin Hood and Sherwood Forest—"

Lance clapped his hands together, hardly believing what he had heard. "Are you certain?"

Agardus shrugged and Leonard looked on, bemused.

While they spoke, a civilian approached. He stood unobtrusively to one side of and slightly behind Agardus, waiting for a break in the conversation. Then he reached forward and nudged Agardus' elbow.

Agardus turned, and his eyes widened in pleasant surprise, but before he could offer a greeting, the man said gravely, "I need to speak with you privately."

Meanwhile, Lance turned to Leonard. "Tell Captain Harry that I'll be right there. I need to check on something, and then I'll be over. And leave a note where I can find you. Sark and Bristol are not far apart as the crow flies." He laughed. "We might have had ancestors who crossed paths and conjoined."

He looked about and spotted Agardus several feet away still talking with the civilian man. Full of enthusiasm for an inkling of something startling and good, Lance walked over briskly.

"I want to check on that chap, Horton," he said, but stopped short on seeing Agardus' ashen face. The civilian man backed away quietly and rejoined the passing refugees.

"It's my father," Agardus said hoarsely. His shoulders fell and his arms went limp. "He was killed during the last battle at Nijmegen." He wiped his eyes. "He's dead. My father is dead."

The sound of another motorcycle rode the slight breeze. Agardus whirled. "That's his. That's my father's bike," he bellowed. "It's got a very distinctive sound, that low, throaty roar. It's an American bike, a Harley-

Davidson, and there aren't many around in the Netherlands. Maybe he's not dead."

"American dispatch riders use Harleys," Lance said cautiously, neither wanting to build up hope nor douse it if it were warranted.

Agardus glanced around frantically and spotted the bike. It was maneuvering slowly alongside the refugee column, which was directed toward a camp being established near Groesbeek. "You see, I was right. That *is* my father's motorcycle. It's red, not green like US Army bikes."

He hurried toward it, and Lance followed. When Agardus reached it, he stepped in its path, blocking it. He stood legs apart, arms folded, and glared at the rider. Then his expression turned to one of relief and he smiled broadly.

When Lance arrived at his side, Agardus and the rider were talking in excited voices. Lance understood none of the Dutch conversation, but gathered that the two men were well acquainted. The rider dismounted and held the handlebars for Agardus to take.

After he had straddled the seat, Agardus introduced the man. "This is my good friend."

Lance shook the man's proffered hand.

"He was a guide for another American unit fighting north of Lent," Agardus said. "He recognized my father's bike. A German had stolen it." He scoffed angrily. "That *mof* is no longer of this world, and my friend was bringing the bike back. He said that the last time he saw my father, he was very much alive. That was yesterday."

"That's great news," Lance said.

"I must go," Agardus said. "I need to return my father's bike and see him for myself."

"Go. I wish you and your family the best." Lance watched as Agardus put the bike in gear and roared off. A staff jeep and driver waited nearby, and Lance directed the driver to take him to the 508th's regimental aid station.

As he walked in, he saw many wounded men in various states of treatment and recovery. He asked a medic about Horton and was directed to the back of an adjoining tent. There, he found the patient sitting on a cot with his back to the entrance.

Lance was positive that he recognized the stocky build, like that of a rugby player, with wide, rounded shoulders and a short torso. White bandages still covered his entire head.

Lance crept slowly toward him with a mischievous smile. When he was directly behind, he called in a low voice, "Is that Sergeant Derek Horton? Or should I say Lieutenant?"

"Huh?" Horton turned stiffly, and Lance saw that his friend had difficulty moving.He circled to the other side of the cot. "Derek, is that really you under all that gauze?"

Horton stared, unable to believe his eyes. "Did someone finally let you out of jail for keeps?" he said, and laughed out loud. Then he groaned. "Sorry for the costume. The medics tell me I got to wear this a few more days, and then I can't stay out in the sun for several weeks. That's going to crimp my combat style a bit. I'm not sure I can jockey one of them staff chairs more 'n about twenty minutes."

"I saw you shortly after you came in here, but you were bandaged. I didn't know it was you." Lance laughed. "Asking how you are is pointless. I can see for myself."

"It only hurts when I laugh," Horton said, "so don't make me laugh." He chortled uproariously, and then groaned. Then he rose painfully to his feet. "The shock wave knocked me against the turret, so I'm a little stiff. My voice is hoarse like this 'cuz the flame got down my throat some. I'm most worried about my face, though. Ya know I'm supposed to marry after the war, and now I'm thinking that Chantal won't have me. What am I going to do? Who the hell else will have me?"

"You? Married? You found a girl who'd consider it? You're not talking about that little girl who was crazy about you and you thought she was a bother."

"One and the same. She's growed up, and as some Texans I met in the 82nd would say, 'she done lassoed and hog-tied me.'" He started to laugh but managed to throttle it to a chuckle. "That probably don't sound right with a British accent. I've got to practice, though, 'cuz when this war is over, I'm movin' to Texas. I told you and Kenyon that when we wuz floatin' around in the bay by Saint-Nazaire waitin' to be rescued after that dive bomber sunk the *Lancastria*."

Horton chuckled again. "You remember how the ship rolled on its side—"

"How could I forget?"

"—and the housing for the screw-drive was like a shelf, and people was sliding down to it, and then jumpin' off into the water. That's how we got out, you, me, an' Kenyon, God rest his soul. Then the oil on the water caught fire, and there was nowhere for the blokes on the shelf to jump to. So they started singin', 'Roll out the barrel, we'll have a barrel of fun.' Could you believe that? They also sang, 'There'll Always Be an England,' but the saddest thing was—"

Horton suddenly convulsed with involuntary emotion. "—the saddest and the bravest thing I've ever seen in my life was when, just before the ship went under, they started singin', 'We'll Meet Again.'"

He sniffed. "I remember the words, 'we'll meet again, don't know where, don't know when—'"

He wobbled, staggered for balance, and almost fell.

Lance caught him and propped him up. "Are you all right, chum."

Horton nodded, but did not move, leaning into Lance's chest. "Too much time to think, Lance." He slipped away, sitting with a thump on the cot. "I've seen such terrible things, mate—done such terrible things. So much blood. I've killed a lot of men. D'ya think God will forgive me?" He dropped his head. "I'm not sure I can forgive m'self."

Lance recognized that his best friend was in a dangerous mental and emotional place. "I think the people of Italy, France, Belgium, and the Netherlands would intercede for you, not to mention all of England, and they'd all thank you."

"Ah, I hope so. I am a truly evil person."

Lance laughed out loud. "You? Evil? You haven't learned the meaning of the word."

Horton guffawed. "Don't laugh at me when I'm bein' melancholy." He half-turned to peer at Lance through the eye holes in his bandages. "Come to think of it, I haven't seen you since you were hauled off by the Germans after we blew up that fuel-oil tank farm near Saint-Nazaire.

"You're the reason I'm alive, Lance. I never would've thought to walk the whole length of France during a German invasion, and even if I had, I couldn't have made it without you. I made sure your family knows that, and I'll never forget it."

"I didn't do anything special," Lance replied. "Plenty of other men escaped the same way we did, and you were perfectly capable on your own." Before Horton could reply, Lance mused out loud, "Let's see, if you marry Chantal—"

"If she'll still have me."

Lance scoffed but otherwise ignored the comment. "If you marry her, and Jeremy marries her sister, Amélie, neither of whom I've met, by the way, that'll make us related somehow. What would we be, brothers-in-law?"

"Brothers," Horton retorted. "There aren't any brothers closer than those forged together in the fires of war."

"Amen to that, my brother. I can't tell you how incredible it is to see you."

"Listen, I'm late for a meeting at division headquarters. I'll get back as soon as I can. Meanwhile, you take care of yourself, and stay away from dark thoughts. You're as dear to me as my own family, and you know how close we are."

On his way out of the tent, Lance cautioned the medic to keep an eye on Horton. Then he hurried to his meeting with Captain Harry, his high spirits for having discovered Horton tempered by concern over his friend's physical and mental state.

"I'm glad you could make it," Harry greeted when Lance met him in the operations room at 82nd's division headquarters. "XXX Corps has a high-priority mission, Operation Berlin, to rescue as many men as possible of the British 1st Airborne Division trapped at Arnhem. The British Army's Corps of Royal Engineers and the Royal Canadian Engineers will carry out the mission. They've requested Agardus Leegsma to go along as a local area adviser."

"Do you think that's prudent, sir? I'm sure he'd be willing, but he's not trained."

"He was on the crossing at Nijmegen, and knows the area well. His ability to bring in local Resistance assets on the far side of the river and his help on getting into the city are considered indispensable. The 82nd might not have succeeded without him. He received on-the-job training under the severest conditions."

Lance acknowledged Harry's comment with an incongruous shake of his head. "Still, sir. That's a lot to ask. He just received word that his father might have been killed in the last battle at Nijmegen, and he doesn't know the status of his brother who was also on that last crossing. He might not be in the best frame of mind—"

"That would be up to him. I'll put it to him. But as you say, he's not trained, which is why I'd like you to go along—"

"Me, sir?" Lance blurted, stunned. "Of course I'm willing, but those are seasoned engineer units. I'd be seen as an interloper."

Harry shook his head. "You're a commando who came up through the ranks and has water operations under his belt. We'd insert you with Agardus as a team to advise on departure points, landing sites, foibles of the river, etcetera—"

"Agardus can do those things without me."

"If he stays alive long enough. We need you to pay particular attention to ensuring he does. The engineers will concentrate on the mission. We need you to pay attention to Agardus, make sure he reacts effectively to combat conditions as they occur. It's no secret that he wants to enlist in the US Army, specifically to be with the 82nd. General Gavin will make that happen, but more importantly now, we'd all like to see this rescue mission be a success."

Lance let out a long, slow breath. "When does it go off?"

"In three days at the Nederrijn River that runs through Arnhem. XXX Corps is still fighting its way north. Getting the logistics in place will take that long."

Lance started to ask a question, but Harry went on. "Your participation is strictly voluntary. The operation is a tough one. The German defenses are thick along the river. They remember how we took Lent. They'll be alert.

"We'll have some small element of surprise because the wounded at Arnhem will be firing weapons and generating radio traffic to create a sense that the 1st Airborne is still fighting there. Meanwhile their healthy fighters and the walking wounded will slip off quietly to rendezvous with the rescue party at a point on the river. The enemy could spot the rescue craft on the way over or at any time on the way back." Harry tossed his head. "Getting everyone out will require some boats to make at least two trips."

Lance listened with rapt attention and a sinking gut. "I get the picture. What happens to the wounded men left there?"

Harry muttered with a resigned expression. "They'll become POWs. We can only hope that the Germans will treat them according to the Geneva Convention and provide proper medical attention."

Lance nodded. "Tell me about the mission."

"The rescue party will go over at two points, equally divided. About half the boats will be Canadian metallic boats with motors. The rest are the same canvas ones used at Nijmegen. They'll have to be rowed and paddled."

Lance interjected with a note of sarcasm. "Hmph. That raises confidence. They provide no protection at all, and they sink with one bullet below the waterline."

Harry ignored the comment and went on. "The combat engineers are battle-hardened veterans. They'll get the job done."

"The 82nd lost half of those who went on the Nijmegen crossing."

Harry nodded with a grim expression. "Nevertheless, we now own Nijmegen, the Waalbrug, and Lent, and we're pushing north aggressively toward Arnhem." He leaned forward to make direct eye contact for emphasis. "Lance, besides owing those men a rescue attempt, the Allies have manpower shortages too. We need them."

Lance scoffed. "So we're going to get some men killed so we can rescue some cannon fodder." He harrumphed. "I understand. I'll go willingly. Far be it from me to refuse when I can be helpful. At least I can be another trigger-puller."

Harry arched his eyebrows in acknowledgment. "I'll advise the operation's headquarters to expect you. It's Operation Berlin. Planning will take place over the next day, followed by rehearsals and positioning the boats. You'll be visible among the staff as an integral part of the planning process. A consultant. Your kayak mission up the fjord in Norway to blow up that mine sweeper provides your credentials."

Recalling being captured on that mission, Lance swallowed a comment, and Harry continued, "We all know that the plan will go out the window as soon as the first bullet shoots our way. The Nijmegen crossing was chaos, and we expect this one to go similarly. The soldiers in each boat will do what they must to survive. No commander will be able to control the whole unit or what happens in—"

"Canvas boats, crossing a river with no cover," Lance interrupted. Another thought flitted across his mind. "How wide is the river?"

Harry's jaw tightened. "Roughly two hundred feet," he said grimly.

Lance launched to his feet and spun around. He blew out a heavy breath and brought his hand up to massage his jaw. "I've never shirked duty," he said, "but this isn't the kind of adventure I had in mind when I joined the army." He closed his eyes and let his head fall back. "I said I'd do it," he muttered. Then he brought his head forward swiftly and thrust his index finger at the Dutch captain. "But you're going to hold my farewell letter to my family and see that it's delivered if—"

"I'll do that," Harry said quietly. "Anything else?"

Lance thought a moment and nodded. "My best friend in the world is in the division aid station right now recovering from burns received on 504th's flank—"

"I heard about that. Is he all right?"

Lance's shoulders drooped. "We don't know the extent of the damage to his face, and he apparently breathed in some flame. He was knocked around in his turret too, so he's bruised and wobbly, but I'm worried about his mental and emotional state. I think he should've been evacuated already. I'm guessing he wasn't because he refused to go. He feels duty strongly, and just as strongly he worries that his fiancée will find him too horrific to look at, and that he's bound for hell because of the men he's killed."

"Hmph," Harry interjected. "We all worry about that latter part."

"I want him to have the best care available, starting immediately. That's my only condition. I'll trust you and whatever authority it takes to make that happen."

Before Harry could respond, Lance asked, "Where do I report for Operation Berlin?"

After leaving Lance and the column of trudging refugees crossing the Waalbrug, Agardus roared on his father's Harley through back alleys, along dirt roads, and across fields, taking routes known only to those who had roamed the area over a lifetime. He noted the absence of fear that had formerly stemmed from possibly encountering German patrols intent on stopping or killing him, but the thrill that should have accompanied that realization of freedom was stymied by the lingering worry for Papa.

People jumped out of the way at the incongruous sight of a rider in full American combat uniform with goggles covering his face, speeding with almost complete abandon on the powerful red motorcycle. However, having lived for four years with the danger of German vehicles, including motorcycles, roaring over Dutch roads with little regard for other vehicular or pedestrian traffic, they were practiced at jumping out of the way. Agardus arrived in his neighborhood without mishap.

He was brought up short on seeing a crowd surrounding the front of his house. Most were dressed in black, but given the ongoing war, such apparel might signify nothing other than the cleanest or most available apparel at the moment. He had coasted to a stop a block away, and now kicked the bike back into gear and accelerated to a slow approach. Recognizing the bike but not the uniform or goggled rider, people moved out of his way as he reached the front of the house. He recognized many of the long, sorrowful faces regarding him with questioning eyes.

Frits appeared in the doorway, also still wearing the combat uniform Captain Wilde had provided ahead of the Waal River crossing. He rushed to meet Agardus, dried tears streaking his face, joined by new ones.

Agardus' heart dropped even before he dismounted. "It's true?" he gasped, seizing Frits by the shoulders. Frits only nodded and then closed his arms around Agardus' neck and sobbed while their sympathetic neighbors surrounded them.

"How?" Agardus asked when Frits' emotions had subsided.

"The Germans fled," his brother replied. "An officer stole the bike. Papa tried to stop him. The officer emptied his pistol into Papa's chest."

Agardus sucked in his breath at the mental image. "Where's Mama?"

"Inside. She's safe."

Sitting in a worn, overstuffed chair, their mother greeted Agardus with outstretched arms amid a fresh round of shared grief. "I don't know where Papa's body is," she cried. "So many dead were lying around, German soldiers and our people. And they gathered them all up in a truck and took them away."

"Who, Mama? Who took them away?"

"The city government. They said they had to prevent the spread of disease."

"Stay with her," Agardus shouted to Frits as he rushed out to the people milling outside the front door. "Where did they take the bodies?" he blurted to anyone whose eye he caught. Most shrugged their shoulders. Some pointed.

"I saw a truckload go that way," one man said. "I think they've dug a mass grave on the edge of town."

Others indicated different directions.

Agardus roared off on the Harley, headed to the town hall. People crowded its doors, some seeking answers to Agardus' own question: where were the bodies of the deceased being taken?

He soon realized that his American combat uniform gained him deference, and he found a clerk willing to find answers. Various sites were being prepared, and the bodies from his neighborhood would most likely be in a field to the west of town. Fifteen minutes after arriving at the municipal offices, he rode onto the designated field.

The scene was one he feared would haunt him for the rest of his life. Three flatbed trucks with waist-high slats waited in a row. Out to their front, a pair of bulldozers and two backhoes had already dug deep, wide trenches with a graded end so that the trucks could drive down inside.

The cargoes of dead bodies, carefully placed in rows stacked to the top of the slats, had been jolted enroute into horrendous positions. Each corpse appeared so small and flat, but their aggregate appeared enormous.

The smell of death permeated, threatening nausea. Agardus shook it off, gunned his motorcycle, and sped to the front of the first truck. No bodies had yet been placed in the mass grave.

"My father is on one of your trucks," he yelled to the first driver. "I must find him."

The old man, who had probably retired before the war and had little stomach for his current job, regarded him sadly, taking in the uniform. "Wait over there," he said. "We'll put the bodies down. If you see your father, let us know."

Amid the stench of oozing blood, entrails, and brain matter, rather than stand aside, Agardus helped, picking the bodies from the trucks' beds by the arms or legs, and toting them with another helper to lay them in a line on the floor of the trench. After two hours of shared labor, he recognized his father's face, expressionless, drained of blood, a stiff, swollen corpse.

Agardus dropped to his knees over Papa, absorbing painfully the reality and the loss of hope. He reached under the stiff neck and pulled the face to his chest, cradling the head in his arms, and wept. "We're winning, Papa," he cried. "We're so close."

The old driver from the first truck patted Agardus' shoulder. "How will you get him home? I suppose you want a proper burial."

Agardus stood and nodded. "Yes. Thank you. That is exactly what we want. My mother—" His voice trailed off.

"When we're finished here, I'll drive him. You tell me where."

Next Day

Papa Leegsma's funeral was as stately as it could be under the circumstances. Gloomy weather had settled in with overcast skies, but being a well-respected community leader, his family, friends, and neighbors attended the internment en masse to honor him and comfort his widow.

That evening, having changed out of the clothes he wore for the burial, Agardus appeared in front of his mother once again attired in his combat uniform. From her chair, she glanced up at him in surprise. "Why are you wearing that? For us, the war is over."

Agardus knelt in front of her and shook his head. "Mama, the war's not over. It's just moved past Nijmegen."

"But it's over here, and I already lost—" She held back tears.

"Mama, the Netherlands will soon be free, all of it, but only because hard men came from across oceans to fight for us. I can't leave the fight until it's finished."

Frits stood across the room watching, his own face forming a questioning look.

"Frits will stay and take care of you, Mama, but I will continue in combat. I'm enlisting in the US Army with the 82nd Airborne Division."

23

_____

September 23, 1944
Stony Stratford, England

A soft knock on the front door startled Claire. She had heard no car come up the driveway. Then again, she had just come in from the backyard where she had been playing with Timmy on a rare Saturday morning off from work. Although happy for the rest, she was unusually nervous because the man who had left a message with Elsie earlier in the week concerning Timmy had called back two days ago.

Introducing himself as Mr. William Davis, he had sounded elderly and was courteous, and even warm, but he had struck terror into Claire's heart when he said, "We'd like to come out to see Timmy, if it's all right. We're family, you see, and we have all the papers, but I thought I should give you a call first. It's just my wife and I. Would Saturday work out? We could drop by early in the afternoon."

"Certainly," Claire had replied in a voice as charming as she could manage while gripped with anxiety. "Would you be able to stay for tea?"

"Thank you, that would be kind. We should come a little later then. We don't want to take up too much of your time."

They had set arrival for mid-afternoon, and it was now only mid-morning. Claire glanced out the window as she passed through the sitting room to answer the door and saw a sedan was parked in front of her garden. It was a government car.

Color rose in Claire's cheeks as panic seized her. The reaction was rare for her, but the sudden, unexpected appearance of the vehicle threatened to overwhelm her.

With the constant pressures of her work and concern for her parents, new dread over what might transpire with the Davises added to her ever-present anxiety that any day an official visitor might come to inform on the death of one or more of her brothers.

The soft knocking at the door repeated.

Claire took deep breaths to calm herself.

A voice called out, "Claire, are you home?"

Claire's eyes opened wide, and she lunged for the door, twisted the knob, and threw it open. "Jeremy? Is that really you?"

Without waiting for an answer, she leaped against him and threw her arms around his neck. "Oh thank God," she said, and kept repeating the words over and over, finally ending with, "I can't believe you're here." Then she sobbed tears of happiness against his chest. "I'm sorry," she said at last, "I'm all over the place emotionally."

"It's great to see you, Sis," Jeremy said comfortingly. He kissed her fore-head and squeezed her.

The door at the back of the house opened and closed, and Timmy came running. He slowed when he saw Jeremy and Claire in the front doorway, and then stopped with big, solemn eyes. "Why is Gigi crying?"

Claire burst into laughter and stooped in front of him. "These are happy tears. Look who's here. It's Jeremy."

Timmy stared, wide-eyed, his face exuding a little boy's excitement. Then it clouded with uncertainty, and he looked to Claire for reassurance. "Jermy?"

Jeremy laughed warmly and crouched with his arms out.

With one finger hanging from his mouth and still looking at Claire, Timmy took a step forward, and then another, and another, until Jeremy closed his arms around him.

"I've missed you so much," Jeremy whispered while standing and holding the boy close. Recollections flooded his mind of the *Lancastria* going down; of Timmy's mother, Eva, holding Jeremy's hand while he held Timmy in the crook of his other arm, and then jumping into an open area among a swirl of bobbing heads of people trying to escape the sinking ship before it sucked them under. Eva had never resurfaced.

Jeremy blotted the images from his mind and held the boy tighter.

"Let's go play," Timmy yelled brightly. "Jermy, will you push me on the swing? And then we can play with my trucks."

Jeremy glanced at Claire helplessly. "Go on," she said, "he's thrilled to see you. I'll come with you."

Aware of each passing minute bringing closer the arrival of her afternoon visitors, Claire watched as Jeremy pushed Timmy on the swing, and then the two chased each other around the yard and wrestled in the grass. As noon approached, she sent Timmy grumbling into his bedroom to take a nap.

"My, but you rule a tight roost," Jeremy said in amusement as Claire closed the bedroom door, returned to the sitting room, and took a seat in the divan across from an overstuffed chair where he sat. "Does Timmy normally take a nap on Saturdays at this time? And where's Elsie?"

"I gave her the day off, and no, Timmy doesn't ordinarily take a nap at this time on Saturdays. But I must talk with you."

She explained the situation with the Davises. "Also, Lance was just here a few days ago, but he left and couldn't tell me where he's going." Her inflection rose as she spoke, and Jeremy saw in her eyes the extreme emotional struggle occurring below her attempt at calm. "I'm so worried about Mum and Dad. I don't know where Paul is, and now, if the Davises take Timmy away, they would rip my heart right out." She leaned forward holding her face in her hands, as forlorn a figure as Jeremy had ever seen.

He rose, crossed to sit next to her, and held her. She leaned into him, gasping with sobs. "Ah, Sis. I love you. We'll meet the Davises together and see what happens."

The Davises arrived, Terence and Muriel, a very old couple, bent, and walking slowly up the garden path. They had also come in a government sedan, driven by a man who introduced himself as Mr. Boyd, a member of the foreign office. He presented his credentials. Unnerved by what his presence might bode, Claire greeted the trio, and led them into the house.

Taking in the surroundings, Muriel remarked in a high-pitched voice, "Oh, this is beautiful. I'm so happy that Timmy had a good place to grow up to this point."

Stung by the implication, Claire gulped. She led her guests into the sitting room where, after making them comfortable, Terence Davis said, in a voice affected by age, "I apologize. I should have called to let you know that a third person would join us. At the last minute, we thought that Mr. Boyd should come along to establish that we are who we say we are. After all, you couldn't be expected to turn over a child to just anybody who shows up and claims to be related."

"That's why I'm here," Boyd said. "It's better that you become acquainted without my intrusion, though, so I'll leave and come back later to retrieve Mr. and Mrs. Davis."

Claire stymied a gasp. "I'll get Jeremy and Timmy. They're playing out back."

"Oh," Davis broke in, "would that be Jeremy Littlefield, the soldier who rescued Timmy? I was hoping to meet him but thought he'd be away in the war."

"Yes. He's my brother. He came in quite unexpectedly this morning for the weekend. We haven't had time to catch up. The last time I saw him was last January."

Davis and Muriel reacted in consternation. "Oh then, we shouldn't stay long."

"No," Claire exclaimed. "We want you to stay and visit. I'll go get them, but first, may I ask—" She paused, picking her words carefully. "How are you related to Timmy?"

"How silly of me," Davis said. "I meant to tell you. We're his mother's parents."

"Eva," Claire said softly. "Jeremy told me about her. He said she was lovely and wholly committed to saving her son. I'm so sorry for your loss."

Muriel sniffed and pulled a handkerchief from her sleeve to dab her eyes. "Thank you." She took a deep breath, let it out, and said with a broken smile, "If you wouldn't mind, I'm so anxious to see my grandson. It'll be my first time."

"Of course." Stemming her own emotion, Claire started away.

"Wait," Davis interjected. "If it's not too much to ask, could we see him playing? We could watch through the window." He turned to Muriel. "Would you like to do that?"

Muriel's eyes lit up. "Yes, yes, that would be wonderful. And perhaps we could visit with him in the garden?" She directed her request to Claire.

"I'm sure he'd like that. Follow me."

While Claire led the way, Boyd excused himself and departed.

At the window, the old couple watched, captured by the sight of their beautiful grandson running and jumping, and squealing with excitement as he and Jeremy ran about. "Stay there as long as you like," Claire said. "I'll prepare the tea."

As she started for the kitchen, Muriel laid a hand on her arm. "I want to say thank you for taking such good care of our grandson. We'd have come earlier but for the war. We live in India, you see. We're sorry for the troub—"

"I knew that." Claire took a deep breath. "Mrs. Davis—"

"Please, call me Muriel."

"All right, Muriel. Timmy has been no trouble at all. He's a treasure. I love him dearly. My whole family does."

———

Claire and Jeremy talked in the sitting room until late into the night, long after the Davises had left and Claire had put Timmy to bed. "I'm glad you were here for this," she said. "I'm not sure I could have handled the Davises' visit alone."

"They were very warm," Jeremy replied. "I liked them, and Timmy did too. He was thrilled to learn that he had grandparents." He imitated Timmy's reaction. "'Just like the other children in my kindergarten.'"

Jeremy noted the anxious shadow that passed over Claire's face in reaction to his comment. "What happens now?"

"I don't know," Claire replied in a strained voice, her eyes hollow with exhaustion. "The last thing Muriel said to me was that Timmy should be with his family." She dropped her head into her hands. "This is so frustrating. We are his family, you, me, and our brothers, not to mention Amélie, Chantal, Horton, Elsie, and even our cousins Zack and Sherry, as well as Madeleine Fourcade. He's seen all of them as very close to us, and they love him. Together, we're the only family he's ever known." She added in a low voice, "Until now."

She glanced at Jeremy. "They were so impressed with you, and that their grandson is connected with such a recognized war hero, and their gratitude to you for saving his life was real."

Jeremy shrugged off the comment and squeezed his sister's hand. She remained quiet for a time. "I want to hate them, Jeremy," she murmured. "I really do. The idea that they could take him away, and all the way to India. We'd never see him again.

"But I could see the pain in their eyes over the loss of Eva. And you should have seen them watching Timmy playing together with you. They were mesmerized."

Suddenly angry, she stood and paced. "This war has torn up so many lives, and for what? Will anything good come of it?"

Jeremy sat quietly, listening. When she paused, he said, "Our people will live as they choose, and they'll rebuild."

"Yes, well, there is that," Claire said grudgingly. She glanced at Jeremy. "But tomorrow you'll go away again to who knows where or for how long."

Jeremy rose from his seat and went to comfort her. "I don't know who suffers more," he said, "the soldiers who fight in the war, or their loved ones struggling for a good place for veterans to come home to." He took her face in his hands and looked into her eyes. "But there's one thought I want you never to let go of."

Claire sniffed. "What is that?" she asked.

Jeremy smiled. "Things will get better. You'll see."

24

September 25, 1944
Arnhem, Netherlands

A week of fierce combat had bestowed an indescribable but distinct smell of death and decay from German, British, American, and Dutch bodies among pools of spilled blood strewn on the bridge and along the banks of the Nederrijn. Heavy rain drove a mélange of the acrid stink of gunpowder and smoke accompanied by pungent odors of burned-out buildings, scorched war machines, and rising diesel vapors along with the oily smell of spent ammunition. The nauseating fumes joined with the polluted stench of debris and carcasses of wild and domesticated animals floating on the river.

At six o'clock that evening, the 43rd Wessex Division's field artillery unleashed hellish salvos that continued hour after hour into the night with the intention of keeping the German defenders on the north shore and beyond buttoned up and preparing for an assault. Thick smoke joined the stomach-churning swirl that filled the nostrils of the British Royal Engineers and the Royal Canadian Engineers as they prepared the daunting task of extricating the British 1st Airborne Division's remaining able-bodied paratroopers and walking wounded still trapped on the northern end of Arnhem's bridge.

"I was sorry to hear about your father," Lance told Agardus. The two fought nausea from breathing the putrid air along the river's shore as they sheltered from the rain in a bombed-out overhang of a boathouse awaiting mission-start. Heavy clouds blanked out the light of a quarter moon. A stiff early-autumn breeze raised a chill in the air, but brought with it occasional wisps of fresh air.

"Papa died defending our country," Agardus replied. "He would be proud of that."

"And your brother survived the crossing at Nijmegen?"

"Thankfully, yes," Agardus responded, nodding. "He'll stay home to care for our mother. He wasn't pleased. He thinks he should do more in the war, but we're a traditional Dutch family. He'll do as I say because I'm the eldest, and we love Mama."

He sighed and listened to the rushing current and the water lapping on the shore. "I'm glad you're coming along, Lance," Agardus said. "Your commando experience will help. I heard about your raid in a Norwegian fjord."

Lance paused before responding. "That mission was very different. We had only three kayaks in the assault group, and I wasn't part of it. My job was to prepare the escape for the raiding party." He grunted sardonically. "We all ended up in POW camps, and some of our group were executed. So much for the value of my experience."

"But you escaped, and you chose to be back in the fight."

Lance grunted. "I suppose there is that. I'm a glutton for punishment." He shrugged. "We went in at night like we're doing here, and learned some things. The German gunners will follow the spotlights that are guided by a different crew. So, if they start shooting, we'll row hard when the beams are not aimed at us, and duck low and stay still when they pass over us. I'll be watching for them.

"One thing we have going for us is that the water's warm and the current mild. If a boat spills or sinks, the men have a fighting chance of swimming to the southern shore."

"That's good," Agardus agreed. He looked around. "I'm amazed at how quiet the men are. All those boats, and each one with a crew of four, but we can't hear any of them."

"The rain and normal river noises help muffle the sound, but the soldiers are trained to tie down equipment so it doesn't rattle, and to move quietly. Before we cast off, the field artillery will start its salvos to keep the Germans hunkered down and also to prevent them from hearing our movements. When we leave shore, the other boats will key on you for direction—"

Agardus exhaled sharply. "Guiding them is a hellacious responsibility."

"We were fortunate that Canadian boats were added to the mix, and we'll be in one of those," Lance said. "They're metallic and sturdier, and they have motors. About half are the Canadian type. The canvas boats will have a harder time, but the soldiers can follow compasses and they'll paddle hard. And the 43rd Division's field artillery will drop red flares over the intended pickup points, so it's not all on you. In fact, you're the backup in case the big guns can't fire or their aim is off."

Agardus started blowing air into his fist in nervous anticipation.

"You're up to this," Lance stated firmly for encouragement. "I'll be right beside you. Not everyone is going to make it to safety. That's a given. It's not all on you, got it?"

Agardus nodded.

"I've been involved in the planning and I'll tell you what I can," Lance went on. "That should ease some pressure. First off, another British unit, the Dorsets, landed on the far bank last night to help broaden the bridgehead. That should increase the margin of error."

Lance did not divulge a tragic fact that he had learned about the 4th Battalion of the Dorsetshire Regiment of the 43rd (Wessex) Infantry Division. Their mission had failed. Of the more than three hundred soldiers sent on the mission the night before, most were killed or captured. Only seventy-five had returned to safety.

"The next thing to know," he continued, "is that another landing is taking place simultaneously farther west, below Oosterbeek, so the rescue is divided into halves, and they'll have their own guide.

"The artillery will deliver massive fire, non-stop, throughout the night to hold the Germans in their current positions. The *moffen* will think a major assault is about to follow. Meanwhile, 1st Airborne's wounded men left behind will fire off weapons and send radio traffic to create the appearance that their division is still fighting. While all that is going on, the ones escaping will make their way along the opposite shore to the rendezvous."

Agardus heaved a sigh. "That's all good to hear, but the machine gun fire? It was murderous on the crossing by Nijmegen."

"If the rain continues," Lance explained, "combined with our artillery, we shouldn't encounter much from the machine guns. The rain is uncomfortable and makes coordination between boats and people on shore difficult, but it also conceals us. The *moffen* don't go in much for night operations anyway, and with the rain, they're more likely to stay indoors, but if they come out, we'll be harder to see. The rain is our friend."

Agardus chuckled involuntarily at Lance's last comment. "I hadn't ever thought about the rain like that before."

"We'll have to work fast. Sunrise is at 07:15 hours, and first light is well ahead of that. At daybreak, we'll become visible to the German gunners, and they'll be posted along the shore. They won't need to aim so much as sweep their fire through the general area where the boats are." He let out a small laugh. "We have the advantage that this crossing is much shorter than at Nijmegen. Only two hundred feet this time."

"Without even a blade of grass for cover," Agardus said grimly. He sighed. "That was an awful operation at Nijmegen. We only had twenty-six boats for a two-company assault. That wasn't enough, so some boats had to make multiple trips."

Lance grunted. "Some boats will have to make several trips this time too."

Agardus seemed not to have heard. He continued, almost trancelike. "Someone told me that a chaplain went on the Maas River crossing. He didn't have to do that. I was told that he kept praying 'Hail Marys' and thumping the side of the boat, like coxswains do, to help keep rhythm for the rowers. I wonder if he's still alive."

"But you guided the raiding force across the Waal and into Lent, and because of that, the 508th captured the north end of the bridge," Lance interjected. "That was quite a feat."

"It cost a lot of lives," Agardus said sadly. "Great soldiers. I don't know how my country will repay them for their sacrifices. I hope we rebuild in a way that's worthy of them."

"Well, you're with us *now*, and you're enlisting with the 82nd. That's a good start."

The two stood quietly, contemplating. "How's our friend Horton?" Agardus asked, breaking the silence.

Lance sighed. "He should be back in England by now, getting rest and treatment."

"I enjoyed knowing him. He had a way of being funny and deadly serious at the same time, and his men loved him. You could see that. They'd do whatever he said with no grumbling because they knew he cared about them and would do everything possible to keep them alive while meeting the mission. You and he were close?"

Lance's jaw tightened as an image of his stricken friend formed in his mind. "Like brothers," he said tautly. "We escaped from Dunkirk together."

"I'll keep my thumb in my fist for him." Seeing Lance's puzzled expression, Agardus added, "That's a Dutch gesture for good luck."

A runner, ghostly and deadly quiet, materialized out of the darkness. "We launch in five minutes," he whispered, and dissolved into the night to alert other crews along the Nederrijn.

The 43rd Division's big guns unleashed elevated fire and brimstone at the stroke of 22:00 hours. Their explosive rounds descended on known German positions, pounding their defenses and casting flames high in the sky, followed by billows of smoke in defiance of the rain and dark storm clouds. The artillery ranged to the right and left of their original targets and crept to the German rear. And repeated. And repeated...

At the sound of the first salvo, Lance and Agardus jumped into their boat with two other crewmen, one of whom started the motor and steered the boat slowly out into the current. To their left and right, they heard the whine of other motors starting up and settling into a purr as they followed Lance's lead boat farther into the river and formed loosely behind him.

"I can't make out any landmarks on the other side," Agardus said anxiously.

"No worries, we have a compass and the azimuth," Lance reassured him calmly. "All we have to do is keep the nose of the boat pointed in the same direction as the arrow on here," he said, showing Agardus the luminous dial. "If we hit the shore at the wrong spot, you'll guide us to where we need to go."

At that moment, they heard a distinct but muffled shot from the friendly side of the river. A red streak arced across the sky and came down beyond the far shore.

"That's a signal flare to give us direction," Lance said, glancing at the compass. "We're on course. We'll see a couple more of them before we get to land. Win or lose, mate, we're a team." In the dark night, Lance could not see Agardus' face, but he heard the young Dutchman's relieved sigh.

As the small flotilla approached the far shore, the rain paused, and the clouds parted enough to let moonlight through to shimmer off the water. It also provided a view of a scene onshore that was beyond surreal. Rows of what appeared to be short trees that Agardus did not recall seeing before stood along the banks, but as the boat drew closer, he realized that they were not trees at all, but soldiers, all standing stock still and silent, separated into groups numbering exactly the available seats on each boat.

The watercraft pulled in. The waiting soldiers moved forward quietly, deliberately, and clambered aboard, careful neither to rock the boats nor produce undue noise. Agardus marveled at their discipline. In one case, a big soldier carried another over his shoulder and placed him gently on a seat before sitting next to him. "A piece of shrapnel caught him on the way down," came the whispered explanation.

Friendly artillery barrages continued non-stop as more boats arrived and more soldiers filled the motorized Canadian boats first, and then the British canvas ones. When Agardus' boat was full, he looked around for Lance and spotted him nearby helping with another vessel. Agardus called to him.

"You go ahead," Lance shouted back, unconcerned now about being heard above the deafening explosions in such close proximity. "I'll see you on the other side. I'm staying to help load these here. Some of the walking wounded are in sad shape."

Agardus cast him a sharp, uncertain look, but Lance waved him off. "Go," he called. "We'll need your boat back here for more. You know what to do."

Lance watched Agardus' boat head into the darkness. The young Dutchman stood at its front staring back at him, but the clouds opened up, spilling more heavy rain on those soldiers, now at the mercy of fortune, the weather, and obscured views.

Murmurs of impatience were few among those still on the north shore awaiting their turns, and when such expressions arose, they were quickly doused by others standing in line. Quite surprising to Lance, he learned that placement within the queue had been by drawn lots, and he was more astonished to find senior officers, including a commanding general, waiting in line behind non-coms and other ranks.

"I'm part of the rescue team," Lance explained in a whisper when questioned about why he was out of line. "I'm supposed to help stragglers."

The gaunt faces he encountered in rare breaks of moonlight attested to the horrendous conditions visited on this haggard lot for over a week. He knew of reports that air drops of supplies, including food, medical provisions, and ammunition, had drifted into German-held territory and had been recovered by the enemy. Thus, the British and Polish troops, being compressed into a smaller and smaller area that the *moffen* referred to as "the cauldron," had gone days without meals.

Lance walked slowly up the path, offering words of encouragement and ensuring that the escaping soldiers moved steadily toward the boats, realizing that as he went, he came closer and closer to the targets of the ever-present German field artillery, evident by the power and tremors they delivered with their terrible clamor.

He listened to whispered regrets over mates lost, of wounded left behind even while the chatter of small-arms and machine gunfire from Arnhem indicated that badly injured soldiers still fought to mask the safe extraction of their able-bodied mates.

"Could you believe it?" one man whispered. "There I was, just yesterday, shooting the machine gun out the window of a house and receiving heavy return fire. The house had been all but destroyed, and Troy was makin' cabbage soup in a tin over a fire on the concrete floor. He used a picture frame over the mantel for firewood. He even wrote an apology to the owners on the back of the photo." His voice quivered. "And now he's back up there all shot up and unable to move."

Lance commiserated quietly with the exhausted audience, and continued up the line. He had no orders for his spontaneously executed mission. He had become concerned that these men who had dropped from the sky with orders to occupy and hold the Arnhem bridge for two days had done so without support for nine days. While time remained to roust any who might have stumbled in the night and dropped behind, or fallen into sleep from exhaustion, he sought to find them and send them to the rendezvous on the river.

As he worked his way up the line, he encountered white tape strung between trees that had guided the escapees down to the river. The many glider pilots among the fighting force had gone ahead of the main group, scouted the route, located the landing point, and placed the tape to mark the route.

Lance reached the top of the embankment and continued on into Arnhem, taking shelter where he could find it against the artillery bombardment crashing all about him. By the flashes of flame with each explosion, he beheld the absolute destruction meted out on this small town. Rows of houses had been obliterated, some with parts of walls still erect, appearing as ghostly apparitions against roiling dust clouds that ascended around them.

He came upon a small stone church that had obviously been targeted by both sides as a likely observation post. In the brief glimpses between flashes of light, he saw that it had been pounded by small arms, heavy machine guns, and field artillery. Its roof was crashed in, most of its walls demolished, and its spire badly damaged. Yet the steeple still stood.

Then, in pitch-black darkness, he heard a terrible screech followed by a rumble. At that moment a salvo of artillery rounds hit in the church's vicinity, and from behind a brick wall and peering below his helmet, Lance saw the stone bell tower acquiesce to the destructive forces surrounding it, and it crashed to the ground.

Lance's self-imposed, evolving mission suddenly became clear: to reach the small area in Arnhem at the north end of the bridge and see what final aid he might offer. He had seen the zone outlined on the planning maps designated as a place on which no Allied artillery would fall. The wounded were gathered there in rubbled buildings and basements, and they continued their gallant hold-out against the overwhelming 9th *Panzer* Division bearing down on them.

Keeping low and feeling his way through the wreckage and debris, orienting himself by the launch and crash of artillery fire, the rush of the river, and the buildings from which the sound of small arms emanated, he at last identified the headquarters. A few German soldiers in close proximity returned fire on the building, but the main enemy force probably had been pulled back to participate in a final assault to capture or kill the 1st Airborne. However, if the wounded men's ruse had worked, the *Wehrmacht* believed that the paratroopers still presented a sizeable force and would approach with caution.

Careful to stay outside the line of fire from either side of the battle, Lance managed to infiltrate the British perimeter, such as it was, consisting of soldiers lying in positions from which they could not move for fear of opening massive wounds and bleeding out. The first ones he encountered stared at him in frozen terror and then relaxed into states of obvious pain as they realized that he was a friend, and they provided whispered directions to the headquarters where Colonel John Frost, the commander, also lay in dire physical straits from three wounds.

Reaching his destination, Lance was appalled at the conditions. With no sanitary provisions, deluged by rain, and with the dead lying about, the stench was horrendous even against the standard he had experienced at the river. He ducked in, and made himself known to men lying on cots, couches, the floor, some bandaged, some moaning, some delirious. "Where is Colonel Frost?"

Wounded men pointed, and he followed their gestures to a narrow hall behind a grand staircase that had collapsed. Stepping over debris and soldiers, he picked his way down the hall until nearly at its end. "Colonel Frost?" he called out.

A voice responded weakly. "That's me."

"Lieutenant Lance Littlefield at your service, sir."

Weak eyes stared up at him from the withered face of the large man who had already become a legend to the forces south of Arnhem. Dropped in nine days earlier to capture and hold this position for two days, he had fought the Germans to a standstill, refused an offer to surrender, and rallied his men against increasing odds until he himself had been shot multiple times. Yet he still refused to give in.

Frost held a pistol in his hand. He glanced at it and then up at Lance and let out a small laugh. Obviously, he was too weak to lift the weapon. "My orderly gave me this as he was leaving. He told me that if I saw any Germans, to shoot them."

He laughed again, and then asked, "Whatever are you doing here? I don't know you. You're not in my command."

"No, sir, I'm with the rescue party. I came to look for stragglers and to see if you could be moved."

"That's wonderfully good of you, and there might be some who didn't get the word to evacuate." He coughed, his breathing labored, his speech broken. "As you can see, I won't live through going anywhere without medical attention, and the same is true for the others here. We have a few padres and medical people who stayed on. We'll all surrender in the morning, after the evacuation is complete."

He struggled to glance at his watch, and brought it close to his eyes to focus on its luminous hands. "Shouldn't you be getting out of here? First light is less than two hours away, and you'll have small chance of getting across the river after that." He glanced up at Lance without moving. "Go on. Be off with you. Keep up the good fight for king and country. That's an order."

Surprised that so much time had passed, Lance straightened to full height, and saluted. "It's an honor to meet you, sir. I'll look for you after the war, if you'll allow a visit."

Frost chuckled and returned the salute as best he could. "If I make it, my boy, I'm sure I won't forget you, and I'll be pleased to receive you. Now get on with you. I hope you find others who could use your assistance, but you're helping no one here."

Stepping carefully through the dark hall, Lance made his way back to the front entrance with a terrible sense of desertion for leaving the wounded behind. As he reached the door, he encountered a healthy soldier, visible by a slight increase in light outside. Daylight was even closer than the colonel had thought.

"Sir, what's goin' on?" the soldier asked. "I woke up, and was gettin' ready for stand-to, but no one else was about, aside from the wounded. I stopped off at the buildin' where we're holdin' German prisoners. They informed me that everyone had left."

"You spoke with German POWs?"

"I did, sir. They were quite positive that their guards had left, and I didn't see any."

"What's your name?"

"Private Stan Turner, sir."

"Take me to them."

Careful to watch for incoming hostile fire, they scurried through the debris to a nearby house that had been all but leveled. The German prisoners were hunkered down in the basement.

"There's no one guardin' them, sir," Turner said, "and they know it." He showed Lance where the door to a staircase was, just inside what had been a foyer.

Lance checked his Sten gun and ordered Turner to follow with his weapon ready. Then he started down the stairs. "Who's the senior officer?" he called in German. "I wish to speak with you."

A German captain presented himself at the bottom of the stairs.

"He's good," Turner called over Lance's shoulder. "His men were bellyachin' about the lack of grub and quotin' the Geneva Convention. He told them that we had no more food than they did and to stop moanin'."

Lance studied the officer. "You could have overpowered this soldier, sir," he observed. "Why didn't you?"

The captain looked at the ground and shook his head before looking up and meeting Lance's eyes. "What would be the point? For hours, your artillery has hit all over Arnhem, but not here. And then your guards disappeared. We figured out that an evacuation must be taking place, leaving only the badly wounded. We have no weapons or food. Your army treated us as well as they could under the circumstances. Ours will soon re-occupy this area. Meanwhile, this is the safest place to be.

"Let me add that, despite that the *Wehrmacht* is winning this battle, the war goes badly for us, and I don't care to make it a personal one. Under other conditions, we might be friends."

The captain was a slender man with classic Aryan blond hair and blue eyes, but he carried himself with an air of humility and courtesy uncharacteristic of the stereotype.

Lance gazed at him momentarily. "That would have been much more preferable to this situation."

"Lieutenant, I have one more thing to say, and then a piece of advice, if you'll allow me."

"Go on."

"Our country, our people, our army, and even the *Waffen*-SS—we were misled. That's all I have to say on our circumstances. Make of my statement what you will.

"Now the advice. Get out. Go. Now, while you still can. These men are under my command, and they will not try to follow or impede you. We will see that your wounded are cared for. But if you are to have a chance, you must go now."

Lance and Turner crouched behind some bushes on the shoreline, staring at the last boats still visible across the waters. Although the sun had not yet crested, its long rays reached into the sky. The rain had stopped, the artillery was sporadic, visibility already stretched for miles. The new element that joined the diminished cacophony was the regular and voluminous staccato of German machine guns sweeping just above water level and aimed at the boats. The spray of the bullets striking the water was visible, as were sinking boats. The cries of newly wounded soldiers was clear, albeit faint.

"We're going to have to swim for it," Turner said. "I'm not going back into that cauldron of Arnhem, and I'm not waiting to be captured." He waded into the river.

"Wait, Private," Lance commanded, and added tersely, "That's an order."

Turner halted and turned to Lance, obviously angry.

"Listen to me," Lance said. "Look around at the dead soldiers floating in the river. They were your comrades, your mates, and they're dead, but not because they were wounded. They drowned. They were weighted down by their uniforms and kit."

Bewildered, Turner scanned the water, noting bodies scattered near the shore. Aside from being dead, they appeared unharmed, but they were numerous.

On the way down to the river, Lance had seen that the queue had diminished to nothing, but apparently some soldiers had become impatient and had jumped into the water fully clothed and with all their combat gear. He registered the fear and uncertainty now on Turner's face.

"Let's go upstream," he said. "We'll put more distance between us and those machine guns, and then we'll swim across, naked."

"Sir?"

"I'm an escape artist, Turner. I survived Dunkirk, a sinking ship, and I've escaped from POW camps three times, maybe four. I've lost count. If you do as I say, you'll have the greatest probability of getting home safely.

"The water's warm, so it won't incapacitate you for being too cold, and if the enemy spots you and shoots, you can go underwater. We'll take our time and hope that we're not seen."

Turner waded the few steps back to shore. "After you, Guv'nor."

Though mild, the river's current carried Lance and Turner downstream as they made for the southern shore. Lance, a strong swimmer from his days in the Channel surrounding Sark, hung behind Turner to support him if need be. He was gratified, however, to find that Turner needed no help, and the two made steady progress.

They heard sporadic shooting as they went, but thus far, no bullets had come their way. They had drifted past the debarkation point for the flotilla, and they saw boats still scattered along the bank. Lance noticed the bombed-out boathouse where he and Agardus had waited together the previous evening. However, Lance and Turner were still too far out, and the current too stiff, to make shore there.

They had progressed by swimming below the surface as much as possible, only coming up for a few seconds of air, but the effort drained them of strength. As they came closer to the southern bank, they tended to surface more often and linger longer.

Finally, they were within a few feet of shore. Brush grew onshore near the waterline offering concealment, and they had seen the ruins of a village above the embankment, providing hope of scavenging something to wear. They approached the shore in low crouches.

Suddenly, Lance saw small sprays of water erupt near him. A split-second later, he heard the powerful reports of a Mauser machine gun firing short bursts at Turner, who was closer to the waterline.

"Get down!" Lance shouted, but Turner was already scampering the few remaining yards for the concealment of the bushes.

In that instant, a searing jolt to Lance's left shoulder and another one to his right arm knocked him off balance. His body jerked spasmodically, and he was catapulted forward by the force of the bullets that riddled him. He fell face down in the water. The current took hold and carried him away from shore, downstream.

25

Same Day, September 25, 1944
Éloyes, France

A heavy rain beat a rhythm on Lieutenant Zack Littlefield's canvas pup tent. He hunched, cross-legged, over an unopened cardboard C-ration box he used as a writing surface while penning a letter to his girlfriend, Sonja, back home in New Jersey. His company commander's driver had just arrived and crouched at the mouth of the tent.

"Sir, the ol' man needs to see you asap."

Zack glanced down at the letter and scanned the four sentences he had completed. It read, "It's been a long slog from Montélimar, but once again, the 36th Division's soldiers were the first Americans to set foot in another large French city. This time, Lyons, so it's liberated. That was a couple of weeks ago, but I've lost track of time. So much rain and so much mud!"

While wondering if he sounded too boastful or doleful, he sighed and grabbed his field jacket. "All right, let's go see what Captain Bellamy wants."

He crawled out of his tent into crisp air and a stormy night. The weather had turned abruptly from balmy to cold and damp five days ago as the 36th (Texas) Infantry Division assaulted across the Moselle River under heavy enemy fire.

The distance to Captain Bellamy's field headquarters was short, less than a mile, but Zack was glad for the jeep ride. It saved him from stumbling around on a drenched, muddy road, on a pitch-black night in which only mountain peaks were visible by the light of a quarter moon obscured by clouds. Besides, a ride was a good thing when available. The driver knew the way, and Zack had done enough trekking to last a lifetime, up Italy's boot and across France from Saint-Raphaël on the Mediterranean coast, and fighting the *Wehrmacht* every inch.

"You wanted to see me, sir?" he said on entering Bellamy's tent.

"Have a seat," the captain said, and gestured to a folding stool next to his cot. He was dark-complected and somewhat smaller than Zack, who had been a high school football star.

Zack sat down and eyed his boss expectantly. "Have we got another patrol?"

Bellamy shook his head with an air of reluctance. "I've enjoyed working with you, Zack. You're easily one of the best platoon leaders in the battalion if not the division."

Zack regarded him uneasily. "Thanks for the nice words, but why do I suddenly feel like a load of crap is about to dump on me?"

Bellamy grunted. "You're perceptive, I'll give ya that, right off the top. I'll hate losing you."

Zack sat up straight, his eyes wide. "Where am I going?"

"Over to the 141st, unless you say otherwise." Bellamy let out a deep breath. "You know the drill. Someone gets taken out, someone steps in."

Numbness crept through Zack's limbs and his heart beat hard against his ribs. He swallowed to quell sudden ringing in his ears. "Who was it? How'd it happen? Was he KIA?"

The captain nodded somberly. "I don't have details, and I didn't know the officer. He was with his regimental commander, Major Hanson, about a mile south of Noir Gueux where their unit's main body crossed the river. Hanson's party came under fire, he was killed, and so was that officer."

"Tough times." Zack shook his head and exhaled. He looked at the ceiling and rubbed his arms to relieve tension. "Sir, why can't the 141st replace him from its own men. I've been with my platoon since Italy. Those of us still alive and not wounded know what to expect from each other. We're teachin' the new guys the ropes."

"We go where we're needed, Zack, you know that," the captain said, not unkindly. "You came over from the 142nd, remember?" He looked at the floor and his shoulders drooped. "The empty slot isn't for a platoon leader," he said gruffly. "It's for a company commander. He and his exec were taken out."

Zack leaped to his feet abruptly and stared. "You can't be serious, Captain. I'm not trained for that. I just turned twenty and I came straight to the war from high school."

"I know."

"I shouldn't even be an officer. I was the lone survivor in battle three times. When I came to the 36th Division, no one wanted to work with me. They thought I was jinxed, and frankly, so did I."

"You're a survivor, Zack. You're steady, and you get the job done. No one ducks from fighting alongside you now. If anything, they jockey to be in your platoon. Some men are alive today who might have been killed but for you. You know what you're doing—"

Zack re-took his seat and stretched his legs out in front of him. "You said I could say no?"

Pursing his lips, Bellamy nodded. "I almost wish you would. Like I said, I'd like to keep you, but here's the thing. The division isn't stopping. We're moving forward. We don't have the luxury of waiting around and picking from among replacement officers. Where we're going, we need proven experience. The division is short on captains. All three regiments were ordered to submit their best lieutenants, and we're short on those too. You got the job."

Zack's head reeled. "Sir, you said 'where we're goin'—'"

"You know where that is," the captain interrupted. He grunted. "Hell, you spend as much time in the battalion operations tent as I do. You know the big plan and the subordinate ones. We're going into those steep mountains, Zack, the High Vosges, just like the ones we came through in Italy. Maybe worse. And winter is on the way.

"That mountain range was fought over a lot in ancient history. War hasn't touched it since Roman times, until now, because the attackers never succeeded." The captain tossed his head, grimaced, and said his next words distinctly. "And we're attacking."

He remained silent a moment to punctuate his point, and then continued. "The Germans bypassed the Vosges on their way through France. They took possession of it when the country capitulated. Now they intend to use it to anchor their line of defense in front of their own border."

Zack let out a breath. "Sir, I've never commanded," he muttered.

The captain gave him a soft, quiet smile. "How you survived the killing fields at Kasserine Pass and at Saint Pietro are campfire stories. The way you organized your platoon positions and executed a massive ambush at Montélimar caught attention up the chain. And you've been a bug on my ass since I took over command of this company, Zack, always butting your way into my planning meetings—nicely, I have to say, but you never let go of a single detail, and you made good suggestions."

He watched Zack's face as Zack struggled with the decision. "No one is ever as ready as he'd like to be for combat," Bellamy said gently, "not down where the boots pound the terrain. I'll tell you this, though, Zack: you're as ready for company command as any junior officer I know. If ordered to, I'd serve under you without hesitation."

Zack swung his head up and looked directly into the captain's eyes. "You can't mean that, sir. Don't bullshit me."

The captain laughed and met Zack's gaze. "You know my reputation, Lieutenant."

Zack locked his eyes on the captain's. "Yes, sir, you don't bullshit." He took a deep breath. "But you've been trained for this. You're a West Point officer." His voice went hollow, barely above a whisper. "The responsibility. A hundred and fifty men—"

"You've been trained for it too, Zack, in the hardest school, the battlefield. Forged in fire, as they say." He cocked his head to one side. "And if it makes you feel better, you'll only have a hundred guys. We're at two-thirds strength across the division, the corps, and probably across General Patch's whole 7th Army and the rest of our Allied forces."

Zack listened glumly.

"Look, Lieutenant, command is within your capacity. It's a matter of planning your actions, following your plan, adapting to changing conditions, using your resources, including both ways up and down your chain of command, and meeting your assigned objectives. You've been doing all of that on a smaller scale." Seeing continued reluctance, he clapped Zack's shoulder. "I have full confidence in you, or I wouldn't have put you in for the job. But look, you don't have to make up your mind this minute.

"Go back to your tent. Sleep on it. At 06:00 hours, I'll send the driver there to pick you up. If he comes back without you, I'll know you decided the assignment's not for you, and we'll never speak of it again. Otherwise, he'll bring you here so we can say our fare-thee-wells, and I'll send you on your way."

They spoke a few minutes longer on administrative details, particularly regarding who might replace Zack, and then the lieutenant rode in dazed silence back to his platoon area. He wondered about the company commander he was proposed to replace. *Did the man have a family? How did he die? Was it from a mistake he made? Just bad luck?* He grunted at the last thought, reminding himself that the enemy's constant intent was to kill that captain, and Zack, and any other adversary on this side of their long guns.

Although arriving at his tent exhausted, he slept fitfully. Then he sat upright, cross-legged in his bedroll, in the dark, reliving the crossing at the Moselle.

As the 142nd Infantry Regiment of the 36th Infantry (Texas) Division had approached the river from the west near Remiremont, torrential rain had turned the ground into a mire. Zack's soldiers had plodded through mud that coated their boots and ankles, and soon seemed to coat everything they touched. Rest breaks became extended times to clean weapons once again, keeping them prepared for instant use against an entrenched enemy on the opposite shore.

As they drew closer to the Moselle, the rumble of distant artillery reminded them of the reception that awaited any attempt to reach the eastern bank. The village of Remiremont was itself situated on a bend in the river. Zack had spotted the topography on a map, and he recalled a similar bend and the debacle along the Rapido River in Italy back in

January. There, to his mind, poor senior command decisions had sent hundreds of American soldiers to their deaths, perhaps needlessly. *Are we doing it again? Was that only eight months ago? Really?*

His concerns were heightened when, upon nearing the riverbank with his platoon spread in line abreast, he saw that the heavy rains had swollen the waterway into a wild, serpentine creature roaring by ferociously, and on the opposite side, the thunder of enemy field artillery had joined that of friendly barrages in incessant, deafening exchanges. For a fleeting moment, Zack imagined Remiremont's terrified villagers huddling in musty cellars, their children covering their ears and hugging teddy bears under blankets, dampened by fog, on cold, hard floors.

The fording operation had begun at dawn with a heavy white mist blocking the rising sun. River crossings had become hated events, never going as planned, always treacherous, and invariably fatal for many.

Haze prevented enemy field guns from targeting effectively, but moisture seeping through the seams of combat uniforms joined with perspiration generated from rapid motion. Braced in the wind, and with direct fire streaming at them, the moisture chilled soldiers to the bone before they even encountered the raging torrent.

The day before, the reconnaissance platoon had found a suitable place to ford, and overnight, the engineers had placed the boats in location. When Zack approached his assigned launch point, images of the disaster at Rapido entered his mind once more. He stared aghast at the rushing water, the eighty feet to the opposite shore, and the smoke rising from enemy guns spewing hot steel.

As the sun rose higher, the mist thinned, a chorus of mortar whoomphs joined the barrages of field artillery, and their deadly rounds erupted among the assaulting soldiers. Sharp-edged shrapnel growled through the air along with the hiss of bullets, accompanied by green-glowing enemy tracers from small arms. Most terrifying were MG 42 machine guns, "Hitler's Buzz Saws," aptly nicknamed due to their distinctive ripping sounds and rates of fire, averaging twelve hundred rounds per minute.

In the fields leading to the river and along its edge, men fell. Some were silent, others screamed in fear and agony. Medics rushed to downed soldiers.

Zack had coached his squad leaders to keep his men dispersed until just before entering their boats and to keep them low and using available cover and concealment. During maneuver exercises in rehearsals for this operation, Zack had been amazed to see soldiers, even combat veterans, crouch behind trees with diameters of no more than three inches. "Get your butts down," he had roared his warning, "and get behind something that will hide or protect you, if it's available, or get flat and crawl on your bellies. Sitting behind a three-inch twig ain't gonna save you."

When other platoons had retired for the day, Zack had kept his men rehearsing, ignoring their moaning and groaning. "You wanna go home alive and in one piece?" he admonished them. "You've heard this before, but I promise you it's the truth: how you train is how you fight, and as sure as the sun rises in the morning, you're gonna see combat veterans who should know better ducked behind three-inch trees during the hottest fire-fights. A lot of them will go home in body bags."

The icy water had sucked the breath right out of Zack when he entered it up to his waist to climb aboard the boat. Much of it had descended from the mountains and was even colder than the rain that drenched them on their approach. Then, the craft with 1st Squad was in the stream, and the soldiers paddled hard against the stiff current.

Enemy fire increased as Zack's boat reached mid-river. Struggling soldiers who had fallen into the water swept by in the current, panic on their faces. Others washed past, their eyes vacant and staring.

Seemingly by a miracle, Zack's boat reached the opposite shore. He was joined by his platoon sergeant, Tech Sergeant Wilbur, in a hollow place on the bank, out of enemy direct fire. " We lost two," Wilbur reported. "One fell overboard. He might have made it. The other one was shot in the face. His body is in the boat."

"Any wounded?"

"Surface wounds. None that will keep them out of combat."

Up and downriver, the 36th Infantry Division's regiments had continued to fight, and by nightfall, they had firmly established a foothold on the east side of the Moselle from Épinal, south of Remiremont. The 142nd had scrambled up the muddy embankment, secured its position, and turned north to support the 141st at Éloyes.

Zack relived the crossing ordeal in excruciating detail and yet also in a blur of motion, sounds, and ghastly smells. His soldiers had executed his every order with only the normal amount of protest and grunts that is a soldier's right. As he now sat in the dark of his pup tent under the steady drum of rain and contemplated his transfer, each of his soldiers' faces passed by in his mind. To him, they were all brothers. Fighting for "hearth and home" had been displaced by fighting to keep each other alive.

At 05:00, Zack went to Sergeant Wilbur's tent. "Roust the men," he said. "I need to see them formed up in thirty minutes."

"Something up, sir? I heard you went to see the ol' man last night."

Zack exhaled. "You'll hear it with the platoon. Just get 'em up."

A half-hour later, he stood before the soldiers he had led in so many battles. "At ease. Gather round," he said, and then related his previous evening's conversation with the CO.

"So what did you decide?" a voice popped up from the rear.

"Don't leave us," another soldier cried out in a mock-wailing voice amid other jocular protests of dismay.

Zack looked around at the combat-weary creases lining the aged faces of these very young men. He had fought alongside some of them since embarking from Italy. Several had joined him as replacements while fighting north from Saint-Raphaël on the Mediterranean coast and had fought through Grenoble, and then at Montélimar and Lyons, and just days ago, they had crossed the Moselle River together.

Other faces flickered in and out of focus in the formation, those of men not physically present, fallen comrades now seen only in Zack's mind, yet seemingly very real. All those present as well as those viscerally imagined regarded him with anxious eyes.

"I could never expect to serve with better soldiers than those of my platoon," he said as resigned groans rose among the soldiers. "We all want this war to be over so we can go home and beat Jody's ass." A trickle of mirth spread at his reference to the mythical and legendary interloper who, back home, sought the affections of every wife and girlfriend of every soldier in the US Army.

"You're going, sir," a soldier in the front rank asserted. "Why? I git that it's nice to git promoted and be a company commander, but—"

"That's not why he's goin'," Tech Sergeant Wilbur interrupted in a firm voice. He turned to Zack. "The ol' man convinced you that it's your duty, right, sir?"

Zack put his hands in his pockets. His head dropped, and he nodded. "Look," he said, standing straight again and facing the formation, "the whole time I've been your platoon leader, I've wondered why I got the field promotion instead of Tech Sergeant Wilbur." He re-directed his attention to the sergeant. "The fact is, he's fully qualified, he's been part of your leadership since Italy. I couldn't have done the job without him, and now he's replacing me. That was part of my agreement with Captain Bellamy last night. I'm leaving you in good hands." He turned to the sergeant. "I'll go in a few minutes, but I told the ol' man that I'd take the liberty of doing this…"

Zack reached into his pocket. "Stand at attention, Sergeant Wilbur."

As the shocked tech sergeant stood straight, Zack pinned a second lieutenant's bar on his collar. "Take charge, Lieutenant. The captain will handle the formalities later."

26

September 27, 1944
Bletchley Park, Bletchley, Milton Keynes, Buckinghamshire, England

Oddly, Commander Travis stood when Claire entered his office. His manner was solicitous, even going so far as to come around his desk and hold her customary chair as she took her seat.

"You asked about enemy defenses in the Vosges?" she asked, puzzled at his behavior.

"Yes, yes," he responded as he returned to his side of the desk and sat down. "The US 7th Army made good progress coming up from the south." He paused and gazed out the window distantly. "Of course, the XV Corps was transferred from General Patton's army to General Patch's, but French General Leclerc managed to keep his 2nd Armored Division out of de Lattre's French Army and remain under Patton's command. Isn't Leclerc's division the one where your brother Paul is?"

Claire stared in alarm. "Y-yes," she stuttered. "He's a liaison for Leclerc. Have you heard news about Paul?"

"What? Oh no. Sorry to give you a start." Travis gestured with his hands to calm her concern. "I'm trying to get a grip on the larger picture. Things are moving so fast now, you know. Leclerc's troops captured Épinal and crossed the Moselle two weeks ago, and the bulk of the 7th Army crossed south of there three days later. Both Leclerc and the 7th Army appear intent on getting to Strasbourg. We'll see who gets there first."

He pondered the point a moment. "I meant to say that the 7th Army is on a trajectory toward there through Saint-Dié and Molsheim, and Leclerc is bent on fulfilling his Oath of—" Travis struggled for the word.

"Kufra," Claire interjected. "The Oath of Kufra."

"Ah, yes. Well, our units in the Market Garden salient in the Netherlands are holding their ground while Montgomery reorganizes his 21st Army Group. My guess is that, when the time is right, he'll relieve the airborne assets, and his ground units will be reinforced and push east.

"Eisenhower is committed to his broad front, so with the Allied right flank squeezed against the Swiss border and moving north, a point of convergence is shaping up along the French-German border running northwest of Switzerland. Those troops will spill into Germany once we get past the mountains.

"I believe that Leclerc is already pushing into the Low Vosges, the hilly country between the Moselle River and the German border. It's less mountainous than the High Vosges farther south. Unfortunately, the American 7th Army's 36th Division will have to attack through the high peaks. Very rugged country. The command requested any intel we have regarding German defenses in the Vosges. What do you have on the matter?"

Claire quietly bit her lip to avoid thinking of personal implications: *Paul is with Leclerc, and Cousin Zack is with the 36th Infantry Division.*

She rummaged through a set of notes in her lap. "I get the impression from decoded intercepts that the Germans are preparing a stiff resistance there," she said, sublimating her anxiety. "In essence, they don't intend to retreat any farther. They'll make us pay for every square inch the rest of the way into Germany and on to Berlin."

She glanced at her notes again, and continued, holding her voice steady. "Their morale is terrible. The 36th hounded and depleted the *Wehrmacht's* Nineteenth Army all the way from Montélimar in southern France. But with our own fuel shortage slowing us down, that *Wehrmacht* element escaped into the High Vosges."

Claire continued, informing Travis that a new commander, General Hermann Balck, had taken over Army Group G. He had been appalled at the poor fighting strength and lack of discipline that had beset the Nineteenth in its headlong flight north. "He's taking steps to address discipline, and thinks that solving the issue will improve morale. Part of their problem is that Germany is running out of replacements, so they've closed any state and commercial entity, where lots of men were employed, including their navy and air force schools. They've pressed those poor chaps into the *Wehrmacht*."

She paused to scan her notes once more. "One reason the 7th Army made such good progress from the Mediterranean was that the enemy's coastal defenders were units made up largely of conscripts from conquests in Eastern Europe. Those soldiers don't want to die for Hitler any more than they wanted to die for Stalin—"

"Good point."

"Most of them have deserted," Claire continued. "So, the *Wehrmacht* is now composed mainly of Germans defending their homeland." She creased her brow. "They have a lot of seasoned veterans, though. We shouldn't underestimate them." As an afterthought, she added, "The infantry unit that Air Marshal Göring organized from his ground crews on Hitler's orders gained a reputation as an effective fighting force."

From Travis' expression, Claire perceived that, while interested in the information she related, he had something else on his mind. "Am I missing anything?"

Travis sighed. "Do you have any specifics on the High Vosges' defenses?"

Again, Claire referred to her notes and nodded. "General Balck assigned construction of two concentric rings of hardened defenses to General Erich von Kirchbach, who had developed a solid reputation in building such defenses against the Soviets in the east. Our side considers him to be an able and professional soldier.

"He's building the defensive rings with steel-reinforced concrete spaced about a mile apart, complete with pillboxes, tunnels, and cleared fields of fire."

Claire glanced up at Travis and caught a concerned look on his face while he regarded her steadily. "Sir, is there something I've done? I have the distinct impression that you're reluctant to tell or ask me something."

Travis nodded slightly, exhaled deeply, and frowned. "You've caught me," he said with a doleful smile. "I've thought over and over how to tell you this—"

Claire drew back in alarm. "Have I done something—"

Travis shook his head sadly. "There's no easy way." He took a deep breath. "It's your brother—"

Claire leaped to her feet. "Which one?" she gasped, clutching her hands to her mouth. "Paul? You said—"

"It's not Paul," Travis said gravely. "It's Lance. He was in that operation to rescue the trapped paratroopers at Arnhem. He's missing in action."

Stony Stratford, England

Wrapped in her overcoat with a scarf over her head against autumn weather, Claire rode the bus in agonizing silence, and then, with shoulders drooping, she ambled through the town past the old stone buildings with its narrow streets and sidewalks.

While going past the Cock and Bull, the pub that had been her favorite in times past, she stopped and stared, seeing only visions of happier times, when she had played the piano while her brothers and their pilot friends, British and American, had gathered around to regale patrons with lusty drinking songs and patriotic ones, including "We'll Meet Again," and "There'll Always Be An England," and even "God Bless America."

A wisp of memory floated through her mind of Eugene "Red" Tobin, one of the American pilots who had come to England four years ago to fly Spitfires during the Battle of Britain and the *blitz*. The group had become known as the American Eagles and were among those honored by Winston Churchill as "The Few," those five hundred British, American, and Polish fighter pilots who had staved off the months-long German bombing attacks and saved England.

Claire had fallen for Red, and he had fallen in battle. Then, one by one, so had so many of those other pilots and soldiers, friends all, some of whom she had known since childhood. Although well aware of the dangers to her brothers, the idea that one of them might actually be killed had seemed an impossibility. And yet...

She tried to remember a time that Lance had been part of those gatherings at the pub, but no such image emerged. He had joined the army before the war began, he had escaped Dunkirk, and then he had been captured during a raid in which he had participated with the fledgling French Resistance.

She chuckled involuntarily, even as tears spilled, and she caught her breath. *He's been captured and escaped so many times I've lost track of the number.*

On one occasion, Lance had managed to evade recapture and come all the way home, thin, worn, but nonetheless her alive, adventurous, loving brother. And then he had immediately volunteered for the commandos, and on his first mission in that role, he had been captured yet again.

Claire stifled an involuntary sob. "Lance, why did you have to go back?"

A brisk wind blew through the town, and gray clouds threatened rain, sure signs of the transition from summer to autumn. The front door of the pub opened and a couple emerged holding each other closely, bringing once again to Claire's mind thoughts of Red. The aromas of ale and warm fish 'n' chips wafted, adding to her nostalgia for a fading, happier past. Every element of her characteristic optimism drained away.

As tears welled in her eyes, she covered her face with her scarf. Pulling her overcoat tighter, she trudged on, oblivious to greetings and friendly glances from villagers. Jeremy's escape from Dunkirk and his heroic rescue of Timmy had been the subject of front-page news. The townspeople knew of Jeremy's heroism and of Claire's kindness in having made a home for the boy in a rented house on an estate within walking distance of the town.

Despondently, Claire made her way up the gravel driveway toward her house, barely noticing a light misty rain, or that flowers in her garden had begun dropping petals and surrounding trees had begun to fade into russet colors, and many of their leaves floated down to be swirled away by gusts of wind.

The house came into view.

Claire stopped dead in her tracks, dread forming in the pit of her stomach.

A small government coupe had parked in front of her house.

Then, as she put one heavy foot in front of the other and closed the distance, she had to smile in spite of circumstances as she spotted Timmy running toward her. "Gigi, Gigi," he cried, "there's a man waiting for you in the sitting room. He looks very strange."

Must they send someone else to inform me officially *about Lance?* A more alarming thought caused her to choke. *Has another brother...*

Timmy ran up to her, panting. "He's nice," he said, "but his face is shiny, and he told Nanny that he must stay out of the sun." He grabbed her hand and pulled her past the car toward the garden path.

Elsie appeared in the door, her face a mask of anxiety. Behind her, a man loomed, wearing a wide-brimmed hat. The skin on his puffy face gleamed. He regarded her with no expression.

"Sorry," he croaked, "it still hurts to smile," and in that small utterance, Claire recognized Derek Horton's voice, hoarse though it was.

She stared, stunned. "Horton?" she cried, barely above a whisper. She brought her hands to her eyes, unable to stem the flow of tears.

"Somewhat worse for wear," he said, grinning, and then groaned. "I got a little burned. Nothing serious, but the docs sent me home against my protest." His tone of voice changed to one of mock-indignation. "I'm positive your miscreant brother, Lance, had something to do with it."

Color faded from Claire's face; her eyes closed. She wobbled on unsteady legs and leaned against the doorframe.

"Mum, are you all right," Elsie asked, grasping Claire's arm with a supporting hand.

Horton stepped around the nanny and wrapped his arm around Claire's back. "Easy there," he said. "I didn't mean to startle you."

"Your burns—" Claire murmured. "I can't touch you."

"It's just my face," he said, and drew hers into his chest.

She broke into uncontrolled weeping, and then fainted.

Timmy pulled on her skirt. "What's wrong, Gigi?"

While Elsie scurried into the kitchen to fetch smelling salts and make strong black tea, Horton swept his free arm below Claire's knees and carried her gently to the sofa in the sitting room.

Claire opened her eyes. Horton, Elsie, and Timmy hovered over her. "I'm sorry, Miss," Horton said worriedly. "I didn't mean to shock you. I must look a bit worse than I thought."

Claire stared, slowly comprehending her surroundings and circumstances, and recalling with a jolt the news Commander Travis had delivered. As through a haze, she saw Horton's face, taking in its noticeable redness, the puffiness around his eyes, and slightly blistered lips. Most strangely, his skin gleamed.

She pulled herself up to lean on her elbows. "Horton," she gasped, "what have they done to you?" She broke into sobs again, and pivoted her hips to plant her feet on the floor while resting her forehead in her hands. Timmy had watched from a safe distance and now moved over to sit next to her and hold her hand.

Sitting on Claire's other side and bewildered, Horton looked on, unsure that he could console her. "I'm so sorry, Miss," he said softly. "I should go."

"No," Claire exclaimed in alarm. "It's not you." She wiped her eyes and took deep breaths to control her grief. "It's Lance."

Horton bounded to his feet. "What about Lance?"

Speaking in broken phrases and occasionally weeping, Claire recounted what Travis had told her. Horton re-took his seat and listened carefully.

"Let's go over it again," he said when she had finished. "He was at Arnhem and helped men escape. He swam the river with one man and was apparently shot." He pondered a moment. "You know, I saw him just a few hours before that operation. He looked quite fit."

Claire reacted with surprise, and Horton explained the circumstances. "Well I'm glad the two of you got to spend some time together and that he was healthy. That gives some small comfort." She sniffed. "Commander Travis said that Turner, the other man in the river with Lance, heard the shots and ran for the bushes. When he got there, he turned for Lance, but

Lance had disappeared. And then Turner saw what looked like a body floating into the main current."

Horton stood and paced the room. Then he gazed out the window. "So Turner didn't see a dead body for certain." He swung around to face Claire. "He couldn't confirm that Lance had been killed."

"That's right," Claire said while wiping away a tear. "Commander Travis said Lance was missing in action. I dare not hope—"

Horton strode back to the sofa, sat down next to Claire, and took her hand. "Miss Claire, listen to me. You've been a rock for so many of us, holding us together through this war. The most precious things about you are your optimism and your care.

"Don't give them up. When we think of home and why we fight, we think of you. I can't tell you that Lance is alive. If he's not, I'll always be grateful to him for my life, and we'll celebrate his memory and be glad we knew him, but—" He drew himself around to face her. "I can say without a doubt that if there's the slightest chance for anyone to survive and come home to us, Lance has it."

Claire took several deep breaths and leaned against him. "Thank you, I do hope you're right."

Horton kissed her cheek. "Miss Claire. We're winning this war, and soon we'll have the whole lot back home with us."

Claire sniffed and sat up straight. "Would you please stop calling me 'Miss Claire?' My brothers call me 'Claire.' You're as dear to me as any brother could be. Or should I call you Lieutenant Horton?"

He chuckled. "Horton will do. Just please not 'Derek.' I'll try my best to meet your wish, but old habits die hard."

Claire gazed into his face. "Tell me what happened to you. Why the burns?"

"It was nothing, really," Horton said, grimacing. "I exposed myself when I shouldn't have, and an anti-tank rocket exploded nearby. The problem was that the medics didn't treat my face properly. They bathed it in a cool saline solution, which was the correct procedure, but then they wrapped it in gauze. They should have just coated it with a light petroleum gel like I have on now. I don't blame them. They did the best they knew how. Burn treatment is still evolving, as I learned when I got to hospital here in England."

"The gel is why your skin is so shiny?"

Horton nodded. "Unfortunately, the initial treatment set the healing back with a bit of infection, but now I'm on the mend."

Claire studied his features. "Will there be any scarring?"

"Hopefully not much. We'll know in a month. It'll be that long before I can safely be out in the sun for more than a few moments. Most of the burns were first degree, but in a few spots they were second degree. That's where the infections were. The doctors say they might have to graft some skin."

"So if Lance somehow caused you to be evacuated for treatment, he did you a favor?"

"That he did, now that you mention it." Horton cocked his head to one side. "I'm doubly in his debt." As another thought formed, he laughed with a slightly sardonic note. "I was already an oaf for Chantal to take on. She might not have me once she sees the new me. Did you know we were to be married?"

Claire leaped to her feet. "Are you? That's wonderful news. And don't be silly about your burns." She reached over and jostled Horton's shoulder playfully. "Chantal's been bonkers for you since she was fourteen. She's had to mature quickly because of the war, but I assure you, she met the challenge. Her insight is spot-on. She didn't fall in love with just a very handsome man. She loved the courage and the character—"

"That's nice of you to say—"

"It's the truth."

Timmy had sat in Elsie's lap in an overstuffed chair for the conversation's duration, and now with it evolving into a celebratory air, he jumped to the floor and ran to Claire. "Are things getting better, Gigi?"

Claire stared down at him, the happiness and sadness of the moment descending in palpable irony. She kneeled in front of Timmy, drew him close, brushed a lock of hair from his forehead, and smiled into his eyes. "I think so," she said softly, and gestured toward Horton. "Look, your uncle is getting married."

Timmy regarded Horton with wide-eyed surprise. "He's my uncle too?"

"Of course he is."

Horton suddenly leaned forward. "Oh, I almost forgot to mention that I might have run into a distant cousin of yours on the battlefield. Corporal Leonard Littlefield from Bristol. He's a dispatch rider, and a right nice chap, but I didn't get to spend much time with him. I heard the name and got curious, so we chatted for a few minutes."

"I don't know of any relations from Bristol," Claire said, "but that doesn't mean we have none." She was quiet a moment, and then asked, "What happens after you heal?"

Horton sucked in a quick breath, obviously reluctant to answer. Finally, he said steadily, "I'll go back."

Claire rose slowly to her feet, her eyes fixed on his face. "Surely you don't have to. You've already done so much, and you're wounded."

Horton tossed his head. "I suppose I could stay, but that wouldn't feel right. The war's still on. My men are there. Chantal is still fighting in the Resistance somewhere."

"And that," Claire murmured, "is why she loves you so much." Smiling down at Timmy, whose face had scrunched in bewilderment, she stroked the boy's hair. "This must be so confusing for you. Sad one minute, happy the next, and then..." She glanced across at Horton resolutely. "We must enjoy every minute of your time with us."

27

Same Day, September 27, 1944
Brabant-en-Argonne, France

Chantal gunned the engine of Dragon's Motobécane motorcycle and hurtled over a low bluff on a field among the gently rolling hills that created a shallow valley where Brabant nestled. Earlier in the day, accompanied by Fourcade, she had arrived in Verdun, site of the bloodiest battle of the Great War. Then, on being informed that Paris' top *Gestapo* officials had occupied the hotel on the opposite side of the same street where they had intended to stay, they quickly continued to this dot-on-a-map agricultural community twelve miles southwest of Verdun.

Brabant was a good choice. It held no strategic value for the Germans who hurriedly pushed their forces east to defend along the Rhine, but the hamlet was close enough that Fourcade had quick access to her agents who had moved into the surrounding areas to collect intelligence on German dispositions and movements, and when possible, their plans.

Chantal had found the journey nerve-wracking at first. Fourcade had borrowed an ambulance and created a new alias for herself, "Marie-Suzanne Imbert." As they made their way to the enemy's rear, expecting that it would soon move east past them, they represented themselves at each successive checkpoint as French sympathizers of and collaborators with the Nazi cause intent on caring for German soldiers as the *Wehrmacht* retreated. Not sure whether to be amused or disgusted by the enthusiastic approbation that greeted their explanation, the two women smiled stoically, and they were allowed to continue.

When they arrived in Brabant, Chantal was pleasantly surprised to encounter Jean Sainteny, codenamed "Dragon." He had been her Resistance section chief in Normandy when she had been assigned there to assist the artist Robert Douin and his son Rémy in sketching eighty miles of German defenses, in detail, along Normandy's beaches for the Allies ahead of the invasion.

Chantal had grown so attached to the father and son team that she had regarded Rémy as a younger brother and Douin as a second father. She had been the courier to carry the sketches to the Allies and had almost been captured with the damning intel. She had also been devastated to learn that, on the same day as the invasion, the Nazis had summarily executed Douin. Rémy had gone into hiding.

Chantal was thrilled to see Dragon. He had been kind to her at the time that she accepted the Normandy assignment, and he consoled her when the worst happened to Douin just as the Allied ships unleashed barrages and sent the invasion force ashore.

"Papillon," he said fondly when he saw Chantal, calling her by her codename. "I'm happy to see that you're looking healthy."

Fourcade was also pleased but surprised to see Dragon when he walked out of the farmhouse where she and Chantal would stay. "Why are you here? You were supposed to be on a flight back to England."

Dragon, tall, slender, clean-shaven, and with dark, wavy hair over a high forehead, smiled. "General Patton was so impressed with information we provided on enemy dispositions east of Paris that he changed his direction of advance. He was very pleased to learn that the approach to Verdun was only lightly defended, so he's also moving up his timetable. And he wants more intel, particularly on the Argonne Forest."

Fourcade whirled on him. "Patton's not thinking of coming through there, is he? That forest is thick, and it's the site of one of the worst battles of the last war—"

"It might be thick with *les boches*," Dragon countered. "He doesn't want them on his flank as he closes in on Verdun. Not that he necessarily expects that the *Wehrmacht* has much in there, but he wants to be certain, and he wants to know what's between here and Strasbourg."

"Ah, Strasbourg," Fourcade exclaimed with a determined gleam in her eyes. "We are getting close, aren't we? Where is that 'impatient lion,' Leclerc, these days?"

"His division is thrusting that way from the southwest, and he's hell-bent that a French division will liberate that city."

"His oath," Fourcade said, nodding.

"That, and the credibility he established by liberating Paris. Technically, he was part of 1st Army at the time, but he came to France as part of Patton's 3rd Army, and that's whom he credits with his support. He was already one of Patton's favorite commanders, and now he's taken the reins in his mouth, so to speak. You know he refuses to serve under de Lattre."

Fourcade shook her head. "I hadn't heard."

Jean de Lattre de Tassigny had been a senior general in the French Army in North Africa when Germany invaded France and allowed the unoccupied part of the country to organize as Vichy-France under pro-Nazi Marshal Philippe Pétain. When the Vichy army in North Africa switched sides to join the Allies, de Lattre had been the only major commander to remain loyal to Vichy. He escaped arrest, and at a later date, he joined General de Gaulle in Algeria, who appointed him to command French Army B, which then came ashore in the Mediterranean. He subsequently liberated Marseille and Toulouse, essentially intact.

By contrast, Leclerc had been wounded during the German invasion. He had escaped to England in 1940, joined de Gaulle there, and had fought the *Wehrmacht* all across North Africa and Italy. He also led the thrust that liberated Paris.

"The 2nd French Armored Division was supposed to have been assigned to de Lattre's army, but Leclerc refuses to take orders from anyone who ever swore allegiance to Vichy," Dragon went on. "He pushed to come back under Patton's command, and now he's intent on fulfilling his oath in Strasbourg. Patton allows him almost a free hand."

"I can see why," Fourcade interjected. "He's freed a lot of French ground.

The people love him. If anyone can liberate Strasbourg, he can." She chuckled and added, "He's the French Patton."

Dragon smiled obliquely. "I prefer to think that Patton is the American Leclerc."

While Dragon and Fourcade conversed, Chantal wandered about the farmhouse garden, taking in the view of the wide, gentle hills surrounding it. For a few moments, she savored the fresh air while wondering if life would ever return to a time when she could enjoy her beautiful France without concern over mortal combat or losing loved ones. Her thoughts went to Horton and Amélie. *Where are they now?*

The ache she had endured in times past from missing them had dissipated, a change that she did not necessarily welcome. *Am I maturing or becoming callous?*

Absently, she picked a red geranium from the fading garden and held it to her nose for the faint scent. Then she spotted the Motobécane leaning against the house. The small motorcycle was known for easy handling, making it ideal for fast deliveries and evading capture.

Chantal strolled over, eyed it, pulled it upright, placed her hands on both grips, and tried the clutch and hand brake. Then, she gazed over the handlebars across the fields, recalling pleasant moments on bicycle rides with Rémy along Normandy's coast as they moved from place to place to prepare the coastal sketches.

Seized with sudden excitement, she ran back to where Dragon and Fourcade continued in deep conversation. "Is that your motorcycle?" she asked, interrupting Dragon in mid-sentence.

He turned to her with an amused grin. "It belongs to my Resistance organization. Would you like me to take you for a ride?"

"I want you to teach me how to ride it myself," Chantal blurted. She gazed back and forth between him and Fourcade. "You've both said that I'm one of your best couriers. I could do it so much faster on a motorcycle. When I was in England, I saw hundreds of women dispatch riders. They were called 'Wrens.' I know women ride for the Resistance all over our country, don't they?" She looked to Dragon for confirmation.

"Some do," he said noncommittally.

"Then teach me." Chantal looked to Fourcade for support but was met with a concerned frown.

"It's too dangerous," Fourcade said.

Chantal stared in disbelief and then laughed in a way that began as a single chuckle and built to uproarious. "Are you serious?" she said between gasps. "You're worried about danger? You, who built the largest Resistance organization in France, who dodges the *Gestapo* constantly, and who just recently escaped from their jail?

"And what about me? I rode bicycles among *boche* troops with Rémy on all those roads in Normandy, and we went through their checkpoints.

"I'm a spy, trained in England by the Brits. I've been on combat raids, and I escaped from jail just like you did." She stopped to catch her breath, and then added, "I've killed three men, including a German officer—" She stopped talking, realizing that her voice had grown shrill and that a sad look crossed Fourcade's face.

"You've done all of that," Fourcade said quietly, "and you're only eighteen. Amélie—"

"Amélie isn't here," Chantal retorted stubbornly, "and I'm almost nineteen."

Fourcade smiled wistfully. She moved closer to Chantal and put an arm around her shoulder. "Amélie isn't here," she repeated, and sighed heavily. "You were fourteen when you and your sister came to me. I've watched you grow." Rare tears formed at the corners of her eyes. "My heart is torn out whenever I send you on a mission." She sniffed and regained composure. "Don't worry, I anguish over all my agents."

Chantal gazed at Fourcade with deep affection. "I could not have asked for a better second mother."

"Third," Fourcade interjected brusquely. "Amélie—"

Chantal chuckled, wrapped her arms around the legendary Resistance leader, and squeezed her. "She's my older sister, and you both watched over me."

Fourcade took a deep breath. Turning to Dragon, she said, "I'll allow it, but make sure she's trained by the best."

"*Bien sur, Madame.* You forget, I was her surrogate father for a while."

Dragon took Chantal out later that afternoon, showed her how to operate the controls, and ran alongside her to hold her steady as the bike sputtered while she learned to manipulate the gears. "Now listen to me," he told her. "We run training for motorcycle couriers, and usually they already know how to ride. We don't have any courses this close to the Germans, so I'm bringing in a trainer, one of our best.

"He'll put you through every exercise you'd see at our sites. You'll have to learn operation and maintenance of the bike, how to lean into curves and make fast turns, what to do if you start to spill, or if you have to go cross-country. It's a rough—"

Chantal interrupted with a wry smile. "Do I need to bring up spy school again or the operations I've been on?"

Dragon grinned sheepishly. "Go practice on your own now, but be careful."

Chantal rode down the driveway and turned onto the main road. No traffic was there, so she need not fear colliding with other vehicles for the moment. Gingerly, she pulled the clutch and moved the gear into second. Then she speeded up until the engine's tone let her know to change into third gear. That done, she leaned into the wind and turned the throttle full open until her fast-beating heart, gasping breath, and watery eyes convinced her to slow to a cruising speed.

Smiling from ear to ear, she drove on, loving the stream of wind through her hair, the rush of landscape, and the sense of freedom. *Ah, freedom. What we all fight for.* Hers, she recognized, was curtailed as she drew near to Verdun. That she had gone that distance so quickly surprised her, but going farther in that direction was taking an unnecessary risk, despite that *les boches* had ceased patrolling toward the farm.

Seeing no place for a novice rider to turn around gracefully on the narrow road, she brought the bike to a halt, dismounted, and walked it to face the opposite direction. Then she re-mounted and rode back, slower now, enjoying the autumn colors, the sense of self-control, and the roar and vibration of the motorcycle's engine.

As she pulled in front of the farmhouse, on impulse, she turned into an open field and gunned the engine. The motorcycle surged forward on the uneven ground. Exhilarated, she opened the throttle and bounded over several berms before deciding to return to the farmhouse. She arrived grinning broadly.

Dragon hurried out to meet her. His grim expression quelled her exuberance. "What's wrong?"

"Set the bike against the house, and then I'll tell you. How was the ride?"

"I loved it," Chantal replied, but she studied Dragon's face as she spoke, noticing that he barely listened. His interest had been perfunctory.

After she had carefully put the bike in its place, Dragon informed her sorrowfully, "We just learned that Georges Lamarque is dead. A courier brought the news. The Germans executed him three weeks ago. Madame Fourcade is devastated."

Chantal took a deep breath, holding back tears as she absorbed the tragedy. "Where is she?"

"In the front room. She's inconsolable right now. Go in quietly. She'll appreciate that you're here."

Georges Lamarque dead. That was inconceivable to Chantal. He had been the mathematics professor at the Polytechnical Institute in Paris who had become Fourcade's closest lieutenant. When *Gestapo* infiltration had reduced her organization of thousands to a mere five people including Fourcade herself, it was he who had very quickly helped her rebuild a stronger organization with better security. He had recruited Jeannie Rousseau, his brilliant and talented star pupil who had delivered into Allied hands the German plans to invade the United Kingdom and the V-1 and V-2 rockets' technical sketches. She was the same woman whom Amélie now sought to rescue from Hitler's house of horrors in Ravensbrück.

Georges' apartment had been where Chantal and Amélie had reunited after months apart on separate missions, and where they had gathered and celebrated Paris' liberation with Jeremy, Paul, and Fourcade. That was where Chantal had received her last news of Horton, including his letter proclaiming his love and desire to marry her.

With a gasp, Chantal quelled thoughts of Horton and what might have come of him. Under the circumstances, thinking of him only brought more pain, and right now, Fourcade needed comforting.

The house was dimly lit by the day's waning sunlight as Chantal entered the front room followed by Dragon. Fourcade sat motionless on a sofa, her arms bent at the elbows, her head resting in her hands.

Chantal sat next to her but remained silent. After a few moments, she put an arm over Fourcade's shoulder while Dragon pulled up a chair in front of them.

"I told him not to go," Fourcade murmured after a while, her voice hollow. "He insisted on setting up a Resistance organization inside Germany. The time wasn't right. If the Germans were going to rise up and overthrow Hitler, they'd have already made moves to do it. They're suffering under him too."

She caught herself mid-sob and retreated to silence once more. Dusk turned to night, and the three sat in the dark. Chantal's mind had numbed, at first refusing and then seemingly incapable of thinking. She knew Fourcade's greatest fear, that she might have already lost the love of her life, Léon Faye, the handsome French fighter pilot who had been her chief of staff, and about whom she had sensed a premonition just before his disappearance aboard a night flight from Britain to France.

Other losses over four years of leading Alliance through the war had affected Fourcade deeply. Two that came to Chantal's mind were Maurice Coustenoble, a former air force pilot and intelligence officer who had co-founded Alliance with Fourcade, and who now languished in a German prison; and Henri Schaerrer, a dare-devil naval officer who had come to a sad end. Chantal had never met either of them, but she had heard their names and knew that both had been close confidantes and that Fourcade grieved deeply over their plights.

Georges and Faye struck to the core of Fourcade's heart. Not knowing whether Faye was alive or dead preyed on her mind mercilessly, and now Georges...

"How many more are we to lose?" Fourcade whispered hoarsely into the darkness. "*Mon Dieu*, how many more?"

She stood, walked to the front window, and stared out. An almost full moon rode high in the night sky, illuminating the low hills in a ghostly light toward Verdun. "Our enemy is twelve miles over there," she said in a low voice. "Only weeks ago, they lived among us. They're out of Paris and gone from most of our country." She was quiet again, staring into the night.

Chantal joined her and took her hand. Dragon also rose and stood behind them.

"Neither Léon nor Georges would want us to take time from the war to mourn for them until we have driven *les boches* all the way back to Berlin," Fourcade said, and her voice grew stronger and resolute as she spoke. "Tonight we grieve. Tomorrow we fight. We never give up."

28

October 15, 1944
Roville-aux-Chênes

Amélie and Danièle sat on a wide panel of plywood at the edge of a field of caked mud, enjoying a break in the weather. Dark gray nimbostratus clouds had moved off to the southeast toward the High Vosges, revealing a blue sky.

A French soldier, Marc, approached, bearing a beat-up tin tray with chipped crockery. "Tea, m'ladies?" He bowed slightly at the waist, and with mock-dignity, he handed down cups and poured the dark liquid from a pitcher that matched the dishes in style and pattern as well as in its worn state.

Another soldier, Roland, stood behind Marc, and when the first had finished, he stepped forward. "Biscuits, *mademoiselles*, the finest from Paris." He too bowed at the waist and bore a similar expression as he offered C-ration crackers.

"*Merci beaucoup*," the two women said in unison with exaggerated politeness while feigning tittering as the men sat on the plywood opposite them.

"Finally, a dry day," Amélie said, and took a sip of tea.

"I wonder how long it will last," Marc mused. He gestured at the clouds trailing to the southeast toward the High Vosges and already floating over its distant foothills. "I pity anyone fighting in those mountains. As if those bastards weren't miserable enough, those clouds will pour freezing rain on them."

Roland agreed. "I wonder how much longer we'll be sitting here. It's been three weeks since we crossed the Moselle. Rumors are flying that Leclerc is clawing at higher command to turn us loose."

"I'm ready," Marc said. "Strasbourg is only sixty miles away. I can feel it." He closed his eyes and let his head drop back. "It's been a long trek from Chad."

"Through Paris, can you believe it?" Roland exclaimed. "We could be in Strasbourg within two hours if *les boches* would just get out of the way."

"Or surrender, but that won't happen while that crazy Nazi is alive."

"I think the delay is still a matter of logistics," Amélie broke in. "The American general, Patton, and Leclerc are like two drops of water, just alike, at least militarily." She leaned back on her arms and enjoyed the cool breeze on her face.

Squealing brakes caused her to sit upright and look across the street where a jeep came to a very rapid halt. Her companions followed suit.

A British officer with lieutenant colonel's pips on the shoulders of his battledress emerged from the vehicle, his beret partially obscuring the side of his face. He strode into a parking area of combat vehicles and engaged in conversation with soldiers, several of whom gathered around him.

As Amélie's group watched in curiosity, the soldiers pointed their way, and the officer trotted across the muddy street. When he saw Amélie, he stopped and stared. His dirty-blond hair was unmistakable.

"Paul?"

He closed the distance. The two soldiers jumped to their feet. They knew him as the British officer who accompanied Leclerc almost wherever the general went.

Paul stood gazing at them, and Amélie saw in his expression either distress or anger, or both. He greeted the group with a polite nod, and then turned his attention to her. "Hello, Amélie. Might I have a word?"

"Here?"

"No. We can walk."

She chuckled. "Where? Why do you think we're sitting on a piece of plywood in a muddy field?"

Paul gazed around. They were indeed at the edge of a mud field that during better times probably nourished corn or wheat crops. A narrow strip of higher ground formed the base for a four-strand barbed-wire fence that ran between the meadow and the road, which was itself a long bed of caked and drying mud. On the other side of the lane, as far as he could see before curves blocked his view, were bivouac and parking areas where soldiers grouped, visiting or working on weapons or vehicles, or involved in training or other work.

Paul let out a spontaneous laugh. "We can visit inside the jeep, then."

"Sir, we can leave and you can stay here," Roland offered.

Paul shook his head. "Thank you. I wouldn't want to spoil your afternoon."

Minutes later, when he and Amélie were in the jeep, Paul said, "I apologize. I thought I might be interrupting—"

Amélie put her hand to her mouth and laughed spontaneously. "A rendezvous? What the Americans call 'a date?' Look at me, Paul. I'm wearing battledress and combat boots. My face is creased from stress, and my hair... don't even talk about it. Do you think any soldier—"

"You don't know soldiers."

"That's not fair, Paul. I do know soldiers. I'm sitting next to one, and if you'll recall, I'm engaged to be married to one. Your brother."

She spoke with conviction. "Let me tell you about these soldiers. They're aggressive in combat. They've taken high casualties on their way to Strasbourg. You've seen it, standing next to Leclerc. But off the battlefield, they are the sweetest men, and what they want most is to win this war, free their country, go home to their wives and families, and live out their lives in peace.

"They protect the Rochambelles, and we take care of them when they're wounded. They're our friends, our brothers. We laugh together, and we cry together." She sniffed and her face tightened. "We've lost so many people we love. Letting our regard devolve into something it shouldn't would destroy friendships. We all know that."

She took a deep breath. "Those two soldiers you met just now, Marc and Roland, are on the tank crew that goes ahead of us. Our ambulances drive near the front of the convoys so that we can get to casualties quickly. That crew always insists on its position ahead of us to shield us."

Amélie suddenly stopped talking and leaned away to observe Paul. "Did you come to check up on me? Is that why you came to find me?"

Paul shook his head with a sad expression. "No." He sat quietly while Amélie waited. "You're the closest thing to family I have out here."

Perceiving turmoil below his controlled expression, Amélie took his hands in both of hers and kissed them. "Of course we're family. What is it, Paul?"

Moments passed before he could answer. "It's Lance," he said dolefully. "He's been missing in action for a month. I just learned of it."

Involuntarily, Amélie sucked in her breath. "I'm so sorry. Did you hear it from the Red Cross?"

He shook his head. "No. I got a letter from Claire. It took a while to get to me. The Red Cross had received no notification about Lance. All I've been able to find out through SOE sources is that he was last seen in an operation called Market Garden in the Netherlands. I've heard of it, but I've been too busy on this side of France to pay it much attention. I gather it was a fiasco. Many captured, killed, wounded, and many missing, and the main objective was not met."

She continued holding his hand, and they sat in silence for a time. Then Paul asked, "What about you? How are you getting along?"

Amélie let go of Paul's hand and sat facing straight ahead. "Me? I haven't given that much thought. I can tell you that I think of Jeremy every waking minute, and I dream about him at night. We don't really know where he is either. Is he even in France? I don't know."

"You haven't heard from him?"

"No, but under the circumstances, that's to be expected. This war wears on everyone. I joined the Rochambelles to get to Berlin and find Jeannie Rousseau. I'm as dedicated to that as I've ever been. I worry that she'll die in that prison before I find her.

"My job along the way is to drive and fix ambulances, getting dirty and greasy and giving first aid to soldiers at a moment's notice, stopping their bleeding, and treating their wounds without introducing infection. Even enemy troops. And do it under fire from both directions. It's nerve-wracking and heart-wrenching, but when I've saved a life or given comfort, I feel good. I'm doing something worthwhile."

She stopped to contemplate. "Every day, I'm with the bravest of the brave women and men. They're my friends, my comrades. We rely on each other. When we're bivouacked, we, this gaggle of nurses and ambulance drivers, entertain the soldiers, and they entertain us." She turned to him with a firm look. "You must know that we also enjoy General Leclerc's protection."

Paul nodded. "Of course."

"With or without him, God help any man who seeks to abuse us. Our brothers will take them apart, limb from limb." Amélie suddenly chuckled. "Have you ever heard of Toto's rules?"

Paul pursed his lips. "No. I'm clueless on the subject."

Amélie started by explaining the proscription against exclusive tooth-brush ownership by any particular Rochambelle and the absolute need to stay at least twenty feet away from some officers for fear of being burned when they self-combust from alcohol. She also mentioned an admonition that helmets are reserved for foot baths, that no one should lose more than one kit of clothing per week, and an inviolable decree that no one must ever borrow and sleep in Toto's bedroll while wearing boots.

Paul chuckled with increasing amusement, but when Amélie told him the rule of receiving no male visitor wearing less than army-issued long underwear, his face turned red, he lost his breath, and he bent over the jeep's steering wheel, shaking with laughter.

When he had recovered, he gazed through the windshield at nothing. A motorcycle roared by along with other military traffic, but neither he nor Amélie paid it any mind. "Ahh, thank you for that. I feel better."

Amélie smiled. "I appreciate that you were concerned about me on behalf of Jeremy. I saw it on your face when you walked up, and why shouldn't you worry? But keep this in mind: I love Jeremy with all my heart. I will never jeopardize that, irrespective of Leclerc's protection and that of our brothers, the soldiers." She grinned. "And if all that fails, we still have Toto's rule about long underwear."

Paul burst into another fit of laughter. When he recovered, he said, "Jeremy is a very lucky man to have you. We don't know where he is, but for the moment, no news is good news, am I right?"

"That's what I believe," Amélie replied. "As for Lance, from what Jeremy and Claire told me, he's probably somewhere scheming how he's going to get home."

"I hope you're right." Paul grabbed the handle on the jeep's door. "I should let you get back to enjoying this weather with your friends."

Amélie unlatched her own door, pushed it open, and stepped out. Then her eyes opened wide in astonishment as a grinning Chantal stood in front of her.

"What a surprise!" Amélie wrapped her sister in a welcoming embrace. "How did you find me? How did you get here?"

"Finding you wasn't difficult," Chantal replied. "Everyone in the country knows where General Leclerc has been and where he intends to go. Strasbourg. I just followed his path, and when I got close, I asked for the Rochambelles. I found your bivouac area, and someone named Toto sent me across the street to your friends, who told me you were in this jeep."

"So much for security," Paul said, coming around the front of the jeep.

Chantal chuckled. "I was trained to breach it. Hello, Paul."

"Welcome, Chantal," Paul enthused. "The last time I saw you was on Paris' liberation day. It's so good to see you." He opened his arms and embraced her.

"How did you get here?" Amélie persisted.

"On that." Chantal pointed to a motorcycle parked on the roadside.

Amélie stared with concern. "My sister," she murmured. "Whatever happened to that scared little girl I once mothered in Dunkirk?"

Chantal took a deep breath and let it out while glancing around at myriad soldiers, many of them scraping mud from endless numbers of combat vehicles or clambering under open engine hoods with screwdrivers and wrenches. Others cleaned weapons, or worked flat on their backs under tanks and trucks, changing oil.

Chantal returned her gaze to Amélie and responded distantly, "The war."

"Bring me up to date," Amélie said after the surprise had dissipated and normal greetings had passed. Paul had returned to headquarters, and the sisters now sat together on the plywood panel at the edge of the mud field. After enthusiastic introductions to Chantal, the trio of friends, Danièle, Marc, and Roland, had slipped away, allowing the sisters time to converse privately. "How's Madame Fourcade?"

Chantal told the sad news of Georges Lamarque. Amélie took it stoically, staring into the distance. "He was my contact with the rest of the Resistance in Paris," she said quietly, "my connection to reality and hope. He was a wonderful friend and a great patriot. I will miss him." She shuddered involuntarily and murmured, "So much grief."

They remained quiet for a spell, and then Chantal said, "Madame's biggest fear is that Léon Faye is dead. She doesn't say so, but I know her."

"Nothing's been heard of him?"

"Nothing at all."

Amélie sighed. "Where is Madame now, and what's she doing?"

"She has her headquarters near Verdun. I just came from there. She moved to there after the battle at Arracourt. We're heavily involved in supplying local intelligence to General Patton's headquarters. I'm working with Dragon again. He's with Madame Fourcade now. Hence the motorcycle." She smiled impishly. "I'm riding dispatch."

Amélie turned to give Chantal a faint smile and exhaled deeply. "I suppose there's no stopping you."

"It's different now," Chantal said, "and not nearly as dangerous. I'm behind our own lines and don't have to worry about the *Gestapo* or the *gendarmes* or informers—"

"But you're on that bike," Amélie said reprovingly.

Chantal burst out laughing. "You sound just like Fourcade, and I have two mothers to answer to." She reached out and rubbed her sister's shoulder. "You've both looked out for me. I'll never forget."

They lapsed into silence again, and then Chantal said, "You asked what Fourcade is up to now. I think her days of running a Resistance organization are waning. She hasn't said so. She keeps up her Alliance network, and she'll be wherever she's needed, but she's turned her attention to finding lost agents and tending to the welfare of their families. And of course, despite her fears, she's always searching for news of Léon Faye. I take my direction now from Dragon, and General Patton has been so pleased with his results that he turns to him regularly."

"Have you met Patton?"

"No. I'd like to, but the occasion hasn't come up. I'm usually taking messages between Resistance organizations to the intelligence sections of his subordinate commanders. It's been helpful during the battle in the Argonne Forest, which right now seems never-ending."

Amélie gazed at Chantal for an extended time in silence. Then she grasped her hand. "Be careful, little sister. The war is not nearly done. I think the worst of it might still be ahead of us. But we're winning. I wouldn't want to lose you in the final months."

She took a deep breath. "Enough melancholy. Tell me about Horton."

Chantal's expression dropped. "I've got nothing to tell. I don't know where he is."

"Fourcade can't find out?"

"Things got so confused after an operation in the Netherlands—Market Garden, I think. His unit moved up into Belgium and the Netherlands, and the SOE people she works with in London don't have connections up there. All I know is that Horton was with the Sherwood Rangers, and they went in up there." She laughed quietly. "I should tell you, though, that I told him in a letter that I'd accept his marriage proposal."

Amélie's eyes widened in excitement. "Chantal, that's wonderful. You two were made for each other."

Chantal shook her head in mock exasperation. "It took me long enough to convince him of that."

"Well now, you couldn't expect an eighteen-year-old combat soldier to get excited about a fourteen-year-old girl. Not one with any sense of—"

"Don't be condescending," Chantal retorted, grinning. Then her face turned serious. "It's funny. I love him every bit as much now as I ever did, and I think of him all the time, but—"

Amélie looked at her curiously. "But?"

"I'm worried," Chantal said. "About myself. I wonder if I'm getting callous. Horton used to live in my brain all day, all night. Missing him was sometimes a physical pain. I learned to push him out of my mind so I could work effectively, but I think I've developed that skill too well."

Amélie chuckled. "It's all right, little sister. It's called maturity. Tell me, where are you off to now?"

"More dispatches for Patton's headquarters. It's located nearby. I'm carrying Resistance reports about an area west of a town called Geilenkirchen, just inside the German border and right on the Siegfried." Her eyes suddenly sparkled mischievously. "Tell me about Jeremy."

Amélie shrugged and her expression fell. "I know as much about him as you do about Horton," she said with a forlorn note. "I hope he's still alive and healthy."

Chantal jumped to her feet. "Look, there's a rumor that the mail between Paris and London will start up soon. Write a letter to Jeremy. I'll call and ask Fourcade to tell me who at SOE in Paris can get it in the right channels. I can drop it in the mail at headquarters. I'll do the same for a letter to Horton. It's worth a try."

Chantal's face broke into a wide smile. "You're brilliant, little sister."

"Do it now," Chantal urged. "I have to get on the road." She displayed a sly smile. "I get a lot of independence in this job, and on whatever day that the impatient lion flies that flag in Strasbourg, I intend to be there."

29

October 18, 1944
Hollandia, New Guinea

While flying his Hellcat across the shoreline of Humboldt Bay's azure waters, Lieutenant Commander Josh Littlefield sucked in his breath at the magnificence of the island's verdant undulating hills before him. Cyclops Mountain stretched along the northern coast, providing a buffer against the extremes of Pacific storms. As he reached the landward side of the crest, he marveled at a sparkling waterfall plunging a thousand feet onto boulders below, creating a brilliant rainbow spray.

Looking farther to the southeast, he was astounded to see a sprawling patchwork of olive drab and gray tents and buildings, and around them, remaining scars on fresh terrain caused by hurried construction. New roads snaked through the jungle to connect a burgeoning military presence.

Josh banked left and descended for final approach into Sentani Airfield.

Knowing where to look, he located Engineer Hill. Atop it, a white building stood in sharp contrast to the deep green of the surrounding jungle. There was his destination, the headquarters of Supreme Commander, Southwest Pacific Area, General Douglas MacArthur.

He returned his eyes to his glide path, and as the hill rose above him on his left, he completed his descent onto the runway on the valley floor and taxied to the parking area. Being a major transportation hub, aircraft of all sorts were parked about, including transport planes, light and heavy bombers, and fighters belonging to the US Army Air Corps, Navy, and Marines.

An Army corporal met Josh at the flight line. "I've got a jeep waiting, sir. Admiral Halsey sent me down. The conference starts in an hour." The soldier snickered. "He said to tell you that, 'You'd better have your ass in the seat before Pinky walks in.'"

Josh chuckled. "Pinky" was a term of endearment bestowed on the child who later became the legendary General MacArthur. The moniker was picked up by the troops who loved him, and it was used disparagingly by those who did not. "Dugout Doug" was another appellation for MacArthur, stemming from his custom, in the early days of the war, of commanding campaigns from the confines and safety of a bunker. Admirers attributed the habit to strategic thinking. Detractors drew other conclusions.

In Halsey's case, Josh knew that the admiral and the general were great friends. Their fathers had served together in the Philippines many years earlier and had enjoyed a close friendship. Josh had heard Halsey remark that he had felt a kinship within five minutes of first meeting MacArthur last year at Brisbane, Australia.

Halsey had also been a mentor to Josh since immediately after Pearl Harbor. The cantankerous admiral was a legend in his own right among the American public. With bulldog tenacity that earned him his nickname, "Bull" had taken his carriers and fighter planes to battle the Japanese in the Solomon islands immediately after the infamous raid. Tall, lean, and known for his large head, he was beloved among his men despite his aggressive and sometimes explosive temperament.

Josh had been one of his pilots then and had since served in the operations room, run his intelligence analysis center, and gone back to flying. During that time, Halsey had sent Josh out on various special assignments, and recently, he had appointed Josh to command one of his squadrons.

Josh had never seen General MacArthur in person. Most of what Josh knew of him came from news reports and common gossip. He knew of the heroics in WWI after which MacArthur was awarded seven Silver Stars and two *Croix de Guerres* for actions at the Battle of Saint-Mihiel and during the Meuse-Argonne Offensive. The citations particularly mentioned courage and tactical acumen.

Long before US entry into WWI, while still a major, MacArthur had conceived and sold the secretary of war on the notion of a new organization. His idea materialized into the 42nd "Rainbow" Infantry Division, composed of national guard units from across twenty-six states that could be formed and deployed rapidly while avoiding concerns over favoritism between states. Despite his junior rank, he became its chief of staff, and the division was heralded for its performance in Europe.

Beginning in 1936, MacArthur served as the military advisor to the Commonwealth of the Philippines, and it was his commitment to defending the islands in the early days of the current conflict that raised his stature—lauded by some, hated by others. Then as events developed in the Pacific, he influenced military thinking significantly, developing the concept of "triphibious warfare," the strategy of bypassing heavily fortified enemy positions, as happened with great effectiveness at Rabaul, Halmahera, Wewak, Hansa Bay, and other strongholds. Doing so isolated Japanese forces on those islands and left them to fend for themselves. Great savings in American lives and resources had resulted.

"I guess we'd better get going, Corporal," Josh said with a grin. "We don't want to keep Pinky waiting."

"Don't worry on that score, sir. The general doesn't wait for anyone."

Before getting into the jeep, Josh took a moment to glance around. At the southeast end of the runway was Lake Sentani, for which the airfield was named. To the southwest, the ground was flat with a few rises, and to the northwest, low hills sloped down to the lake. To the northeast, Engineer Hill rose sharply, and behind it loomed Cyclops Mountain.

An overriding feature all around was the deep green of the lush landscape punctuated by red, yellow, and orange flowers, and others of myriad colors. Josh took it all in as he mounted the jeep, and the corporal drove away. The drive from the airfield to the crest of Engineer Hill surrounded him with the atmosphere of a paradise, with brightly colored birds flitting through tall palm trees, their musical calls breaking through thick foliage. Occasional kingfishers darted into babbling streams while cicadas raised a raucous racket. Josh imagined that the evening breeze must bring with it wonderful scents, but right now, this close to airfield operations, the pungent smell of fuel pervaded.

As they left, Josh noticed a transport plane disgorging a gaggle of bedraggled Marines. "What's going on there?"

"They're probably here for R&R," the corporal replied. "They come from the front lines, and I can tell you, they usually look frazzled."

"And they deserve to rest and recuperate," Josh remarked. Fresh in his mind was an image from three days ago when he had flown over Peleliu. He recalled the Marine he had seen trying to make his way out of an artillery crater while lugging long mortar legs on his back. That man had been headed into gunfire despite his load and the deadly fusillade targeting him. *I wonder how he is now.* Josh sighed. *Maybe dead.*

Corrugated metal and wooden shacks appeared along the road as they headed across the upward sloping ground toward Engineer Hill. In some places, the huts had grouped into shantytowns. Children played in the dirt road while women cooked on open fires. Obviously, these were families drawn by the US military presence, hoping for lives better than they had known in the recent past under Japanese occupation.

The road suddenly turned steeply uphill, bringing into sharp relief the valley below and Cyclops Mountain behind Engineer Hill. Through a thin mist, Lake Sentani glimmered in the distance. Josh then understood why MacArthur's headquarters was sometimes called a "million-dollar mansion." The view was uplifting and worth far more.

They reached the crest where the dreamy feel of illusion dropped away, replaced by a sense of organization. The purposeful white building he had seen from the air was surrounded by well-ordered outbuildings and paved areas with military vehicles parked in neat rows.

After dismounting and before entering the headquarters, Josh ambled to a lookout point. A slight wind blew past his ear. Far below, and farther out than he would have imagined, Sentani Field abutted the lake. *What a peaceful place to plan more war.*

From this vantage and with his knowledge of Pacific geography, the strategic advantages that MacArthur sought became clear. Hollandia, in the far distance, on New Guinea's north coast, was a strategic staging point for operations in the Philippines and the Dutch East Indies. From there, Southwest Pacific Command controlled maritime routes crucial to advancing into enemy territory. With a deep natural harbor, the port provided the only anchorage between Wewak and Geelvink Bay, making it ideal for launching amphibious assaults against Japanese positions in the theater.

Further, Japanese forces had built several airfields on the flat ground around Hollandia that, having been captured, positioned the Allies for increased air superiority, essential for ground support and supply-line security. Additionally, the airfields provided forward basing for strikes deeper into Japanese shipping lanes and strongholds.

Seeing the physical layout of the island and envisioning the strategic advantages it offered, Josh had to admire the forethought of leadership and the tenacity of the fighting men that brought it about. Although not having been a direct participant in this theater, Josh knew the sacrifices that had resulted. With MacArthur in mind, he muttered, "You've done well, General."

The corporal interrupted his musings. "Sir, the conference? If you're late, I don't need Bull Halsey blaming me."

Josh grinned. "Lead on."

Most of the participants were in their seats when Jeremy entered. Except for MacArthur himself, the major commanders, including Halsey, already sat at the main table with the staff seated around the room. The admiral made eye contact with Josh and nodded without expression. Josh found a seat behind him among other officers of Halsey's staff. From the chatter, Josh surmised that the purpose of the conference was to hear MacArthur's plans for invading and liberating the Philippine island of Leyte.

His summons to attend this briefing had arrived as a surprise early that morning. It came as a handwritten note delivered by a runner before dawn. The message merely directed, "Attend Pinky briefing, 13:00 hours, Hollandia. Take good notes. Halsey."

Short on time to get to flight operations, chart a flight plan from the

Essex with fuel stops along the way, pre-flight his Hellcat, and fly seven hundred nautical miles to Hollandia, Josh had rushed to get into the air. He had little concern about encountering enemy aircraft. The front had moved far westward, and he was well behind the lines. Only while cruising at altitude did he have time to look at a map and discern Hollandia's topography and strategic position among the Pacific Island nations.

This would be Josh's first encounter with MacArthur, albeit as a junior attendee on Halsey's orders. Technically, he was not on Halsey's staff, but his previous stints in working directly for the admiral had earned Josh the crusty commander of the 3rd Fleet's trust as a pilot, squadron leader, and operations planner and supervisor. *What does Halsey have in mind for me this time?*

Previously, the admiral had sent him to observe the experimental takeoff of two B-25 bombers from an aircraft carrier, the *Hornet*, to determine the viability of a concept that became the Doolittle bombing raid over Tokyo. Then Josh had been sent to Guadalcanal as an air liaison officer and found himself in the then bloodiest ground battle to date, at Edson's Ridge. Then, on the basis of having amphibious landing experience, and at Eisenhower's request for a flier with such background, Halsey sent him to North Africa where he found himself briefing a French general during negotiations to flip the Vichy French army from Germany to the Allies.

The best part of the latter excursion was that Josh had been pleasantly surprised to find his British cousin, Paul Littlefield, there for the same mission. They had been able to visit and develop a familial relationship, and fortunately, Paul had been nearby to offer support when Josh received word of his own mother's passing. That had been two years ago, and on the same day, the cousins had been ordered on assignments that took them to opposite sides of the planet, and communications between them were relegated to wartime mail service. *I wonder where Paul is now. For that matter, where are Zack and Sherry?*

30

MacArthur's aide stepped inside the conference room. An expectant hush fell over the gathering. The officer called for attention, and everyone dutifully scraped chairs while scrambling to stand straight.

MacArthur entered, his famous corncob pipe protruding from his mouth, a distinctive man, even at age sixty-four. His six-foot frame bent slightly despite his apparent intent to carry himself upright, and his close-cropped, smoothly combed hair and Roman nose lent to his chiseled stone-like visage. As he made his way to the main table, his eyes, narrowed by age, scrutinized the assembly.

He carried the aura of a man with unfailing confidence in his own destiny. Rumors circulated that the supreme commander was related to both President Roosevelt and Prime Minister Churchill by way of a great-great-grandmother common to all three men, but Josh had no way of knowing the veracity of the notion.

Josh *did* know each of the subordinate flag officers by sight and surmised their command relationship to MacArthur. Halsey was there to support MacArthur's planned operations as a matter of cooperation. His direct boss, Admiral Nimitz, had been briefed on the plan at Pearl Harbor four months earlier. He had agreed to a command scheme wherein Halsey maintained independence for his 3rd US Fleet but accepted MacArthur's directives on a cooperative basis. Fortunately, Halsey and MacArthur's fast-formed friendship allowed the unorthodox command structure to work effectively, at least so far.

Also at today's command table were Vice Admiral Thomas Kinkaid of the US 7th Fleet, Lieutenant General Walter Krueger of the US 6th Army, Lieutenant General Franklin Sibert of the US X Army Corps, and Lieutenant General John Hodge of US XIV Corps. MacArthur took his place at the center of the table and remained standing, scanning his audience.

"Take your seats, gentlemen," he said. Amid more scraping chairs, he nodded to his aide, who flipped off the lights and turned on a projector. A map of the Southwest Pacific Area appeared on a screen at the front of the room.

MacArthur waited solemnly until everyone was seated and silence had descended. Then he removed his pipe and held it in his hand. "Two years, seven months, and one week ago," he began, "I was forced out of Corregidor by the Japanese invading force. I vowed then that I would return to the Philippines. In two days, I will do just that. Our next target lies at Leyte. It will be the door that opens the Philippines and everything beyond."

He let a moment elapse as he continued to gaze over his audience. "We're here to lay out the plan to seize that objective. Accomplishing that, we will be in good position to bypass Mindanao for the time being, and hopscotch on to Luzon and Okinawa on the way to the Japanese homeland."

Josh listened carefully for mention of the vicious battle just fought at Peleliu. MacArthur continued, describing the enemy situation.

"We know from decoded intercepts that the Japanese expect us to attack in the Philippines. If they did not think so before, our capture of Palau last month probably removed any doubt, but they're not sure where we'll strike. Their overall plan, as we have deduced it, is to converge all land and sea forces to counterattack in a massive knockout punch. Essentially, a grand *banzai*."

On cue, the aide changed slides to one showing the long chain of island nations east of China, and the general continued. "These landmasses protect the home island and its supplies of oil and other materials." He traced the area with his pointer. "They include the islets north of Japan's mainland, Honshu, and the Dutch East Indies. It had included Formosa, but for reasons that I'll mention momentarily, we just took it out of this plan.

"I should note here that they threw a lot more air power at us than we expected at Formosa, probably around eighteen hundred aircraft, and we know they have a huge pilot training program."

He pointed to the southern islands. "The southwestern area is crucial to them, starting at Singapore, running south of and including Borneo and the southern Dutch East Indies, and up north of the Philippines. That's the area where they get the bulk of their raw materials, especially fuel, and that's what we must cut off."

The general paused to look at his notes, and then went on. "Their Southern Force Fleet is stationed to protect those islands. Meanwhile, their Center Force, which includes their super-battleships *Yamato* and *Musashi*, are believed also to be southwest of us and able to threaten us."

He paused to make a point. "Remember, those two ships are the largest ones ever built. They went under construction long before Pearl Harbor but in anticipation of going to war with us. Since Japanese high command did not believe their ship production would be able to keep up with ours, they ordered these two to be fast, far more armed and armored than anything else afloat, and able to deliver and receive punches that would cripple any other warship. Together with their groups, they comprise the bulk of the remaining Japanese naval strength, and that is still a formidable force.

"We cannot afford to underestimate these ships. Each is nearly nine hundred feet long, a hundred and seventy-two feet wide, and weigh seventy-two thousand tons. They both carry a battery of nine 18 In. guns, the largest ever used in combat, and more anti-aircraft guns than you can imagine. We will have to deal with them."

A pall settled over the room. MacArthur gazed around stone-faced. "The good news is," he went on, "their radar is inferior, and Japanese fighter pilots and aircraft have been severely depleted, which is why they have such a robust training program."

Amid a stirring of comments among his audience, MacArthur raised his palms to compel silence. "Our best guess is that they intend to deliver their knockout punch when we land our invasion force. They are a wounded tiger. They will fight tenaciously."

The general placed the stem of his corncob pipe in his mouth. He struck a match, held it to the bowl, and drew in air until the tobacco glowed and its scent wafted across the room. "So now," he resumed, "let's talk about our own situation."

Once again, the general nodded to his aide, who changed the slide to project a map of New Guinea on the screen. "We've pushed the Japanese further into the western Pacific and destroyed most of their navy. Vice-Admiral Mitscher neutralized Japanese forces on Formosa two days ago. We didn't occupy the island, but we depleted its forces to the extent that they are effectively out of the equation, including the air power that had been based there. So, our right flank is mainly secured. I say 'mainly' because those two battleship groups still threaten us."

Josh leaned in, expecting mention of Peleliu and its role in securing the same flank. None came.

MacArthur continued. "We're here," he said, indicating Hollandia near the midpoint along New Guinea's northern coast, "and we have now secured this shoreline from one end to the other. That positions us well to launch into the Philippines. And that is what we are going to do."

The aide changed slides again, this time showing the far-flung Philippine chain stretching for eleven hundred miles. "To completely secure the islands, we are going to have to take Mindanao to the south and then Luzon in the north, but we are going to start right here at Leyte Gulf." He snapped the pointer at the location on the map. "And when we have completed the Philippine campaign, we will have severed Japan's oil supply line. After that, they will be operating almost entirely on reserves."

While he spoke, Josh noted MacArthur's very precise articulation and voice modulation. The general had seldom resorted to contractions in his speech.

MacArthur nodded to his aide again, who complied with the unspoken order, and a closer map of Leyte appeared on the screen. The general moved the pointer over the map as he continued. "Admiral Halsey's pilots flew multiple missions over the Philippines during the summer and found

Japanese defenses to be weak. His perception is that the Japanese fighting spirit is at a low ebb." He directed his attention to Halsey. "Is that accurate, Bull?"

Glancing at Halsey, Josh recalled that ahead of the battles at Guadalcanal, Tarawa, and Peleliu, similar assessments had been made. The opposite proved to be the case, and despite the victories, the results were tragic in terms of casualties.

Halsey nodded in response to MacArthur's query. The general continued, "Leyte would give us several advantages. As you can see, we would be protected by landmass, to a degree, against sea attack from the north and south. But the gulf has some deep-water approaches and sandy beaches favorable to an amphibious assault, and in the absence of a strong Japanese naval presence, as is the case now, an opportunity exists to seize the Leyte Gulf.

"The Battle of Leyte has already begun. Yesterday, our minesweepers began clearing the gulf. Meanwhile, our underwater demolitions teams have been reconnoitering sites suitable for amphibious landings. By 08:00 hours this morning, the 6th Rangers had secured two small islands in the bay, Suluan and Dinagat, and I've received word that they are encountering no resistance on Homonhon. The Rangers set up aiming lights to guide the ships bringing in our ground forces.

"Of course, that all means we have confirmed the enemies' suspicions about our intentions. They are preparing countermoves, I am sure, but their fleets are still too far off. This morning, our Admiral Kinkaid's 7th Fleet's big guns started pummeling Japanese installations on Leyte itself, which, being so lightly defended, justifies confidence that our initial landing there in two days will be against light opposition."

That last piece of information about light opposition caught Josh by surprise. He leaned forward to listen intently.

"Once ashore, our infantry and armor can maneuver along Highway 1 and its adjoining roads," the general went on. "It runs north-south along the coast between Abuyog and the San Juanico Strait that separates Leyte from the Samar Islands. We will have lots of flat ground there to build airfields and use them to strike anywhere in the archipelago."

MacArthur glanced out a window, his eyes scrutinizing the clouds.

"This late in the year, we are likely to encounter monsoons..." He went on to describe the likely effects of weather and Leyte's topography that favored his operations.

Josh listened absently with a growing sense of dismay regarding Peleliu. It had been billed as a crucial element in defending MacArthur's right flank, and it had been won at great cost in Marines' lives, but so far, it had received no mention as a supporting element of the overall plan.

MacArthur continued describing the terrain features, relating them to their military considerations. He pointed out a tall mountain range running north and south. Cloaked in heavy forest, it divided the island into Leyte Valley in the east and Ormoc Valley in the west. Highway 2 wound through the mountains, connecting the valleys, and eventually intersected Highway 1. Together, the two valleys and the mountain range occupied the northern two-thirds of Leyte.

"Most of the population, roughly nine-hundred thousand people, lives in that area," the general said, "and when we secure those main routes, we will dominate the northern part of the island." He tossed his head and frowned. "The same cannot be said for the southern third. It is sparsely populated and largely undeveloped."

He described mountain peaks rising to over four thousand feet. Their steep slopes were marked with rocky outcroppings and cut through with deep ravines. Volcanic caves offered formidable defensive positions and seemed not to be used in great profusion by Japanese forces. However, they prevented a Japanese southern assault.

"Leyte's people are magnificent," MacArthur concluded. "Despite tortures and executions, they've conducted guerrilla warfare against Lieutenant General Shiro Makino and his twenty thousand troops of the Japanese 16th Division. Our operation will give the islanders a huge boost, and we can count on their support."

He looked at his watch. "We will take a break in a minute, after which my staff will brief on details, but I will close by telling you that our invading force includes over eight hundred ships, over fifteen hundred aircraft, and over two hundred thousand men."

He paused to let the numbers sink in before concluding. "While the invasion is taking place, our long-range bombers based in China, Saipan, and New Guinea will hit the Japanese oil fields, troop concentrations, and airfields in the target areas. I do not believe there has ever been a larger armada of men and equipment."

MacArthur took a deep breath. "Before I close, I should note that we believe Japan is changing its strategy. Always before, its main targets have been our capital ships. Now, we think they will be seeking to destroy our invasion force. They want to kill as many of our soldiers and Marines as possible before they can get to Tokyo."

The general turned the conference over to his chief of staff, who laid out the rest of the agenda and adjourned for a break. Meanwhile, Halsey turned around in his chair, made deliberate eye contact with Josh, and nodded slightly. Josh read the gesture to mean that the admiral wished to speak with him during the recess.

When Josh complied, Halsey merely said, "Follow me," and led him across the room, out the door, down a hall, and up two flights of stairs.

"Sir, do you mind my asking why I'm here? I received no instruction in that regard. What should I be paying most attention to."

"You'll see," came the brusque reply. "We don't have much time."

31

On the top floor of MacArthur's headquarters, Halsey and Josh emerged into a foyer. They crossed in front of an orderly sitting at a desk who made no move to impede them as the admiral led Josh to a door and entered without knocking. Bewildered, Josh followed him into a large, wide office.

General MacArthur stood across the room with his back to them, looking out over Hollandia, Lake Sentani, the airfield, and the green, low hills in the distance. He turned as Josh and Halsey entered.

Josh restrained himself from gaping.

"Sir, this is the officer I mentioned earlier," Halsey said.

MacArthur regarded Josh coolly. "So, you're the pilot who liaised with Doolittle for the Tokyo raid?"

"I followed orders, sir," Josh managed. "That was my honor."

"And you were with Mark Clark when he flipped the Vichy in North Africa?"

"Admiral Halsey sent me."

"Edson's Ridge?"

"Couldn't be helped, sir. I happened to be there at the time."

MacArthur let out a rare chuckle. "Do you ever take credit for anything?"

"It's a family weakness, sir. I'll try to do better."

MacArthur laughed spontaneously. "What about Truk?"

"He was insubordinate regarding that one, sir," Halsey growled. "I let it slide because he developed the plan and led the raid, and it worked. He had figured out that the Japanese radar was inadequate."

"All right, Bull, I'll let you explain to him what's going on."

"I lost an air group commander yesterday," Halsey told Josh flatly. "I need an immediate replacement for this Leyte campaign. You're it. Nimitz approved, and I've asked the supreme commander to do the honors."

Disbelieving, Josh inhaled sharply. His mind spun as he struggled to respond. "Sir, you're talking about leading several squadrons into battle. I'm not ready—"

"You're as ready as any officer in my command," Halsey retorted. "Hell, you've been in ground combat, air combat, you've been shot down, you've worked in ops, intelligence, you've led squadrons—"

"We're running out of time," MacArthur said impatiently while glancing at his watch. "Lieutenant Commander, either dispense with the modesty and accept the assignment or decline it now."

Halsey regarded Josh expectantly.

Josh took a deep breath and let it out. "All right, sir, I'll do it."

"Stand at attention," MacArthur ordered. As Josh complied, the general reached into his desk drawer and removed two silver oak leaf clusters, the insignia of rank for a US Navy commander. "We don't have time for formality, but I'll pin these on your collar to make it official." While he did so, he asked, "Do you have anything to say?"

Josh spoke without taking time to think. "One question, sir, about Peleliu."

MacArthur stepped back and eyed him with his renowned cool stare. "Go ahead."

"Why did we do it?"

Behind Josh, Halsey coughed. "Sir, I—"

MacArthur raised a hand. "It's all right, Bull. It's a fair question." He returned his attention to Josh. "Continue."

"Sir, going into that operation, we were told that Peleliu was crucial to securing your right flank. I was in that battle three days ago. I saw the carnage. We won, but—"

Josh quelled his rising anger, and continued. "I studied the map on the flight down here. I know the distances. Now it seems that we didn't need that battle, that those men died in vain. We could have bypassed that island as we have so many others, per your triphibious warfare strategy."

MacArthur gazed at Josh wordlessly for several moments. Then he sighed. "You're right," he said, "but we didn't know that when the decisions had to be made. Formosa had not yet been neutralized."

He ambled over to gaze out the window and half-turned to add over his shoulder, "If it helps, Peleliu will not be my only regret. I can assure you of that. I read the casualty reports, and not just so I know our strength. I feel every loss. Is there anything else?"

A sense of having overstepped bounds gripped Josh. "No, sir."

"Congratulations on your promotion, Commander. I know you'll rise to the responsibility that comes with it."

Next Day

Josh trudged stiffly out to the flight line with his gear slung over one shoulder. The days of combat and the long flight down to New Guinea wore on his physique. He had slept in a visiting officers' quarters near the flightline.

Long into the night he had wrestled with the dilemma of conscience presented by the battle at Peleliu. Scenes of wrecked machinery, dismembered and bloated bodies, black smoke... They rose palpably in his mind, and now he struggled with the horror of what he had previously suspected, that the battle had been unnecessary.

Josh and Halsey had returned to the meeting in silence, but when the conference ended and before they parted ways, the admiral steered Josh to a quiet corner. "That was a gutsy question you asked up there. Be sure you take to heart the lessons implied in the response." Halsey had thrust his hand forward. "Congratulations, Commander. I personally selected you for your new assignment. I trust that you'll live up to my faith."

As dawn approached, Josh had sat on the edge of his cot. "Someone had to make decisions," he muttered to himself, "and someone had to take responsibility. General MacArthur did both." *Will I—* He shoved the thought away.

After breakfast, which he barely touched, Josh set out across the flight-line. As he approached his Hellcat, a voice called out, "Sir."

Josh turned. A Marine corporal ran up to him and stood at attention. The man's face bore the strange look of prematurely aged youth character-istic of frontline combat veterans. Bright but tired eyes gleamed from sun-darkened skin. His clean uniform hung on a gaunt frame.

"Rest, Corporal," Josh said. "What is it?"

The Marine relaxed and pointed at Josh's aircraft. "Is that your Hellcat?"

"It is. Is something wrong with it?"

"Oh, no sir. I've been checking with every Hellcat pilot I've seen since I arrived yesterday. I flew in for R & R."

Josh acknowledged him with a nod, and took a closer look at the Marine. "I might have seen you. A planeload of Marines landed yesterday shortly after I came in. Where did you fly in from?"

"Peleliu, sir."

Jeremy's heart skipped a beat.

"What's your interest in the Hellcats?"

"Well you see, sir, I was in combat on Peleliu. I'm an assistant mortar gunner."

Josh stared, and then scrutinized the Marine's face. "What's your name?"

"Corporal Sledge, sir. They call me Sledgehammer—"

A spontaneous smile broke across Josh's face. It turned serious again as images flashed through his mind of Peleliu's bloody beach passing below him, of a lone Marine struggling—

"Sledgehammer, did you happen to be crawling up the beach out of a bomb crater with mortar legs on your back?"

Sledge's face broke into a jubilant grin. "Yes, sir! I can't believe I found you. I wanted to say thank you." He thrust his palm forward. "May I shake your hand, sir? I thought I was done for, and then you flew over. I'll never forget your engines roaring so close over my head, your guns blazing. You saved my life."

Overcome, Josh grasped Sledge's hand as his own jaw tightened. Then he threw his free arm around the Marine in a bear hug. "I promise you," he said tightly, "you've done every bit as much for me."

On Josh's return to the *Essex*, he found Commander David McCampbell of Bessemer, Alabama, waiting for him in the ready room. "Congratulations," he said in a heavy Southern twang. "Bull Halsey called. He asked me to meet with you to kinda get your feet firmly planted on a rockin' deck, so to speak." He laughed at his own joke.

When Josh had brought his squadron to the *Essex*, he had fallen under the command of McCampbell's Air Group 15. Several years older than Josh, he was widely known within the navy for being its most skilled and prolific ace to date. He carried himself with a jauntiness and affability that had won the affection as well as the respect of superiors, peers, and subordinates. Josh and his squad members had been pleased to be in his command.

"Thanks," Josh said while shaking McCampbell's hand. "Frankly, I find the notion daunting."

"Of commanding an air group?"

Josh nodded. "That and—" He hesitated.

"Spit it out."

Josh laughed. "The notion of being your peer, your colleague. That's difficult to get my head around. You're the most successful ace in the navy. I haven't been a squadron leader for very long, and people will write songs about you. They'll probably make a movie about your life. And now, I'll be responsible for several squadrons." He took a deep breath. "I'm going from leading four Hellcat drivers to commanding a bunch of Wildcat, Helldiver, and Avenger pilots."

McCampbell chuckled. "I know your record. You'll do fine. Just remember, in most cases, the Hellcats go in first to soften up the target, clear the skies, get the enemy runnin' for cover on their ships, and knock out some gun crews. Then the Helldivers drop down from on high to hit 'em with bombs. An' finally, the Avengers go in low, after everythin' is mayhem, and try to punch torpedo holes in their hulls. That's it, and you already knew all of that."

Josh chuckled. "You know it's not that easy. I've flown all those aircraft types , and there's always a hiccup."

"Ah," McCampbell said with a sly tone in his Southern drawl, "the voice of experience. You might know more than you think. Your job is to minimize the hiccups and know how to recover from them through trainin' and plannin'."

Seeing tired uncertainty in Josh's eyes, McCampbell said, "Look, you and I ain't talked a lot. You had barely arrived when we went into Peleliu, but I can tell you this, Bull Halsey ain't one to mince words, and he wouldn't put you in the position if he didn't think you could handle it. I could give you a few pointers, if you're interested."

Josh blew out a breath of air. "Please do."

"Okay. First, trust your squadron leaders and pilots. They're highly trained, disciplined, and dedicated, and the bad apples are few and far between.

"Next, in combat, treat your squadrons as you would individual planes. You've got your wingmen and competent leaders in each squadron deploying single fighters. They know what they're doin'. That leaves you free to fly your own airplane and coordinate actions and timin' over the battlefield.

"Finally, all of that points to good plannin' and makin' sure each pilot knows the scoop and his individual role before a mission."

McCampbell grinned. "You know every good plan goes out the window when the first shot gets fired. But"—he jabbed a finger in the air—"when that happens, your pilots will know what to do. Trust 'em." He laughed. "One more thing. Pilots are a wild bunch. Sometimes, you gotta be a little crazier than they are."

Josh laughed with him. "I'll try to keep that in mind."

"For me, that comes naturally. *You* might have to practice."

"You might be right," Josh said wryly.

They talked into the night about tactics at air group level. Then McCampbell wished Josh luck, and they went their separate ways. Early this morning, Josh bid farewell to his squadron, took off from the *Essex*, and flew to the *Intrepid* to take command of Carrier Air Group 18.

32

October 24, 1944
Sibuyan Sea, Philippines

Josh could not believe his luck, and he had not yet determined if it was good or bad. For better or worse, he led the first wave attack against the battleship, *Musashi*. It had been spotted by a reconnaissance flight from the *Intrepid* two hours earlier.

Josh's air group of eighteen F4F Wildcat fighters, an equal number of Dauntless "Helldiver" bombers, and nine Avenger torpedo bombers had sortied immediately after the first reconnaissance report was received that identified the battleship. His orders to his pilots had been short and direct. "Wildcats clear the airspace of enemy fighters above the battle area. Helldivers follow, drop your bombs and scoot out. Avengers, hang back until I call that the air is sufficiently clear of enemy aircraft, and then roll in and launch your tubes. Then we hightail back to our mothership to refill and repeat. We've got a two-hour trip each way.

"We're the first wave. Air groups from *Cabot, Essex,* and *Franklin* will follow with Hellcats in their mix to suppress fire."

He had not had time to become well acquainted with any of his pilots. When he landed on the *Intrepid* after leaving the *Essex* two days ago, preparations were underway to provide close air support for the amphibious landing the next day. He had spoken briefly with the ship's captain, gone into immediate briefings with operations, and then met his pilots as he briefed them on his plan of attack.

As MacArthur had predicted, resistance had been light that day, and the general had waded ashore, stone-faced, with a smiling Philippine President Sergio Osmeña. Hours later, Josh listened to the general's radio address. "People of the Philippines," he said in a clear, steady voice, "I have returned. By the grace of Almighty God, our forces stand again on Philippine soil, soil consecrated in the blood of our two peoples." He went on to state that the Philippine seat of government had been reestablished in their own country.

The next two days had been fairly routine, sortieing to provide cover for troops pushing farther inland. Reports had come in informing that part of Japan's Southern Force had entered the Sibuyan Sea northwest of Leyte.

This day had started similarly to the previous two, with preparations for sorties that had come to feel routine. Then, at mid-morning, as Josh's group prepared for another foray, the urgent message from *Intrepid's* recon flight had been received. "The *Musashi* and the *Yamoto* are in the Sibuyan Sea."

Within thirty minutes, Josh's CAG-18 tore across the sky toward the coordinates. The weather was ideal for flying, with a few scattered clouds against light winds varying from southeasterly to northeasterly, and the azure waters sparkled. But for his presence in the aircraft and his group spread out behind him, at the moment, Josh would be hard-pressed to make the case that a war existed at all.

With nearly two hours to fly before reaching the target, he had time to wonder at the sheer scale of the battle shaping up. Between Tokyo and Singapore were more than thirty-three hundred miles, and from there to Leyte were fifteen hundred more. Back to Tokyo was twenty-six hundred. Within that triangle, opposing forces of monumental size were being drawn together, nearly a half million men and untold tons of steel and ammunition, to be expended in a deadly struggle spanning one hundred thousand square miles of air, land, and sea.

Admiral Kinkaid's 7th Fleet alone composed the largest armada ever assembled. Added to Halsey's 3rd Fleet and a special carrier group, the total number of warships amounted to eight hundred and fifty-one, including eight fleet carriers, six battleships, eighty-seven destroyers, and myriad other lethal vessels. They were complemented with a fleet of twenty-two hundred assault aircraft consisting of Wildcats, Hellcats, Helldivers, and Avengers.

Josh could only guess at the size of the Japanese forces. Despite their being severely depleted, its leaders believed them sufficient to deliver a fatal blow to US forces. For the past two days, reports had streamed in of their Southern Force sailing up in two groups between various Philippine islands in a possible attempt at a pincer maneuver at the mouth of the Leyte Gulf. Meanwhile, Halsey's fleet had stationed at the mouth of San Bernardino Strait to protect against Japan's Northern Force, believed to be sailing down from the northwest to engage in the battle.

Just yesterday, Josh had stopped into Ops for an update and found the staff ecstatic. Two US submarines, the *Darter* and *Dace*, had spotted the *Yamato* and its escorts traversing the Palawan Passage on the west side of the Philippines. They had attacked and sunk the heavy cruiser, *Atago*, which happened to be Japanese Center Force Commanding Admiral Kurita's flagship. Later intercepts reported Kurita having been fished out of the water and transferring his flag to the *Yamato*.

So now, US forces knew the precise positions of both monster battleships.

As the first vessels of *Musashi's* battle group came into view, Josh searched the sky above the ships for the fighters that should be providing security patrols. He saw none. He squawked his mic. "Anyone seeing overhead cover?"

"None," came back a reply, followed by other similar responses.

Josh flipped his radio to a fleet frequency. "Wannabe here. We're not seein' air patrols over the target. Is that possible?"

"Wait."

Moments later, the disembodied voice came back over Josh's headphones. "Bandits are active in other parts of the AO, but none showing on radar in your sector. The Japs must have sent them out on patrols."

Astonished, Josh acknowledged the message and took a second to think. The big battleship was still many miles away, and suddenly he saw two huge puffs of smoke spew horizontally over the water. "Spread out and go high," he called over the radio. "They're shootin' at us with their big guns."

Meanwhile, he pulled back on his own stick to start a steep climb and jinked back and forth to frustrate enemy targeting. Mentally, he ran through his Wildcat's capabilities. He had been dismayed that his air group did not include Hellcats. They were faster and more robust than the Wildcats, which was why they typically went in first to knock out anti-aircraft fire.

Wildcats were slightly slower but more maneuverable, and thus better in dogfights, so they generally went after enemy aircraft. That usually meant flying in after Hellcats had been through, and then dogfighting with enemy security patrols, allowing cover for the dive bombers and torpedo bombers to try to rip holes in the steel hulls with their explosive payloads. This time, because of the imperative for rapid response, CAG-18's Wildcats were out front. They would face the full force of the Japanese defenses.

Josh keyed his mic again. "Wildcats, we're swooping in. Keep looking for bandits. Drop your bombs as planned. Helldivers and Avengers, you know what to do. See y'all on the other side."

Then Josh saw the *Musashi*. At first, it appeared as a speck on the far horizon that grew rapidly in perspective. Followed by his command of forty-four other aircraft, Josh soared high over waves and enemy warships at over three hundred miles per hour. He gaped as he took in the ship's size, fully three football-field lengths from bow to stern, and at least half a field across at the beam. It bristled with cannons, anti-aircraft guns, machine guns, radar disks, and radio antennas, a true monster ship.

Its guns fired non-stop, all aimed in his direction.

The ship's main cannons continued to fire, but Josh's group was too close for them to effectively track his aircraft. He surmised that the second wave from the US 3rd Fleet carriers must be entering the zone, and the Japanese guns were attempting to engage those fighters as they came within range.

Amid the whir of the wind and the roar of engines, Josh dropped his Wildcat's nose, picked one among many anti-aircraft and machine gun nests on the *Musashi's* starboard side, and pulled his trigger. His Wildcat bucked through the air as six .50 cal machine guns in his wings delivered withering fire on the Japanese gun crew.

Josh could see the men plainly. Their bodies slumped against the steel forecastle. Bright red blood poured from multiple gaping holes.

The *Musashi's* superstructure filled his vision. Josh pulled a lever releasing twin two-hundred-and-fifty-pound bombs, and then rolled left to avoid colliding. Keeping the ship in sight, he climbed high, jinking, rolling, and banking all the way until he reached an altitude above anti-aircraft gun range where he could watch the action below. He was amazed that, thus far, he had lost none of his aircraft. He was soon joined by his Wildcat squadrons.

Crisscrossing tracers and smoke streams and the continued boom, boom of the big guns testified to the ferocity of the battle below.

"Helldivers, you're on," Josh called. He watched as they dove in from high altitude while Japanese anti-aircraft guns spat unceasing streams of steel. The aircraft dropped their thousand-pound armor-piercing projectiles. If the bombs struck the deck, they would drill through and explode somewhere deep in the ship's interior, hopefully inside one of the ammunition magazines.

Josh recalled how, during the Battle of Midway, he had suddenly been jerked from duty in the *Enterprise's* combat intelligence center to fly an Avenger in an all-pilots' desperate sortie against *Hiryu*. He had never flown a dive bomber before, but he understood the basics. He had been astonished at how a target the size of an aircraft carrier could seem so small from high in the sky and then loom so large in a matter of seconds. Yet, with a slight change in direction, the mark was missed altogether. The sad fact was that most bombs failed to hit their targets.

He watched in dismay as that scenario played out against the *Musashi*. "Not this time," he muttered as, one by one, the rocket-shaped munitions splashed into the sea and erupted within yards of the mighty warship.

"Avengers, you're up," he called to his torpedo bombers.

Far below, Josh's torpedo-bombers lined up, looking like gnats ahead of the smoke-spewing behemoth. He watched as they flew as close to the water's surface as they dared and at an angle to *Musashi's* length to give the greatest chance of a hit.

From this distance he could not see the release of the tubes, but he knew they had taken place when the Avengers veered away and climbed. Clearly visible, though, were the torpedoes' underwater wakes streaming behind them.

Josh was once again dismayed to see that, with odds similar to those of the Helldivers, none of the Avengers struck their target. The good news was that all of his planes were out of range of the ship's ack-ack with no losses.

"Wannabe, this is Alabama." Josh recognized McCampbell's voice and twang. "We're comin' in right behind you. Bandits inbound. Good job. We'll take over."

Despite continued danger and the disappointment over having no hits, momentary exultation raised Josh's spirits. All his pilots were alive, and he had survived his first engagement against a major target as commander of CAG-18.

"Roger," he replied to McCampbell. "We'll be back."

Josh's radio squawked with transmissions between fighters, bombers, and their ships all the way back to the *Intrepid*. On landing on the pitching deck, he left his Wildcat to be checked out and replenished with fuel and ammo, grabbed a bite to eat, and dropped by Operations. There, too, the radio crackled with voices of pilots still in mortal combat with the *Musashi*.

He was surprised to find the atmosphere decidedly optimistic. Prominently displayed were the hits on *Musashi* delivered by *Intrepid's* pilots after CAG-18 had left the scene. They painted a picture of a badly damaged battleship.

Also displayed were the counts of downed enemy aircraft. Josh sucked in his breath. *The Zeros must have swarmed there right after we left.*

He viewed the situation map on the wall in the ops center. "Brief me," he told a young seaman attending to it. His shirt bore the name Alexander.

The sailor viewed the map. "You prob'ly need to know that the *Intrepid* will be movin'." He spoke with a decidedly Southern accent, and he pointed to a spot on Leyte's east coast. "That's San Bernardino Strait, about eighteen miles northeast of where General MacArthur landed. Admiral Halsey's scouts spotted four enemy carriers northwest of there. That's got to be Northern Force.

"He thinks the *Musashi* is crippled and that we'll sink it by nightfall. He's sure that the *Yamato* turned around after the *Atago* went down, so he thinks he could leave the strait lightly defended while he sends three carrier groups, including the *Intrepid* and a bunch of destroyers to deal with the carriers. But to be honest, sir—" He hesitated.

"Go on," Josh urged. "What were you going to say?"

"This is my personal view, sir," Alexander said in a subdued voice. "The Japs don't seem to have many planes on those northern carriers. They laid a bunch of smoke and they're steamin' southeast, but they're not comin' aggressively after our ships or fighters." He leaned in and lowered his voice conspiratorially. "I think it's a feint. The Japs are drawin' us out. Somethin' else is goin' on."

Josh studied the map, trying to see what Alexander saw. Once again, the scale of the battle awed Josh, but he had no time to reflect further.

"You might be right. You should run your observations up higher. I have to go. I'm due for another sortie."

"Be sure to check with ops for coordinates before you try landin'," Alexander joked. "Your runway might be somewhere else."

Before returning to the flight deck, Josh checked the casualty board. A pang of dismay hit him when he saw that two Avengers from *Intrepid's* other air group had been lost, including the pilots. Saddened, and wondering if he had met them, he returned to the flight deck. CAG-18 was ready and waiting.

Once airborne, Josh listened to the chatter. A celebratory sense had taken hold from the notion that the *Musashi* was crippled and would soon be a fatal casualty. Multiple direct hits had been reported from both Helldivers and Avengers. The few Zeros that showed up were soon gunned down.

When his air group arrived at the battlespace, Josh could scarcely believe his eyes. The big ship was riding low in the water and listing at least fifteen degrees to port, but she still sailed under her own power. She had no air cover, and all about her wake were wreckages of support ships. Also trailing behind her were thousands of men bobbing in the water who had abandoned ship. Some flailed, some treaded water, and many were face-down, not moving.

Gripped by melancholy, Josh keyed his mic. "Helldivers and Avengers, go in and get her. Wildcats, we'll pull topside security while the others finish her off."

Minutes later, against pitiful ack-ack and machine gun fire, two torpe-does and two dive bombs from Josh's group struck with resounding booms. The *Musashi* rolled to port, and sank slowly below the waves.

33

Next Day, October 25, 1944
Aboard The USS *Intrepid*, Vicinity of Cape Engaño, Philippine Sea

Before dawn, coffee in hand, Josh ambled into the operations room to glean whatever pertinent information he could before the morning battle briefing. He found Alexander at the map.

"Good morning, sir," the sailor said. "I saw that you were at *Musashi's* final moments. That must'a been a sight to see. Did ya hear that Commander McCampbell made ace again? He shot down nine Zeros in less than fifteen minutes. The news is all over the fleet. So is the news that CAG-18 delivered the final blow to Musashi."

Despite heavy fatigue, Josh scrutinized Alexander. The sailor was slender and small, with bright eyes, a ready smile, and thin blond hair. "No," Josh replied, "I hadn't heard." Recalling that McCampbell was rolling into the battle just as Josh and his group were leaving, he knew for certain now that he had just missed the aerial dogfights. "That's amazing." He sipped his coffee and glanced at the map. "Where are we?"

"In the Philippine Sea, coming up east of Cape Engaño. We're closing on Japan's Northern Force—"

Josh had landed back on the *Intrepid* late in the evening and enjoyed an unusually long sleep while the carrier cruised from the San Bernardino Strait and headed northwest into the Philippine Sea. "You were concerned about how few enemy aircraft had been encountered. Is that still a worry? Fewer Zeros should be a good thing. Did you run your thoughts up the staff?"

Alexander nodded. "I tol' my boss." He laughed sheepishly. "I'm no officer and I ain't got no college, so I'm prob'ly wrong. My boss said the Japs wouldn't send four carriers out here without fighters." He heaved a sigh. "I just take info when it comes in and post it on the boards. I had noticed that we didn't git a lot of spot reports on enemy aircraft sightin's from the Northern Force direction." He grinned. "The Japs're prob'bly holdin' back so's we don't know how strong they really are."

Josh scrutinized the young sailor. Intelligence gleamed from his eyes despite his "aww shucks" persona. "Where are you from, Alexander?"

"West Virginia, sir." Alexander beamed with pride. "Best damn state in the whole union."

Josh had to smile. "Well, Alexander from the best damn state in the whole union, let's compare notes after my next sortie. You might be on to something."

San Bernardino Strait, Philippines

The sun glinted through a mist hovering over the Philippine Sea as it peeked above the eastern horizon, sending shafts of light into the bridge on the destroyer, USS *Johnston*. The ship's captain, Commander Ernest "Big Chief" Evans, stared at his radio in disbelief, sobered by an air reconnaissance spot report just being received.

"I'm seein' a massive Japanese fleet coming through San Bernardino Strait by Samar," the static-broken voice called in urgent tones. "They're turnin' southeast toward Leyte Gulf. I cain't count 'em all, but there's a bunch of cruisers, light cruisers, destroyers, an' there's three battleships, including the *Yamato*."

Evans recognized a calamity in the making. Most of Admiral Halsey's fleet had sailed through the same strait many hours ago to pursue Japan's four-carrier North Force near Cape Engaño, seven hundred miles in the opposite direction.

The USS *Johnston* was one of three Fletcher-class destroyers belonging to Task Group 77, commanded by Rear Admiral Clifton Sprague and dubbed "Taffy 3." The group also included four destroyer escorts and six escort carriers. Its current mission was to provide air support for the troops who landed inside the gulf at Leyte.

Evans sucked in his breath as the implications struck home. Taffy 3 was insufficient to counter the vastly larger enemy force. One hundred and thirty thousand troops already on Leyte could be massacred. The Pacific war could be lost.

The radio crackled again with the reconnaissance pilot's voice. "I'm seeing no enemy aircraft, carriers, or troop transport ships."

Once again incredulous and not comprehending the reasoning behind such a task force organization, Evans did a quick mental analysis. Obviously, the Japanese admiral's intention was to enter the Leyte Gulf, loiter offshore, and pummel the beachhead into either submission or oblivion. But with no aircraft to speak of, the Japanese Center Force was blind and vulnerable to air attack.

Taffy 3 had limited combat power. Its one hundred and fifty fighters, dive and torpedo bombers, and ten fighting ships were insufficient to stop the approaching juggernaut. The escort carriers were small and intended to transport aircraft, not engage in combat. With only light onboard defenses, they were of no value in a close-in fight; quite the contrary, they needed to be defended.

The radio emitted more static. Admiral Sprague came on and ordered all aircraft into the sky to attack and harass the enemy fleet. He also directed the destroyers and destroyer escorts to screen and protect the escort carriers.

Evans took a deep breath while he took stock of his situation. His nickname, "Big Chief," had derived from his size and his Cherokee and Creek lineage. Classically good-looking with wavy hair and a Clark Gable mustache, after graduating from high school in Pawnee, Oklahoma, sixteen years ago, he had been declined enlistment by the Marines for an injured knee. Subsequently, he won an appointment to the US Naval Academy, and by the time Pearl Harbor was attacked, he had served on active duty for eleven years and commanded several ships under enemy fire.

Just under a year ago, after overseeing the *Johnston's* commissioning, Evans took command of the vessel, declaring at the ceremony, "This is going to be a fighting ship. I intend to go in harm's way, and anyone who doesn't want to go along had better get off right now."

As Evans remembered his bold proclamation, he grunted at the irony. *I didn't have in mind what this fight is gonna be.*

He issued orders, pushed through a door into the morning air on a small deck off the bridge, and took in the sights, sounds, and smells of a destroyer readying for battle. Already, his executive officer had alerted the crew with sirens and various PA announcements preluded by, "Now hear this. Now hear this..."

The ever-present smell of diesel permeated everywhere aboard the ship intermingled with the aroma of strong coffee almost anywhere and warm meals near the galley. On this small, private domain of the ship's captain, however, Evans could breathe in fresh air, enjoy the view of the magnificent sunrise on blue waters under this morning's clear sky, and wonder for a few brief moments about how bad things might get. He stopped himself. *No time for that.*

The roar of Wildcats and Avengers ground by overhead as they flew northeast. He shook his head and grunted. "A hundred and fifty of 'em," he muttered. "Barely three air groups, and no Hellcats or Helldivers." Yesterday, it had taken at least eight air groups five hours and multiple sorties each to kill the *Musashi*.

The *Johnston's* normal vibration deepened as its powerful engines kicked into gear and it set out in the same direction as the aircraft formation. Together with the other two destroyers and four destroyer escorts arrayed abreast of it, it turned to attack the Japanese naval onslaught.

As the morning haze lifted, the first glimpse of the Japanese fleet came into view, appearing as dark blips marring the distant horizon. Evans stood on the bridge, squinting through binoculars at the armada of towering battleships, heavy cruisers, and destroyers steaming his way, and among them, the *Yamato*.

Updated reconnaissance had revealed more of the fleet's composition. In addition to the three battleships, it included six heavy cruisers, two light cruisers, eleven destroyers, and large numbers of support vessels bearing down on the tiny flotilla of thirteen small American warships, the only line of defense that stood between the enemy and the exposed troops on Leyte's beach.

"Smoke," Evans ordered, and almost immediately, his ship speeded up. Down in the engine room, his engineers deliberately burned high volumes of fuel in a boiler to create thick black smoke spewing from the *Johnston's* funnel. On the deck, crewmen fired up smoke generators, streaming long layers of black, dense clouds that hung over the sea's surface. The other ships of Taffy 3 followed *Johnston's* lead, spewing smoke across the battlespace, cloaking their assault on the mammoth fleet.

From beyond the billowing dark clouds, loud booms announced the big guns of the Japanese battleships. Explosive rounds splashed near Taffy 3's vessels, raising geysers marked by red, pink, and greenish-yellow dyes.

With the sun all but blotted out by the mix of fiendishly colored billows, Evans wondered if this battle was a preview of hell. He muttered, "I might know soon enough."

He whirled to his helmsman. "Zigzag," he ordered.

The sailor spun the wheel to his left, stopped it, and spun to his right.

"Keep it up," Evans called, "but maintain the general direction straight ahead." He turned to his exec. "We're going in. Let the other ships know."

An ear-splitting whistle descended. A projectile crashed through the ceiling. Evans found himself pinned to a wall by a steel panel. Searing pain shot through his face. Blood oozed from his left hand where two fingers were severed.

Crewmen rushed to pull away the sheet metal. Smoke filled the bridge, and debris littered its floor. While one seaman grabbed Evans' arm to stop the bleeding, he shouted out, "Increase speed. I saw the *Kumano*. It's a heavy cruiser. We need to get closer. When we get a break in the smoke, hit her with the 5 In guns, all of 'em, and don't stop until she goes down.

"Get me commo to the skippers on the *Hoel* and the *Heermann*."

The *Johnston* broke through the smoke. The destroyer's 5 In guns opened up on the *Kumano*, firing incessantly as the destroyer weaved back and forth, coming ever closer to the heavy cruiser despite volleys of enemy fire from multiple enemy ships.

Flames leaped above the *Kumano's* deck. It listed to starboard. Men jumped overboard. Its guns silenced, its bow dipped into the frothing water, and it sank.

Evans barely took note, now a man driven, seeking his next target.

"Sir," his radio operator yelled, "all of Taffy 3 is in the fight. When the other ships saw us attack, they followed."

Oblivious to sharp shrapnel cuts across his face, Evans acknowledged the info with a quick nod. "Good." To the helmsman he called, "Keep weaving," and to the exec, "Keep that smoke pouring out."

For two hours reminiscent of Sir Francis Drake fighting the Spanish Armada, Evans and the other captains of Taffy 3 crisscrossed the battlespace between the much larger enemy ships, sinking more of them amid a furious rate of fire, but also receiving devastating blows. Then, shot up, running out of ammunition, and surrounded by hostile fire, *Johnston's* engines failed.

Evans ordered his crew of three hundred and sixty-seven to abandon ship. Only one hundred and eighty were alive to do so. Surviving crewmen last saw Evans in the water. He was later listed as missing in action, and he was never found.

Aboard the *Intrepid*, Philippine Sea

When Josh returned to the operations room at mid-morning after his first sortie of the day, he was surprised to find that the morale of the staff had turned dramatically south. He made his way straight to the status boards, and found Alexander there in his normal place. "What's happened? Why is everyone so down in the mouth?"

Before the sailor could reply, Josh added, "I came to let you know that you were right. We found hardly any enemy aircraft to shoot at, and when we saw 'em, they turned tail and ran. We managed to sink one of their carriers, though—"

Expecting an enthusiastic response, Josh was surprised at Alexander's continued glum nod. "What's wrong?"

Alexander grimaced. "The four carriers *were* a diversion. Admiral Kurita turned his Center Force back around in the Sibuyan Sea. He sailed through the San Bernardino Strait behind us to attack at Leyte Gulf. His fleet includes the *Yamato*."

Josh listened, stunned. "The invasion force. It's unprotected." In a daze, he gazed at Alexander. "You were right again."

Alexander shook his head glumly. "I'd rather have been wrong. Taffy 3 intercepted them by Samar Island."

"Taffy 3?" Josh said, bewildered. "That's just three destroyers and—"

"Exactly, sir, and we're too far away. We cain't git back there to save 'em."

Josh took a deep breath and let it out slowly while the implications worked their way through his mind. The status boards provided no additional information. Clearly, America was heading for a resounding defeat.

He reached over and grasped Alexander's shoulder. "We should have listened to you, Sailor."

"I wasn't the only one, sir. I found out today that Admiral Bogan and several other commanders saw it the same way I did. They wanted to stay at Leyte to defend there, but Admiral Halsey overrode them."

Late that night, after a full day of more sorties against the Japanese carriers, Josh sat at a small desk writing a letter to his cousin, Paul Littlefield. He seethed with anger, but just as frustrating was a sense of bewilderment, of not knowing whether or not his wrath was warranted and feeling helpless to react even if it was justified.

After normal greetings, he wrote, "This war, regardless of purpose, has an evil effect that drains both morality and morale. I spent all day in the air shooting at the enemy. The carrier task force I'm with north of the Philippines sank four Japanese aircraft carriers today, *Zuikaku, Zuihō, Chitose,* and *Chiyoda.* I should be ecstatic, right?

"The problem is that we faced hardly any aircraft at all. So, where were they? Several of our senior commanders advised against this maneuver, perceiving it as a feint. In fact, the ruse was so apparent that an enlisted man in our operations section whose job it is to post status boards figured it out. Yet Admiral Halsey, my mentor, overrode the advice of his subordinate commanders.

"Meanwhile, to accomplish this excursion, we left an amphibious landing force already ashore unprotected from a Japanese armada that included the *Yamato,* two other battleships, and various heavy cruisers, destroyers, etc. By the time we learned of the threat at Leyte, we were seven hundred miles away.

"Fortunately, three destroyers and four destroyer escorts left behind to protect six escort carriers were in the area. Unbelievably, those seven ships attacked the Japanese battle group, and after two hours of fighting, for reasons that are unclear, the Japanese turned away.

"I could conjecture why the enemy withdrew. Perhaps Kurita believed that a larger fleet was close by and on the way. The truth is, we don't know his reasons, but our strength there was not nearly sufficient to coerce that end.

"The good news is that our invasion force at Leyte was saved, and we sank those four of the Japs' carriers. The sad news is that we lost some very brave men off the coast of Samar Island. Another sobering element of the tragic events is that we were hoodwinked into pursuing those carriers. But for Taffy 3, the ramifications of what could have happened are unthinkable. That thought infuriates me.

"Then again, I don't know what Admiral Halsey knew or thought he knew. If I had been in his shoes, would I have done any different? I don't know, and that is the source of my bewilderment. Ahh, the fog of war."

Sleepless, Josh tossed on his cot well past midnight. His letter lay unfinished, and he knew it was one he could not send. It contained too much information that could be considered sensitive.

He needed sleep. Tomorrow, CAG-18 would join other 3rd Fleet formations to hit targets on Luzon.

At some point during the night, Josh tore his letter into shreds and flushed it down the toilet. He lay back down to try to sleep, but his frustrations persisted.

34

One Day Earlier, October 24, 1944
Hill 617, East of Biffontaine, France

Zack and his new command, Charlie Company, had barely swept over their objective when, with no time to consolidate and establish a security perimeter, heavy enemy artillery rained down, and a German counterattack commenced. Harsh weather had impeded the 141st's approach. Thick clouds descended to ground level, bringing visibility to zero, and with it, incessant near-freezing rain that beat against soldiers' helmets, seeped under their collars, and trickled down their backs as they crawled up a near vertical incline, clinging for handholds to shrubs and low-hanging branches and the long leaves of dense willow trees.

The oppressive smell of gunpowder clung to the fog and mixed with earthy odors released from mud created by hundreds of soldiers scuffing the steep ground with their boots as they ascended the steep slope in the night. They breathed hard from strenuous effort, and their own sweating bodies added to the stench.

They received no reprieve from climbing blind until nearing the summit. Then, flashes of light lit up the sky intermittently as artillery and mortar bursts softened the objective ahead of the assaulting force and were answered in kind by the enemy. The sporadic flicker bounced through the fog, followed immediately by loud explosions, friendly and enemy, or from crisscrossing green and red machine gun and small-arms tracers. Some of the artillery and mortar rounds struck heavy branches high in the seventy-foot willows, sending molten shrapnel flying in all directions. In their aftermath, screams of agony and calls for medics added to the tumult.

But the soldiers of the 141st of the 36th Texas Division kept climbing.

From the time that Zack left his platoon with the 142nd until one day ago, the 141st had been held in reserve while it rested and prepared for its next mission. Eight days earlier, the 36th Division's attached 100th Infantry Battalion of the 442nd Regimental Combat Team had been ordered to attack and secure Bruyères, a village so small that it had to be penciled onto the map. The hamlet was nestled in a narrow valley between steep forested peaks that rose to an altitude of four thousand feet above sea level.

The 100th Battalion led the assault on Bruyères, supported by the 142nd and 143rd regiments. From his bivouac area at the rear, Zack had heard the sounds of battle, and reports filtered back that the Germans refused to cede a single inch easily. Thus, the fighting was particularly intense, moving from house to house. The battle lasted for eight days, and while it continued, images filtered through Zack's mind of his former platoon sergeant, now 2LT Wilbur, and the soldiers they had led together for all those months. He shoved the thoughts aside, also smothering pangs of guilt for not being with them and wondering how many still lived and how many were wounded.

Returning his attention to training his new company, he muttered to himself, "Got to keep these men alive."

After liberating Bruyères while supported by the 142nd and 143rd, the 100th Battalion had again led in battle to liberate Biffontaine, six miles east of Bruyères. Once again, reports of fierce fighting, slow progress, and high casualties reached Zack, and once again he lamented not being with his erstwhile comrades.

The battle had ended in victory yesterday, and right on its heels,

General Dahlquist, commanding general of the 36th Division, decided to press forward two miles farther into enemy territory. His senior staff officers and subordinate commanders advised against doing so, arguing that only the 141[st,] Regiment, which currently constituted the 36th's reserve, was rested and prepared to pursue the offensive. They stressed that the division should take time to consolidate its gains and prepare for a deliberate attack through the mountains. Rumors circulated among the troops of heated discussions that escalated to loud, angry voices in the division's command tents.

Enemy strategy in the area had become clear and was confirmed by interrogating German POWs. The German high command considered the High Vosges to be eminently defensible with economies of force, seeing that enemy armored vehicles would be confined to narrow roads and could be more easily engaged at closer ranges with 50 mm, 75 mm, and 88 mm antitank guns.

The *Wehrmacht's* newly appointed commander in the High Vosges, General Balck, had arrived with his "*Führer Befehl,*" the direct order from Hitler, to hold the those mountains to the last man. To that end, and despite a late start that coincided with the US 36th Division's action in Bruyères barely a week earlier, Balck had poured in construction supplies, equipment, and slave labor, and had rapidly built his two concentric rings of steel-reinforced fortifications, including machine gun nests and indirect fire positions. He had also cleared wide swaths of forest to expose the fields of fire on the most likely enemy approaches.

Those defenses were east of Biffontaine, toward Germany. Breaching them was imperative if the 36th was to burst through the Vosges Mountains, cross the Alsation Plain, and be the first major unit to ford the Rhine and enter Germany. Apparently, that vision was General Dahlquist's ambition, or at least that was a perception of his intent seeping among the foot soldiers, and it was shared by the 141st's junior officers. It reminded Zack again, with a tightening stomach, of the tragic events at the Rapido River crossing in Italy.

Twenty-four hours ago, the 141st was ordered to advance during the night to seize Hill 617. Orders had gone out, preparations made, and coordination accomplished to move through the areas currently controlled by the 142nd and 143rd Regiments and the 100th Battalion.

As Zack's driver maneuvered his jeep through a narrow street of rubble that had been Bruyères, he kept a watchful eye out for anyone from his former platoon but saw no one. Behind him a column of big trucks followed, transporting Bravo Company's troops. Dusk approached as the convoy rolled into Biffontaine, six miles farther on.

Zack found himself becoming inured to the sight of bombed-out homes and shops, although the sense of lives destroyed had not yet left him. He remained sensitized sufficiently to be bothered that blight seemed normal. Chiding himself for hardening senses, he kept watch for his former platoon comrades in the 142nd.

As the convoy traversed the debris that littered Biffontaine's main street, Zack observed soldiers in their defensive positions, and then noticed a curious sight, one he should have expected but nevertheless surprised him. In various places, grouped soldiers seemed smaller in size than average, and when he looked closer, he saw that their eyes were slanted, Oriental.

He suddenly recalled that the 100th Infantry Battalion and its parent unit, the 442nd Regimental Combat Team, was made up almost entirely of Japanese-American volunteers who had been recruited out of internment camps. President Roosevelt had ordered Japanese-Americans living in military exclusion areas on the US west coast to report to the camps shortly after the attack on Pearl Harbor. The only non-Japanese-descended members of the 100th were its leaders above company level, who, per the mandate that created the unit, were not allowed to be of Japanese ancestry.

Seeing these troops had caught Zack so off guard that, driving behind a machine gun nest manned by a crew of them, he halted to observe them. The soldiers noticed, and stared back. Zack waved a loose salute and his driver moved on.

His convoy had nearly reached the east end of town when he heard his name called and turned to find Lieutenant Wilbur panting alongside his jeep. Zack ordered a halt and got out. He took one look at Wilbur's haggard figure and bearhugged him.

Zack had known Wilbur to be always in high spirits under horrific conditions. He was unusually handsome, a favorite among women across

France as the towns and villages were liberated. Zack recalled having to pull him from a bevy of girls in Grenoble to plan for the mission to Montélimar. Wilbur had come away in good humor, but his admirers had audibly expressed their dismay at his departure.

Wilbur looked nothing like that now, and his appearance shook Zack. The platoon leader's skin was dark, as if embedded with soil. His eyes had sunk deep into his face, which was deeply creased.

"I heard the fighting was rough," Zack managed.

Wilbur's lower lip trembled and he looked away. "We lost three," he muttered.

"Who?"

"Mikey, Jeb, and Ted."

Zack swallowed hard. Those seasoned veterans had been with him since Italy.

He sniffed and turned away. After a few moments of silence, he turned back to Wilbur. "I'm glad to see you in one piece," he said hoarsely. Then he gestured back the way he had come. "I saw some of those guys in the 100th Infantry back there. How're they doing?"

"They're incredible fighters. You'd be lucky to share a foxhole with any one of them. We didn't know how to take it when we heard that they'd be attached to the 36th, but we're sure glad they're fighting on our side. They're disciplined, they know what they're doing, and they never give up. Their motto is, 'Remember Pearl Harbor.' Their parent unit, the 442nd, has the motto, 'Go for broke,' and they do it, every time."

"I read reports about them," Zack said. "Our Echo company is an all Mexican-American unit. They're tremendous fighters too.

"Come to think of it, I recall bumping into an all-black outfit around Montecassino. The Buffalo Soldiers. You'd be happy to have them fighting on your right or left too. I'm glad we're all fighting on the same side."

Wilbur nodded grimly. "Me too. We all bleed red."

Zack sighed. "Anyway, this 100th Battalion has one hell of a reputation. They took me by surprise, though, when I first saw them."

"Us too, but we wouldn't trade them away." Wilbur turned and scanned in the direction that Zack's convoy traveled. He sighed. "You'll be glad to have them at your back. Where you're goin' is gonna be rough. Ya know, the villagers started calling this area '*les trapin des saules*.'" He took a deep breath and exhaled. "That translates to 'the trap of the willows.' Let's hope that isn't prophetic."

He dropped his voice. "We shouldn't be sending *anybody* farther east yet. We're not ready for it. After two straight weeks of house-to-house fighting in these villages, all three regiments are worn out and need to replenish. We won't be much of a reserve for the 141st." He swore softly. "I hope Dahlquist's lunacy doesn't get you killed."

Zack took in a deep breath and let it out. Then he grasped Wilbur's shoulder and rocked him in a comradely manner. "Get some rest, my friend. You look like you could use it." He forced a grin. "I'd better go. Can't be late, ya know, to the line of departure."

As he started to get back in the jeep, Wilbur gave him a searching look. "Hey, sir, why are you still wearin' lieutenant bars?"

Zack pursed his lips, arched his brows in a jocular expression, and held his palms forward in the universal expression of, "I have no clue." He laughed. "I go where I'm told and follow orders. So far I haven't needed the extra pull. The men are good."

Wilbur shook his head with a tired smile. "Well, I'll see you on the other side." He lifted his eyes to the heavens and added, "Wherever that is."

Zack waved and climbed into his seat, and the jeep drove on. He blew off Wilbur's last comment about where they might see each other next, but the conversation about the 100th Infantry Battalion prompted reflection.

Drawing on memory of what he had read about them, Zack suddenly realized that the path of the battalion through the war had paralleled his own, at least since landing at Salerno. They had faced the buzzsaw of defenses that the Germans had seized there upon General Eisenhower's ill-timed announcement to the world that Italy had capitulated. That had been the 100th's first combat, and they had paid a bloody price, as had the entire invasion force that had expected a relatively easy landing.

They had fought at Belvedere in the battle for Montecassino, the ancient Benedictine abbey high on a mountain overlooking the only route up the Italian Peninsula that could support armor. The fighting for all Allied elements in the area had been intense and prolonged over weeks, with tragic casualty rates. So many of the 100th's soldiers were wounded that the unit earned a new moniker: "The Purple Heart Battalion." But they met their objectives and went on to liberate Lanuvio, just short of Rome, thus adding to their growing reputation as a tenacious combat force.

A bump in the road jostled Zack and disrupted his attention. "Sorry, LT," his driver said.

"Not a problem," Zack replied, but the reference to him as "LT" diverted his thoughts to Wilbur's comment about Zack's rank. When Zack had arrived at the 141st regimental headquarters, his reception had been cordial, but just short of perfunctory.

The commander, Colonel John Lundquist, had himself just arrived to take charge of the regiment as a result of his predecessor's death. He greeted Zack with a firm handshake, but he appeared as a man with too many things on his mind at once. "I've heard good things about you," he had said. "I chose you, but that was from paper and comments of commanders who knew you. We'll get to know each other later. You'll have Bravo Company, and the top sergeant is great. I know him. He'll steer you right.

"Your immediate commander, Lieutenant Colonel Bird of 1st Battalion, is at a conference with the 2nd Battalion commander. You'll meet him later.

"Meanwhile, go take command of your company."

Zack had gone to the assigned bivouac area somewhat taken aback and unsure of where to begin. He remained a lieutenant with no written orders for taking command of Bravo Company, and obviously, no ceremony would take place to install him.

Fortunately, First Sergeant John Huberth greeted him warmly. "We know about you, sir, the stuff about Kasserine, Rapido, and other places. We're happy to have you. We're only sorry about the circumstances. You're replacing a good man.

"I'll get you introduced around. This is a great regiment. Quite a few of us have been with the unit since it shipped out from Texas. The camaraderie is terrific."

Later that afternoon, at 1st Battalion headquarters, Zack met LTC Bird. The other company commanders were there too, and Zack was surprised to learn that all were lieutenants. None had an executive officer. The most respected among them was Martin "Marty" Higgins of Alpha Company. He had landed with the regiment at Normandy and fought in every regimental engagement across France.

Higgins was a quiet, dark-haired man of average size who laughed easily, asked insightful questions, offered sound advice, and conducted himself in a way that instilled confidence. He greeted Zack with a warm handshake.

"I'll help you settle in. You've got a great bunch of guys to work with, particularly your top sergeant, Huberth. He's worth gold to you."

———

While climbing Hill 617, Zack saw that it occupied a commanding position in the Vosges, providing visibility from the southern end of a wide valley into smaller tributary valleys and their roads. His understanding of General Dahlquist's view of the hill as a strategic objective was to disrupt German operations and continue his drive to the Alsation Plain and the Rhine River beyond.

Zack watched his men closely. Their faces displayed their deep fatigue from months of combat despite their three weeks of rest. "Why the hell is Dahlquist sending us so deep into enemy territory?" he muttered to himself. "We should be consolidating our gains in Biffontaine."

Breaking through the High Vosges was a necessary objective. Zack saw that, but he did not understand going after it so soon, except to mollify Dahlquist's apparent desire to be first to the Rhine. *I hope the payoff is worth it.*

Zack had read reports from reconnaissance patrols that confirmed the intelligence that the German general, Balck, had very quickly built formidable defenses to halt the American advance through these mountains. He shook his head in resignation. *And our lot is to seize and occupy that damned hill.*

He had helped develop a simple plan of attack. Relying on surprise, Alpha, Bravo, Charlie, and Delta companies would work their way along a logging road on a high ridge. There, they would set up defensive positions overlooking the crossroads village of La Houssière in the valley below, still in German hands.

All was quiet aside from the crunch of combat boots on the gritty road. Then Zack heard the unmistakable pops of distant enemy artillery barrages. They rose to a crescendo, joined by the whispers and whistles of rounds flying toward Hill 617.

"Incoming," Zack shouted, joining a chorus of voices calling out warning along the line of trudging soldiers. "Take cover."

The troops scattered, diving behind tall willows on both sides of the road.

All night, the artillery continued, hurling jagged, hot steel onto the men hunkered in their hastily dug, shallow foxholes. Then, as early morning dawned, reports filtered in that the road they had used to mount the hill had since been mined and blocked with felled logs.

During a lull, Zack sought out Huberth. "Surprise is blown. I just got an order from Colonel Bird to dig in."

Huberth grunted. "Dig in, huh? We just went from surprise offense to defense."

"Yep. Balck must have figured out what Dahlquist intended and led us into a trap. We're surrounded, cut off from higher headquarters, any support, and our supply line."

The first sergeant groaned. "And we've only got rations and water for a day."

"The krauts are bound to stage a counterattack. Get the men digging defensive positions. Use whatever the Germans left behind. I'll go coordinate left and right and see what Battalion HQ intends."

Just then, from a few feet away, Zack's radio operator called urgently, "Sir, it's the battalion XO." He held up the mic.

"I'll get the men settled in," Huberth interjected. "Go do what you need to do."

Zack grimaced. "Thanks, Top."

Zack spent less than a minute on the radio, and when he was finished, his head spun. Major McCoy, the battalion XO, had informed him that LTC Bird had been seriously wounded by artillery shrapnel. McCoy was taking command of the battalion, but the Germans had cut off the roads surrounding Hill 617. "You're surrounded by six thousand crack German troops, six hundred of them between you and us. Our 2nd Battalion is organizing a rescue, but until they get to you or we can figure something else out, you're on your own. Get over to Alpha for a meeting of commanders."

As he turned around, Huberth returned. "The platoon leaders are looped in an' gettin' after it."

Zack related his conversation with McCoy. "Take charge here," he directed. "I'm headed to Alpha."

Dodging from one covered position to the next while artillery continued to descend and the sky turned from black to gray with smoke and dust, Zack and his radio operator arrived at Higgins' CP. It was a small, non-descript, newly constructed concrete structure, apparently built to house troops. Already gathered inside were the COs of the other companies. Consternation showed on all faces but one, Higgins'.

"Listen up," Higgins said loudly enough to be heard above the din of battle outside. "We're short on time, and you know the lowdown. We're on our own. I just got off the radio with the XO. He's taken command of the battalion, but he's down there and we're up here. I told him that, barring your protest, I was taking charge up here."

He looked around at the four commanders. "Any objections?"

The lieutenants glanced at each other searchingly and returned their gazes to Higgins. "We're behind you, Marty. No one else has the combat experience you do, except for maybe Zack—"

"Not me," Zack said firmly. "I'm new to this outfit, I haven't had the training in the Army's schools that Marty's had. I didn't feel ready to be in charge of a company, and now—" He turned to Higgins. "Effectively, you're taking command of a battalion. I'll be happy to follow your orders."

"Anyone else?" Higgins searched the faces of his comrades. When none offered further comment, he said, "All right, I'll relay that to McCoy. Now, this is what we're going to do. We don't know how long the siege will last. We've got to outlast it. So immediately, get the rations from all your men and bring them to a central location. Come to think of it, I wish we'd brought more than a single day's worth.

"My First Platoon leader will designate a location. He'll also take command of Alpha. From a chain-of-command perspective, we're covered.

"As for water, as long as the rain keeps up, we're good, but monitor your soldiers' intake against supply. We might have to ration that as well if the weather clears.

"Your men didn't get much sleep last night, so put 'em on a sleep plan and make sure the awake ones keep their eyes peeled, and check on 'em frequently. We can't afford anyone fallin' asleep when they're posted on the perimeter. We've got to conserve our ammo too. Our troops can't shoot at every bush that moves. Keep 'em in deep cover. Get everyone improving our defensive positions constantly. I'll make regular rounds, and if you need anything, you know how to find me. Any questions."

"We should have a plan for commo too," Charlie Company's commander observed. "Batteries won't last forever. We can run landlines between us up here, but we can't do that down to headquarters. So, commo to higher will be radio only."

"Good point. Take charge of that issue and get me some recommendations." Higgins asked for more questions, and when they had run out, he heaved a sigh. "Buds, we're in a tough spot. We'll have to rely on each other and count on higher headquarters to get to us. Keep your spirits up and keep those of your soldiers up too."

35

Same Day, October 24, 1944
Biffontaine, France

Private George "Joe" Sakato sat with his friend, Corporal Rudy Tokiwa, in a machine gun nest on the village's eastern edge overlooking an avenue of approach that the Germans could use in a counterattack. Heavy fog had burned off, rain had ceased to fall, and the sky had cleared to deep blue. "You okay, Joe?" Tokiwa asked kindly.

Sakato nodded, but clearly absent was the humorous disposition for which the private was known among his fellow soldiers of the 100th Battalion of the 442nd "Go For Broke" Regimental Combat Team. He nodded while staring glumly out over the sector he was detailed to watch. He was a rifleman, not a machine gunner, but casualties had imposed the need to serve in various capacities. In this instance, the machine gun was already set in place, so he had no need to carry it or lug the heavy load of belted ammo.

Not that he would have minded. He was known for jumping into any task cheerfully, but he was diminutive, even by Japanese-American norms. He was so small that during basic training at Camp Shelby, Mississippi, he had run around vertical walls on the obstacle course because he could not jump high enough to grasp the top and pull himself over. Such limitations, however, had never quelled his tenacious spirit.

Oval-faced with an angular chin and dark complexion, Sakato had characteristic Japanese eyes. At the beginning of the war, he could not have imagined that, three years after Pearl Harbor, he would be fighting Germans among the deep valleys and high ridges of the Vosges Mountain. He remembered the infamous day well, and the reverberations that reached far beyond Hawaii. He could thank his father that the Sakato family had not suffered the humiliation and confinement visited on other Japanese-Americans. As soon as the attack was announced in the news, the elder Sakato, acting on instinct, loaded his family and whatever belongings that could fit into the family car, burned or gave away the rest to astonished neighbors, and moved to Arizona.

Larger than Sakato and with the same dark skin, Corporal Tokiwa was square-faced. His family had been less fortunate. As the Sakatos and nearly all Japanese-American families had done across the country, the Tokiwas lit large fires and burned family photos, ancestral shrines, and exquisite Hina-matsuri dolls and other treasured memorabilia, and they gave away, hid, or destroyed valuable heirlooms and anything else that could be construed as showing even tacit support for the Japanese Empire.

The day after the Pearl Harbor attack, on his way to school in Salinas, California, Tokiwa was jeered at and challenged to a street fight for being Japanese. Fortunately, his teammates on the football team intervened for him. At home that afternoon, he watched as FBI agents, with no evidence, detained his own father, a decorated US WWI veteran, on suspicion of spying.

Then, ten weeks later, President Roosevelt issued a proclamation requiring all people of Japanese ancestry within specified military zones on the West Coast to be forcibly removed from their dwellings and transported to internment camps. Thus, while Joe Sakato found a job selling fruit in a grocery store in Arizona, Rudy Tokiwa languished in the unforgiving sun at Poston War Relocation Center in the same state under the watchful eyes of armed guards. There, Tokiwa nursed resentment against his government. He was, after all, *Nisei*, a second-generation American, born and bred in the USA. *And my parents are loyal citizens who never broke any law.*

Sakato eagerly sought to fight for America and had nursed dreams of flying fighters, but when he applied for the Army Air Corps, he was declined for possibly being an enemy agent. In the confines of the detainment camp, for Tokiwa, even entertaining the thought of joining the fight seemed a concept beyond reality.

Meanwhile, during 1942, President Roosevelt reacted to conflicting political pressure. Due to the public backlash resulting from the attack on Pearl Harbor, he had caused the internments to take place. In the months following, more kindly indignation built among the American public opposed to the ill-treatment of Japanese-American citizens who had been deprived of their Constitutional rights.

To address those concerns, beginning in February 1943 and for the rest of the year, the War Department and the War Relocation Authority together administered a loyalty test to the one hundred and twenty thousand internees across the ten camps scattered over seven states. Included in the questionnaires was one inquiring about the detainees' willingness to serve in the United States military. Another asked about their willingness to swear unqualified allegiance to the US and forswear fidelity to the Japanese emperor.

Then in January 1944, Roosevelt ordered the formation of the 442nd RCT, with its members to be recruited from among those internees who had responded with a willingness to serve in the US armed forces and swear allegiance to the United States. Rudy Tokiwa jumped at the chance, deciding that languishing in the camp and nursing resentment served no one. He volunteered and was tested for becoming a linguist. Preferring to be in combat, he deliberately failed the test and was sent to the 442nd.

Never having been interned, Joe Sakato had not been required to take the loyalty test and was not recruited. However, he got wind of the 442nd's formation and showed up again at an Army enlistment station. This time he was accepted.

"I heard about your friend," Tokiwa said, peering at Sakato, who continued to gaze stoically over his sector. "I'm sorry. Can you talk about it?"

Sakato's face contorted as he struggled with grief. "We trained and fought side by side since Camp Shelby," he said finally, barely above a whisper. "Can you believe that was only nine months ago?"

"He was always to my left, at Salerno, at Belvedere, that village by Rome —" Sakato's body shook, and he leaned over in his crouched position, holding his face in his hands. "We always talked about our families and what we'll do after the war. Most of all, he wanted to prove that he was a good American. Not Japanese-American. *American.* He was the best friend I ever had."

Moments of silence passed, and he continued haltingly. "We were fighting our way into Bruyères. I heard the whistle of an artillery round. I yelled, 'Incoming!' The explosion threw me ten feet, and when I came back up, my friend was on his back and bleeding from his neck. I ran to him screaming for a medic and tried to stop the bleeding, but it was coming too fast. The litter guys took him—" He gasped. "He died on the way to the aid station."

"That's rough," Tokiwa said. He leaned back against a wall and sighed. "We've lost so many friends." He sat quietly for a time and then said, "Maybe after this war, we'll be accepted as Americans who love our country."

The two men remained silent for a time. Then, as if to change the subject, Sakato said, "The 141st passed through our lines here yesterday. A jeep stopped by this position. Its top was down, and a lieutenant just stared at us. He didn't look mean, just curious."

Tokiwa laughed. "We're still an oddity."

"I suppose so," Sakato mused. "Do you think they'll ever accept us?"

Tokiwa shrugged. "I can tell you that the 142nd and 143rd Regiments do. They were happy with what we did in the fighting through Bruyères and Biffontaine. We were the spearhead for those operations and took the most casualties."

Having collected his composure, Sakato turned to Tokiwa inquiringly. "You're one of our dispatch couriers. What's the news? What's going on?"

Tokiwa grunted. "I don't read the messages, and I'm not supposed to hear things." He flashed a grin. "But I do. It's not that I intend to, but the brass don't pay attention when I'm there. They keep talking while I'm delivering dispatches."

"So what's going on? We heard tremendous rumbles and saw huge flashes up the road toward Saint-Dié. I suppose that was the 141st?"

Tokiwa nodded grimly. "They sent their 1st Battalion up a big hill last night. They took the objective, but the Germans counterattacked quickly. Now those guys are cut off. The 2nd Battalion tried to break through to them, but were beaten back. The 142nd and 143rd also went in to rescue them —" He shook his head and muttered, "No dice."

Sakato mulled the information without expression. Then he turned to Tokiwa with a look of dawning realization. "That only leaves us. Dahlquist is going to send us in."

"That's the kind of stuff I'm not supposed to hear, and I didn't say that."

Sakato scrutinized Tokiwa's face. "You didn't have to." He glanced at Tokiwa. "When do we pull out?"

"Soon."

Sakato returned his gaze to his sector. "Go for broke," he muttered.

36

October 29, 1944
Biffontaine, France

Private George Sakato peered up the front of Hill 617 on its east side, hoping for a glimpse through the night of anything that might be used as a hand-hold or a firm place to put his feet on his ascent up the steep slope. The weather had cleared the day before, providing much better conditions under which to scale the rough terrain, but the torrential rain of previous days and volumes of spilled blood had seeped deep into the soil, and the resulting fetid mud had not yet fully dried. Enemy fire continued its deluge as the battalion fought to rescue the 141st and refused to forsake their trapped comrades.

Sakato had been with the 442nd at its inception, when its only subordinate unit was the 100th Battalion. As it had fought across Italy and France, it expanded by adding 2nd and 3rd Battalions, but the 100th had so distinguished itself in battle that it kept its original designation. Otherwise, it would have been 1st Battalion.

As the 442nd grew, the original four thousand *Nisei* soldiers, now seasoned combat veterans, were spread among the new units. Thus, Sakato transferred to 2nd Battalion while his friend, Rudy Tokiwa, moved over to K Company in the 3rd Battalion.

The nearly full moon, obscured by heavy clouds, offered no increase in visibility as the troops continued their climb. Only flashes of field artillery explosions provided any view uphill. For a fleeting moment Sakato thought about the irony of nearby artillery explosions becoming so commonplace that he barely took note of them. So dark was the night despite battle flickers and red and green tracers that squads had resorted to climbing close together, each member holding onto the man ahead of him with one hand, a prescription for losing ten or more men with a single burst of an artillery round.

After Corporal Rudy Tokiwa had departed back to 442nd headquarters four days ago, the regiment's 100th Battalion and three more companies from the regiment's 2nd and 3rd Battalions had, just as Tokiwa intimated, received orders to prepare to assault Hill 617 and effect a rescue of the 141st. Departing that same night, the assault force had road-marched through torrential, freezing rain on a route cleared by the 143rd Regiment, and it arrived in its assembly area early the next morning.

Reconnaissance patrols went out during the day, reports came in, and the leadership solidified their plans. At dawn the next morning, the assault began.

Unfortunately, the 442nd battalions did not accomplish their mission that day. As they commenced their grueling climb, inching their way uphill, hours-long barrages dropped on the *Nisei* soldiers. They had intended to reach the crest that night. Instead, they spent it on the hillside among the willows in treacherous weather, attempting to gain yet more inches.

The weather cleared on the second day of battle, but otherwise, as a bitterly cold winter night closed in, the tactical situation mirrored the first night, with more casualties. However, the *Nisei* soldiers had reached within a few hundred feet of the crest.

Rumors floated back to Sakato and his compatriots of horrendous casualty figures. The blood-soaked ground gave testament to the numbers of ultimate sacrifices already made. Those troops still able continued to fight.

The battle went into its third night. Sakato huddled with a buddy in a hastily dug foxhole that was really nothing more than a shallow carve-out on the hillside. Artillery whistled by overhead in concert with the staccato rattle of machine gun fire and the crackle of Garand M-1s and Karabiner 98K rifles.

As first light spread across the sky, Sakato heard the order to push forward again. Adrenaline drove him now, and he shoved to his feet and started forward. As his squad proceeded, they encountered battle-weary enemy soldiers only too happy to surrender. More than once, he saw them kneeling in front of their *Nisei* captors, pale, shaking with cold and fear, their arms over their heads in pitiful surrender. With no time or resources to handle the prisoners, they were searched and instructed to make their way down the hill to be directed to a POW holding area.

As his squad continued to fight up the hill, it encountered and subdued enemy positions. In one machine gun nest, Sakato found an intact German MG 42 machine gun and a P-38 pistol, both with full loads of ammunition. He picked them up and carried them forward into battle.

The companies of 2nd and 3rd Battalions continued uphill, taking more prisoners, but also absorbing more of their own casualties. Enemy machine guns fired down on Sakato's platoon. For a period that seemed to him to last for hours but was probably only minutes, the firefight built and then waned.

Images of his best friend, bleeding at the neck and gasping for air, flashed through Sakato's mind. Suddenly furious, he leaped to his feet and charged the enemy nest while firing both his captured MG 42 and the P-38. As he ran, holding down the trigger of his machine gun and firing off pistol shots, wild cheers and suppressive gunfire to his left and right erupted from his squad mates, aimed at the enemy position.

Panting, struggling under the weight of his weapons and ammo, Sakato raced up the rugged slope, dodging from side to side as he went to frustrate return fire. Then, he was at the side of the nest and firing into it. When he finally stopped and leaned exhausted against the concrete wall, no one inside stirred.

Sakato's audacity inspired his squad mates, who surged forward, over-running adjacent positions. However, before they could consolidate on the objective, the Germans counterattacked, and Sakato's squad leader went down. The squad froze.

Sakato took charge. In a calm but loud voice and drawing on instinct he had never known he possessed, he directed his squad members where to direct their fire, and as the tide returned to their favor, he secured the position, thus meeting his squad's objective.

When the dust had cleared and casualties were counted, Sakato had taken down a dozen of the enemy. With his squad members, they had captured thirty-four prisoners. As the acknowledged tacit leader, he set about preparing for the final assault on the summit.

On the opposite side of Hill 617, Tokiwa struggled laterally along the side of the steep slope through the dense willow forest. Radio contact had broken down and he had an urgent message for 3rd Battalion headquarters.

He moved carefully along his own lines to reduce chances of being mistaken for the enemy and shot by his own comrades. Stepping across the slippery hillside was less difficult than climbing up it, but he still had to listen and take cover from artillery rounds. He knew the way though, for having made the trip several times since the battle was joined.

His battalion was nearing the ridge, but the Germans fought more fiercely than he had ever experienced before, probably, he guessed, because if they lost this High Vosges mountain range, the way was clear onto the Alsation Plain, and the Allies would be within twenty miles of the Rhine River.

At last, he arrived at the battalion headquarters, which at this point consisted of the executive officer and a radio operator. The commander and sergeant major were out checking the line.

Tokiwa stumbled in, panting and streaming sweat, despite the cold. "Sir," he said, "an urgent message from my CO."

Gaunt and fatigued, the major gazed at him through sunken eyes. "Let's have it."

With the faces of fallen comrades rolling through his mind, Tokiwa reported robotically, "Captain Masayuki says immediate reinforcements are imperative. K Company is almost combat-ineffective on the left flank."

"What's your current headcount?"

Tokiwa's jaw trembled but he maintained composure. "When I left, it was less than thirty."

The major visibly paled. "Out of a hundred and fifty men?"

"That was as of when I left the captain nearly an hour ago. Combat was fierce then. We're close to the summit, sir, but we're not there yet."

Comprehending the implications that would follow the collapse of either flank, the major mulled silently, but only for a moment. "I'm sorry," he said grimly. "Tell your captain that we have no more men to provide. All our forces are in the fight."

Tokiwa stared into the major's eyes a moment. Then he bowed slightly from force of cultural habit. "I'll tell him, sir."

Captain Masayuki received the news stoically. "I anticipated as much." He extended his hand and shook Tokiwa's. "Go back to your squad. We are about to execute the final assault. And good luck. Your father and mother would be proud. You're a good soldier."

Daylight broke, and the assault began. The men of E Company, in coordination with adjacent units, started creeping uphill. Gunfire paused, and all was quiet, aside from, ironically, the music of early morning songbirds and leaves rustling in the wind.

Suddenly, a burst of machine gun fire broke the stillness, muzzle flashes spewed against the half-lit sky, and hot steel hissed through the air. Tokiwa lunged behind a fallen log. Almost as soon as he landed prone against it, bullets bit into its upper side, showering him with dead bark. Moments later, a massive barrage of artillery arced through the sky and exploded on the summit.

Pinned down behind the log with bullets whizzing over his head and bark splintering around him, he was sure that his time on earth was ended. Then he heard a hand grenade explode, the machine gun stopped firing, and his squad leader yelled.

"Let's go," the sergeant roared. "We're almost to the top. We have these guys beat. Get on your feet and follow me."

37

October 30, 1944
On the Summit of Hill 617, East of Biffontaine, France

Zack stood under an overhang outside his headquarters, a bare concrete structure the *Wehrmacht* had built and then vacated three days ago as the 141ˢᵗ moved onto the summit. He rubbed his hands together, blew into them to warm them, and watched the vapor of his own breath join heavy fog that limited visibility to just in front of his face. He listened carefully, but all he heard was freezing rain drizzling onto the roof of the hut.

He turned to the dark figure standing next to him, First Sergeant Huberth. "Top, you take the left this time, and I'll head to the right."

Huberth acknowledged his directive, and the two stepped into the dark for the umpteenth time to check on the readiness of their men. On this night, all of them occupied dug-in positions on the perimeter. The same was true for all of the 141ˢᵗ Regiment.

As Zack moved quietly from position to position offering encouragement to his soldiers, he scanned downhill, careful not to expose himself. His message for each man in all the foxholes was the same. "The krauts are comin'," he whispered in a low voice accompanied by a comradely slap on the shoulder, "and so is our rescue. This will be over soon."

He saw the faces only in shadows, but he knew the hopes and aspirations of each man, and their hometowns and family backgrounds. He knew which ones nursed wounds even as they waited in their foxholes to defend against an enemy attack. In his mind's eye, he saw the exhausted, emaciated, and in some cases agonized faces and the mix of hope and determination in their eyes.

Over the past two days, gunfire originating from the valley floor and moving uphill at an excruciatingly slow pace had erupted, aimed at the German enemies between the summit and the valley floor. Reports came in from the perimeter of small soldiers in US Army uniforms flitting from position to position. Hope surged among the 141st troops that rescue was at hand.

Immediately after Higgins adjourned his meeting on the first morning of the siege, the company commanders, including Zack, had set about developing defensive positions. The perimeter was established, left and right boundaries set for interlocking fields of fire, adjacent unit coordination done, and communications procedures set up.

Fortunately, having departed the assembly area just the day before on full bellies, the troops were not then ravenous, but Higgins' mandate for pooling food and cutting rations still raised groans. A patrol found a muddy bit of stream off the left flank. It was outside the perimeter and could be approached cautiously, and if the water that the battalion brought and collected from the rain ran out, the muddy hole could be the only source.

Further investigation revealed that the Germans used the same watering hole. On being informed, Higgins immediately ordered a twenty-four-hour observation post to watch it, and he mandated that no German soldier should be shot when approaching it. "Look," he said, explaining his rationale, "we don't want them poisoning it, and they won't, as long as they also need it. Now if our OPs see one of them about to dump something in it —" He cocked his head and pursed his lips. "You get my meanin'."

The commanders did, and put out the word.

Throughout that day, small German patrols tested the entire 141st perimeter and were met with fierce resistance on each assault. Zack, moving along his lines, saw his own men rally under fire with surprisingly high morale despite the grim circumstances.

A significant problem arose by the second day of the siege. Litter teams and volunteers had brought in dead and wounded. The corpses were splayed on the ground to be buried when conditions allowed, but those same conditions, clearer weather, brought more aggressive ground assaults and more accurate artillery. Proper burials were difficult. Digging graves was life-threatening.

Medical supplies ran out early that day. Men cried out in agony for lack of sedatives, infections turned to gangrene, and as yet, the weather had not provided a reprieve that would allow air-dropped resupply.

Food, already sparsely rationed, ran out later the same day. Radio messages, clipped short to conserve batteries, pleaded with higher headquarters for air drops. The 36th staff promised that supplies would come, but weather proved prohibitive.

Stored water ran low by the third day, and frequent patrols had to be dispatched to bring in more from the muddy watering hole. A filtration system of sorts removed most of the gunk, but the unpurified water brought on physical problems of another sort.

Zack's respect for Higgins grew enormously. The acting battalion commander circled the perimeter tirelessly, even as artillery barrages and ground attacks escalated into seemingly unending hisses, whistles, ground-shaking explosions, dust clouds mixing with fog, small-arms clatter, and the buzzsaw of MG 24 machine guns. And casualties mounted.

Zack learned from Higgins how to analyze the flow of battle, where weak spots were, when actions might be only feints, and how to encourage his commanders, their platoon leaders, and the soldiers in their foxholes.

Despite the remorseless enemy pressure, each attack was rebuffed until nightfall, when the Germans, characteristically, fell back to their own lines. Then, with hunger gnawing and thirst threatening, Higgins nudged the soldiers to fortify their defenses further against attacks that were sure to resume the following day.

Zack had accompanied Higgins on many of his rounds, admiring his manner that was both commanding and gregarious. Higgins liked the troops, and they liked him, despite the conditions. Nevertheless, as night settled in, Higgins startled Zack and caused momentary panic when he remarked, "You know if anything happens to me, this command falls on you."

Zack stopped dead in his tracks. "Don't say that. Don't even think it. What you do is far above my ability. Nothing's going to happen to you."

Higgins grunted. "You're the logical choice. You *do* have the most combat experience among the commanders—"

"But you've had the schooling—"

"Which you've picked up on. As a soldier, you're a natural."

Zack scrutinized Higgins' face, looking for signs of humor. "You're not kidding?"

"I'm not."

Zack breathed in and out hard. "That's not going to happen. The weather will break, supplies will get air-dropped, a rescue team will come through."

Higgins laughed. "I hope you're right. Our own 2nd Battalion couldn't get through, and neither could the 142nd or 143rd. That's why we can't get out."

Then, early on the fourth day, the deep, throaty roar of aircraft engines caused every man to scan the skies with immediate hope. No German aircraft had been seen for weeks, and the weather had cleared sufficiently that an airdrop of supplies might be feasible. Four P-47 Thunderbolt fighters appeared initially as dots on the sky, and as they approached, they were met with heavy enemy gunfire from below the ridge. The fighters responded with thunderous bursts from a total of thirty-two .50 Cal machine guns, four to both wings of each aircraft, spewing onto the enemy six hundred and thirty two rounds of lead per second.

Their roar grew louder, and they cleared the crest to wild cheering and joyful antics of the beleaguered men below. Those on the perimeter stayed in position and returned fire as the enemy attempted to exploit the distraction with a hasty assault.

Zack watched as the aircraft flew over the summit, and he recognized the markings of the 405th Fighter Squadron of the 371st Fighter Group. The unit had flown air support for the 141st previously, and he waved a jaunty salute in gratitude as they passed over. In place of extended-range fuel tanks normally attached under each wing for longer flights, each carried a large canister capable of transporting one hundred and fifty pounds of supplies.

They released at the near edge of the perimeter. Immediately, air drag forced open the parachute canopies attached to the cylinders, and they floated to the ground, landing with a hard crunch. Soldiers quickly surrounded them and carried their contents to Higgins' designated central location.

More reasons for optimism occurred later when the sounds of military vehicles in the valley below the eastern ridge indicated military preparations for a large operation. The besieged men on the hill's summit believed them to be a rescue effort in the making. Their hopes were bolstered by another resupply flight of six aircraft that flew over in the early afternoon.

Zack watched his soldiers' faces light up with anticipation, and then saw disappointment approaching despair settle in as the day waned, and evening shadows lengthened with no more drops. The combined deliveries provided only enough food to ease hunger for two hundred and fifty men for a day, and ammunition and medical supplies to last for roughly the same time.

"We've been promised more tomorrow," Higgins told the company commanders. "We'll see. The weather doesn't look promising."

Four more flights of six to ten planes attempted to drop additional supplies the next day, but did not reach the besieged soldiers. Thick fog and strong wind currents conspired to prevent delivery on-target. In one instance, a P-47 crashed into the hillside. The pilot did not bail out, and the accompanying explosion told the story of a young life ended. Another fighter sputtered within sight of the summit, obviously damaged by flak, and turned away to limp back to its airfield. Canisters that *did* drop floated into enemy territory.

Plans communicated from the rear were obviously hatched in desperation. "They're going to do what?" one of the commanders demanded incredulously when Higgins explained the scheme. "They really intend to fire artillery rounds filled with chocolate bars?"

"The idea sounds crazy to me too," Higgins admitted. He grinned. "If it succeeds, it's food, and we live to fight another day. At least it'll be a sign to the men that they're not forgotten." He shrugged. "It's all we've got for the moment. The 405th is gonna try to do more airdrops too, but again, the weather doesn't look good." He shrugged again. "Another assault up the hill is supposed to be coming soon."

He glanced at the circle of grim faces and took a deep breath. "Let's hope for the best."

At the appointed time the next day, with wind swirling thick fog over Hill 617, the men of the 141st took cover. In the distance, they heard the 36th Division's artillery rounds launch, and moments later they heard the quiet hiss and whistle as they dropped to the ground. The wind had intensified and deflected the rounds away from their intended drop zone, and in some cases, in close proximity to where some soldiers took cover. Despite that the shells were non-explosive, when they impacted on the ground, jagged pieces of them and the chocolate bars flew in all directions, becoming other forms of shrapnel that hit soldiers.

Observing the fiasco, Higgins grabbed his radio operator and called HQ with a waning battery. "Cease fire," he yelled into the mic. "That chocolate is hitting our men. Now I've got more casualties."

Watching from the side, Zack could not decide if the situation was humorous or tragic, and his body was too spent for a spontaneous reaction. Despite the kerfuffle, each conscious man enjoyed at least a taste of chocolate that evening with his last scraps of food.

One other event occurred that day that set Zack's nerves on edge. Huberth approached him with a private whose face dripped with sweat. The soldier heaved from exertion.

Before Huberth could say anything, the private blurted, "Sir, I shot a German at the watering hole."

Zack stared at him in consternation and then whirled to the first sergeant, who nodded. "He did, sir," Huberth said. "I've already investigated. The kraut had a box of poison. He was about to pour it into the water." He gestured toward the private. "Mac here stopped him with one shot."

Zack's mind flew into overdrive. He grabbed a small notebook from his jacket pocket, scratched out a note with the nub of a pencil, tore off the page, and handed it to the private. "Good job, Mac. Now get this into Lieutenant Higgins' hands. Make sure he reads it. Go."

After the soldier left, Huberth inquired, "What was that about?"

"The krauts don't need that watering hole anymore. They're going to assault in a big way tonight, probably at dawn. Let's get every man on the perimeter."

Massive and repeated explosions and large volumes of gunfire jarred Zack to full alertness. He bounded to his feet from sitting against the wall in his headquarters where he had rested while fighting to stay awake after his last round of checking troops on the perimeter. "It's started," he yelled to Huberth, who grabbed his own gear.

The sun had not yet risen above the mountain ridge across the valley, but its light was sufficient for limited visibility out to twenty feet, and it cast a ghostly pall over Hill 617's summit. The freezing rain had abated, but drops dripped steadily from the roof of Zack's headquarters and surrounding willows.

While he hunkered down, awaiting the end of the artillery barrage that would serve to warn of an imminent ground attack, he thought back over his parting conversation on the rubbled street of Biffontaine with Lieutenant Wilbur regarding the trap of willows. *It has certainly become that.*

Quiet descended on the hilltop, but it lasted only moments. Then furious machine guns, small arms, and mortars cut loose from below the ridge. Almost simultaneously, the soldiers on the perimeter returned fire. As Zack crept up to the line, he saw the muzzle flash of German weapons, but as he peered through the fog, he noticed that along the enemy line, some weapons appeared to be firing downhill. And barely visible through the mist and farther down, he saw dim flashes aimed uphill.

He hurried back to his nearest platoon leader. "Help is on the way. Tell your men to hold steady. Reinforcements are closing in."

He found Huberth and related the news. "Top, get the word out."

Just then a voice called to him, "Lieutenant Littlefield!"

A private, panting and staggering, trotted up to him and held out a scrap of paper. "Sir, the commander at A Company told me to give this directly to you. He says it's urgent and needs your immediate attention."

Zack took the message and scanned it. Stunned, he stared at the private. Then he called urgently to Huberth, who had started back to the line. "Top, hold up."

As Huberth returned, Zack turned to the private. "What happened to Lieutenant Higgins?"

"He was captured, sir, right after the last barrage. The krauts broke through the line and overran his headquarters. We beat them back, but they took the lieutenant and several other prisoners with them."

His mind in a whirl, Zack handed Huberth the note. It read, "Lieutenant Zack Littlefield, if you are reading this, I've been removed from battle. This is my written order to take command of the companies on Hill 617 until relieved by proper authority. The other company commanders will have been advised by the same method. Major McCoy approves. Best of luck, Lieutenant Higgins."

Dumbfounded, Zack asked the messenger, "How did you get this note?"

"The commander of A Company had it, sir. He sent me over here with it as soon as I informed him of Lieutenant Higgins' capture. He sent other runners with messages to the other commanders."

Zack took a deep breath. "All right," he said, turning to Huberth. "Top, get the First Platoon leader over here. Tell him he's in command of Bravo Company and to be ready to send reinforcements if I call for them. I'm heading over to see where the break happened." He turned to the private. "Do you know where that is?"

"Yes, sir."

"Lead the way."

The breach had occurred in Delta Company's sector. The commander there, Lieutenant Riley, was disconsolate. "We don't have time for blame," Zack told him. "The krauts were bound to come through somewhere. Our rescue party is fighting up the front side of the hill now. Show me your position."

While the fight raged downhill of the perimeter, Riley guided Zack cautiously through D Company's area to the specific place where the attack had succeeded. The ground there was a shallow downward slope with many trees, and it dropped off sharply sixty yards out.

"The problem here," Riley explained, "is that with the steep hillside beyond the shallow area, the enemy is almost impossible to see until he's right on us. If we extend the perimeter out that far, we're creating vulnerable flanks, which could also be in our own line of fire. I had observation posts out there, but the Germans coming our way were crack troops." He dropped his head and strained to speak again. "They took out both of my OPs." He let out a long breath. "Both KIAs."

Zack regarded Riley with a long, searching look. "We'll grieve later, I promise. Right now, we've got this hill to defend. That's how we keep the rest of your men alive. Are you up to it?"

Riley took a deep breath as he straightened up. "Yes, sir," he replied resolutely.

"Good. We've got to close this vulnerability. We'll draw in from the left and right side of the breach and I'll bring over two machine guns from more defensible terrain. Meanwhile, pull your perimeter back and reinforce where it was penetrated and make sure you've got good fields of fire down that slope. If they come through there again, pour it on." As an afterthought, he added, "We'll get some more men over here too."

As the battle increased in intensity, Zack maneuvered around the perimeter of his four companies, reduced in size by casualties. By his estimate, the 141st had occupied the summit with two hundred and fifty men, some already incapacitated with wounds, and some killed. Among those on the front line, many had taken hits that left them just barely combat-capable. Besides being depleted in numbers, even the soldiers so far untouched by bullets or shrapnel were weakened by hunger, thirst, and lack of sleep. All approached their physical limits.

Zack checked in foxholes and fighting positions along the line. Ammunition was running low, but there was no more of it to distribute. He grunted at the irony of reminding troops to conserve it in the midst of a determined assault. "Use your own judgment," he advised. "We don't know how long this will last."

All the food had been consumed, and the gunky liquid from the watering hole hardly fulfilled the need to quench thirst. The notion sank deep in Zack's psyche that all he had to offer was encouragement and advice on positioning.

The battle raged on. Then Zack noticed German firepower being diverted downhill, away from the summit. Increasingly, firefights below took place across the hillside rather than up and down it.

Thrill surged through him. "We're winning," he shouted to those nearby. He was in Charlie Company's area, and the commander was there with him. He stopped and looked around. "No one's firing this way at all now. The krauts have stopped shooting at us. Tell your men to hold fire."

A soldier emerged from between the willows. His Oriental features identified him immediately as someone not of the 141st, but he wore a US Army uniform with corporal stripes. He stared at Zack, his rifle held at the ready. Zack stared back.

"Are you with the 141st, sir?" the corporal asked.

"I am. Are you with the 442nd?"

"Yes, sir. I'm Corporal Tokiwa of Company E." He pointed his weapon away.

Zack extended his hand and gasped, "For the rest of my life, yours will be the most beautiful face I'll ever see. Where's the rest of your unit?"

Tokiwa smiled sadly. "What's left of us is right behind me, sir." He turned and gazed down the hillside where gunfire had waned to sporadic. "The rest are down there somewhere."

Another soldier of the 442nd appeared, and then a captain. "This is my squad leader, Sergeant Yamamoto," Tokiwa said as the noncom approached. When the officer arrived next to them, he said, "This is my company commander, Captain Masayuki."

Zack came to attention and saluted. Masayuki returned the salute. "No need for formality, Lieutenant," he said.

"Sir," Zack replied, "that was an expression of gratitude."

Masayuki scrutinized him and returned a distant smile. "Our mission is to relieve you on this hill. Take me to your commander."

Zack stood straight and swallowed hard. "I'm it, sir."

Masayuki stared at him without reaction. "What happened to Colonel Bird?"

"Wounded enroute."

"Major McCoy?"

"We were cut off before his headquarters arrived."

"No captains?"

"The regiment is short of them. All the commanders are lieutenants without XOs."

"And you've been running the show all this time?"

"No, sir. That would be Lieutenant Higgins. He was captured this morning right after the first barrage."

Masayuki looked around at the haggard, soiled soldiers resting in their positions and returning his scrutiny. "Walk me through your defenses. We'll take over while we still have enough daylight to get you back behind friendly lines."

As the pair walked along the front edge of the ridge, the exchange of gunfire faded completely, and more soldiers of the 2nd and 3rd Battalions of the 442nd RCT climbed to the summit. Masayuki took in the poor physical condition of the 141st soldiers and their wounded, and he radioed immediately for emergency food and medical supplies to be brought forward with the 442nd's headquarters.

"You and Higgins did a remarkable job," he told Zack. "I'm not sure that we could have done better."

"That's a tremendous compliment, sir. Thank you."

Suddenly, the smallest soldier Zack had ever seen clambered over the defenses along the eastern edge of the summit.

Zack stared.

The soldier noticed and scrutinized Zack. Then he called, "Sir, I saw you the other day in Biffontaine." He walked over, presented himself, and saluted. "I'm Private Sakato. You stopped your jeep behind my machine gun position."

Simultaneously feeling very tall yet very small, Zack gazed at the diminutive soldier. "I did, didn't I." He reached out his hand. "I was curious. Now I'm in your debt forever."

Sakato smiled with lingering sadness. "Sir, I'm with the 'Go For Broke' Regiment. We do our duty for honor and our country."

"You do," Zack said in a broken voice, and saluted. Sakato returned the salute.

Tokiwa and Sakato sat on a low step to the side of the entrance into the building that had been Zack's headquarters. Sakato had gone looking for Tokiwa, and after finding him, the two helped members of the 1st Battalion of the 141st gather their gear and form up. Then they watched as the unit road-marched out of the area along the same logging road they had used to enter it.

Sakato nudged Tokiwa. "We made it through that hell."

Tokiwa leaned back against the wall and let out a long sigh. "We did, didn't we."

They were quiet for a time, each with his own thoughts. Then Sakato asked, "What's the news? What happens next?"

Tokiwa shook his head. "It's mostly bad."

"Tell me. I want to know."

"Our casualty numbers were high."

"How high?"

Tokiwa sighed. "I'll tell you, but you didn't hear it from me. The numbers will come out anyway."

"How high?" Sakato asked stubbornly.

"Eight hundred," Tokiwa said softly.

Sakato gaped. "Eight hundred? To save two hundred and fifty?"

Tokiwa nodded and let out a long breath. "After the final assault, my company came out with only nineteen members out of a hundred and seventy." His voice caught, and he rasped, "So many buddies. Gone."

Sakato reached over and grasped his friend's shoulder.

"There's more," Tokiwa said. "Another unit is on its way to replace us here. We go back into action in two days."

Sakato whirled on him. "You can't be serious. We've been in constant combat for three weeks, since Bruyères." He leaned his back against the wall, shaking his head in disbelief. "Two days, huh," he said after a while. "We'd better rest up while we're here. Anything else?"

Tokiwa brightened a bit. "Yeah, as a matter of fact. But you can't say anything to anyone. It's about you."

"Me?" Sakato said, visibly concerned. "Why?"

"Your company commander put you up for a Congressional Medal of

Honor. Something about charging a machine gun nest and saving the lives of your whole squad."

Sakato pursed his lips and shook his head. "That was nothing. I was mad because of what happened to my friend at Bruyères. The brass will never award something like that to me."

Tokiwa gave his friend a jocular punch in the shoulder. "Why not?"

Sakato laughed uproariously and turned to face Tokiwa. "Because, my friend, I look like you."

38

One Day Earlier, October 29, 1944
RAF Lossiemouth, Scotland

As he began taxiing his modified Lancaster, Jeremy returned Andrew's salute through the windshield, as well as those of Sky and Mark. The three men, visible only by dim positioning lights and braced along the tarmac against a stiff wind, watched his departure in the dark at three hours past midnight.

While Jeremy maneuvered the bomber onto the tarmac for Operation Obviate, he recalled soberly all the activity that had occurred to bring about this moment during the six weeks since last month's RAF attempt against the *Tirpitz*. To make the aircraft lighter for this mission, the responsibilities covered by the navigator, bombardier, and flight sergeant had been modified, streamlined, and transferred, leaving a crew of four to carry out the mission: pilot, navigator, wireless operator, and tail gunner.

Within days of the raid at Kåfjord, Jeremy had attended a formal briefing on the results of their previous mission and passed along the information to his crew in a meeting. "Intel came down from above that the *Tirpitz* sailed to Tromsø," he explained. "As far as we know, the ship is still operational, but needed major repairs. Resistance observers on the ground at Kåfjord and Tromsø reported a large hole in its bow, which must be why it needed tugboat assistance to make that two-hundred-mile trip.

"The fjord at Tromsø is not nearly as defensible as Kåfjord, but we're hearing that the town itself is important to the jerries to defend against an Allied invasion they expect in that vicinity. So their idea is to use the *Tirpitz* as a static artillery base, at least until repairs are completed. The water there is shallow, so the ship won't completely submerge when it sinks. We'll have to utterly destroy it to remove it as a German asset, free up our navy to protect shipping along those northern seas, and continue to supply the Soviets."

They had gathered in the squadron briefing hut at RAF Bardney in Lincolnshire during the week after Jeremy had stayed at Claire's and met with the Davises, and the implications of that visit weighed on his mind. He dreaded the notion of losing Timmy, but the effect on Claire was terrible to contemplate. For now, though, he had to dismiss those concerns and concentrate on the task at hand, and it was a formidable one.

"Both 9 and 617 Squadrons will fly at full strength for Operation Obviate," he said after providing the latest update on the *Tirpitz* location and status, "but I'm sorry to say—or happy to say, take your pick on which best suits you—that the requirements of the mission dictate that we can't take everyone along." Amid puzzled glances between crew members, he continued. "The location is close enough from RAF Lossiemouth in the north of Scotland that we can fly from there to Tromsø and back without refueling. But that's a twenty-two-hundred-mile roundtrip, so we'll have to take on extra fuel. Each plane will be carrying a single six-ton Tall Boy, so you know what that means."

"No Johnnie Walkers," Mark chimed in.

Andrew groaned. "Weight reduction. That's what it really means. Who and what gets jettisoned?"

Jeremy frowned. "For starters, Flight Sergeant, you do."

"That figures. You can do without me for a single sortie, even one that long. But for that distance, you'll need two blister tanks of extra fuel and probably a long-range fuel tank taken from a Mosquito and slung under the Lancaster. Plus you need room for the Tall Boy." He looked around at the other crew members. "That takes out Sky in the mid-gunner's turret. You'll need Sparks on the wireless, though.

"With that much fuel, you'll still be overweight for takeoff, so you'll have to cut more weight." Andrew paused and stared at the ceiling while he did mental calculations. "You need your bombardier and your navigator, but you can't take both, so which one will it be?"

Jeremy had listened with increasing astonishment while Andrew spoke. "My word, but you are a wonder, Flight Sergeant. That's almost precisely what Operations figured out with their maps, slide rulers, and protractors. The one piece of information they had that you didn't was that, using known pieces of geography related to time, velocity, and distance, they've determined a new way of pinpointing targets."

Now it was Mark's turn to groan. "That means I'm out." He exhaled, though whether from relief or dismay, Jeremy could not be sure. "I should feel lucky," Mark commented, "but I hate the thought of all of you flyin' off to a party without me."

"Yeah, yeah," Sky cut in, "so much bravado. You, me, and the sergeant will just have to drown our sorrows at the local pub until they return."

After much jocular shoulder-punching and hoo-hawing among the crew, Jeremy continued, "Even after all that, we'll have to remove the nose and mid-upper turrets." He glanced toward his tail gunner. "Stal, we'll have to cut your ammo load by half."

Stal frowned noncommittally without remark.

"We'll have to cover the holes left by those empty positions," Andrew growled.

"We will, but that's not all." Jeremy's facial expression changed to one of "believe it or not." He furrowed his brow. "Our Rolls-Royce Merlin V-12 engines won't do the job. We'll have to trade them out for the newer and more powerful Merlin 24s."

He looked across the stunned faces. Six sets of eyes stared back in stupefied wonder. "Sir," Andrew said, scoffing, "is Ops out of its bloody mind? You're talking about, what, forty aircraft, each with four engines, and none of them have those new Merlins on them now. That's a hundred and sixty engines to trade out. Do you have any idea how many man-hours that'll take or the number of mechanical errors?"

Jeremy replied somberly, "I *don't* know, Flight Sergeant. That's why I have you. Where our particular aircraft is concerned, I'll need you to watch over and make sure the job gets done right." He chuckled. "I don't have a death wish. I have a fiancée to come home to."

"We've all heard about Amélie, sir," one of the crewmembers quipped.

Startled, Jeremy asked, "How? How have you heard?"

"The mail just started running between here and France again," another called. "There's a letter postmarked from Paris waiting for you at headquarters. It's all perfumed up with 'Amélie' in the return address. Doesn't take a genius to figure it out."

Jeremy's heart took a leap. He turned red, and his crew teased him further.

"Hey, we haven't dubbed our Lancaster yet," Sparks called. "How about "*Amélie's Hope*?"

Amid laughter and bantering, Sky volunteered, "I can do the artwork."

Andrew had been listening with a frown. He stood and glanced around at the crew with the air of having something profound to say. The men quieted down. "I've seen Amélie's picture on the instrument panel ample times," he said gruffly. "Perhaps I can pry it away from Major Littlefield long enough that Sky can make a fair likeness."

The crew cheered. Jeremy flushed a deep red, and tried to hold back an irrepressible grin. He let the revelry continue for a few minutes. Then he raised his hands for quiet. "All right, all right, let's get on with the matter at hand. Air Group 5 has the number of engines we need, but they're on aircraft scattered about its area, and as Andrew indicated, the effort to switch them out will be monumental. Then, each aircraft will have to be recertified for flight. And finally, we'll have to do practice runs so we know how to fly the new configuration."

Questions abounded with much pertinent comment and an equal amount of grousing. After the briefing, Jeremy hurried to squadron head-quarters where, just as his crew had said, a letter from Amélie awaited. He tore it open and read.

"Dearest Jeremy, I hope this gets to you. Chantal assured me that, some-how, she could get it into the hands of Madame Fourcade, who would forward it to SOE, and then, magically, it would come to you.

"I'm healthy and well, and wanted you to know that, and I hope you are too. I will say that this ambulance-driving experience is one I would not wish on anyone. I've gained insight into the lives and sufferings of front-line soldiers. Those men are unbelievable. Their countries don't appreciate them enough. I even feel for the German soldiers. I've picked up many. They're just like our own. In their case, they fight because they have no choice, and all they want now is to go home. The arrogance they displayed in Paris months ago is gone. Like us, they want this war over.

"I love you, Jeremy. I always will, Amélie."

Jeremy re-read the letter several times, imagining Amélie's honey-colored eyes and auburn hair. He was happy that, somewhere, Amélie and Chantal had been together in one place, at least for a time, and they were in contact with Fourcade. For a moment, he allowed worry to cloud his thinking. Then, he tucked the letter in his jacket, where it remained to be read repeatedly as weeks passed and he prepared his crew.

He had been astounded over the next few days at the massive effort and organization to complete the engine transfers. Nineteen bombers of various types from across the United Kingdom flew into RAF Bardney, propelled by Merlin 24s. Once there, swarms of mechanics worked around the clock to dismount, transfer, and mount the newer M 24 engines onto the Lancasters. The visiting aircraft flew out three days later powered by the older Merlin V-12 engines. Similar action took place on twenty Lancasters for No. 617 Squadron at RAF Scampton.

Andrew had thrown himself into his oversight tasks, watching the mechanics that did the transfer closely, and then checking tolerances and tightness. The flight sergeant leaned in with the technicians under bright lights in a hangar long into the nights, turning wrenches and screwdrivers, scraping knuckles, and making certain that Amélie's Hope received the best attention.

His own crew had removed the nose and upper turrets and sealed the cavities with metal plates customized for the purpose. They had also wrestled in two huge rubber blisters for extra petrol and connected them to the main fuel line. Electronics were re-worked so that Scout could handle both navigation and bombardier duties. And finally, they slung a long-range fuel pod from a Mosquito below the airframe.

When the engine transfer and all other modifications were complete, Andrew ran each of his subordinates through their systems checks several times. Only when satisfied that every component operated as it should did he sign off on a certificate stating that the bomber was ready to be flight-tested. Jeremy had monitored the progress of each aircraft in his flight and was pleased to see that all of the flight sergeants oversaw their aircrafts' modifications with competence and dedication that matched Andrews'.

Jeremy had managed to get away twice more to see Claire. She maintained her optimism, but whereas in the past that had been her natural disposition, now she struggled for it.

The nanny, Elsie, went to see friends when Jeremy visited so that the two siblings could talk without constraint. Jeremy played with Timmy for hours while Claire watched with sad eyes that turned deliberately bright over a forced smile when Timmy caught her eye.

The Davises had been back to visit twice more while Jeremy was away, but they had given Claire no indication of their desires or intentions regarding Timmy, and Claire dared not inquire for risking a response that would leave her heartbroken.

"This stress is worse than all the others you've shouldered," Jeremy told her.

With a pinched face, Claire nodded and wiped her eyes. In a hollow voice, she said, "Timmy's like my own child. I couldn't bear to think that I'll never see him again."

That had been two weeks earlier, and because of security prohibitions, neither Jeremy nor Claire could talk about work to lighten the mood. Neither had time for hobbies, and talk of family and friends, despite fun memories, led to wondering when the pain would end.

As he had left Claire's house last weekend, Jeremy picked Timmy up and held him tightly. "I love you, little man. Don't ever forget that. Wherever you are, I'll find you."

"I know, Jermy, but I'll be right here with Gigi." He looked solemnly into Jeremy's eyes. "And my granny and grandpa can come visit. I like them."

Claire had been standing a few feet away and overheard. She turned away sharply, and her body shook from stifling sniffles. After a moment, she turned back to them. "You're going on a mission again, aren't you, Jeremy?" she said. "You don't have to answer. I can sense it. Please take care of yourself."

With that, she embraced Jeremy while he still held Timmy, and then they parted.

That farewell bore down on Jeremy as he pulled the stick back on *Amélie's Hope* with the likeness emblazoned below the cockpit window. As the aircraft lifted into the sky, he glanced down at Amélie's photo in its place on his instrument panel. Then he keyed the mic on the intercom. "Tromsø," he announced with forced confidence for the benefit of his crew, "here we come."

Tromsø, Norway

Jeremy tensed in anticipation as *Amélie's Hope* approached the target area. As missions go, this one had been easy so far. A de Havilland DH 98 Mosquito had been sent ahead for weather reconnaissance and had reported clear skies all the way.

To avoid alerting either the *Luftwaffe* or the *Kriegsmarine* of large numbers of aircraft heading north, each bomber assigned to Operation Obviate had flown separately, following Norway's coastline well out to sea at only fifteen hundred feet above the choppy North Sea. At one point, Jeremy listened over the radio as a 617 pilot reported engine trouble that required a return to Scotland. Aside from that, the mission proceeded smoothly.

Fortunately, No. 100 Squadron, an RAF unit that specialized in electronic countermeasures, had probed German radar along Norway's coast and found a gap in coverage between Namsos and Mosjøen. At the latitude that bisected the distance between them, Jeremy turned east and ascended to thirteen thousand feet, well above the mountain peaks.

The mission planners had chosen this route to reach a rendezvous point over Lake Torneträsk. From there both squadrons would attack from the southeast, a direction they anticipated that the Germans would not expect. However, since the lake was inside Sweden, that country's sovereignty would be violated.

Thus, when Jeremy crossed the Norwegian-Swedish border, he was not surprised when he drew anti-aircraft fire. He heard the flak. However, it was too far below his flight path to cause concern. His aircraft was not hit, and he heard no radio traffic indicating that any others had been casualties.

Three weeks before mission launch, Jeremy had been called into his squadron's headquarters. There, Wing Commander James Bazin informed Jeremy that he would be commanding a flight. "You came over from the army, and given your record, reducing you from your rank of major seemed unfair, but your flight experience was dated, and flights are usually led by lieutenants or captains. You've proven yourself and we're short a leader, so you're it."

The move was made without fanfare, and it was heralded by Jeremy's own crewmen, who were proud to serve with their acknowledged hero. Rumors had been whispered around both squadrons that:

"He's the chap who escaped Dunkirk and rescued that little boy during the *Lancastria* bombing."

"He flew Spitfires in the Battle of Britain and nightfighters during the *blitz*."

"He was in the Saint-Nazaire raid."

"He was an undercover operator for the SOE in France."

Jeremy's expanded responsibilities required his oversight of three additional planes and crew. The interaction on the present mission would be minimal, however, due to the separate flight paths taken by each bomber. Until the squadron rendezvoused over Lake Torneträsk, Jeremy had little to do other than monitor their progress. That left him plenty of time to take in the view of the breathtaking expanse of mountains and valleys surrounding the lake, the low hills in its closer proximity, and the gentle slope that descended on its south side and flattened out near the shoreline.

As Jeremy orbited over isolated villages, he wondered about what neutral Sweden's citizens must be thinking. The war was not supposed to touch them.

Several miles north of him, a flight of Lancasters had formed and was ascending northward to its attack altitude. His flight was next.

Four hours after departure from RAF Lossiemouth, Jeremy had heard disturbing news over his radio. The attack was then just beginning. No. 617 Squadron had led, and its first aircraft had departed from Scotland two hours before Jeremy's flight on the same route. "The weather's changed," came the transmission. "It was clear over the target when we first came into the area. An unexpected front blew over Tromsø and the *fjord*. It's obscured everything. We can see nothing of the town, the water, or the *Tirpitz*."

Jeremy had continued on, as he knew both squadrons would, wondering if the mission would be called. He doubted that such would happen because the *Luftwaffe* would already have been alerted to the route of attack as well as its radar gap between Namsos and Mosjøen. Another chance to attack might not occur.

"Proceed with the mission," he heard.

Six hours after takeoff, at mid-morning, Jeremy's flight formed in a V-formation over the vast Lake Torneträsk, with one Lancaster to Jeremy's left rear and two to his right. They banked north, and began their climb to attack position.

The weather for most of the remaining distance was clear. They flew over multiple mountain ranges that crossed their flightpath laterally, as well as valleys and deep gorges running generally north. Then, as Wing Commander Tait had reported from 617's lead aircraft, the area around the fjord was fully obscured by heavy clouds.

"What's the plan," Scout called over the intercom. He now doubled as navigator and bombardier.

"Let me know when you think we're over the target."

"Roger."

They flew on. The bad weather buffeted the aircraft. Jeremy and Sparks listened carefully to incoming transmissions. So thick was the cloud cover that, in nearly three hours of bombing, not a single aircrew had seen the battleship.

"By my calculations," Scout called after several minutes, "we're over *Tirpitz* now, but I can't be certain. I have no landmarks to go by."

"Hold up," Jeremy responded. "We'll go around, get our bearings, and come back in." He called to his squadron leader, Bazin. "Dogwood, this is Labrador. Has the forward squadron cleared the area?"

"Roger. They dropped their payloads, and two of my flights ahead of yours have as well. So far, no big bangs."

"Roger. I'm at fourteen thousand feet. Is it clear to fifteen thousand?"

"Roger."

"Request permission to circle and come round again. Will stagger my flight above for a second attempt."

"Understood. Granted. Come back in one piece. Out."

"Scout," Jeremy called. "We'll circle north and keep going around to clear skies. Then, get us some bearings, and we'll head back in."

Scout acknowledged the order, and Jeremy called to the other pilots in his flight. "You heard my transmission with Dogwood. Stagger behind and above, drop at will or circle. Your choice. Head home when ready."

Three electronic squawks in his ear let him know that he had been understood, and his orders would be followed.

Turbulence tossed *Amélie's Hope* about. By Jeremy's calculation, she was nearly alone in the sky, or soon would be. No. 617 and two of No. 9's flights had cleared. That left only his own flight and two others still in the target area, a total of twelve bombers of the original thirty-nine.

The flight broke into open air. Scout determined position, plotted a course, and relayed an azimuth to Jeremy. Forty-five minutes after their first attempt, Scout announced that they were again over the target area—"or should be," he qualified.

"If you're not sure, then let's wait and go around again," Jeremy called, but two of his pilots had already dropped their Tall Boys. "Too late," one called back. "Sorry, Skipper."

"Head for home," he called back. To his navigator, he said, "Keep a close watch on fuel. We're making another run. We need enough to get home."

On the third go-around, the sole remaining bomber in Jeremy's flight also dropped its Tall Boy and departed. "I think it's just us up here now," Sparks called. "I'm not hearing any cross-talk from the target area."

"And still no big bangs," Jeremy replied. "We're going around again."

Normal chatter on the aircraft's intercom ceased as a sense of dread pervaded *Amélie's Hope*.

"Sir, you know the jerries must be sending out fighters by now," Sparks called.

"And they're as blind as we are," Jeremy replied. "Scout, keep a fix as best you can on our position relative to the target and I'll pull tighter circles."

The lone bomber's fourth pass yielded no better result, and neither did the fifth. "Sir," Sparks called again, "the fuel."

"Roger. Scout, drop at will and plot a course for RAF Sumburgh."

Next Day, October 30, 1944
RAF Sumburgh, Scotland

Jeremy entered the flight hut to his crewmembers' stoic faces, rendering a subdued atmosphere bordering on hostile. Flight Sergeant Andrew had taken him aside and warned him of the crew's attitude. "They feel like you unnecessarily and recklessly risked their lives," he said grimly. "I'm not saying that you did. I don't know. I wasn't there. I'm just letting you know the way they feel."

With Andrew standing behind him, Jeremy faced five sets of stony, accusing eyes. Crew members lounged back in their seats, arms crossed, glaring.

"You're upset with me," he began. "You've lost faith in my judgment."

No one moved or said a word in response.

"Hear me out. After that, I'll approve any request for transfer."

No one stirred.

"The situation as we know it is this," Jeremy continued. "We, the 9 and 617 Squadrons, dropped thirty-nine bombs. As far as we know, not a single one hit. Intelligence reports are still coming in, one of which indicates that a near miss caused some damage to the *Tirpitz*, but we don't know how much.

"That means we'll have to run the mission again."

Silence continued.

"We don't know yet if the *Tirpitz* is operational, if it can sail on its own power, or if its guns work. We do know that if it can run on its own steam, it will have survived thirty-three attempts to destroy it to date, and it continues to threaten our navy and our merchant shipping in the North Sea. That means Soviet initiatives in the east will grind to a halt, either prolonging the war or ending in an Allied defeat. Our families will suffer longer. Meanwhile, a single direct hit from a Tall Boy can destroy that ship.

"Recall that the *Bismarck* took out the HMS *Hood*, our own largest battleship, with a single shot. Granted, it was a lucky shot, but any endeavor owes its success to a measure of luck. However, just getting that ship in the right vicinity to take the kill shot took an inordinate amount of skill. In that case, the *Bismarck's* round struck on top of *Hood's* ammunition magazine. The secondary explosions sank our ship within minutes."

Jeremy paused to let the implications sink in.

"Our whole mission was based on luck. Of course, the Tall Boys are more precise than previous bombs, but the reason why two squadrons flew thirty-nine of them was to increase the odds. Tall Boys are not, as a matter of fact, precise, especially in a fog. Yet if a single one hits, chances are good but not guaranteed that it will put the *Tirpitz* out of commission.

"Winter approaches and could obliterate our possibilities of success this year. On our final two passes at Tromsø, we carried the last chance of destroying or disabling that ship, at least during Operation Obviate."

Jeremy took a deep breath and squared his shoulders. "I had to take that chance."

He paused to let his statement sink in. "My final point is this: given the same information and what we know now, I'd do the same thing again."

He gazed across the crewmembers' faces. They exchanged implacable glances.

Jeremy turned to Andrew. "That's all, Flight Sergeant. I'll be on the flight line checking the other crews. Please inform me by day's end which of *Amélie's Hope's* positions need replacements."

39

Same Day, October 30, 1944
Baccarat, France

After transporting severely wounded soldiers to a field hospital west of town, and with Amélie at the wheel, she and Danièle drove toward the battlefront on a rubble-strewn road on the southwestern edge of Baccarat at mid-morning, their fourth trip of the day. Colder weather had arrived behind unusually heavy rain, and trees lining the lane on either side had shed their autumn leaves, aided by fierce crossfire that had raged there. The town had been exploited by *Wehrmacht* forces as a center of operations due to its defensible terrain resulting from low-lying hills and forests and a wide river.

Fighting exhaustion and dejection from the terrible injuries she had witnessed and from seeing yet another centuries-old treasure of a town lying desolate from the ravages of war, Amélie understood why it had become a major objective for General Leclerc. It was the last town of size to be liberated on his drive to Strasbourg.

Sitting astride the Meurthe River and surrounded by agricultural fields in a wide valley between the Low Vosges' hills, it had been famous since the 1700s for its glassworks fabrication, particularly its crystal. Tinted windows created there adorned cathedrals across France, and exquisite chandeliers, sets of wine glasses, and other works of crystal art fashioned in Baccarat graced many fine houses and palaces.

Driving through, Amélie tried to imagine the town as it had been before the war had blighted the stately stone buildings lining the streets and the elegant gardens and pathways along the river. Her mind wandered to recollections of better times and places, of the Dunkirk of her childhood, of Paris on her visit there with her father, and of France as it had been. *Will it ever be restored?*

Her musings were interrupted by the distant sounds of heavy guns.

A French soldier darted in front of the ambulance and waved frantically. Amélie slammed on the brakes. In the passenger seat, Danièle braced against the dashboard. The battered vehicle squealed to a stop.

The soldier stumbled to the driver's side window. "We need your help," he cried, and Amélie recognized, by his pallor, that he was in shock. His legs wobbled as he leaned against the door and pointed to a nearby hill. "Up there," he gasped. "The lieute—" He panted as he struggled to speak. "Direct hit."

Amélie looked where he pointed. A single tank smoldered, black wispy smoke rising from its turret.

Danièle was already out of the ambulance with her kit and heading for the hill. Amélie, careful not to knock the soldier down, opened her door, slid out, and put a supporting arm around his back. She led him to the back of the vehicle, opened the panel doors, helped him lie down inside on one of the stretchers, elevated his feet on the inside of his helmet to aid blood flow to his head, and drew a blanket over him. "Stay here," she said. "I'll check you out when I get back."

Grabbing her kit, she took off after Danièle. The route led through the ruins of a bombed-out dwelling, identified by its foundation and part of a wall still buttressed by a fireplace situated between what had been a kitchen and a front room.

She hurried over the cement floor, leaped down a back step, and ran through a small barren garden, taking fleeting notice that the back gate, ironically, was untouched. She raced on, reached the hill, and slowed to a labored walk on the bare incline, panting heavily.

Glancing up the slope, she saw two more soldiers and the outline of the tank, but the sun's glare prevented her from making out any detail. She scanned the area, looking for Danièle, and spotted her holding herself upright with one hand against a tree and bent over, retching convulsively.

Amélie hurried to her. "Danièle, what's wrong?"

The nurse looked up with red eyes streaming tears, and sobs compounded her spasms, causing a coughing fit. She pointed at the tank.

Amélie turned to take a deliberate look. Having been around other war machines destroyed by fire, she thought she had been inured to the worst cases, but as she approached cautiously, she fought off spasms similar to those that afflicted Danièle.

The tank had taken a direct hit, as the soldier on the road had said, but whether from an enemy tank or artillery round, Amélie could not discern. It had been ripped open, and the scorched upper torso of a man lay splayed over the lip of the turret. Steeling her nerves and holding her breath against the stench, Amélie drew closer and saw the lower torso and legs in a similar state in the hull of the tank.

One of the soldiers drew alongside of her. "That's our lieutenant," he said morosely. "He was alone in the tank. We were on ground watch farther out. Marcel, the soldier you met on the road, was the closest, and he was thrown by the blast. The battle had moved on through town and was nearly over. Our unit was pulling rear security. And then—wham. It came from a tank across that field." He indicated the direction of the retreating German army. "We thought another counterattack was coming, but none showed up."

The soldier stared at the tank, disbelief on his face. "We don't have commo, so we couldn't contact anyone, and we couldn't move the body for the heat. Your ambulance was the first vehicle to come by in several hours."

Danièle had steadied herself and joined Amélie and the soldier. "Sorry," she murmured to Amélie.

"Take a few minutes to catch your breath," Amélie replied. "None of the soldiers have external injuries. The two up here are in mild shock, but who wouldn't be? The one below in the ambulance needs a thorough checkup."

She turned to the soldier. "We'll move the body to where a recovery team will find it. Then we'll take the three of you to an aid station."

"Thank you," Danièle said as she and Amélie drove from an aid station well away from the front. "You were very strong back there. I wasn't—"

"*Ah, n'importe quoi,*" Amélie replied. "We've all had our moments. If I'd been the first one to reach the site, I'd have been worse."

"Saving lives keeps me going," Danièle muttered. "I don't think I could recover bodies on a regular basis. It's gruesome."

"Especially that one. The lieutenant never knew he was hit."

The ever-present smell of spent munitions and unrecovered corpses thickened as they emerged on the eastern side of town. With deliberate stoicism, Amélie steered toward the rat-tat-tat of machine guns, the pops of rifles and pistols, the explosions of tanks, mortars, and artillery, all adding to the strident clamor that had become the routine of front-line soldiers and the Rochambelles.

They came to the aid station from which they had transported the earlier casualties to field hospitals. A stream of wounded soldiers, some carried on stretchers, limped and plodded their way into the stone building, which had been an infirmary.

Amélie had no sooner parked the ambulance than a counterattack erupted, aimed at a nearby bridge across the Meurthe. Mortar rounds exploded, indicating close German proximity. An MG 24, with its buzzsaw sound, spewed fire onto a supply truck crossing the bridge. Return fire streamed from the near side of the river. The line of wounded soldiers hurried as best they could to gain the safety of the building.

Amélie jammed the vehicle into reverse and backed the ambulance into an alley next to the building. Then she and Danièle hopped out and ran inside.

Firing along the river spread, and its volume built into a full-fledged firefight thundering all around the aid station. Bullets flew in both directions, many of them striking the infirmary's stone walls. Inside, wounded soldiers screamed in agony.

Since her first encounter with the dead and wounded at Dompaire, Amélie had seen more carnage than she would have thought was possible. She had stiffened her spine and forced a cheerful disposition when administering aid, but she was always aghast at the horrific wounds, and these soldiers were typical of battlefield injuries. Some had caught bullets in their legs, others in their arms, or both. One had a sucking chest wound, others had deep gashes from shrapnel now embedded deep in their flesh. Still others...

The two women and a pair of regular army medics covered as many as possible with available blankets, provided first aid, and comforted as best they could, but with no place to go, they were left with coping until the battle ended. They moved the men away from windows, gave them water, held their hands, and dragged three who died to another room. And they waited.

"If the Germans win this skirmish, we'll all be POWs," Danièle observed.

Tired to the bone, Amélie acknowledged her words with a nod. She dropped her head and covered her ears with her hands, but the effort was useless. The thunder of big guns and the sound of striking bullets continued.

The afternoon wore on. The battle waned, built again, repeated the pattern several times, and at twilight, it finally ceased.

Daring to peek outside the door, Amélie saw French soldiers maneuvering about to secure the area. Baccarat was safe, at least for the moment.

She and Danièle made several roundtrips to the field hospital, trading off at driving, and then headed to the coordinates they had received for the night's cantonment, which, fortunately, was in a dry vacant home. The furnishings were sparse, they were told, but at least they would sleep on cots out of the cold wind and rain.

On their way to the house, Amélie gripped the steering wheel, fighting to stay alert. The rough road kept her awake, but once in a while, she found herself veering off, and she swerved back at the last moment. Danièle tried to keep up conversation, but she too fought exhaustion, and found trying not to yawn a losing proposition.

At last, they arrived in the area where the other Rochambelles' vehicles were parked. Because the drivers and nurses had learned a soldier's skill for sleeping under any conditions, and given the hour and the long day under fire, the two latecomers expected that everyone would be asleep.

Instead, they found most of their comrades awake and consoling Zizon Sicot, who, with her partner, Denise Colin, had just arrived from their own last trip of the day to the field hospital. As Amélie and Danièle joined the group, Denise was speaking. "That doctor should be drawn and quartered," she declared. "We save lives, not decide who we should *try* to save and who is too far gone."

"What happened," Danièle asked.

"Tell them," Denise said.

Still distraught, Zizon glanced briefly at the group, and then covered her eyes.

"All right, then I'll tell them," Denise said. Her eyes burned with anger as she spoke. "For most of the day, we were northeast of Baccarat, up at Badonviller and in the surrounding areas. We were between the front lines in no-man's land for much of it, and we picked up wounded men from both sides.

"One German told me he refused to be carried in the same ambulance with French soldiers." She harrumphed, relishing telling this part of the story. "Can you believe it? I stuck him with a healthy dose of morphine, and that was the end of that."

Amélie listened as Denise continued to relate the details of the day, but her mind went to what she knew of Zizon. Of all the Rochambelles aside from Toto herself, Zizon was the one that Amélie would have least expected to be unnerved by something on the battlefield. She was tiny, five feet two inches, quite beautiful, with big eyes, a turned-up nose, and short-cropped hair, but she was very tough. Ironically, she was also very fashion-conscious even to the extent of having suede boots custom-made when the ones issued to her were several sizes too small.

Her prominent family had escaped from France to Rabat, Morocco, ahead of the German invasion. There, they invited French soldiers training in the area to their large house. That led to Zizon's learning of the Rocham-belles, whereupon she became enamored with their work and decided to apply. Her size and driving skills gave some concern, but she had competed in a cross-desert race and overcame any objections.

Always an outspoken supporter of de Gaulle, Zizon had famously worn a medal bearing the symbol of the Free French, the Lorraine Cross, to a dinner with Florence Conrad and General Giraud. The general had ardently opposed de Gaulle. However, instead of being offended by Zizon's effrontery, he had insisted on seating her next to him, and they conversed all evening.

On reporting for duty with the Rochambelles, Zizon announced that she had given up her past life and was ready for her new adventure. She had subsequently traveled with them and Leclerc's forces across North Africa, landed at Normandy with his newly formed French 2nd Armored Division, and crossed France with it.

"That doctor's actions were unconscionable." Denise's angry tone jarred Amélie back to attention. "On our last trip to pick up the wounded, there was one man who was shot in the heart and both arms. A machine gun burst had sprayed right across him."

Groans of commiseration rose from the listeners.

"Somehow," Denise went on, "he was still alive and conscious. We got him into the ambulance, but he wouldn't let go of Zizon's hand. She was driving with one hand and leaned sideways to hold his with her other hand, and he kept saying, 'Please don't let go. You know I'll never hold the hand of another woman.'

"We got to the field hospital and carried him inside. The doctor took one look at him, followed us out, and scolded Zizon. He said, 'Why did you bring him here? You know he won't live through the night.'"

Denise put her arm around the tiny driver's shoulders and squeezed her. "Our precious Zizon was heartbroken. I've never seen her shaken at all, until now."

Zizon had remained silent with her face still hidden while Denise related the story. After Denise's last comment, Zizon lowered her hands. Her face was puffy and her eyes red, but she sniffed and said, "Thank you. I'll heal."

Later, Amélie snuggled in a bedroll on the cot in the darkness of the vacant house thinking about the day's events. She had believed that no battlefield experience could be worse than the one of that morning with the two scorched halves of the lieutenant's body. *How would I feel holding the warm hand of a young man, shot through the heart, who knows he is about to die.*

Deliberately, she forced her thoughts to Jeremy, picturing his face smiling into her own. *Where are you, my darling. Are you alive?*

She sat up, thinking of writing to him, but that would require rummaging about the room for a flashlight, pen, paper, and a writing surface. The noise might awaken Danièle, who was already fast asleep across the room. Amélie dismissed the idea, and within minutes, overcome by exhaustion, she slept.

40

November 5, 1944
Château de Gélacourt, Baccarat, France

Although the château had a rich history dating back to the founders of the celebrated glassworks and crystal factory, and despite its classical French architecture with elegant façades and landscaped grounds, Paul Littlefield did not care to stay in it. The palatial abode needed major repairs. Dry space for General Leclerc's planning staff was an unmet imperative, and even the room where the general slept required buckets to catch rainwater dripping through the ceiling.

However, Leclerc's adjutant had requisitioned the place with short notice, and the general did not expect his headquarters to stay there long. Every day he grew more eager to meet his most cherished objective.

Paul knocked on the general's office and entered. "Sir, you sent for me."

"*Mais oui.*" Leclerc rose, smiling broadly, gestured to a seating area across the room, and joined Paul. After they were seated, he said, "Strasbourg is nearly within our grasp. Only one obstacle remains before liberating the city and fulfilling my oath."

"Saverne? I've studied the map and the terrain model you ordered of the Baccarat area. The route to Saverne looks challenging. The pass is narrow, and the *Wehrmacht* built impressive defenses."

"Agreed, but I have a plan that I'm confident will defeat those defenses quickly. Unfortunately, that's not the biggest obstacle."

Paul drew back, puzzled. "I don't understand."

"I sent for you because there's a role for you to play in meeting my vow, but before going into that, I need to discuss philosophy."

Paul looked at him quizzically without speaking.

The general stood and paced with a furrowed brow. Normally, he supported his tall, trim frame with a cane due to the effect of his old wound, but in this office setting, he just limped. "You've been with me since Normandy, Paul. You know how I operate. I'm loyal to our allies, but I am French first, and I will risk our position with the Allies in the best interest of France.

"In the drive to liberate Paris, you saw that I disobeyed my corps commander at risk of a court-martial. I was prepared to disregard de Gaulle, which could have been viewed as treason, but I *knew* that the way to Paris was open, and that if we did not act immediately, the city would be destroyed by demolitions *les boches* had planted there."

"You put your division on the road before you received the order. I knew that."

"I don't apologize. The fact is, events moved swiftly and the results were much better than if the Allies had waited or bypassed Paris for later deliverance, as General Eisenhower intended. Instead, the city was saved intact."

"I can't dispute that, sir."

Leclerc continued to pace while he reflected. "I despise Marshal Pétain. He deserves credit for his heroism in the last war, but he betrayed France when he surrendered most of it to the Germans and then had the audacity to pretend to govern the part of France *les boches* didn't occupy. And he did it from a resort town, Vichy. I was a French army officer when all that happened, and by law, I had a duty to obey him. I chose not to."

His tone had risen, and he lowered it as he continued. "I'm a moral man, Paul, raised in a Jesuit school. My core belief is that the eternal struggle between good and evil takes place in a man's soul. The practical implication for an officer is that a debate should always exist in his mind to distinguish between mindless obedience and moral duty to his country."

Paul listened intently, but with a sinking stomach. *He's going to ask me to do something he thinks I might object to.*

"The situation is this. The Oath of Kufra binds me and my command to refuse to lay down our arms until the French flag flies once more over Strasbourg Cathedral."

Paul nodded. "I know, but I've never grasped why Strasbourg. Why not Paris? That was an amazing victory. Several generals claim it, but I know it was yours."

Leclerc shrugged. "I'm satisfied with the victory. I don't need the credit. I'll answer your question, but first, let me finish explaining a dilemma and how you can help."

He paused to gather his thoughts. "The Allies pushed rapidly across France. Several other divisions of Patton's 3rd Army now operate in the Vosges. When they emerge on the other side, they'll be on flat terrain and poised to strike Strasbourg from the northeast. Patch's 7th Army is in the mountains too, and approaching from the south. They'll also break out of the mountains soon.

"We're only sixty miles west of Strasbourg, but we face very rugged terrain—"

Paul peered sharply at Leclerc. "Your concern is that Patton or Patch might liberate the city before you've had a chance."

Leclerc let out a long breath and nodded. "That is exactly the point. It is crucial that French forces liberate Strasbourg. French soldiers, my division, led the campaign to liberate Paris, and de Gaulle's provisional government is recognized as the legitimate authority in France. Yet even now, our Allied diplomats treat him and his appointees with less than normal diplomatic courtesy. We're not seen as full Allied partners, even though our army fought alongside them in North Africa and all the way here."

His exasperation grew. "Our oath doesn't specify that French forces must liberate Strasbourg except by implication, but under the circumstances, I think French forces *must* lead, or our provisional government will wither. Long-term stability across Europe will be at risk."

Paul leaned back in his chair. To gain time while he mulled, he asked again, "But why did your oath center on Strasbourg? Why not Paris?"

Leclerc sat back down facing Paul and spoke ardently. "The reasons are simple. First, our Allied forces would logically invade either across the English Channel or on our southern coast." He smiled. "The Allies did both, and Paris was the halfway point to Germany. Strasbourg is almost on the border. By the time it is free, most of France will have been liberated.

"Secondly, Strasbourg was the capital of Alsace before the Germans annexed it years ago, but it was French for most of its history, and Lorraine too. The Germans seized the region in 1870 during the Franco-Prussian war. It came back to France as part of the Treaty of Versailles at the end of the last big war, but Germany annexed it again in 1940 when it invaded France.

"So, Strasbourg is culturally and historically vital to France. It had its beginnings under Charlemagne, the Father of Europe, who turned it into a trading crossroads."

Paul listened closely. Then he chuckled. "General, I must say, if your facts don't carry the day, your passion should. What do you want me to do?"

Leclerc inhaled deeply. "As you know, my 2nd Armored Division is now attached to General Haislip's XV Corps as part of Patton's 3rd Army.

"As we speak, Haislip is negotiating 3rd Army's boundaries on behalf of his boss, General Patton. He's having meetings with Generals Bradley and Eisenhower for that purpose. My division is deployed along the southern edge of Patton's battle area. If that limit were widened to include Strasbourg, the task of liberating it would fall naturally to me. I need to influence the discussions to cause that result."

He moved over to a large wall map and swept his hand across a swath of central France. "As you can see, we're moving through the Low Vosges, and once we've cleared Saverne, we'll be in a perfect position to strike Strasbourg."

He indicated a wider swath of France. "Some elements of Patton's army pushed north of us to Haguenau, closer to the German border. Three of his divisions are almost positioned to move on Strasbourg." He lowered his voice almost to an urgent whisper. "None of them are French."

Paul studied the map. "I see. And you must still get through Saverne."

Leclerc nodded, stepped close to Paul, and spoke insistently. "I *know*

Patton's thinking. He wants Strasbourg, and he's as impatient as I am." He straightened and resumed pacing. "He's a great battlefield commander, but he's not known for subtlety."

"That he is not," Paul agreed, chuckling.

"I don't know Haislip well. I hear he's pro-French, but I think he's indifferent to who liberates Strasbourg. He's my immediate superior, and he could agree to stand aside for another division to take the city without knowing the ramifications."

Paul stared as he perceived what Leclerc probably intended to ask of him. "You want me to try to influence those decisions."

"Hear me out, Paul. Eisenhower knows you."

Paul shook his head doubtfully. "That was three years ago. He probably wouldn't remember me."

"He sent you with General Clark to North Africa to convince the Vichy-French army to flip to our side. I think he'll remember you. In any event, this Strasbourg matter must be handled delicately. Patton might want to push for an early assault on Strasbourg. I need time to get past Saverne. That will take two days."

Paul regarded Leclerc in somber silence while contemplating. "Are you asking me to run an intelligence operation on a US higher command?"

Leclerc whirled on him with a tight smile. "You could think of it that way. I know your background, Paul. You'll know how to pull this off. If I go there, my sheer presence will announce my purpose. I'll be seen as another pushy Frenchman insisting on my way for the glory of France." He chuckled. "That's how General de Gaulle is seen in places. In this case, if I did that, I would probably alienate the support I need. We must be more subtle."

While Leclerc had been speaking, Paul recalled other intelligence operations he had worked. One of his first had presented a moral dilemma in that it involved withholding information from a critical ally, specifically President Roosevelt. Further, the charms of a willing vixen had been engaged to affect the vote of an influential US senator who opposed legislation enacting Roosevelt's Lend-Lease program. The result had been passage of the needed legislation, which led to Liberty ship production and convoys that prevented hunger among the British populace by delivering desper-

ately needed foodstuffs. By also transporting weapons, the op was still leading, even now, to a victory in the Battle of the Atlantic.

In another operation, Paul had helped deceive the Germans and Ital-
ians about landing sites for the Allied invasion of Italy. The idea was to
convince the Germans that the attack would come on Italy's eastern coast
rather than on Sicily's southern coast.

The complicated intelligence maneuver had involved a cadaver dressed
in a British Royal Marine's combat uniform and carrying secret war plans.
The ruse worked, and the *Wehrmacht* moved several divisions from Sicily to
mainland Italy, and thus, Allied troops landed on the intended shores
almost unopposed. Countless soldiers were saved from death or serious
wounds, at least for the moment on that beach.

Despite the successes of those and other operations in which Paul had
participated, two of which involved assassinations, his sense of fair play
had pricked his conscience. He had subsumed it in the face of the deadly
threat to his country and against the reality that the enemy exercised no
such scruples. The existential danger to Great Britain was not yet extinguished. Leclerc shared the same concern for France.

"Could you go directly to Patton? You two get along quite well."

Leclerc shook his head. "I tried that once before going into Paris. He
told me point-blank that he didn't care about political considerations, that
he was there to win the war." He sighed. "Besides, I'd be jumping the chain
of command, which could alienate Haislip permanently, and I need him in
my corner."

"What happens if I can't convince Haislip?"

"I'm confident that you will, but delicacy is a must. Approaching him
directly on the issue might close down the conversation. Haislip is probably
receiving pressure from Patton to get on with liberating Strasbourg. I went
to see Haislip myself, but his staff said he was sick. Frankly, I suspect that
was a ruse. I think he just didn't want to have to consider waiting for my
division to get through Saverne."

Paul remained pensive. "You really believe a French division must lead
the charge to buttress France's sovereignty?"

"Without a doubt," Leclerc replied. "You saw the militia groups in Paris.
The largest and best organized were the communists answering to Joseph

Stalin in Russia. De Gaulle has them under control at the moment, but it's been barely two months since we liberated the capital, and he's been busy setting up his government. If the communists sense weakness or see signs that de Gaulle is considered less than an Allied partner, they will pounce. Stalin will replace Hitler as the Continent's strongman."

Paul took a moment to ponder, and then rose to his feet. "All right, sir, I understand the situation. How can I help?"

Next Day, November 6, 1944
Sarrebourg, France

Paul sat outside General Haislip's office feeling very much like a miscreant waiting to see the principal for an infraction. In point of fact, he was sitting outside precisely that office in a schoolhouse, now used temporarily as the XV Corps headquarters while more suitable facilities were being prepared.

He had enjoyed the drive from Baccarat, heading northeast for twenty-four miles. Situated well behind friendly lines, the road wound lazily through wide-open fields and small hamlets. With little fear of being attacked from either air or ground forces, Paul took the opportunity to take in the scenic landscape and breathe in the crisp autumn air.

He arrived at the XV Corps headquarters less than an hour after leaving Baccarat, and he presented his credentials at various security checkpoints. Once inside the school building, he inquired his way to General Haislip's office with the statement, "I'm a British liaison officer with a message to be delivered directly to the general."

After several such iterations at successive internal checkpoints, he arrived at the principal's office. The Corps chief of staff, Colonel Wattinger, scrutinized him. "What's the message?"

"I'm sorry, sir, my orders are to deliver it only to General Haislip."

"Who the hell are you, *Lieutenant Colonel*?" the chief said testily.

"Sir, you have my credentials. If you doubt them, please feel free to call General Eisenhower to check them out."

Taken aback, Wattinger stared grimly at him, and then went into Haislip's office, closing the door behind him. He re-appeared twenty minutes later, ushered Paul into the room, and hovered behind him.

Haislip had been talking on a desk phone and hung up as Paul entered. He leaned back in his chair and eyed Paul suspiciously. "What's your message?"

Paul turned, glanced at the chief of staff, and turned back to Haislip. "Sir, my orders are that you are to be the only recipient."

Behind him, Wattinger grunted in exasperation. Haislip's eyes narrowed even further, but he signaled to the chief with a nod to leave the two of them alone.

When the colonel had departed, Haislip rose from his desk and peered at Paul. "This had better be good. You've got fifteen minutes, but before you start—" He gestured at the phone. "I was talking with Ike as you entered."

Blood rose in Paul's cheeks at the mention of General Eisenhower's nickname.

Haislip continued, "So you've been present in meetings with him and Churchill. You've worked directly for Ike, Mark Clark, and Monty. You've been involved in covert operations, and you've commanded at least two infantry battalions in combat." He folded his arms and lowered his voice to almost a growl. "But Ike didn't send you. He *suggested* I hear you out. So what are you doing here?"

Paul squared his shoulders. "Sir, you're setting up a headquarters here to plan 3rd Army's crossing of the Rhine."

"So?"

Paul indicated a map on the wall. "May I show you?"

Haislip raised an eyebrow but assented.

"As I understand, sir," Paul began, "you're drawing up the corps boundaries, prepping for the campaign to cross the Rhi—"

"Hold up right there. Before you go on, I want to know right now who you represent."

Paul hesitated.

"That's an order, Colonel. It's either that or the stockade. Take your pick."

Paul came to attention. "As you guessed, General, I'm here under false pretenses. I'm the British—"

"Don't tell me, let me guess. You're the British liaison who works for General Leclerc. I'd heard of you before speaking with Ike."

Paul nodded. "Guilty, sir."

Haislip regarded him sternly. Then he chuckled, and finally broke into a full belly-laugh. "So, our impatient lion lives up to his name."

"Sir, he requested that you allow me five minutes to explain what he told me. In his mind, it's a crucial point that might be overlooked." He added, "I've been with the general since Normandy. I can tell you that he acts out of devotion to his country."

Haislip chuckled. "I promise you, he has an ego too, probably as big as Patton's, but he's better at hiding it." He looked at his watch. "I know what he wants, but go ahead. You've got five minutes."

Paul talked fast, relaying to Haislip the pertinent details Leclerc had divulged the day before. After the time limit had elapsed, Haislip wanted to know more and asked questions. When he was finally satisfied, he escorted Paul to the door. "Tell Leclerc that I'll give the matter some thought. In any event, Patton will have to approve."

41

November 12, 1944
Tromsø, Norway

"We've been hit," Scout called urgently over the intercom. "The main tank was punctured on the right wing's leading edge. Liquid is streaming along its underside."

"Roger," Jeremy Littlefield responded. "Keep me apprised."

He checked his fuel gauge, but at the moment it showed no appreciable decrease beyond the level of a minute ago. The main tanks were self-sealing, and unless fuel gushed out, he should have enough to make his bomb run and get home.

As before, they had flown into Swedish airspace and started their approach to Tromsø from over Lake Torneträsk. When they entered the target area, Jeremy had heard anti-aircraft guns and thought he heard dull thuds against the airframe, but above the roar of the engines, he could not be sure. Now he knew. *No second or third passes this time.*

No. 617 took the lead, with Wing Commander Tait out front. Twenty-nine bombers from both Nos. 9 and 617 Squadrons had flown out early this morning for Operation Catechism, following the same plan and route that they had used for the last sortie. Remarkably, the radar gap still existed between Namsos and Mosjøen, but ominously, intelligence had come down reporting that *Luftwaffe* fighter units of unknown type and more anti-aircraft guns had moved into Tromsø's vicinity to protect the *Tirpitz*.

On recalling that part of the mission brief, Jeremy took a deep breath and scanned the skies. "Stal, are you awake. You're all the defense we've got. The anti-aircraft guns are firing at us. We can expect the fighters at any moment."

"Right-o, Skipper. I'm topped up and ready."

Jeremy smiled. He was gratified that his crew had remained intact and had re-coalesced after his meeting to address their discontent with his actions during Obviate. One by one that day, the crew members had appeared on the flight line to carry out their normal maintenance duties. At first awkward around him, Sky had broken the ice by jesting with Scout within earshot of Jeremy, "We've got to stick around, or someone'll paint over my *Amélie's Hope* masterpiece on the kite, and who wants to have that on his conscience?"

"I see your point," Scout replied, "but I would've done a better job of sketching Amélie. Aside from that, what other flight can boast having a major as its commander?"

"You're right, I suppose."

Jeremy had heard without reaction. He watched from the corner of his eye as the whole crew entered the maintenance area, and then he faced them. "You're staying? All of you?"

"They're stayin'," Anderson bellowed. "Enough drama. Let's get to work."

"All right then, I have a piece of good news to share. We'll have some help this time: a homing beacon, courtesy of the Milorg."

The resource had not been available during the first two attempts. This time, a member of the Norwegian Resistance, the Milorg, had assigned an operative to scout along the south shore opposite of where the British aircraft would appear and transmit a radio signal that would guide the aircraft directly over the *Tirpitz*. By gauging airspeed, wind, and travel direction, they could pinpoint the drop with a solid probability of hitting.

The crew reacted enthusiastically, with Sparks declaring, "We'll get the bastards this time."

Jeremy smiled. As he adjourned the gathering, he said with mock severity, "Sky and Scout, please fix Amélie's hair on the aircraft. It should be more auburn than red."

The two men grinned, saluted jauntily, and went to their tasks.

Six days after the failed Operation Obviate of late last month, activity required to fly the next mission against the *Tirpitz* was once again complete. The two squadrons deployed forward to RAF Lossiemouth, intending to take off from there early the following morning for Operation Catechism against the *Tirpitz*. Gale warnings caused the mission to be postponed, and the squadrons flew back to Bardney and Scampton. The crews griped, but took the situation in stride.

Another attempt two days later ended with the same result. The two squadrons had repositioned to Lossiemouth for the mission, but the pilot of a Mosquito flown up to check the weather over Tromsø reported back that more gale-force winds had been encountered along the way. Once again, the bombers returned to their home bases. Frustration grew among the crews. "It's time to get that jerry battleship."

"Oi, don't be such a grump. You've got another day to be on this lovely planet."

Then on November 10, with the autumn window closing, a Mosquito pilot transmitted a meteorological report indicating that the weather should be clear over Tromsø and the *Tirpitz* for the next two days.

On arriving at Lossiemouth and checking with flight operations, Jeremy learned that an updated Mosquito report mentioned clouds forming along the route and over Tromsø. Nevertheless, the Group 5 commander ordered the mission to go forward.

Jeremy shared the counterintuitive release of tension among the flight crews. "Marching off to do battle and possibly die," he muttered to himself, "and can't wait for it. That's what pent-up tension does." The men exhibited their anticipation in their rapid gaits and determined, eager eyes.

The air had been fairly smooth with a few erratic bumps along the way. Each aircraft flew up singly, as they had done before. They navigated through the radar gap with no problem, and assembled into respective flights over Lake Torneträsk.

By the time Jeremy was over the lake, Wing Commander Tait was on his bomb run. Jeremy formed up his flight and headed northwest.

Suddenly, Tait's voice sounded loudly and excitedly over Jeremy's headphones. "Willie here. We nailed her. Direct hit to the bow. Skies clear enough. Some clouds. Homing beacon loud and clear. No sign of bandits."

Only seconds later, another report came in. "I got her too. In the tush."

More reports piled in of hits and near misses until someone called in, "Hey, mates, save some for the rest of us."

As Jeremy flew into the target area, apprehension built in his stomach. It spread to his extremities. Adrenaline coursed through his veins, but for the first time that he could recall, the tension converted to anticipation and became his dominant sensation.

He thrilled to hear that the homing beacon had worked. Tait's attack had been dead-on. *Someone on the ground took a hell of a chance.*

Within seconds of entering the vicinity, Jeremy's aircraft took the anti-aircraft hit. Thin clouds were scattered about, but the view over the target was clear. Thin spirals of black smoke rose into the air.

He watched as the Lancasters in the flight ahead of his dropped their munitions. The sun glinted off the graceful curves of the bombs, their noses dropped toward the ground, and their fins caused them to spin. Moments later, Jeremy heard thunderous explosions and watched black clouds rise into the sky.

Although the *Tirpitz* was fourteen thousand feet below him, its condition was a sad sight to see. As predicted, the water there was shallow, so the ship had not sunk far. Instead, it had rolled with its port side resting on the fjord's bottom. The entire superstructure was underwater.

"We've got the homing signal," Sparks called. "Turn left five degrees."

"Roger. Scout?"

"Ready, sir, although there doesn't seem to be much point."

"We've got to make sure she stays dead. We're on course. Drop when you're ready. Then let me know how that fuel leak looks."

"Aye, sir."

Jeremy glanced at his gauge. The level now seemed noticeably lower than it should be. He checked his trim and continued on his bomb run.

"Bombs away," Scout called.

Amélie's Hope bobbed up from the loss of weight.

"Stal, let us know if we hit," Jeremy called to the tail gunner. He checked his trim again. "Scout, how's that leak."

"Not lookin' good, sir. It's comin' out faster. The self-sealant isn't stopping the flow. The leak must have expanded."

Stal broke in, "We hit just off the *Tirpitz's* stern by the fan tail."

"Understood," Jeremy acknowledged. "Scout, plot the shortest course to the sea. We don't want to go down over these mountains in enemy territory. Sparks, shift as much fuel as you can to the opposite wing."

"I'll do what I can," Scout responded, "but we've already dropped the long-range Mosquito tank, and we can't pump back into the fuel blisters."

"Push as much as you can into the left wing. We'll be off balance, but I'll fly with what I have. Sparks, call ahead and report our status while I work this out. Stal, no sign of bandits?"

"None."

"Well, there's that," Jeremy said. "Everyone listen, we might not make it all the way back to Scotland, maybe Shetland if we're lucky. I'm sure that German fighters are fully alerted, so heading into Sweden isn't an option.

"Go over our ditching procedures and get ready for the dinghy. Sparks, make sure our homing pigeons are well fed."

"Winkletwo's ready, sir. He'll do his duty, and so will his mate, Dora."

Jeremy had to chuckle, suddenly pleased at having the two homing pigeons aboard. *I wonder how they do what they do?*

They were an element of communication that had not been available to him when he flew fighters, but every RAF bomber carried two of them. If he had to ditch in the North Sea, Sparks would write down the coordinates on two pieces of paper, roll them into two small canisters, and attach one to each pigeon's leg. When released, the birds would fly to their home nest, and a guard watching for them would remove the cannisters and communicate the coordinates with the news of a downed aircraft to appropriate rescuers.

Sparks had named Winkletwo for the most famous RAF pigeon, Winkle. Two years earlier, a Beaufighter pilot had been shot up. He went down in the North Sea. Winkle had flown over a hundred and thirty miles with its cannister to its home, and the pilot was saved.

"Winkletwo," Jeremy murmured, "you might be called upon to best your namesake." The bird was not a regular on *Amélie's Hope*. Each bomber that took off from Lossiemouth for Operation Catechism had been allotted two of them from RAF Sumburgh, the birds' home and the designated airfield for emergencies for this mission.

The plane droned on, operating smoothly despite the leak, but against stiff winds. Jeremy maintained high altitude to leave himself plenty of distance to glide if the fuel gave out before they reached Shetland. *Every mile closer is one we don't have to paddle.*

He checked the fuel gauge with increasing frequency, and each time, it had dropped more than it should have. "What's the distance?" he asked Scout.

"Roughly four hundred miles to Sumburgh," Scout replied.

"I'm quite sure we won't get that far in the air," Jeremy said. "Get ready. Stal, gather the flairs, portable radios, food, potable water. Get it all into the center of the aircraft—"

"No worries, Skipper," Stal cut in. "We're well-rehearsed."

"Of course you are."

An hour later, one after the other, the engines sputtered out. "How far are we from land?" Jeremy asked Sparks.

"About a hundred miles from the northern end of Shetland."

"And from this altitude, we'll glide about twenty-eight miles. Winkletwo and Dora will have a challenge, particularly in this wind." He took a deep breath. "Gentlemen, make final preps for ditching. Sparks, double-check our radios. Make sure Sumburgh knows our direction. Scout, keep checking our coordinates. We'll hit water in about fourteen minutes."

Almost to the minute, *Amélie's Hope* descended to just above the choppy high waves of the North Sea. Jeremy pulled back on the stick. The aircraft flared and settled the tail into the water. A wave slapped the fuselage and spun the aircraft, caught its right wing, and forced the nose down.

Rolling waves fractured the windshield. Cold seawater seeped into the aircraft in expanding streams. Jeremy keyed his mic. "Is anyone hurt?"

"Water is coming through the tail fast," Stal called. "I'm in one piece."

"I've dislocated a shoulder," Sparks called in obvious anguish.

Electric sparks flew. The lights and all other electronics went out, and only the tossing waves and strong winds were heard above the creaking and groaning of the sinking aircraft.

Jeremy glanced out the windshield and saw that, on hitting the sea's surface, the dinghy had deployed automatically from its nacelle. "Grab your gear and hit the exits," Jeremy yelled. "The dinghy is open on the starboard side. Sparks, I'm coming aft for you. Stal and Scout, get the hell out."

Jeremy had already ripped off his headgear and safety belts. Water sprayed into his face through the fractured windshield as he climbed over the partition on his right that separated him from the short walkway where his flight sergeant would normally be stationed. Immediately behind his own seat and overlooking the same walkway was Sparks' tiny domain.

As Jeremy's feet touched the floor, cold water sloshed around them. When he reached Sparks, pain was written across the radio operator's face, but he had already removed his belt with one hand and was attempting to wrap it around his back and chest to secure his injured arm.

"Sorry, mate," Jeremy yelled. "No time for that. We've got only a few minutes before she sinks." He stared into Sparks' eyes. "This will hurt." Then he reached up and pulled the airman over the barrier and onto his own shoulders.

Sparks screamed in agony.

"I'll bring the extra kits," Stal yelled. "Scout is already out. He's steadying the dinghy."

Jeremy struggled in the tossing aircraft under Sparks' weight and the now ankle-deep water. Scout had gone through an emergency hatch over the starboard wing. "Listen," Jeremy told Sparks, "I'm going to set you on your feet and lay your upper body through the hatch. Then I'll push your legs up and through. You're going to have to help with your good arm. Can you do that?"

Sparks slapped Jeremy's shoulder in acknowledgment. Jeremy set him down. Sparks gritted his teeth against excruciating pain. Scout appeared outside of the hatch. "I've slip-knotted the dinghy to the wing," he yelled, barely audible above the wind, "but the water's lapping at the flaps. We've got to hurry."

He pulled, Jeremy pushed, and Sparks screamed. By the time they got to the dinghy, Stal was there braced in the crook between the fuselage and the wing, holding the tiny lifeboat as steady as possible. Moments later, with Sparks safely moaning on its floor, Scout pulled the slip knot and shoved away from the plane.

A sudden terrible oversight flashed through Jeremy's mind. "The pigeons—"

"Taken care of, sir," Scout said. "I let them go through the emergency exit as soon as we hit water, with our coordinates attached to their legs. They're well on their way."

Jeremy breathed a sigh of relief. "Good show. Now." He looked at Sparks. "Morphine for you, ol' boy. By the time you wake up, we'll have your shoulder back in its socket, and we'll be in sunny weather."

Sparks shot him a withering look but nodded slightly.

Two minutes later, *Amelie's Hope* sank beneath the waves.

42

November 14, 1944
Maastricht, Netherlands

Supreme Allied Commander Eisenhower, US Lieutenant General William Simpson of the 9th Army, and British Major General Brian Horrocks of XXX Corps had just finished a fine dinner at 9th Army headquarters housed at Henric van Veldekecollege, a Catholic boys' school on Aylvalaan Street, where they conversed in a relaxed atmosphere. Eisenhower held both commanders in high regard. Thin-faced with a full head of light brown hair and intelligent eyes, Horrocks was one of Britain's most respected generals. Equally thin-faced but bald and with piercing eyes, Simpson had proven himself as both an aggressive strategist and tactician and an able commander.

"Taking Geilenkirchen is imperative, Jorrocks," Eisenhower said softly, using the British general's nickname but speaking with firm emphasis. "The town's position on the Wurm River forms a salient right on the Siegfried Line that protrudes at the boundary between your XXX Corps and Bill's 9th Army. We can't bypass it, or the Germans will have an open path into our rear.

"We have the assets in the area to handle it. They just happen not to be nicely arranged for a clean command line. But we don't have time to rearrange deck chairs. It'll be a tough fight that we can win, but it'll take two divisions. You and Bill each have only one available and you're in separate army groups."

"We talked about this yesterday at my headquarters in Beek," Horrocks interjected, addressing his comment to Simpson. "I explained that XXX Corps is almost fully committed. As its commander, my current mission is to hold the line from just north of Geilenkirchen all the way to the North Sea. I don't have the manpower to provide the support you need."

Starting two months ago, after Eisenhower had lifted his operational pause, the Allies pushed aggressively to the German border. During September's second week, the 3rd Armored Division's Combat Command B conducted a reconnaissance in force across the German border, captured the town of Roetgen, and established a position from which it prepared for further thrusts north. Since then, the front's organization had become tortuous for tactical, political, and even personal reasons—General Bradley did not like Montgomery.

Bradley foresaw that he might be required to give up a division to Montgomery and organized his divisions so that, in such an eventuality, he would not lose one of his veteran units. Three weeks ago, after nineteen days of intense fighting led by 1st Infantry Division, Bradley's 12th Army Group had captured Aachen, a city of immense historical and cultural importance.

The psychological blow to Germany's population was inestimable. Founded in Roman times, Aachen was purported to be Charlemagne's birthplace. He established the capital of his Holy Roman Empire in the city during the Middle Ages, a fact from which local residents drew enormous pride.

Ominously for the German people, the city sat behind the Siegfried Line, the vaunted defense system that stretched nearly four hundred miles along Germany's western border, from Kleve near the Netherlands to Weil am Rhein, close to Switzerland. The city's capture was a clear signal to the German population that Hitler's "impregnable" fortifications were seriously threatened.

Construction on the Siegfried had started in 1936 in response to the

Maginot Line a few miles west, inside the French border, which was itself built against fears of German incursions. As opposed to the Maginot's mammoth continuous walls with built-in gunnery sites, the Siegfried consisted of four bands of "dragons' teeth," concrete pyramids ranging in height from three to five feet for the line's entire length. Intended to stop tanks and infantry, the teeth were reinforced by pillboxes and casemates set back at strategic points to stop invasions.

Because the *Wehrmacht* had been so successful in subduing France, the line became unnecessary and was neglected for most of the war. However, as the Allies advanced rapidly toward Germany, Hitler ordered immediate improvements to shore up the Siegfried's vulnerabilities, particularly at its northern end in the area of Geilenkirchen. To the east, beyond the town, were flat ground and a high-speed corridor ideal for armored war machines leading to Cologne, the Rhine River, and Berlin.

"Regardless of current commitments," Eisenhower said, continuing the conversation with Horrocks and Simpson, "Geilenkirchen must be taken, or we'll find the *Wehrmacht* rolling around in our rear." He remained in quiet contemplation, and then mused aloud. "We're about to launch a major offensive all along the Siegfried south of the town. Bill's army will be a significant part of that and he's preparing for it now. His momentum can't be impeded by a major battle on his left flank."

He faced Horrocks directly. "So, General, will you take Geilenkirchen for us?"

Horrocks chuckled. "You do have a charming way about you, sir. Just let me say that the spirit is willing, but the flesh is weak. The only division I have available right now is the 43rd Wessex, which has been pounded in constant battle since Normandy. I couldn't possibly take Geilenkirchen with just that one division. The town occupies one of the strongest positions on the Siegfried."

Eisenhower swung around to Simpson. "Bill, would you give him one of your divisions?"

"I would, sir, if it gets the job done. He can have the 84th Infantry Division."

Horrocks leaned back with mock exasperation. "You bring me here for a banquet and wine, and then drop this on me," he said, chuckling. "To use your American term, I've been 'bushwacked.'" He frowned in contemplation. "You're talking about an American division attached to a British Corps and, in turn, supporting a British division." He paused, still mulling. "Naturally I want to help," he said reluctantly, "but isn't the 84th a new division just making its way to the front? It's never been blooded." He hastened to add, "I'm a great admirer of the way your country mass-produces well-trained divisions, but until they've been in battle—"

"They're all combat soldiers," Eisenhower cut in. "They'll face battle at some point. That objective, Geilenkirchen, is crucial."

Horrocks nodded resignedly. "The command structure will be convoluted."

"At least they all speak English," Simpson interjected with a chuckle. He added with an encouraging tone, "I know your Wessex Division. They're a battle-hardened bunch. And I know the 84th's commander, Major General Bolling. He's a veteran of the last war, and a hard charger. He works his men. He'll have them ready."

Horrocks let out a long breath and arched his eyebrows. "In that case, how can I refuse?" He shot a glance at Eisenhower and chuckled. "Not that I could."

November 16, 1944
Western Outskirts of Geilenkirchen, Germany

A shadow crossed in front of the open flap on Lieutenant Derek Horton's six-by-six officer's tent as heavy rain pounded his canvas shelter. He looked up from his folding seat near the back end next to his cot and was pleasantly surprised to see Corporal Leonard Littlefield grinning at him.

"Welcome back, sir," Leonard said. He dripped with rain and his boots were coated in thick brown mud. "Word's gone round you're in-country and with your mob, so I thought I'd track you down. How's the face? All healed up?"

"It is, it is," Horton said enthusiastically. "It's a little tender in places, some light scarring. Nothing to speak of, so I think my fiancée might still have me. Come in. Have a seat." He moved onto the cot, leaving the canvas folding chair free for the corporal.

"Much obliged, sir. I don't mean to be cheeky."

"Bollocks to that. We're not in the same unit, and with a moniker like 'Littlefield,' I reckon we're practically family." He chuckled. "Course, muscling in on your clan might be seen as brazen, but the Sark branch treats me like one of their own, so I've got a soft spot for anyone with your surname. What's the latest on this dust-up? Still playing postman on your iron horse? Where are you bivouacked?"

With the squishing sound of mud trailing him, Leonard crossed the floor and sat down. "Where do I start? The Wessex is just two fields over. Took me five minutes to walk it, even in this muck. And yeah, I'm still on dispatch. I enjoy it, 'specially when I'm behind friendly lines." His eyes bulged. "But when I'm on forward recce, it can get proper dicey."

Horton stared at him in surprise. "I didn't know you did that. Sounds dangerous. Can't the enemy hear you?"

"Not bloody likely. The battle racket at the sharp end usually drowns out me old bike. There've been some times, though. Once, I was buzzin' down this road, playin' postman between our lot and the one next door. We were trying to button up the gap, but the jerries beat us to it. Crikey, they popped up out of nowhere on foot patrol, right in the middle of the road. I'll tell you what, they looked as gobsmacked to see me as I was to clock them."

"What did you do?"

"I swung my bike around and got the hell out, that's what I did."

"Did they take shots at you?"

"Aye, they did, but I weaved back and forth until I got round a curve, and then I opened to full throttle." He sighed. "It's a bit of a lonely job, though. More often than not when I'm in a spot of bother, it's up to me own devices to scarper. The real bugbear is when I'm stuck bringing up the rear of the column, having to give the dawdlers a kick up the arse." He laughed. "They give me a bit of stick with their fancy name-callin'."

Horton laughed with him. "I can see that. An' here we thought yours was a glamor job."

"The ladies seem to fancy it, and we've got loads of tales to spin to make ourselves look a bit more dashing, if you catch my drift."

The two soldiers enjoyed another laugh, and then Leonard exhaled. "You know, I hear a thing or two in my line of work. I keep my mouth shut and don't spill what I shouldn't. But I'm a bit worried about this scrap coming up in Geilenkirchen."

"Oh?"

Leonard nodded slightly. "I won't blab about what I'm not meant to, but just stickin' to what's common knowledge, it's a bit worryin' beyond the usual fare."

"How so?"

"Well to start with"—Leonard leaned forward with this elbows on his knees—"that town's a right German stronghold. On the other side from us is the Fatherland, the place the jerries will defend like there's no tomorrow, and they're reinforcin'. People think this war is almost over. Not I. Hard fightin' is ahead of us, every bit as bad as the *bocage* in Normandy and at Nijmegen. You know they're bringing in the American 84th Division to fight alongside of us?"

Horton nodded. "Go on."

"That's a brand-new division." Leonard tossed his head in wide-eyed incredulity. "Not a man among them has seen a day in action. And here's a kicker. You're meant to back them up."

Startled, Horton's head popped up. "You mean the Sherwood Rangers?"

Leonard nodded. "I'm not quite sure how it's meant to work, to be honest. I don't reckon you'll be formally attached to them, but your regiment will be in proper support of that division. They'll take one side of the town, and the 43rd Wessex, my unit, will take the other."

He inhaled and let his breath out. "That's a bit of an oversimplification, mate. Today, General Bradley's 12th Army Group kicked off Operation Queen, launching a major offensive against the Siegfried Line south of our position. As part of this push, General Simpson's 9th Army is set to cross the River Roer and advance eastward. He's attached the 84th Division to the Wessex Division to take Geilenkirchen, and General Horrocks plans to execute this operation in four phases."

"Tell me."

"The first regiment from the 84th, supported by the Sherwoods, will assault Geilenkirchen from the east, using the high ground. Five hours after the initial attack, the Wessex will hit from the villages to the west and aim to cut off a main road comin' in from the northwest. Together, the two divisions should effectively encircle the town.

"Then, another regiment from the 84th will attack from the south.

"Finally, once we secure Geilenkirchen, both divisions will clear out the Roer Valley heading north up to Wurm. It's a coordinated effort to tighten our grip on this sector and push deeper into enemy territory."

Horton listened with increasing interest. "Tell me about the Sherman Crabs. Have you seen one? I hear the Sherwoods have some, but I haven't seen them yet."

Leonard nodded. "It's a right strange contraption, a tank with a horizontal tube, like a big barrel, spinning on the front. It's got these chains welded to it, and they're meant to make landmines go kaboom while clearing the minefields."

Horton grunted. "Blimey. I don't recall signing up for that. I mean, what if we miss one and it goes off underneath? What then?"

Leonard laughed. "Ours is but to do or die, eh?"

"If that happens, I'll call you to come on your motorcycle and get me the hell out."

"Not a chance in this muck. It's so deep it comes up over the treads on the Shermans. The drivers are having nightmares with them." He chuckled and shrugged. "As for my bike..."

They talked into the night. Leonard explained that after Horton had been evacuated from the country for burn treatment, the Sherwoods had remained on picket duty for a time east of Nijmegen with the US 82nd Airborne Division. "Then Montgomery launched Operation Pheasant and took Brabant. The fighting was intense. Be glad you missed it."

"Wait," Horton interrupted, alarmed. "There's a French Brabant and a Dutch one."

"Right you are. We're talking about the Dutch one."

"That was southeast of Arnhem, all the way down near Eindhoven. We passed by it on our way north to Nijmegen." Horton looked sharply at Leonard. "You backtracked?"

"We did. We had to shore up gaps that were left during the rapid march to Nijmegen."

Horton's brow furrowed and he shook his head. "I wondered if we were going too far too fast. We didn't get to Arnhem and we had to go back and fix gaps." He shook his head in frustration. Then suddenly, he sat up straight. "And what of Arnhem? Did we finally take it?"

Leonard shook his head grimly.

Horton heaved a sigh, leaving his thoughts unspoken.

Eventually, conversation turned to home, the war, and plans for after the war. When Horton mentioned Chantal, Leonard teased, "Ah, the lass who might have you for marriage."

Horton showed her picture.

Leonard crowed, "Now she, sir, not meanin' to be rude, is worth staying alive for." He sat back and searched Horton's face. "I dunno, you're still puffy under the eyes, and one of your ears—"

Horton guffawed and clapped Leonard's shoulder. Then he sobered up. "I suppose you heard about Lance?"

"I did, sir. The news was all over 82nd Airborne Division's headquarters. You know he is a hero. He absolutely saved the life of the soldier who was with him, Turner." He related the story as Turner had told it. "I was hoping to see more of Lance to find out if we're related."

"I told Lance's sister, Claire, about you while I was in London. She's anxious to meet you. You'll have to come around to meet the rest of the Sark Littlefields after the war. If you're not family, they'll make you feel like you are. Has there been any more news on Lance?"

"None, I'm sorry to say."

Horton lamented in silence, recalling his first acquaintance with Lance north of Dunkirk, then their escape across France on foot, the sinking of the *Lancastria*, a sabotage raid with the Resistance, and Lance's capture. He sighed and blocked the latter memory.

A while later, Leonard went on his way. Horton lay back on his cot looking up at the canvas ceiling while the incessant rain poured down. He took Chantal's photograph out of his jacket and gazed at it. "You really are worth staying alive for," he murmured before touching the picture to his lips. "I hope you're safe."

43

November 18, 1944
Geilenkirchen, Germany

Horton had not expected to be immediately in charge of a troop again, but ironically, he replaced the lieutenant who had replaced him upon his departure. Like Horton, the officer had been wounded and was sent back to Britain. The two men never met.

Not surprisingly, and to Horton's dismay, many of the faces that greeted him were new to him. When he asked his troop sergeant about specific names of those not present, he received back only blank stares followed by a shaking head, and even the troop sergeant was new. Sully had fallen in battle.

Strangely comforting after the sad news, and although worse for wear and battle damage, Horton's Sherman was the same one in which he had been wounded. He recognized old pockmarks and battle scars among new ones, including the scorched paint on the side of the tank where the round had grazed that burned him.

He was glad of Leonard's visit two nights ago. In addition to the camaraderie, without the conversation, Horton would be going into battle almost blind. He attended the mission briefings and made preparations ahead of convoying to the assembly area, but the view of the bigger picture was absent. Essentially, he received his intelligence on the enemy, his objective, his route, and his support. Mention was made of the imperative to seize Geilenkirchen with a nebulous reference to the road to Berlin, but without Leonard's conversation, Horton would have had little context.

He grunted at the realization. *How much context do I need? See the enemy, shoot the enemy.*

As Major Semken briefed his squadron's part of the assault on Geilenkirchen, dubbed Operation Clipper, Horton glanced around at the exhausted faces and beleaguered figures of the other troop leaders. Coming fresh from home, rested, and well-fed, he was an anomaly, but fortunately, friends who had survived the battles that took place during his absence were present in sufficient numbers to make him feel welcome. Among them was Lieutenant David Render.

"It's good to see you, Horton. Did you enjoy your holiday?" he teased.

"Good to see you too, David. I can't believe I'm saying this, but I've missed you." He looked around. "I was going to say, 'and the others,' but we're missing so many."

"That we are," Render agreed somberly. "Well, I'm off to get ready for the next scuffle. Wish us luck."

In the dark of night, the attack launched. Horton's Sherman struggled through mud that threatened to swamp the steel plating overhanging the tracks. And the rain kept pouring.

The operation relied impossibly on stealth. The best that could be hoped for was to get close to the minefields that lay in front of the dragons' teeth before the Germans became aware that the attack was underway. With the clatter of tanks, the roar of their engines, and the squish in the thick muck of treads, tires, and infantry boots, only time was needed to reach the minefields, hopefully before the enemy was alerted.

The saving grace was darkness. The Germans could not see their targets. However, neither could Allied drivers see the roads well. The engineers shined extremely bright spotlights at the clouds that reflected down and gave a semblance of moonlight visibility without pinpointing targets for the enemy, but essentially the military horde was confined to feeling its way forward through the abysmal torrents and muck.

A peppering of gunfire rang out, but they were far off the mark, aimless shots seeking any target. They were followed by mortars with equal lack of effect beyond causing Allied soldiers to button up or seek cover.

Horton took note of the muzzle flashes. "Hold fire," he told his gunner. "No need to help them find us."

For the most part, Major Semken's Squadron A and the 84th's 1st Brigade adhered to the same wisdom. However, as they proceeded, enemy artillery fed into the mix, conducting reconnaissance by fire and gradually zeroing in on the approaching threat.

Near the front of the formation, Horton heard a raucous clanking noise. "The Sherman Crabs," he breathed. He had seen them during the day as he went about preparing his troop. The mine-sweeping Sherman tanks, as Leonard had said, had been fitted with long steel arms on their fronts. Their horizontal barrels spun between them, flailing the ground ahead with heavy metal chains, intending to detonate any mines they encountered.

As they entered the minefields, the Crabs moved at the rate of one and a half miles per hour. Their awful racket had the additional effect of informing the enemy of their precise positions.

Soon, enemy fire rained down, but dawn was still hours away, rendering anti-tank guns useless and limiting the effect of artillery, and the distance the Crabs needed to traverse the minefields was measured in tens of meters, not miles. However, of six such war machines that started out with the Sherwood Rangers, three had broken down enroute. Only three arrived intact to do their jobs.

The night wore on. Exchanges of gunfire erupted intermittently, waned, rose to fever pitch again, and repeated the cycle several times. Meanwhile, the rain poured down, men were wounded, and cries for medics punctuated the night.

At last, the minefields were clear enough for armored bulldozers to move through, push aside the dragons' teeth, and plow a route to the hostile side of the Siegfried Line. Owing to the loss of the three Crabs, it was narrower than intended, but no sooner had the gap opened than the Sherwoods started through, followed by the 84th Infantry.

Two Sherwood troops were ahead of Horton's. Major Semken rode with the second one in his own command tank, and as it maneuvered through the narrow passage, several mines exploded beneath it.

Horton shook his head. *Exactly what I worried about, missed mines.*

He watched from behind, barely able to see the dark figures of the crew jumping from the wounded tank despite the glow of the engineers' lights reflecting off the clouds. One of the men ran back to Horton's vehicle. "No one was badly injured, but our Sherman's disabled and the radio's knocked out," he informed. "The skipper's moving to another tank. He says to continue on as soon as we move off."

"Right-o," Horton replied, but no sooner had the group started off again than he saw a flash of light under a tank ahead, and heard a detonation. Once again, the procession halted and a runner came to inform, "That was skipper's tank again. It's crippled. He's moving to yet another Sherman."

While he waited to proceed, Horton sat low in his cupola, watching the fireworks around him, the orange tracers of friendly fire whizzing one direction, the green ones of enemy fire flying the other, punctuated by irregular artillery searching for targets and exploding rounds nearby. To his right and left, the weird columns of white dragons' teeth glowed in the equally weird effervescence emanating from the luminous clouds.

"We're actually entering Germany," he muttered amid a surreal mix of thrill and dread. "We're storming the *Reich*."

The journey to be here at this moment had been long, and arduous, and if he lived past breaching the Siegfried's remaining yards, he might one day look back and conclude that the struggle was worth it. He chuckled. *This isn't a moment I'd want to share with Chantal, though.*

As he reflected, the rain stopped, and the squadron started off once more. Again, a boom sounded beneath the tank directly ahead amid the clamor of battle. Again, the procession of war vehicles came to a halt in a precarious position. The interval before a runner arrived was longer than the previous instances, and his voice bore a tone of extreme urgency. "The skipper's tank was hit a third time."

Before Horton could respond, the runner added, "This time, he's disappeared."

"Disappeared? Where? How?"

"No one knows, sir. The adjutant has taken charge. We have to push on."

"Roger. We'll follow." The squadron started off again, and Horton wondered what could have happened to the major, a Sherwood Rangers living legend, the man who had led Squadron A across North Africa, Italy, and France. He was not only revered, he was loved.

And now he's been hit by landmines three times in a single night within minutes? What happened to him?

The assault force broke into the fields beyond the dragons' teeth and spread out, headed toward known pillboxes. Tactics had been worked out to overcome the fortified positions, which were spaced to cover each other with interlocking fire. Field artillery would be dropped on them during the advance, and since their precise coordinates were known from reconnaissance reports, darkness was no impediment to accuracy.

As the assault party approached their targets, the tanks were to remain in the lead, and when the pillboxes were in range, they would pummel the entrances and firing ports with 75 mm HE rounds or any others the tanks might be carrying. Meanwhile, under this suppressive fire, the infantry would advance, breach the defenses, and capture or kill the occupants.

Another major hitch occurred. While crossing a field, several Shermans, including Horton's, became bogged down in the rain-soaked muck, which no amount of tread-spinning resolved to forward movement. The crew had no choice but to dismount and dig out.

As they jumped into stinking mire with shovels and entrenching tools and began digging and tossing mud up and over their shoulders, Horton among them, he was surprised by 84th Infantry soldiers filing by. They called greetings and jocular invectives about the superiority of foot soldiers over fat tankers, but their obvious intent was to continue the fight, with or without their armored support.

Awed by their courage, Horton's crew tossed back similar slurs, but kept digging.

Glimmering light seeped over the horizon. The sky cleared of clouds. The sun rose, casting cold November light over a desolate landscape.

Bombs dropped all about, drawing closer, and small-arms fire rained down, but Horton drew some comfort from knowing that, by now, the Wessex Division would have started its attack on Geilenkirchen from the west, the 84th's 2nd Brigade would be assaulting the town from the southwest, and all along two hundred and twenty miles of the Siegfried south to General Bradley's right flank, similar scenes would play out as Allied armies assaulted across the dragons' teeth. *Enemy attention to my corner of the war will come from only what's in front of me right now.*

Infantrymen continued to file by, and so did tanks that had been impeded by similar circumstances and had broken free of the sludge. Two of them hitched chains to the front of Horton's tank and pulled it free.

The sun rose, the engineers' lights turned off, and almost immediately, the distinct whine of RAF Supermarine Spitfire fighters sounded. Moments later, the aircraft zoomed in. They strafed the pillboxes and casemates with much flash and bang, and then flew deeper into enemy territory to hit field artillery positions. On the ground, soldiers cheered.

The Spitfires had barely disappeared in the eastern sky when the roar of P-47 Thunderbolt fighter-bombers rolled in to strafe and drop bombs before heading farther into the Fatherland. More waves of aircraft followed. The men below celebrated. Horton's crew drew a collective breath of relief as they set out to catch up to the infantry.

Late that night, Horton dozed in the seat of his cupola. The day's objective had been met. In support of the 334th Regiment of the 84th Infantry, the Sherwoods had thrust past the line of pillboxes, captured the town of Prummern, and secured the high ground south of and overlooking Geilenkirchen. Word was that the 84th's 333rd Regiment and its contingent of Sherwoods had occupied the town and its defenses, and the 43rd Wessex Division had captured and held the ground to the north, inside the Siegfried Line.

Horton's driver nudged him awake. "Sir, Major Semken called for a meeting of troop leaders. A runner is waiting to guide you to his head-quarters."

"Ah, they found him," Horton said enthusiastically, "and he's alive and calling a meeting. That's a good thing." He clambered down from his Sherman. Then, as he trekked through the darkness with the guide, he asked, "So, where was our fearless leader discovered."

"Sir, I'd rather not say."

Noting his somber tone, Horton did not press further. They walked on in silence, and on arrival at a small barn below a stand of trees, Horton gathered with the other troop leaders. Seeking out Render, Horton queried, "What's happened? Why the meeting?"

Render took him aside. "Chaplain Riley found the major sometime after daybreak. He was in an empty pillbox reading poetry. At first he seemed his normal self, but the chaplain saw that he was in a bad way. He was shaking, unsteady on his feet, and was quite surprised that no one knew where he was."

Dismayed, Horton blew out a long breath. "I'm sorrier to hear that than I can say."

Render grasped his shoulder. "We all are."

At that moment, Semken's adjutant walked to the center of the gathering and announced, "Gentlemen, our commander."

Semken appeared at the door. His men moved aside to allow him through, all eyes watching his face with anxiety. He moved to the center of the floor. Gone was the jauntiness that had characterized him for as long as Horton had known him. He moved awkwardly, as if trying to hide pain, and his eyes were sunken.

He forced a smile as he gazed around the room. "Ah, but we've had some good times together," he said in a weak, broken voice. "It wasn't all bad, was it?"

A palpable cloud of dread descended. No one stirred.

Semken came to strained attention. "I'm afraid my time with you has come to an end. I must go home. My honor has been to serve with you. Carry on."

With that, he ambled slowly out of the barn and into the night.

44

November 21, 1944
Dabo, France

Paul Littlefield's jeep spun its wheels while inching uphill in a valley so narrow that it barely left room for the muddy road. Over two weeks had passed since he had met with Haislip, and five days later, on November 10, as Leclerc had become increasingly insufferable on the subject, Haislip had ordered the 2nd Armored Division to advance on Saverne. Paul had never seen Leclerc more elated, not even over his liberation of Paris. "You did it, Paul," he exclaimed, smiling broadly. "He knows I won't stop at Saverne."

Traveling up this road now in a jeep following a half-track, Paul questioned whether Leclerc had acted wisely in insisting on a French unit leading Strasbourg's liberation. At least three American divisions were already poised in better positions for the operation, whereas Leclerc's gambit had the bulk of the general's heavily armored war machines struggling on tight logging roads between forested slopes through freezing rain mixed with occasional flurries of snow. Conceivably, this entire section of his division could bog down and be rendered combat-ineffective.

Worse yet, this was not the route Haislip had approved.

On receipt of Haislip's orders, Leclerc had immediately set his own plans in motion, ordering a feint to the north on a route through Sarrebourg, Lutzelbourg, and Saverne. The rugged ground along that northern course constricted movement between low hills on a road that ascended among steep mountain slopes until reaching the heights above the Saverne Pass before descending into the Alsace Plains. From there the way was clear to Strasbourg for armored vehicles.

The *Wehrmacht* had built almost impregnable defenses across that narrow approach into the Vosges, including steel-reinforced bunkers and machine gun nests. For that reason, Leclerc sent only two of his sub-groups to engage the enemy along that route. They had passed easily through Sarrebourg, leaving behind a population cheering for their first taste of freedom in four years, but as they approached Lutzelbourg, the weather and the terrain imposed more rugged conditions, and the enemy expected them. However, those sub-groups' real mission was to pin down the Germans and convince them that the French main attack threatened along that route.

Meanwhile, Leclerc's main force, Paul with them, diverted south through terrain so harsh that the Germans, believing that no sizeable force would venture on this route, had left the tiny roads through its coniferous forests virtually undefended. Only Dabo housed German troops along the rugged trail. The town, with barely three thousand residents, nestled along the western slopes of the Vosges massif with crests ranging in altitude from seven hundred to twenty-eight hundred feet.

Paul had set out two days ago with Colonel Massu, commander of the force bearing down on Dabo. Leclerc had grudgingly allowed Paul to travel with the group. Paul had requested to join the forces assaulting through the northern route, but the general had refused. "I can't afford to lose you," he had said simply.

"And I can't sit around in safety while your own soldiers, my country-men, and the Americans are in action all over France," Paul replied. "I came to fight." He blew out a breath in exasperation. "At Normandy, you asked me to be your liaison officer between you and the British and Americans, and I was honored to do it." He looked around. "Out here, there's no one to liaise with."

Leclerc had chuckled. "Strasbourg is the next major objective, my friend, but after that comes the Rhine and Ruhr Valley. We'll be in close proximity to Americans, and most of my subordinate commanders don't speak either English or German. I'll need your language and liaison skills then." Reading Paul's impatience, he added, "As a compromise, I'll attach you to Massu's headquarters for the trek through Dabo. There'll be some fighting there, but it should be lighter."

Paul had acquiesced. Now, after a day and two nights of constant movement uphill, he wondered if the maneuver was not a fool's errand. The pace had been ponderous, the way narrow, and the ground unforgiving.

The tramp that began in Lorraine's lowlands had met rising hills where, under a bleak autumn sky, dense conifer and beech forests enveloped the soldiers. The hills gave way to mountains marked by rocky outcrops. Steep grades had eroded over millennia and evolved into a labyrinth of cliffs and deep ravines. They tested men and machinery and could easily conceal enemy positions.

Then today, at mid-morning, Dabo appeared through ground fog, its red-tile roofs gleaming in sunlight from a momentary break in the clouds. It had materialized suddenly, and Massu's men entered it without resistance. Residents met them with cautious joy and warnings that Germans still occupied the town.

Paul glanced about in amazement. Apparently Group Massu had approached undetected.

That sense lasted barely a moment.

MG 24 machine guns buzzed and bullets shattered windows and struck buildings with sharp smacks. Mortars emitted popping sounds followed by explosions.

People scattered, screaming in panic. Wails of the wounded rose, and blood blotted the cobblestones.

Paul sought shelter and then crept to a place where he could surveil the situation. The bulk of Group Massu was still strung along the thin route trailing out of the forest from the northwest. That included the command section. Paul had been separated from it due to terrain constraints, and he had slowly worked his way forward near the front of the convoy. Those tanks and support vehicles just emerging from the woods diverted left and right, but the enemies' firing positions had not been identified.

Paul grabbed a map from his jacket pocket. When he had studied it on his way up the trail, he noticed a significant land mass, a steep, jagged hill jutting above Dabo on the east side, labeled, "La Rocher de Dabo." The morning fog had obscured not just the town, but also the landscape around it.

With the fog lifting and more structures becoming visible, including the surrounding mountains, Paul looked for a vantage point where he could safely take a wider view. The gunfire was coming from the east. He scooted from cover to cover along the sides of buildings on Dabo's southern edge until he found a place from which he had clear observation of the ground to the east.

He spotted La Rocher de Dabo and sucked in his breath. Less than two miles away, it protruded more than six hundred feet into the sky, and it was flat on top, the perfect place for a gun position to observe Dabo and the entire basin.

Paul squinted to see better. The cloud ceiling had lifted, but it had closed and was still thick, casting a shadow across the landscape and obstructing a clear view. Nevertheless, he thought he saw a structure on La Rocher's summit. Pulling out his field glasses, he took another look, and was dismayed to see a small church, apparently not yet touched by the war.

Behind him, he heard the unmistakable signature of field artillery, and seconds later, he heard an explosion and saw a cloud of dust well short of the hill. Hurriedly, he stuffed his map and binoculars back into his jacket and retraced his steps to the west end of the town. When he reached his jeep, he called to the driver, "Has Colonel Massu made it out of the forest yet?"

The young private nodded. "Yes, sir. Just a few minutes ago. He's set up at the edge of the trees."

"Take me there."

Minutes later, panting, and sweating despite the cold, Paul stood in front of Massu. "Sir, please keep suppressive fire going, but don't walk it to the top of that hill." He explained what he had seen.

When Paul had finished, Massu responded. "That's too far away for mortars and machine guns to be effective against us. They've got positions closer in to the east."

Paul agreed. "But your field artillery suspects that a gun position of some sort, or at least an observation post, is up there."

The colonel's driver ran up to them. "Sir, Dabo's mayor is here. He wishes to speak with you. He says it's urgent."

"Bring him over."

Mayor Mylan Caissie, a portly little man in threadbare trousers and a worn sport jacket, presented himself, rubbing his hands together nervously. "The church—your guns—"

Massu regarded him sharply. "Is the enemy up there?"

Caissie nodded and spoke haltingly. "Not in the church. Another flat place, below the main plateau. *Les boches* keep men there to watch our valley."

"Any weapons there?"

The mayor nodded again. "Two machine guns, to the left and right of the church, but they're farther down the slope on the lower plateau."

Massu turned to his adjutant standing close by. "Tell Operations to hold the field artillery to a line only halfway up that hill. Keep suppressive barrages going, but don't lift to the top of the summit or fire for effect unless I give the order. Go." He turned to the mayor. "We'll save your town and your church."

"Thank you, sir. Thank you. Thank you. People have lived around Dabo since the Stone Age. That church is nearly a century old."

"We'll still need to take out those machine guns and that observer," Massu muttered to no one. "Our convoy will move below the Rocher. That position could halt our entire convoy."

"Sir, if I may," Paul interjected. He had pulled his map out again and pointed out Dabo. "The tree line extends around this basin on both flanks and wraps around below the backside of La Rocher. I think they're only lightly defended. If you keep suppressive fire going, a platoon-sized patrol could work its way over there inside the woods and come up from behind."

"I know a back road," Caissie interjected. "They're not guarding it." He shrugged and smiled. "They weren't expecting you. I can guide you."

Massu exhaled. "We've got to deal with it quickly. By now, the German high command knows we're here and will take countermeasures. This convoy must get to the other side of the Vosges and onto the Alsace Plain by tomorrow. We can't afford delays. Those narrow passages through the mountains disorganized our battalions. I don't know that I can get an intact platoon right now." He turned to Paul. "You've led infantry in combat. Would you take a hastily formed patrol to seize that objective?"

Paul snapped to. "Of course."

Massu turned to his adjutant standing at his shoulder. "Grab the first infantry elements sufficient to form a platoon. Tell them they are to follow Lieutenant Colonel Littlefield's orders. Send them here to form up."

Fifteen minutes later, five half-tracks and the soldiers of a platoon of mechanized infantry from the Chad Column formed in front of Massu's jeep. Two years ago, the regiment had trekked from Chad to Libya as part of that same regiment under Leclerc's command to join the Allies in the fight across North Africa.

Massu addressed their platoon leader. "No time for briefings or explanations," he said. "Follow Colonel Littlefield's orders. He'll explain the mission enroute." He indicated the mayor. "He'll guide you. Make sure to keep him safe."

Turning to Paul, he handed over two tubes. "You've got your radio frequencies. Take these red flares too. When I see both of them go off from La Rocher, I'll know the objective is secure, and we'll fire artillery only for mop-up operations closer to town. You have two hours. Questions?"

"No time, sir."

The platoon from the Chad Column, a regiment of soldiers from across the French colonies, headed north in their M3 half-tracks. Paul and the mayor rode in the front vehicle with the platoon leader, Lieutenant Alain Badon. Mayor Caissie rode next to Paul, appearing torn between sheer terror and having the unexpected time of his life. His eyes intermittently bulged on hitting hard bumps in the road, after which he grinned, baring a wide row of white teeth below a thin mustache.

With no time for chit-chat, and all three men preoccupied with the mission, Paul briefly realized the incongruity of entering battle with soldiers completely unknown to him, and who were expected to execute his orders despite that he was equally unknown to them. Lieutenant Badon, however, appeared as the embodiment of competence, his deep tan, lean physique, and manner with his men instilling confidence that the mission was in good hands. *And he's lived through three years of combat under General Leclerc.*

"There, turn left," Caissie called above the wind, roaring engines, and the creak and rattle of tracks on cobblestone streets.

Badon grasped the mayor's shoulder to gain his attention, pointed at La Rocher, and called back, "Take us on a route that keeps us covered from that hill."

Caissie nodded and proceeded to direct the patrol through the town. They turned onto a long street with a row of houses on the east side that extended almost to the tree line. The lieutenant cast a questioning look at Paul.

"Run the gap one at a time," Paul ordered, "but make it fast."

Badon signaled his men and sent the first half-track across. A minute later, one of its men appeared at the tree line and signaled all-clear. The command vehicle was next, and in quick succession, the other three followed.

"We're going to take that hill," Paul told the lieutenant as the patrol wound its way up a gentle slope through the forest.

"I thought so." Badon's boyish face under blondish hair protruding below his helmet bore an incongruous expression of laconic intensity. "What's the plan?"

"As far as we know, there are two machine gun nests up there, but there might be more. They'll have security around them. On the northeast slope, opposite from Dabo, the woods extend up to the level of the lower plateau. Mayor Caissie will guide us through back roads to get as close as we can. Then we dismount, and it's your show. Send a squad to approach on our left flank, one in the center, and one on the right. We have to move fast and secure the main plateau within ninety minutes. If not, our own artillery will demolish the position. Our forces in the basin will keep the two machine guns busy along with anyone else we encounter. Hopefully, they won't spot us."

Badon grinned. *"Bien sur!"*

They turned onto a narrow dirt road that trailed generally southeast and curved around to the back side of La Rocher, out of sight under the forest canopy. Paul and Badon monitored their progress against the map. To their right, they heard field artillery firing incessantly and the clatter of machine guns and rifles. Paul was glad of the clamor to cover the noise of their own machines.

"There's a wider road farther on that *les boches* use for supply," Caissie informed. "They never come on this one because it's so small. We'll stay on it for just over three kilometers. Then we'll turn right and start up the backside of the hill. It's steep there."

With no opportunity to converse, Paul learned little of Badon, only that he came from a military family that had transferred around the French colonial empire for most of his life. While growing up, he had lived in Indochina and in each of the African colonies. Military life was all he knew, and his father happened to be stationed in Chad when Germany invaded France.

The younger Badon had immediately enlisted when Leclerc arrived to form a regiment and march it north to Libya to fight with the Allies. Hardened over thousands of miles in combat, he had earned a battlefield commission and leadership of this platoon.

His father had remained with the Vichy army. "I don't know where he is now, but I am sure he is fighting for France."

The patrol came to the turn-off that Caissie had mentioned and traversed an even narrower lane scarcely larger than a footpath for a short distance. There, Badon called a halt and briefed his section leaders. Then he gathered his men around him.

"My brothers, we've fought many battles together," he said, and was suddenly quiet. When he spoke again, his voice trembled. "We've lost many friends, great warriors. I was about to say that this should be our last battle before we go to fulfill the oath we took at Kufra. Tomorrow or the next day, Strasbourg!"

His soldiers almost broke into cheers, but anticipating that happenstance, he lifted his hands to quiet them. "We have to get clear of Dabo first," he said, "and Colonel Massu is counting on us to knock out those machine guns and whatever else is up there." He grinned. "I know you don't want to miss tomorrow's party, so be careful, but go fast. We have less than an hour to get to the summit and do our jobs."

Mayor Caissie broke in. "May I come along?"

Watching from the side, Paul had to smile. In the romp across France, and particularly in Paris, he had witnessed many civilians eagerly inserting themselves in harm's way to assist their liberators and participate in securing their own freedom.

Apparently, Badon had too. He nodded at the small figure gazing at him with shining eyes. "Stay well behind us, *mon ami*," he said kindly. "We don't want you to be a casualty, especially not this close to the end of the war."

Caissie beamed. "I'll stay out of your way."

First Section led off, trailing along the base of the hill to the southeast to form the platoon's left flank while Third Section circled to the northwest slope. Paul advanced with Badon and Second Section in the center section. Caissie followed him, well back from the soldiers.

Second Section came to a wide area at the base of the hill. It was no surprise. Paul and Badon had noted it on the map, and Caissie had warned of it.

Anticipating that they might be seen, and per Badon's orders, the sections dismounted and maneuvered on foot in a line-abreast formation. Then a soldier at the extreme of each flank ran weaving paths across the open area.

Almost immediately, shots rang out, distinct against the background of the ongoing battle in the basin. Tiny clouds of dust burst from the ground near the soldier on the right flank. He sprinted forward, and was soon under the safety of the trees.

Two more men raced across the wide area, this time, closer to the center. More shots were fired from above in quicker succession.

"There are at least two riflemen on this side of the hill," Paul observed.

Badon agreed. "We haven't lost anyone, but they know we're coming."

Two more men raced across the opening, both from Second Section.

Once again, the rifles from above attempted to pick them off, but were frustrated by the erratic tracks the runners took.

"I count only two enemy rifles," Paul said.

"That's my count," Badon replied. "But I only hear one machine gun at the front. The one on this side stopped firing. He might be moving to engage us. I'll find out."

He spoke on his radio. Moments later, two men from First Section darted across the left flank. At the same time, one on the right flank ran out. Immediately, the familiar buzz of an MG 24 sounded. The runner on the right sprinted to the safety of the nearest trees.

Badon grabbed his radio. "Second and Third Sections, maximum suppressive fire near the right side below the summit. First Section, get your men across *tout de suite.*"

Paul glanced at his watch and grimaced. Only forty-five minutes remained until Massu's big guns ranged in on La Rocher's summit and the little church. Hearing leaves rustling behind him, he turned to find Mayor Caissie looking up from his watch with anxious eyes.

At the sound of more close-in shooting, Paul whirled. The center and right sections had opened up with all their weapons, and as he watched, more and more men to his left scurried across the open area.

One stumbled and fell, but then he was on his feet and ran safely to the opposite tree line. On the right, the machine gun fired down intermittently, but was apparently held down by the right flank's suppressive fire.

Badon was again on his radio. "Second Section, shift left and follow First Section. I'll move with you. I count two rifles. Deal with them. Then go after the forward machine gun. First Section, when Second is past the clearing, maneuver forward and take out the rear machine gun. Third Section, keep that rear machine gun pinned down."

He handed his receiver back to his radioman and rubbed his eyes. When he looked up, he found Paul regarding him in admiration. "You know your business, Lieutenant."

Badon smirked. "After three years of this, I'd better know it." He glanced along his line where Second Section was already maneuvering to the left. "Let's go, or we'll miss the fun."

Paul followed, briefly recalling that the last time he had been in combat as an infantryman was at Normandy with the French commandos, whom he had technically commanded. However, he had soon found that their leader, who had organized and trained the unit, had little need for his oversight, so he had relinquished command to him and joined Field Marshal Montgomery's operations staff.

Before that, he had replaced a battalion commander in the Sahara. He was wounded in a subsequent battle and had to be returned to England, but his unit had met its objective.

In each case, Paul had been with fighting soldiers, on the ground, and the sense overcame him of the sacrifices they faced daily. Of the various types of engagements he had been in since the beginning of the war, including espionage, diplomatic missions, staff work, and even as liaison with Leclerc, he found the simplicity and straightforwardness of infantry combat to be the most satisfying, once the mission was complete. He grunted at the irony. *That assumes I live through it!*

Gripping his carbine, Paul hurried through the trees and bushes after Badon. Caissie followed close behind them.

Having cleared the open area on the left flank, Paul breathed heavily from the exertion of climbing uphill. Second Section had spread out again in the center of the approach, and Third Section still exchanged heavy gunfire with the machine gun near the back side of the summit. The forward gun continued its loud bursts, but so far, its impact area remained out over Dabo and the basin.

The two riflemen who had first fired down on the platoon had been silent, though whether they had been shot, captured, or were in hiding, Paul did not know. He continued up the slope, struggling to keep pace with Badon and the radio operator.

They reached the back side of the summit, and Paul suddenly realized that the rear machine gun was now below them, and then it fell silent. Badon whirled around, his radio mic in hand. "We got it, the rear machine gun," he exclaimed with a triumphant grin. "The whole crew. Now for the forward one."

Panting heavily, Paul nodded. "What about the two riflemen?"

"One's wounded. We've taken him prisoner. First Section is moving up to support eliminating that forward gun."

"Lead the way."

The going was much easier on the plateau, and the church, marked on the map as Saint-Léon Chapel, appeared untouched. Despite the still-overcast sky, Paul could now make out the Neo-Romanesque architectural structure resting on pink sandstone. Its tall, square belltower rose high over the sanctuary, giving an unobstructed view in every direction. Even at ground level, the view of far-off forest-cloaked hills and mountains was expansive. Despite the ongoing engagement, he could not help sucking in his breath at the magnificent landscape, regardless of the glowering clouds.

Third Section had already maneuvered over the main plateau and was at its forward edge firing down on the German machine gun position. The other two squads had linked up and now swept deliberately over the objective, checking every possible hideaway but finding nothing. Two men climbed the belltower and waved all-clear.

The machine gun fell silent. Paul and Badon moved toward the forward edge of the plateau. Dabo appeared, spread out below among the folds of the valley floor. Dull sounds of the ongoing firefight in the basin rode a stiff wind, but fortunately, no precipitation had further marred the bleak day.

Two German soldiers, their hands held high over their heads, plodded up the path that connected the lower and higher plateaus. Their captors followed closely with rifles trained on them. "There's one sprawled over his gun down there," one of Badon's men called as the group passed by. "He won't be shooting anyone."

Badon nodded grimly. "Put them in the church tower for the moment. Keep them separate and don't let them talk. You know the drill."

As the prisoners were led away, Paul suddenly glanced at his watch. He had almost forgotten to set off the two red flares. He had less than a minute before the artillery barrages began targeting right where they stood. Hurriedly, he pulled the signal tubes from his pouch and uncapped one of them.

Shots rang out from the rear of the plateau. As one, Paul, Badon, and

Cassie whirled. Three German soldiers charged across the flat ground from the eastern flank, seemingly intent on Caissie.

Paul dropped the flares, pulled his carbine up, and fired while leaping in front of the small mayor. From less than fifty yards away he saw a muzzle flash and heard a rifle shot, and then another figure jumped in front of him only feet away, and fell.

Gunfire exploded from behind him, and the three German soldiers dropped dead.

Paul stared at the prone figure in front of him with growing dread. Badon lay face down, and blood spilled from his back. He did not move.

Paul felt for a pulse, but found none.

The unmistakable sound of field artillery guns suddenly reverberated across the valley followed by the whistles of rounds splitting the air overhead. "That's our artillery," he yelled. "They've got the range to the bottom of the hill. They'll be going for the top."

He ran back to where he had dropped the flares, scooped up the one he had opened, and struck the ignitor against the hard ground. Red smoke poured into the air. Quickly, he repeated the action with the second flare.

No more artillery arced their way.

Paul trudged slowly back to where Badon's body lay. Several of the lieutenant's men had grouped around him. Paul crouched next to the body and let out a long breath. "Who's in charge of the platoon now?"

"I am, sir," the First Section leader said.

Paul's voice caught. "Radio in that you're doing another sweep and that unless you inform otherwise, the objective is secured. Your platoon is returned to the command of your company commander."

He remained for a few moments grasping Badon's shoulder, and when he rose, Caissie nudged Paul's arm. "You saved my life," the mayor said plaintively.

"He saved both of our lives," Paul muttered, gesturing toward Badon's still figure. He peered at Caissie. "Those German soldiers looked like they were after you. Specifically you. Why would they do that?"

Caissie held his hands to his face. "I knew them," he said, struggling with emotion. "I knew them all. The Germans. They knew me." He remained silent as Paul continued to scrutinize him, and then he blurted,

"I'm the mayor. I had to deal with them and keep my people safe. They lived among us. We had no choice. They probably saw me as betraying them for leading you up here..." His voice trailed away.

Caissie moved over and crouched next to Badon. He stayed there stroking the fallen soldier's shoulder for a time. Then he sniffed and regained his feet. "We will see that he has a proper burial, and we'll erect a memorial to him. The people of Dabo will never forget what he did." He glanced up at Paul and added, "What you all did."

Two soldiers with a stretcher arrived to take the body away.

Paul glanced out over Dabo and then at the little church. All fighting had stopped. The guns had fallen silent.

He placed an arm around Caissie's shoulders. "Dabo is liberated. The church is secure. I'll walk with you back into town."

45

November 23, 1944
North of Strasbourg, France

Paul's jeep careened through freezing rain and light snow flurries along a muddy road behind a Sherman that threw back large clumps of the brown muck, splattering the windshield. The driver kept the wipers running, but they had the effect of smearing the glass such that visibility was possible only through clear slivers between streaks. Amid the engine's groans, the jeep slipped and slid through the thick mire, managing to keep up only through the driver's tenacity and skill. He dared not slow down or drop back, however, because another Sherman followed not far behind. With no greater visibility than the vehicles ahead of it, the tank threatened the real possibility of overrunning and crushing the jeep.

Despite the fierce weather encountered as Massu's sub-group traversed the mountains of the Low Vosges range, by noon of the day after liberating Dabo, it had pushed through Wolfsberg Pass, and two hours later, its leading elements broke onto the Alsatian Plains and warmer temperatures. The formation set out almost due north across flat, navigable terrain to link with the diversionary elements of Leclerc's division. Those components had broken through German defenses on the northern route and also closed in on Saverne.

Strasbourg was only a few miles away.

Despite the dangers, a sense of exultation gripped Paul and his driver as they drew ever closer to the city that had grown to mythical proportions in the minds of every soldier in General Leclerc's division. The objective that had seemed impossible for four long years, that men had fought for, bled for, and died for, had drawn within sight. The ornate spire that had inspired the general's troops rose high over the city, clearly visible despite the atrocious weather. It was a beacon for the grand thrust to rid France of the Nazi scourge and a major step in liberating the whole country. France and its far-flung colonies had given up throngs of its young for feats of unfathomable courage in the quest to fulfill Leclerc's Oath of Kufra, and it was now within their reach.

One hour before dawn, Leclerc had met with his commanders and staff at a wide place on the main road leading southeast out of Saverne. Paul watched his face closely. The general contained his exuberance, his eyes looking sharply about, taking in every detail of preparedness. Then, when all were assembled, he quieted his small audience with a wave of his hand toward their objective. "Gentlemen," he intoned, "Saverne is taken. Strasbourg lies ahead. Only forty kilometers separate us. You have your orders. Execute."

As word spread across the vast formations, the division's jeeps, tanks, ambulances, half-tracks, tank destroyers, and troop-transport trucks began their trek. Soldiers whooped, engines roared, gears ground, and the division's elements set out on their individual missions. Leclerc dispatched his forces in four sections: Lieutenant Colonel Rouvillois took a battalion to traverse due east and then cut south through Brumath to enter Strasbourg from the north. The route was the longest and circuitous, but it also had better roads and was the fastest.

Lieutenant Colonel Massu led a *groupement*, a combined arms unit larger than a regiment but smaller than a division. It maneuvered along an axis southeast from Saverne, directly toward Strasbourg. He would take a slight jaunt northeast and then turn south to enter the city behind Rouvillois.

Lieutenant Colonel Cantannel headed straight southeast with his *groupement* on a parallel route east of Massu's while Lieutenant Colonel Putz struck on the right flank from Marmoutier rather than from Saverne.

Paul continued forward with Massu. The Strasbourg Cathedral's imposing shape came into view as his jeep navigated through the slurry of open, harvested fields with tanks plowing forward on both sides of him. Rising over five hundred feet into the sky, the spire had been the tallest building in the world, until displaced by St. Nikolai's Church in Hamburg in 1874. American and British bombing raids had damaged the main structure three months ago, but the tower still stood as a daunting beacon.

Resistance was light as French troops crossed the fields and entered Strasbourg, surprised to find that their arrival was entirely unexpected. Normal early morning traffic filled the streets. French pedestrians on their way to work stared in wonder. Sleepy-eyed German soldiers gawked at them in astonishment on recognizing that the tanks rumbling by were Shermans and waved French flags. Trolly-car operators glanced over in amazement as the war machines rushed past them. Their drivers looked about uncertainly on seeing friendly waves from tank commanders, but then they returned the greetings with arms upraised in enthusiastic celebration.

Paul observed the reactions, thrilled. "Leclerc's ruse worked," he exclaimed to the driver. "The *Wehrmacht* didn't expect us to come through Dabo. They thought they'd stopped our advance along the northern route. We caught them napping."

As field artillery rounds arced overhead to drop on German fortified positions, tanks clanked and transport tires squealed on Strasbourg's cobblestone and paving stone streets. Huge explosions erupted around the city at forts and anti-tank defenses, destroying their connecting tunnels and blocking enemy armor and mechanized infantry. Lethal munitions depots blew up, and troop barracks and *Wehrmacht* headquarters crumbled under the barrages, fatally impeding the enemy's ability to mount coordinated defenses or counterattacks. Then Leclerc's M4 Shermans, supported by infantry, roared to the same targets to scout out the forces and drive enemy soldiers into the open to be killed or captured.

Seven hours after Leclerc gave his order, Paul's driver wheeled the jeep into the Place de la Cathédrale. Guns still blazed to the northern and eastern sides of the city, but the western section had been liberated, and people celebrated in the streets.

The enormous Romanesque and Gothic northern tower of Cathédrale Notre-Dame de Strasbourg stood in regal relief against the sky. Built atop it was an octagonal belltower of similar height and architectural style, and above that, its magnificent sloped steeple. Paul gaped in wonder at the majesty of the cathedral and at the thought that someone intended to scale its four hundred and sixty-six feet to unfurl the French tricolors at the pinnacle.

Below its intricate stained-glass sunburst, the massive, arched main door stood ajar. Several yards in front of it, three Moroccan Spahis stood at attention. They were soldiers from the French colony in Morocco, members of the Chad Column who had marched with Leclerc since before they took his Oath of Kufra in Libya. Today, they wore colorful ceremonial uniforms of their country's mounted cavalry, with full Arab trousers of blue-gray below red jackets with black embroidery. Around their waists were wide red sashes, and deep blue cloaks were draped from their shoulders. High red turbans adorned their heads. They stood unmoving while they awaited their commander.

Paul knew about one of the men, Corporal Maurice Lebrun, of the 5th Squadron of the Marching Regiment of Moroccan Spahis. The soldier had hand-stitched together a white bedsheet, a blue skirt, and a strip from a Nazi flag to fashion a French flag, which he now held under one arm as he stood at the center of the trio.

The sound of a single half-track caught Paul's attention and he turned to watch Leclerc, who stood erect in the vehicle. The general braced himself as the vehicle squealed to a halt. Regaining his balance, he once again stood straight and directed his gaze to the three Spahis standing at attention before him.

At his slight nod, all three men saluted smartly, waited for a return salute, and then took off at a run, disappearing into the cathedral.

Leclerc descended from his half-track and joined the officers watching the event. They had moved back a ways so that they could see each level of the edifice. Spotting Paul among them, Leclerc approached. "I'm glad you're here to see this," he said.

"It's thrilling to be here, sir. You've done it. You've fulfilled your vow."

"Almost," the general replied. "The flag isn't flying yet, and the fighting goes on. But"—he beamed—"before this day ends, we'll have done it."

"Sir," Paul said with some hesitance, "I was sorry to hear about your friend, General La Horie. My condolences."

Leclerc turned stiffly and gave a slight nod. "He was one of the best," he rasped through tight lips. "We were at St. Cyr and fought all across Africa, Italy, and France together, and then, just a few days before we were set to enter Strasbourg..."

He paused, and his voice broke. "He was in Badonviller, only seventeen miles away, when I heard that shrapnel had torn into his throat. I rushed over, but by the time I arrived, he was gone." His lips quivered. "All I could do was say prayers over him."

The two were quiet for a while, and then Leclerc resumed the conversation. "I heard about what happened on La Rocher de Dabo. That was a terrible thing. Lieutenant Badon marched with me from Chad as a private. I knew him well."

"Saying 'he died a hero' is trite," Paul said sadly, "but he did, saving my life and Mayor Caissie's."

"Well, we got Group Massu through the Vosges intact," Leclerc said. "He played a large part in bringing that about, and so did you." He suddenly swung about and faced Paul, and when he spoke again, he struck a painful tone. "Ahh, Paul, this war is a terrible thing. It rips the best people and times from our lives. It devours our youth, lays waste to our land..."

He exhaled sharply. "But we must finish it, deal with the evil that causes it, and let our people go back to their lives." He shook his head and sighed. "Then we have to man the ramparts because, unfortunately, evil never rests. War will rage again."

While he spoke, Paul reflected on the losses that had affected his own life most. The first was the only woman he had ever loved, Ryan Northridge. She had been ferrying a bomber from a maintenance facility to a forward airfield when she was shot down and killed by a *Luftwaffe* raid over England.

Paul had always been more cerebral than congenial, and he was thus awkward in social situations. As far as he knew, Ryan had been the only woman who had ever taken an interest in him. As her lovely face crossed his mind along with recollections of working with her at RAF Fighter Command Headquarters, he shoved them aside to guard against the awful chasm that had been left in his heart.

The second loss was a little girl he had never met before finding her still-warm body clutching a teddy bear in a house destroyed by field artillery in Italy. He had carried the child to her grave on the edge of a forgotten village. The memory visited him unbidden in nightmares that often awakened him, striking with horrific grief.

And now Lieutenant Alain Badon. He had been so competent, so dedicated, so eager to liberate Strasbourg, and he died throwing his body in front of a bullet that might have otherwise killed Paul or Caissie. *And barely thirty-six hours before the operation began that he fought across continents and oceans to be part of.*

Pulling himself from his sad memories, and in response to Leclerc's flat statement about the future of evil, Paul muttered, "I'm sorry to say, sir, that you are probably correct."

Leclerc heaved a sigh and switched subjects, seemingly deliberately. "The Rhine is on the east limit of the city, just two miles from here. It flows past our river port. Directly on the opposite bank is the German town of Kehl. Only foot bridges join the two shores, so the Germans will have a difficult time trying to escape." He glanced at the sky. "And that would be true even in clear weather."

While the sounds of battle continued in the background, the two men stood and craned their necks. Observing Leclerc, Paul saw that the general was completely enthralled.

Looking about the square, Paul noticed that three of the Rochambelles' ambulances had pulled in and parked abreast of each other. As the drivers and nurses emerged and took up positions in front of their vehicles, he spotted Amélie. She sat on the hood of her vehicle watching with Danièle, Toto, Denise, Zizon, and others of the group whom he had met.

"Excuse me a moment, General," he said to Leclerc, who nodded his acknowledgement. Paul walked over to greet Amélie.

"This is incredibly exciting," she exclaimed after greetings, "even more than being in Paris during its liberation. Nearly all of France is now free."

"Not quite," Paul said with a cautionary tone. "We still have the Colmar area in the south and other regions in the north to clear—"

"Don't be so pragmatic," Amélie chided playfully. "Enjoy the moment. Today will be a great victory for France."

Paul broke into a reluctant smile. "You're right." He turned and gestured toward Leclerc. "Have you met the general? If not, I'd like to introduce you."

Amélie reacted hesitantly. She glanced at Danièle, standing nearby. "Oh, I don't know—"

"Go on," Danièle encouraged. "Most of us have met him at one time or another. He's always pleased to see us and he doesn't mind showing his appreciation."

"*Eh bien*, let's go," Amélie said, her hesitance turning to excitement. "How would I ever explain my refusal to meet with the general who liberated Paris and Strasbourg." She followed as Paul led the way back to where Leclerc continued gazing up to the base of the belltower.

"I'm so pleased to meet you," he told Amélie as Paul presented her. "The Rochambelles' work is vital and I can never appreciate you enough."

"She's my brother's fiancée," Paul said proudly.

"I had no idea you had someone so close in the Rochambelles," the general said in surprise. Then, with a good-humored glint in his eye, he asked Amélie, "You're marrying a Brit?" He chuckled. "Some good things will come of this war after all."

At that moment, roughly ten minutes after the three Spahis had dashed inside the cathedral, a stirring among the crowd caused everyone to look up to the tall, octagonal belltower resting on the north corner of the main edifice. Three tiny figures appeared at its base, nearly two hundred feet above the ground. The belfry rose another hundred feet, and from there, the ornate steeple soared an additional one hundred and twenty-six feet to a peak. The three men waved. Their audience roared their approval.

"I can't believe they'll climb all the way to the top," Amélie remarked. "And in this wind."

"Only Lebrun will continue the climb," Leclerc said without diverting his gaze from the unfolding drama high in the sky. "He insisted on going all the way up."

Paul held his breath. No rain had dropped since leaving the mountains, but the cold wind must be stiff at that height, and the danger of sniper fire was ever present. Even now, as they watched, the sounds of battle persisted in the east.

With his homemade flag fastened securely on his back, Corporal Lebrun turned and faced the belltower. He stood, apparently studying it for a few moments, and then began his climb, using the intricate architectural features for hand and footholds. Almost immediately, shots rang out from beyond the square. Chips flew from the sides of the spire. Lebrun's two Spahi comrades immediately returned fire.

He continued to climb.

More shots sounded.

Lebrun's mates returned fire again. On the ground, the crowd ducked, and gun crews on war machines joined in raining bullets toward the hostile fire until the snipers' guns were silent.

Against the brisk wind and the sound of distant explosions, Lebrun continued his relentless climb.

He passed the belltower and began to ascend the steeple.

The crowd held its collective breath.

Finally, after many more minutes, he reached the steeple's apex.

Amélie's heart pounded.

Lebrun's figure had diminished to ant-size, barely discernible. For several minutes, he was detectable only as a dark, moving blotch at the spire's zenith.

Then suddenly, the blue, white, and red of the French flag waved over the cathedral. The crowd cheered wildly. Soldiers jumped in the air with exhilaration, hugged each other, and danced about in celebratory antics.

The Rochambelles likewise celebrated in front of their vehicles. Seeing them, Amélie turned to Leclerc. He stood transfixed, his arms raised over his head with tight fists, signifying victory.

"Congratulations, mon *general*," Amélie said. "With your permission, I'd like to be with our crews."

Leclerc glanced toward the Rochambelles. Then he grabbed Amélie in a celebratory embrace and grinned. "Of course. Give them my regards."

Blushing profusely, Amélie made her way through the crowd to the ambulances, she heard the roar of a motorcycle and then saw the bike pull up by the Rochambelles. She stopped, hands on hips, watching as Chantal dismounted and searched about.

With a rueful smile, Amélie headed toward her sister. "You found me," she said. "What are you doing here?"

"Are you joking?" Chantal replied, grabbing her sister's hands, her eyes wide with excitement. "I told you I'd be here. Nothing could stop me. Besides, I was not far away. I ran dispatches to General Patton's headquarters this morning." She leaned toward Amélie and confided, "When I'm done here, I'm going to find Horton."

Startled, Amélie grabbed Chantal's arm. "You can't."

Chantal pulled away. "Why not? All across France, wives greeted their husbands in the streets, soldiers who'd fought with Leclerc. The same thing happened when he liberated Paris. I have my motorcycle, passes to get through checkpoints, permits for petrol, and cash. I managed to find out that the Sherwood Rangers just crossed into Germany up near a town called Geilenkirchen." Her voice hollowed out, and her expression changed to one of anxiety. She grasped Amélie's arm. "If I don't go find him, I might never see him again." Her eyes took on a look of resolve. "So when I leave here, that's where I'm going."

Leaving Amélie speechless, Chantal whirled and gazed up at the tower in exhilaration. "Can you believe it? Strasbourg is free." A far-off explosion followed by rattling small-arms fire prompted her to add grimly, "Almost."

Still standing next to Leclerc with his eyes resting on the steeple, Paul watched in awe as Lebrun began his slow, careful descent. Then, on reaching the spire's base, the Spahi brandished his fists over his head in triumph. The crowd roared its approval and broke into wild, unrestrained revelry.

Paul glanced at Leclerc, who had stood unmoving while Lebrun climbed down. Then the general muttered, "Louis, now I can die."

Thinking he might have misheard, Paul looked around but saw that the general addressed no one close by. "Sir," he said, "I didn't quite catch what you said."

Leclerc chuckled. "I was addressing King Louis XVI. He was the last French king before the French Revolution brought down the monarchy. I was letting him know that French sovereignty and pride are restored, or nearly so. I think he's pleased."

He laughed quietly again and gazed about, acutely aware of the combat still raging across the city's east side. Then he looked up at the blue, white, and red banner flying proudly over the cathedral. "Let's go," he said at last. "We've got a battle to fight and a war to win."

EPILOGUE

November 24, 1944
West of Geilenkirchen, Germany

Lieutenant Render poked his head into Horton's tent. "You're wanted at squadron headquarters."

The summons surprised Horton. He had not expected one and he was officially at rest. In the two days after breaching the Siegried Line, the 84th Infantry Division's 334th Regiment to which his troop was attached had engaged in mop-up operations in Prummern and the high ground east of Geilenkirchen. Meanwhile, the 43rd Wessex Division and the 84th's 333rd Regiment and its attached Sherwoods had fought house-to-house until it was secure. Then both regiments and attachments as well as the Wessex Division had cleared the Roer Valley, as planned, up to Wurm.

Yesterday, they had been relieved in place by the US 102nd Infantry Division and fell back to an encampment well within friendly lines west of Geilenkirchen. The plan from there was to continue west to a reasonably secure location near Nijmegen for complete rest and refit, and to prepare for upcoming operations.

"Any idea why I've been sent for?" Horton asked.

"None," Render replied. "I happened to be there when the order came down and offered to stop by to let you know. I'd hurry if I were you, though. It sounded serious."

Still feeling the effects of three days in combat, Horton cast Render a jocular scowl, clambered into his boots, and clomped along next to him for the short distance to headquarters. "Was anyone else called up?"

"No, just you."

Horton glanced at him suspiciously. "Then why are you coming along?"

Render grinned. "Because if you're in trouble, mate, I don't want to miss it."

"Some friend you are."

They reached the headquarters, a large, unused toolshed on a farm. When they walked in, a sergeant sitting at a field desk shot Horton an expressionless glance. "Through there," he directed toward a door with a jerk of his thumb. "Good luck."

Horton glanced at Render.

"If you need help, mate, I'll be right here."

Horton pushed through the door that he assumed led into the new squadron commander's makeshift office. However, it proved to be empty of furniture and was lit only by daylight streaming through a small window. He paused to allow his eyes to adjust to the half-light and heard a noise from behind the door. Stepping through, he grasped its edge and yanked. A dark figure bolted from its shadow.

Chantal threw herself against Horton, wrapped her arms around his head, and buried her lips on his. Momentarily shocked, Horton stood stock still and stiff, but as Chantal's face came into focus and he felt her warmth, he relaxed and melted into her kiss. Then, without turning around, he kicked the door shut with his heel.

———

"Ah, Chantal," Horton said, savoring her name, when they emerged much later through a back door into sunlight, "how did you ever find me? How did you get here?"

"On that," Chantal said, pointing to her motorcycle.

Horton grimaced. "Blimey. I should have guessed."

Chantal told him of her work as a dispatch rider for Dragon's Resistance group. "I figured out where your unit was when I was at General Patton's headquarters a few days back, and from there…"

Horton embraced her again. "This war needs to end soon so we can keep you alive." A clouded expression crossed his face. "I was going to get down on one knee like I said I would, but—" He gestured toward his face. "I got badly burned. You might not—"

Chantal placed her hand to his lips. "You really are a fool, aren't you. I can see your face perfectly well, and all I see is the one I've loved all these years."

"But my ear. Half burned off. Grafted skin. My left cheek is scarred."

"But you're alive and healthy." She stood back and looked him over. A mischievous light shined from her eyes. "You're not going to get away from me with that as an excuse. You know by now that'll never work."

Horton chuckled. "I do know that, and I would never try anyway because I'm bonkers for you. It's just that, I thought—" Once again, he indicated his face.

"Your scars are a badge of honor, but don't you dare get down on one knee because I've already said yes, and that's still my answer."

Horton held her in his arms and kissed her until his breath all but ran out. "We need to get your sanity checked as soon as this war is over," he muttered.

Then, with recollections of what Leonard Littlefield had told him of the hazards that dispatch riders faced, Horton indicated the motorcycle. "Should you be doing that kind of work? It's dangerous."

Chantal harrumphed. "Somebody's got to do it. Why should someone take the risk, and not me? You go into combat over and over because it needs doing. Dispatch riding is a job I can do, it's necessary, and I'm available. Therefore, I must do it."

Horton laughed and caressed her face. "Ah, but I do love you, Chantal Boulier, the clarity of your thinking and your indomitable spirit, not to mention that you are so mind-numbingly gorgeous. Why you'd want to take up with the likes of me is one of nature's mysteries, but I intend to take full advantage—"

"Please do."

Horton turned red and took a deep breath. "Tell me about your sister and Madame Fourcade and anyone else you've heard about."

Chantal chuckled and asked incongruously, "You've changed the subject. Is there a chaplain about?"

Horton gazed at her uncertainly. "Of course, but—"

"Let's find him and get him to marry us, right here, right now."

Astounded, Horton gaped, unable to formulate a thought.

"I'm serious, Horton." Tears formed in the corners of Chantal's eyes. "I'm here courtesy of Dragon with a promise that I'd return by the day after tomorrow." Her voice shook. "After that, either of us could be killed. You know that. If it's you, I accept that I'll be your widow. What I can tell you is that, right here, right now, I want to be your wife. We can honeymoon in the nearest village."

Horton stared. Then a slow smile crossed his face. "My, my, but you have become a force of nature." He turned and led her by the hand around to the front of the headquarters. On entering, he commanded the sergeant, "Find me Chaplain Riley."

Two Days Later

"I didn't get to spend much time with Amélie," Chantal said. "She was called away on duty shortly after the flag was raised in Strasbourg—"

"And you were there?" Horton said excitedly. "You saw that?"

"I did. It was incredible. I can tell you that Amélie was terribly worried about Jeremy. She's heard nothing of him in weeks. We don't even know if he's still in France or was returned to England."

They sat alone in the early afternoon in the café of a small hotel. The proprietors kept looking their way with barely hidden amusement in the way that people often do with newlyweds. The couple had arrived there shortly after Chaplain Riley blessed their hurried nuptials attended by Lieutenant Render, the cheeky sergeant at headquarters, and the men of Horton's troop. He received a two-day pass and a raucous send-off.

They had created a small sensation on arrival at the hotel, with people gawking at the rugby-type lieutenant in combat uniform riding on a motorcycle behind the small woman with auburn hair. The proprietors, however, had been thrilled to host a honeymoon, and they extended every courtesy as well as kindly inquisitiveness. Fortunately, they kept within civil bounds and left the couple to enjoy each other.

Soon, the time would come for Chantal to drop Horton off at his unit and return to Dragon and Fourcade at Brabant. "I'm worried about Madame," Horton said.

"I am too," Chantal responded. She had earlier explained to him Fourcade's work on behalf of the families of lost Resistance members and her search for Léon Faye. "She's obsessed with finding him, and of course, she's terrified that he's dead." Chantal sniffed. "I think one of her biggest regrets is that she didn't marry him." She reached over and took Horton's hand. "Seeing her suffer drove me to find and marry you now."

Horton squeezed Chantal's hand. "You're stuck with me." He sighed. "I'm very sad over the news about Lance."

"So am I, but Fourcade has inquiries out on him through her still very active grapevine. If it's possible, she'll find him."

When the moment came to depart, with a lump in his throat Horton rode behind Chantal back to his encampment. There, they both suffered the cheers and playful jeers of his comrades.

"Stay safe," Chantal implored with tearful eyes. "I couldn't bear to lose you."

"Ah, m'lady, keepin' you from pain is reason enough to stay alive."

As Chantal rode away, Render approached and stood with one arm around Horton's shoulders. "You've done well," he said. "I mean that sincerely."

"And you don't know the half of who she is," Horton murmured. "She's bewitching," he breathed as Chantal rounded a curve. Then he laughed. "Bloody hell, she bewitched me."

Same Day, November 26, 1944
RAF Sumburgh, Mainland, Shetland

Jeremy shivered uncontrollably. In his half-sleep, he pulled his blanket tighter. Seven days had passed since he and his crew had been plucked from the cold North Sea, but that was after they had floated on its high waves for three days until rescue arrived.

The modified four-man Lancaster crew had been near life's end when the distinctive, deep-throated drone of a Bristol Pegasus engine powering a Supermarine Walrus amphibious-rescue aircraft passed low over their dinghy in the choppy North Sea. At irregular intervals over the previous three days, they had heard low-flying Spitfires, Walruses, and Sea Otters roaming overhead in apparent searches for the downed airmen, but heavily overcast skies and sea-level fog limited visibility, and gale-force winds prevented more frequent flights.

The crews' fleece-lined flight boots, pants, and B3 bomber jackets had done a fair job of protecting them from the elements, but eventually the cold, wet air had seeped through their clothing, moisture had gathered against their skins, and the constant exposure to the elements spanning two nights and three days had worn down their resistance. With no alternative means of protecting themselves against the elements, their physical conditions plummeted.

During the first day, while Sparks was still unconscious from a morphine shot, Jeremy and Scout managed to push his arm back into its shoulder socket, but with bone grinding against bone to accomplish the task, it was something Jeremy never wished to do again. However, during a brief time that Sparks was awake, he groaned in pain less.

Then, early on the third day, the weather had cleared, and upon the first sound of an aircraft, the crew had sufficient strength and presence of mind to toss yellow-dye markers into the waves and turn on a signal light.

The highly competent Walrus crew deftly retrieved the four airmen from their dinghy and flew them to RAF Sumburgh where ambulances awaited and transported them swiftly to hospital. "Winkletwo and Dora did their jobs," Scout mumbled to Jeremy as he lay on a gurney while waiting to be trundled to a ward with their two other comrades.

"They did at that," Jeremy rasped, "and when we're discharged, we'll drink to them and perhaps go see them."

When an attendant started to wheel Jeremy in a different direction, he asked weakly where he was being taken. "To the officers ward," came the reply.

Jeremy held up a hand and shook his head. "I'll stay with my crew."

Unfortunately, the weather had taken a greater toll than originally perceived. On the fourth day after their rescue, Sparks succumbed to pneumonia.

Jeremy accepted the news with outward stoicism, but inwardly, he writhed with grief, and he suspected that Scout and Stal did as well. All knew the anguish of losing comrades, but given their multiple efforts to sink the *Tirpitz* and their three days together among the waves in the tiny dinghy, this loss hit harder than most. Particularly since all four suffered from the same symptoms. Sparks, weakened by his injury and morphine, had lost his natural immunity against infection.

Jeremy started coughing out bloody mucus. A nurse heard him, walked over briskly to check on him, and saw him shaking. She felt his forehead with the back of her hand, and checked his pulse. "We need a doctor here," she called. "This one's in trouble."

Jeremy heard as if in a void. His mind was far away, in the elegant gardens of a villa overlooking Marseille and the sparkling Mediterranean Sea, sharing the view with Amélie. This was the place where their romance had blossomed.

The nurse held his hand.

Jeremy savored the warmth of Amélie's palm.

The nurse leaned over him, checking his vision.

Jeremy gazed into Amélie's deep, honey-colored eyes.

"Hurry, Doctor," the nurse called out. "We're losing him."

In Jeremy's delirium, he reached out and took Amélie's hands and cupped them in his own. Pressing them together, he reached his left hand to his chest and then inserted it between both of hers. "I'll leave my heart right here," he murmured, "where it belongs. I love you, Amélie."

November 25, 1944
Aboard the USS *Intrepid*, Southwest Pacific Area

Josh Littlefield scanned the *Stars and Stripes* main headline, "B-29s Bomb Tokyo." The article related that one hundred and eleven bombers had flown low over Japan's capital city and dropped four hundred and fifty-four tons of primarily incendiary bombs on the city. Since the Doolittle Raid over Tokyo shortly after the Japanese attack on Pearl Harbor, US bombers had several times attacked military and industrial targets in the country. Yesterday's raid, however, had not only been the first to use B-29 Super-fortresses over Tokyo flying from Saipan, but they were indicative of a change in strategy, flying in low, dropping mainly incendiaries, and intending to harm civilians and thus degrade the population's will to fight.

Josh well remembered the campaign and the bloody battles that delivered Saipan and its airfields into US hands. It had been a strategic victory, and some part of it belonged to Marine Private First Class Guy Gabaldon, who had singlehandedly captured more than eight hundred Japanese POWs and limited the effect of a massive *banzai* against US forces. The Marine, of Mexican descent, had grown up in a Japanese neighborhood in Los Angeles and learned his neighbors' language and culture. He thought of their people as gentle and peace-loving, a view that was at odds with the empire's aggressive war-making.

On his own initiative, he had gone into Saipan's jungles at night, found the enemies' cave hideouts, and convinced the occupants to surrender. As a result, his company commander nominated him for a Congressional Medal of Honor. No word of whether he would receive the award had yet come down.

Josh had flown missions over Saipan. He knew the horrific casualty numbers that had resulted. He had also seen the devastation at Pearl Harbor immediately after the attack. The idea of bombing civilians rankled him not just a little, yet the war needed to be prosecuted to a successful end. With those conflicting thoughts in mind along with the newspaper article, and what he knew of Private Gabaldon's initiative, he picked up a letter from his desk and read it again for the third time. It was from Zack, and it was less than a month old.

"Dear Josh, I miss you, big brother. This war needs to end, and soon. I'll be careful with what I write here, but most of it is already in the news, so I'm sure there won't be anything classified in it.

"If you've read about the 'Lost Battalion' in the Vosges Mountains, Josh, that was us! We were the ones that the 442nd Regiment and its 100th Battalion rescued. I say that with nothing resembling pride. We can talk about decisions that brought about that debacle at a later date, and it certainly needs discussion.

"If you haven't read about the 442nd Regiment, let me tell you that they are the finest fighters you'll ever meet, and loyal to America like no one else I've met. From where I stand, they're true-blue Americans in every sense of the word, but they're of Japanese descent, mostly first generation. They don't like to be called Japanese-Americans—just Americans—and that is amazing since most of them were ripped from their homes and held in detainment camps after the war began.

"Hell, there was one guy of theirs, the smallest soldier I've ever seen. All alone, he charged a German machine gun nest with one of their own guns he'd captured. He got 'em all. That's who I want with me in my foxhole.

"I understand the need for security and I don't have any answers about how things could have been done better, but I will tell you this: I owe them my life, and so do all in my battalion who survived. But for them, you wouldn't be reading this letter because I wouldn't be writing it. I'd be six feet under.

"Glad that's not the case. Love you, Zack."

Josh set the letter down. Then he sat back with a sigh. After thinking for an extended time, he rummaged through his desk for stationery and a pen.

"Dear Zack, it's great to know that you're still able to pick daisies rather than push them up from below. I struggle with some of the same moral dilemmas that might be crossing your mind. I don't have answers, just questions. I can tell you this much, though: Errors and bad decisions in this war are not confined to your side of the planet. We didn't seek this conflict, and maybe the Japanese people are not to blame. But their military followed orders, and to my mind, it would have attacked our western shores if we had not stopped them. Regardless, they hit our sovereign soil without warning or provocation. That can't stand, or we'll cease to be a nation and lose the opportunities and protections it affords.

"Unfortunately, I don't see any way around an invasion of Japan. I wish I did, because I've seen the initial casualty estimates, and they are mind-numbing, for us and for them.

"I'm glad to know that those who've come across to live among us wish to be unhyphenated, loyal Americans. Theodore Roosevelt was a big proponent of exactly that, and frankly so am I. I'm happy to accept them on that basis, and I'm sure most of our countrymen feel the same way, particularly after reading the stories of how they sacrificed to save our lost battalion. So if you see those guys again, tell them that they are welcome, and we're proud to have them. For saving my little brother, they have my undying personal gratitude. Love you, Josh."

Josh scanned the article and both letters one more time. Then he put the one he had written in an envelope, addressed it, and went to drop it in the mail. He took with him his flight gear and personal belongings for a long flight aboard a Douglas C-47 Skytrain to Hollandia, New Guinea. He was being transferred again.

Admiral Halsey had personally called Josh in to inform him of his new assignment. "General MacArthur was impressed with you. He asked for you."

"But sir," Josh had protested, "I just took over my air group."

"I knew you'd say that, so here's the deal. If you'll take your new post without a lot of kickback, I'll see to it that you get another command when we execute."

Josh knew there was no arguing with Bull Halsey, but he mulled for a few moments for no better reason than because he could. At last he said, "All right, sir. What's the assignment?"

"You'll be on the planning staff for the invasion of Japan."

Christmas Eve, 1944
Sark, Guernsey Bailiwick, Channel Islands

Dame Marian Littlefield sat alone in the storage room at the back of her home among stacks of suitcases left in her care by residents who had been deported to German detainment camps on the Continent. Her poodles faithfully took up their stations by the mansion's front door to provide early warning of anyone approaching while she listened to BBC war reports over her illicit radio.

Hopes for an early end to the war raised three months ago upon the liberation of Paris had been dashed by an Allied pause in forward action toward the German border. Operations had resumed, with reports of soldiers fighting in sub-zero weather all along the mountain ranges and in the northern plains in the vicinity of the French-German border. Then, several days ago, reports came in about a new German offensive in the Ardennes. The American 101st Airborne Division had been sent to Bastogne to block the *Wehrmacht* advance that had caught Allied commanders by complete surprise, both in timing and strength. The belief had been that the *Reich* had been too weakened to organize and field an army capable of such an aggressive operation.

"Apparently Hitler hopes to force the Allies to negotiate a peace settlement that allows him to focus on fighting the Soviets on the Eastern Front," Alvar Liddell, the announcer, had said. He went on to relate German objectives as the Allies had deduced them, and they were to break through Allied lines in the Ardennes Forest, cross the Meuse River into Belgium, recapture Antwerp, drive a lethal, physical separation between the British and American forces, and then encircle and destroy the British 21st Army Group and parts of the US 1st and 9th Armies. They would thus disrupt Allied supply lines and stall the enemy advance into Germany. "Hitler seems to believe that achieving those objectives would deliver a blow to the Allied war effort so momentous that it could turn the tide in Germany's favor."

Since that broadcast, Marian had listened as often as she dared with a sinking heart. The reports intensified her sense of being alone at Christmas while her family was scattered across Europe in life-threatening wartime pursuits. With no news about them, she had descended, for the first time, into hollow despair.

Nevertheless, despite the threat of death should she be caught listening to news reports, she was drawn inexorably to the BBC. *Like a moth to a flame.*

She had sat at her kitchen table eating her breakfast of stewed potatoes with no condiments, washed down with ersatz tea made from a mixture of linden tree bloom, beech buds, and pine tips. A blustery wind moaned past her window, blowing snow flurries across her garden. As the time approached for the news reports, she picked up several blankets from her parlor while staring glumly at the few pieces of firewood in the holder next to the fireplace. Then she plodded to the rear of the house to the storage room, set up the radio, and listened absently to the electronic bleeps and bloops in her earphones as the tubes warmed up. She sighed as she settled in to hear the news. Then came the BBC's signature three dots and a dash, Morse code for V for "Victory."

"This just in regarding the days-old German offensive in the Ardennes," Lidell announced. "We are hearing from our sources that the 101st Airborne is completely surrounded and cut off from its supply lines. The Germans have demanded the immediate surrender of the entire division."

Marian stared abjectly at the radio and dropped her head into her hands. "It's never going to end."

"However," Liddell continued, "we have word out that the commanding general—and we currently don't have his name—the 101st's commanding general sent back a one-word written reply. He told the Germans, 'Nuts.'"

Marian's head bobbed up, and once again, she stared at the radio, hardly knowing what to think.

"We're told that, in American jargon, a reply of 'nuts' means an absolute refusal of whatever is proposed, in this case a surrender, and American forces are rallying to cut off the *Wehrmacht* in what has come to be called the Battle of the Bulge, with the additional objective of rescuing the soldiers at Bastogne."

Marian stood, still staring at the radio. Then she packed it up, carefully placed it in its hiding spot, and gathered her blankets. That done, and her face set with renewed resolve, she walked briskly back to her parlor. "General," she muttered, "if you can take what's coming, then so can I."

Same Day
Stony Stratford, England

Claire stared at her radio, hardly believing what she had just heard. The commanding general of the Americans in Bastogne had profoundly communicated his intent by his one-word response to the Germans. His division would stand firm against all odds.

She had followed the story in the newspapers as well as in intercepted messages at Bletchley, and what had astounded her was the level of secrecy the Germans had maintained prior to launching the offensive. Not one word had been breathed outside of German sanctioned quarters, and yet the whole of *Heeresgruppe* B, a *Wehrmacht* army group of four hundred thousand men, had been reorganized, equipped, and transported without Allied knowledge.

The Allies had responded quickly, she knew, and General George Patton's 3rd Army was marching to the rescue, but the fact remained that the ambitious maneuver had the potential to tilt the war back in Germany's favor. That was not only plain to see from public news reports but also from intercepted communiques at Bletchley since the fighting in the Ardennes began.

The news, despite the American general's obstinacy, added to her concerns. She still had no word of Lance, and what she had received regarding Jeremy was extremely disturbing. He had been on the widely publicized mission that sank the *Tirpitz*, she learned several weeks after its occurrence, and his plane had gone down in the North Sea. He was rescued after three days, but his life had been in the balance from pneumonia. He was still in hospital in Shetland, and far from out of danger. No positive prognosis had yet been available.

Adding to her worries, William Davis had called just before the news broadcast, and he requested to drop by. "It's important that we speak," he had said in a grave tone. Always before, he had been friendly, and he was not hostile this time, but he sounded strained, hesitant. "May we come by in the early afternoon?"

Being a Sunday, Claire consented and suggested an early tea, but as the time approached, she became more fidgety. She had given Elsie the day off, and playing with Timmy only raised her anxiety. *They're coming to take him away.*

The child sensed her apprehension. "What's wrong, Gigi?"

She tried to answer, but emotion overcame her, and for several minutes, all she could manage was to hold him close. Then, to relieve tension, she took him outside and pushed him on the swing.

When the Davises arrived, she greeted them and took them to the back garden where Timmy still played. He ran to them with open arms. "Granny, Grandpa."

Claire choked back emotion.

While the old couple played with their grandson, Claire made tea, brought it into the garden on a serving tray with some precious, rationed Huntley and Palmer cream crackers, and set them on an ornate table. "I'm sorry, this is all we have."

Davis raised his eyebrows over a kindly smile. "No apologies needed. We came on short notice, and those biscuits are as good as anyone can get these days." He held a chair for Muriel, and then took his seat next to her.

Deciding that bad news was not made better by delay, Claire looked directly into Davis' eyes. "You said we needed to talk."

He nodded. Curiously, tears streamed down Muriel's face.

"This is hard—" Davis began, but was interrupted by Claire.

"I'll make it easier. You came to take Timmy."

Davis held her steady gaze. "We must go back to India—"

"I understand." Claire now spoke from an empty place where acceptance of the inevitable left her devoid of emotion. "I'll help you pack."

"We—we wanted to ask you," Muriel broke in. "Of course it's an enormous imposition, and you've already done so much." She sniffed and labored for words. "Would you consider keeping him here while we're away?"

Claire barely heard. She had diverted her eyes to Timmy swinging merrily on the playset.

"You see," Davis cut in, "we know we're old. The thought of leaving

Timmy for strangers to care for—Well, you and your brother are the only family he's ever known."

Their words pierced through Claire's trance. "I'm sorry. What did you say?"

"If it's too much trouble—" Muriel said.

Astonished, Claire broke in. "Timmy is never too much trouble. Did you say you want to leave him with me?"

"Well of course we don't want to abandon him," Davis said. "We intend to go back to India to sell the house and move back here. But we know we're too old to care for him properly while we travel—"

Claire leaped to her feet. "Timmy always has a home with me. If you're asking if he can stay with me, the answer is yes, yes, and yes. A thousand times yes."

"We didn't dare ask before," Muriel said. "We'd like to be able to come visit you after our return, if that's possible, and bring Timmy along—"

"You're welcome here anytime," Claire assured her. "You needn't even wait for an invitation. Timmy is so proud of having grandparents." She called to him and he came running. She tousled his hair. "Then it's done."

Uneasiness settled into her stomach as the unspoken implication of the conversation impinged on her mind, and she added, "At least until your return."

Christmas Day, 1944
Oflag IV-C POW Camp, Colditz Castle, Germany

Windows banged, cups clattered, and men roared, their clamor echoing resoundingly from the walls of the five-story prison castle's smaller of two inner courtyards. Barely larger than a basketball court, it was where prisoners of war could lounge, play stoolball, engage in other pursuits approved by the prison *commandant*, or seek a smidgeon of solitude in shadowed corners, all under the watchful eyes of a contingent of guards who outnumbered the prisoner population. The larger courtyard was for the Germans' recreational use.

Colonel William Tod, a Scotsman and the senior British officer present, sat at a small table that served as a desk in his room. He heard the outside ruckus, but given that not much was needed to elevate the POWs to such spontaneous outbursts, he paid only passing heed. However, when it was sustained longer than usual and the volume rose to thunderous decibels, he walked to his window and peered out.

A German *kübelwagen* had entered the courtyard through the double gates on the opposite side. Because of the freezing weather, the area had been empty, but suddenly, as Tod watched, men began spilling into it from all directions. They were held back from the vehicle by a detail of guards, but they were uproarious in their festivity, twirling clothing over their heads, whistling, and making catcalls. They were joined by men at every window who were frenzied in their celebration.

Such displays were not unusual and were the way that the prison population welcomed new POWs. They had become more frequent as the war had progressed, more Allied soldiers were captured, and more of them escaped from other prison camps and were recaptured. Colditz was a special prison, conceived, manned, and equipped to hold Allied POWs with a propensity for escape.

Because of the freezing weather, the *kübelwagen's* top was up, so Tod could not see into it, but based on the heightened enthusiasm of the inmates, he perceived that some had seen and recognized the vehicle's passenger. Whoever it was had to be someone they recognized and considered to be one of their own, and very popular.

As he watched, two guards moved to the back passenger door. It opened, and a single figure emerged. The man was bent and moved stiffly, as if in pain. From the distance, his features were difficult to discern, but he at once seemed familiar to Tod.

The prisoner straightened, ambled with a limp to the front of the *kübelwagen,* and looked across the crowd. Then he lifted his fists over his head and pumped them in a gesture of defiance and triumph.

The volume elevated to unimaginable levels as the prison population roared back its appreciation and pressed against the guards to welcome the newcomer.

As the senior British officer, Tod had a duty to welcome arriving inmates. They would not be released into the prison population until he had greeted them and been present in interviews with the prison *comman-dant*. With that in mind, he picked up his jacket and cap and climbed down the stairs and entered the courtyard.

He was a tall man with a thin face, known for professionalism and strict discipline, but he was also fair, loved by his fellow prisoners, and respected by Colditz officialdom. As he proceeded across the square, the crowd parted to make way. Tod strode past the line of guards and stood in front of the prisoner. Then he turned and raised his arms for quiet. The celebratory noise receded to a low clamor.

Tod faced the soldier. As he had suspected, the man was one he knew who had escaped and had been recaptured. Tod recognized the medium build, reduced by physical trauma; the light-colored skin, apparently bruised from beatings; the dirty-blond hair, long and unkempt; and the green eyes, peering at him with undaunted spirit.

The prisoner straightened to attention and saluted.

Tod returned the salute, and then extended his hand. "Lance Littlefield. It's good to see you again," he said. "I wish the circumstances had been better."

Lance gripped Tod's hand. "It's my pleasure to see you again, sir."

Crossing the Rhine
Book #9 in the After Dunkirk Series

In late 1944, as Allied forces grind their way toward Germany's Siegfried Line, the Littlefield family finds themselves caught at the center of a desperate struggle.

Jeremy, the daring pilot, flies dangerous missions across Europe and beyond, risking his life and his heart as he battles a waning and desperate empire. Beside him stands Amelie, the courageous ambulance driver dedicated to saving soldiers' lives at the front—Allied and enemy. She is equally devoted to Jeremy—undaunted by the chaos around them.

Claire, the brilliant cryptologist who is stationed at Bletchley Park, races against time to crack enemy codes that could save thousands. Her sharp mind unearths enemy secrets, but she is haunted by the fear that her warnings could be ignored—leading to catastrophic consequences.

Paul, the steady and determined soldier, advances through France, uncovering Nazi atrocities as he liberates war-torn villages. The discovery of a hidden Nazi prison camp forces him to confront the unimaginable, fueling his mission to expose the truth and bring freedom to the oppressed.

And in the brutal confines of Colditz, Lance, the bold adventurer, is willing to risk everything, escaping and joining forces with the French Resistance as he fights to defy Nazi rule. As he and his comrades endure unspeakable conditions, Lance's spirit burns fiercely—a defiant spark of rebellion behind enemy lines.

Will their collective strength be enough to silence the guns of war?

Get your copy today at
severnriverbooks.com

AUTHOR'S NOTE

I love finding and writing about true stories of strength and courage. This entry into the *After Dunkirk* series contains more than a few of them. Most of the stories contained herein are based on fact—I dramatize but avoid embellishing. The Littlefields' roles, along with Horton's and the Boulier sisters', tie together disparate events into a cohesive narrative. Some readers look up the names of characters and are pleasantly surprised to find that, regardless of prominence in the story, many are real, and their full stories are intriguing.

I can't go into detail on all real characters I include, but in the interest of closing open questions, I've written up a few from *Storming The Reich*, included below.

A fun and notable exception to the role of the Littlefields is that of Corporal Leonard Littlefield, the dispatch rider. A close friend, Lisa Marinus (wife of my West Point classmate, Bradley Rotter), enjoyed my books and was surprised to learn the name of the protagonists' family, "Littlefield." That was her grandfather's last name, and she let me know that he had fought with the 43rd Wessex Division. Researching did little to provide information on him personally, but Horton was already involved with the Sherwood Rangers Yeomanry, which were attached to that division, so tying Leonard in with Horton and Lance was too enticing not to indulge.

Two other results of that research were that I learned much more about what dispatch riders did and to include an expanded telling of what took place with Market Garden than originally anticipated.

One of my favorite anecdotes is that of Jan van Hoof, the presumed savior of the Waalbrug, the bridge at Nijmegen. (After the war, the Dutch people renamed it as the John Frost Bridge in honor of the British lieutenant colonel who defended the north end so tenaciously and at such great personal cost. While researching, I ran across an old episode of *This Is Your Life* that featured him, and was struck by that British officer's humility and humanity.)

I call Jan's story a true one because I believe it to be true, at least the broad brush. As an author of historical novels, I try to be accurate. So, the broad brush of Jan van Hoof's story as I've written it is factual. I believe that the good people of the Netherlands would agree. He is celebrated as a national hero. However, I filled in with fictional details.

What is known is this: Jan had been very concerned about the Waalbrug, seeing the threat of its destruction as a major danger to Nijmegen, its people, the success of the Allied thrust northward, and thus to the probability of Allied success in Europe. He expressed his concern to Captain Harry and provided much information about it. (The nickname "Harry," the Dutch officer attached to it, and the reason for its derivation is factual, as is the part about the telephone number workaround. Harry's son, by the way, settled in northern Virginia, and his grandson married and lived in the same neighborhood and was friends with another of my classmates who first told me of the Dutch officer's wartime exploits.)

On September 18, Jan disappeared for hours. When he reappeared, he was as filthy as described, and told his sister and several others who saw him that day that the bridge was safe. He provided no other details.

The bridge was wired for detonation. The local senior *Wehrmacht* commander at Nijmegen, General Bittrich, had ordered that if and when Allied tanks made it to the north end of the Waalbrug, it should be blown up. The tanks arrived, they pushed across the bridge, and Bittrich gave the order. The detonator was plunged, but nothing happened.

No one proved conclusively that Jan disarmed the bridge. He never claimed that he did, though as stated, he told several people that the bridge was safe. Sadly, he was executed by *Wehrmacht* troops two days later after they ambushed a patrol he was guiding.

Regardless, he was honored by his countrymen and by Allied countries. In 1945, the US recognized him with a Medal of Freedom with Bronze Palm. In 1946, the Netherlands awarded him the Order of William, Knight 4th Class. And in 1947, the UK awarded him the King's Commendation for Brave Conduct with Silver Laurel.

If he did save the bridge, how he did it is unknown. I gave it my best shot.

Next, in chronological order, is Agardus Leegsma. Suffice it to say, that he really did those things as described in the story, and he did join the US Army in the 82nd Airborne Division and enjoyed a long and sterling career.

One of my favorites is that of George Sakato. The facts of his story are quite accurate. He was awarded a Silver Star initially, and then, many years later, he received a posthumous and well-deserved Congressional Medal of Honor.

Another favorite is Marine Private First Class Guy Gabaldon. I wrote about his exploits at greater length in Book #7 of this series and summarized in this one. Reports of his achievements vary between eight and fifteen hundred Japanese POWs. He was immediately awarded a Silver Star, which was later upgraded to a Navy Cross, that service's second highest honor. On the certificate, he is credited with personally capturing over one thousand enemy soldiers. Many supporters tried to have his award upgraded to that of the Congressional Medal of Honor, but as of February 2025, that has not happened.

I would be remiss not to include Commander Evans of the USS *Johnston*, and the other men and ships of Taffy 3. As implied in the narrative, his body was never found. He led that impossible attack knowing the odds, and the other captains of that small fleet followed his lead without orders from higher headquarters. Without their actions, the course of the war in the Pacific might have turned out much differently. For his actions, he was awarded the Congressional Medal of Honor.

One other that must be included here is Lieutenant Martin "Marty" Higgins. Not only is his story as presented true to the record, but after his capture, he was interrogated by Heinrich Himmler and remained a POW for the remaining duration of the war.

I tussled with whether or not to include Zizon Sicot's story in this book, but ultimately included it because, as remarkable as her courage was in the anecdote related herein, the rest of her story is mind-blowing. I think it will be included in the next book.

Two actual characters whom I feel I must include here are Lieutenant Alain Badon and Mayor Mylan Caissie. Aside from the insertion of Paul Little-field into the battle to seize La Rocher de Dabo, that event is described fairly accurately. Badon was assigned the tasks of taking out the two machine guns, positioned as described, and saving the church. Mayor Caissie did volunteer to guide the platoon, and did express his concern for the village and the church.

I found no record for how Badon took his objective, but not only did he do so, he also saved Caissie's life in the way described, and the village built a monument to him as the mayor promised to do.

I can't go into the specifics of each such hero because that would take several more books, but I invite you to look up the individual stories online to learn more about those that are just as true. Readers have enjoyed learning which characters are real and their backstories. I'm in awe of all those true heroes and heroines.

ABOUT THE AUTHOR

Lee Jackson is the *Wall Street Journal* bestselling author of The Reluctant Assassin series and the After Dunkirk series. He graduated from West Point and is a former Infantry Officer of the US Army. Lee deployed to Iraq and Afghanistan, splitting 38 months between them as a senior intelligence supervisor for the Department of the Army. Lee lives and works with his wife in Texas, and his novels are enjoyed by readers around the world.

Sign up for Lee Jackson's newsletter at
severnriverbooks.com
LeeJackson@SevernRiverBooks.com